He passed through the living room into the kitchen, where he mixed himself a drink. He made it very stiff; it would be his last before retiring. Something to help him sleep.

As he drank it, he sniffed the air. Perfume. Still sniffing, he went into the bedroom, which was empty. Then back to the living room.

"Bon soir," said the husky voice.

She was seated in the corner, in darkness, smoking a cigarette. Her legs were tucked up under her in a rather girlish fashion. In the flare of her cigarette he saw the haughty face—high cheekbones, dark eyes, firm mouth. Her hair was glossy, dark blond, falling over her face. Impatiently she swept it back.

"Hello," he said.

She smiled. "How are you getting on?"

"Fine."

"Does he suspect?"

"No. He suspects nothing."

"Excellent," she said, puffing on the cigarette. "Now come and kiss me hello..."

ALSO BY MICHAEL CRICHTON
WRITING AS JOHN LANGE:

BINARY
DRUG OF CHOICE
EASY GO
GRAVE DESCEND
ODDS ON
SCRATCH ONE
ZERO COOL

SOME OTHER HARD CASE CRIME BOOKS
YOU WILL ENJOY:

CHOKE HOLD *by Christa Faust*
THE COMEDY IS FINISHED *by Donald E. Westlake*
BLOOD ON THE MINK *by Robert Silverberg*
FALSE NEGATIVE *by Joseph Koenig*
THE TWENTY-YEAR DEATH *by Ariel S. Winter*
THE COCKTAIL WAITRESS *by James M. Cain*
SEDUCTION OF THE INNOCENT *by Max Allan Collins*
WEB OF THE CITY *by Harlan Ellison*
JOYLAND *by Stephen King*
THE SECRET LIVES OF MARRIED WOMEN
by Elissa Wald

The VENOM BUSINESS

by Michael Crichton

WRITING AS JOHN LANGE

A HARD CASE CRIME NOVEL

A HARD CASE CRIME BOOK

(HCC-MC5)

First Hard Case Crime edition: November 2013

Published by

Titan Books
A division of Titan Publishing Group Ltd
144 Southwark Street
London SE1 0UP

in collaboration with Winterfall LLC

THE VENOM BUSINESS™
by Michael Crichton writing as John Lange™

ISBN 978-1-78329-122-9

Design direction by Max Phillips
www.maxphillips.net

Typeset by Swordsmith Productions

The name "Hard Case Crime" and the Hard Case Crime logo
are trademarks of Winterfall LLC. Hard Case Crime books
are selected and edited by Charles Ardai.

Printed in the United States of America

Visit us on the web at www.HardCaseCrime.com

For Herman Gollob,
who asked for it,
And for Robert Gutwillig,
who got it.

PART I *The Snake Man*

PART II *The Snake Convention*

PART III *The Venom Business*

THE VENOM BUSINESS

Part I:
The Snake Man

1. YUCATÁN

It was not a very good hotel, but it was the best in the town, and it had a fine old bar with overhead fans which rotated slowly, casting shadows across the ceiling. He was partial to that bar, with the creaking fans, and he liked the bartender, Henri, so whenever he came to Valladolid he stayed in the hotel.

The girl said, "Do you come here often?"

"Every month," he said.

"For snakes?"

"For snakes."

"Snakes have made Charles very rich," Henri said. Henri was an old Parisian; he loved to talk, long into the night. He particularly liked to talk to Raynaud, because he traveled so much.

"Pour yourself a drink," Raynaud said, "and shut up."

Henri laughed delightedly.

"And pour another for the girl," Charles Raynaud said.

The girl was sitting there, wearing trousers and a shirt with the sleeves rolled up. She was rather pretty, long blond hair pulled back casually; Henri introduced her as Jane Mitchell. She seemed quiet and reserved and a little stuffy.

"Miss Mitchell," Henri said, "just arrived today."

Raynaud said, "You're with a tour?"

She shook her head. "Hate tours."

He was genuinely surprised. "You came alone?"

"I can take care of myself," she replied quickly.

"Miss Mitchell," Henri said, "is on her way around the world."

"Vacation?"

"Escape," she said.

"From whom?"

"From New York," she said, pushing her glass across the bar to Henri.

"And how did you happen to choose this gay resort?"

"I wanted someplace out of the way."

"That," he said, sipping tequila again, "you definitely have."

Henri said, "Miss Mitchell was expressing great interest in your work."

"You'll have to excuse Henri," Raynaud said, "he is an incorrigible matchmaker."

"Nonsense," Henri said.

"Well, it's true," the girl said, "I was curious. I never heard of anybody collecting snakes before."

"Oh," Raynaud said, "I don't collect them. I sell them."

"Sell them?"

"To zoos," Henri said, "and to scientists."

"And snake farms," Raynaud said. "You might say I'm in the venom business."

"Is it interesting?" she asked.

"No," he said. "It's really quite dull."

"How do you catch them?"

He shrugged. "Prong, sometimes. Or a trap. But usually just bare hands."

"That," she said, "sounds interesting."

He smiled. "Only if you make a mistake."

"And you don't make mistakes?"

"Not if I can help it."

"You are very sour tonight, Charles," Henri said. "Invite the girl along. You can see that she wants to go."

"Oh, I couldn't—"

"Nonsense," Henri said, raising his hand. "Charles would be delighted to have you. He would say so himself but he has not had enough to drink. He's very shy."

"Really, I don't think—"

"You mustn't be put off by Charles, as you see him now. He is actually quite charming. Charles, be charming."

Raynaud grinned. "Miss Mitchell," he said, "you are cordially invited to a snake hunt tomorrow morning."

She hesitated.

"If you don't accept, I shall go to my room, which I now know to be second best in the hotel, and hang myself from the ceiling fan because I lacked the charm to convince you."

She smiled back at him. "That sounds awful."

"Then you accept?"

"I accept."

"Good. But you must understand two things. The first is that we leave at five in the morning. Sharp."

She nodded.

"And the second is that you will probably be very bored by the whole thing."

She smiled, and said, "I've been bored before. I think I can stand it."

"Then," Charles said, "allow me to buy you a drink."

When the girl had finally gone to bed, Raynaud stayed at the bar to have a last drink with Henri.

"You shouldn't have done that," Raynaud said.

"You were disgraceful," Henri said.

"I didn't want her to come."

"Absolutely disgraceful. Are you getting too old?"

"I have a tight schedule tomorrow."

"But she is very pretty, Charles."

"She is attractive."

"And besides, she is so unhappy. I think she has had bad luck with love, and now she needs to be happy."

"You think catching snakes will make her happy?"

"I think," Henri said, "that it will divert her."

"And I think that she will sleep peacefully until noon."

Henri looked at him slyly. "One hundred pesos?"

"One hundred pesos." He took the money from his wallet and set it on the bar.

"I fear you have just lost a bet."

"We'll see," Raynaud said.

He sat hunched over the wheel, concentrating on the driving. The Land Rover bounced over the muddy ruts of the jungle road as the first pale rays of dawn broke over the corozo trees along the horizon. They were huge trees with forty-foot fronds, glistening after a week of hot rains.

Alongside him, the girl sat smoking a cigarette, watching the road. Ramón, the boy, dozed in the back seat with all the gear.

"How much?" she said.

"A hundred pesos."

"Why did you bet?"

He shrugged. "Why does anybody bet?" he said.

"And now you're angry because I made you lose?"

"No," he said. In fact he was not. The usual girl he took hunting showed up in a cotton dress and sandals, and had to go back to change. But this one had arrived in heavy twill trousers and high boots, very businesslike. And in a way he was glad for the company.

"Where are we going?" she said.

"Chichén."

"Chichén Itzá? The ruins?"

"Yes."

"But is it open yet?"

He smiled. "I have a key."

"You seem to know your way around."

"I don't lose all my bets, if that's what you mean."

"No," she said, looking at him. "I don't think you do. But when Henri was talking about you…"

"You expected a little potbellied man with a pith helmet and a butterfly net."

"Very nearly."

"And instead you are dazzled by my wit and verve."

"How old are you?"

"Thirty-four. How old are you?"

"I'm not supposed to tell," she said.

"Yes. But then I'm not supposed to ask."

"Twenty-five," she said.

He took the left fork at the monument turnoff. Here, for no particular reason, pavement began. The road was good all the rest of the way to the ruin.

The girl brushed her hair back from her face. "It's already getting hot," she said.

"Yes. It will be a good day. The natives will refuse to work."

"Why?"

"Because a hot day after a rain brings the animals out."

"Then it should be perfect."

"Depending on your viewpoint," he said.

She finished her cigarette and lit another from the glowing tip. He glanced over at her and she said, "I'm not nervous. It's just how I wake up."

They came to the edge of the ruins; the pyramids could be seen to the left, rising over the trees.

"Have you ever been bitten?" she said.

"Yes."

"Often?"

"More often than I wanted to be."

"Are you married?" she said.

"No."

"Why not?"

He did not answer. They parked by the gates in front of the sign, glistening damp: "I.N.A.H. Departamento de Monumentos Prehispánicos, Zona Arqueológica de Chichén Itzá, Yucatán." They got out; around them the jungle was noisy with howler monkeys and the shrieking chatter of parrots. The ground underfoot was damp and steaming as Raynaud walked to the back of the car and began unloading the gear: a long, pronged aluminum stick, a machete, a heavy canvas bag, double-lined, and a small battered metal box.

Ramón, the boy, crawled yawning from the back seat. Jane Mitchell looked at the gear laid out, and said, "You don't have a gun."

"I do," Raynaud said. He produced the heavy .45 revolver. "But the boy gets it."

He handed it to Ramón.

"He comes with us?"

"No, he stays here. To make sure the car isn't stolen."

"But then you won't have a gun…"

"Won't need it," Raynaud said. He threw the bag over his shoulder, picked up the aluminum stick, and handed her the metal box.

"What's this?"

"Antivenom set."

"Just in case?" She opened the lid and surveyed the tourni-
quets, syringes, and rows of small vials.

"Just in case," Raynaud said.

They walked to the gate, unlocked it, and stepped inside.

She watched the way he moved through the tall grass. He
was a big man, well over six feet, and powerfully built, but he
walked with a slow grace. He kept his eyes on the ground, his
neck bent, and she noticed again the pale white scar that began
behind his right ear and disappeared down his collar. The scar
bothered her; many things about him bothered her. He did
not fit into any of the expected categories: too nasty to be a
zoologist, too subtle to be a bush hunter. She wondered if he
had done other work before.

"Where did you get the scar?"

Absently, he touched the line. "An accident."

"What kind of an accident?"

"When I was a child," he said vaguely, and moved ahead,
forcing her to hurry after him. He seemed to her a suddenly
mysterious figure, standing to his knees in tall grass and clinging,
steamy mist; he seemed almost to be floating, with the pyramids all around them. The jungle on the perimeter was now
silent as a tomb: all sound from the animals had stopped as soon
as they had entered the gates. Now there was nothing but a
faint swishing as they moved across the grass.

"Have you been in Mexico long?"

"Ten years."

"Always working with snakes?"

"No. I began as a foreman for archaeological digs. I was good
with languages, you see."

"Spanish?"

"And French. German. Russian and Japanese. A smattering
of English."

"Where did you learn them? College?"

"The Army."

He was frowning; her questions seemed to bother him. He
had a pleasant, almost boyish face, but it took on an ugly aspect
when he frowned, something dark and faintly sinister.

"But you *are* American."

"Oh, yes. Born and bred. The Bronx, actually."

And then he doubled over in a quick jackknife and was lost in the mist and grasses, and she heard a nasty hissing sound.

"Got him!"

He raised up with a long black snake dangling from one hand. He had caught it right behind the head. The snake wrapped itself about his forearm in sinuous coils.

"How do you like it?" he said, holding it so she could see the head, the gaping jaws, the pink grainy mouth.

She knew he was trying to shock her but she was not shocked. The snake was large but not half so ugly as the rattlesnakes she had grown up with.

"Very pretty," she said. "What is it?"

"Genus *vera ribocanthus*. Quite deadly. The natives call it the rollersnake, because of the way it moves." He examined it critically. "This is a fine specimen."

He dropped it into the bag and moved on.

"The poison," he said, "is a potent anticholinesterase. Interrupts nervous transmission at the neuromuscular junction. The victim dies of asphyxiation, by respiratory paralysis."

"Have you been doing studies?"

"No. Professor Levin at LSU. I supply him."

"You supply a lot of universities?"

"Quite a few."

They walked on. In a few minutes, the pattern was repeated again—a swift darting down, a scramble in the grass, and another snake. It seemed to be the same kind. He dropped it into the bag.

"You're very good at this."

"Practice," Raynaud said.

As he moved through the grass he was hardly aware of her. The questions annoyed him because they broke his concentration, lifting his attention away from the grass, where he was watching for small movements, small disturbances which moved counter to the wind.

As he walked he wondered about her, because she did not seem repelled by the snakes. Or fascinated: she watched them with a kind of cold, almost clinical interest. She showed none of the horrified thrill that the others had demonstrated.

Odd.

He bent forward slightly. He needed a third snake, and it might as well be a *vera*. They were cumbersome animals, easily caught. And there seemed to be many of them today.

In a few minutes, he saw another, sliding away. He darted forward and gripped it swiftly, catching the damp slimy body behind the head, squeezing the scaly flesh, feeling the coldness. He always had a moment of revulsion when his fingers touched it— just the briefest moment of elemental disgust, and then it passed.

Still bent over, he held the snake firmly as it wriggled and hissed. The tongue flicked out.

And then he froze.

Just three feet away was a diversnake, its orange and blue body coiled around a clump of grass. The diversnake was reared back to strike, the head high and moving from side to side, the mouth wide, the fangs showing whitely.

He did not move.

The diversnake was fiercely poisonous. No one had been known to survive a bite, and people had died of the most superficial scratches.

He waited.

For a moment he thought the diversnake, having been startled up into an attack stance, would lapse back. But then he realized that it was not going to, that it was pulling back in the last smooth gesture before it flung itself forward to strike....

A shot rang out, and another.

The first bullet caught the snake in the head, tossing it to one side. The second hit it as it fell and buried the head deep into the mud. The animal was dead, the body continuing to writhe reflexively.

He looked back over his shoulder. The girl was standing there with a gun in her hand, looking pale. Her purse was open and the gun was smoking faintly.

For a moment neither of them spoke, and then she said, "Are you all right?"

"Yes. Fine. Thanks to you."

"It looked…mean."

"It was. About as mean as they get."

He straightened up and dropped his snake into the bag. The girl slipped the gun back into her purse and clicked the latch shut.

"You, ah, had that with you all the time?"

"Yes. I always carry it."

He set the bag on the ground and took out his cigarettes. He shook one out for her, lit it, and took one for himself.

"Why?"

"You never can tell," she said, "when you'll need it."

"You obviously know how to shoot." He glanced back at the snake. She had fired from thirty feet, perhaps more. Most people couldn't hit a building at that distance, with a handgun.

"I learned young," she said, sucking on the cigarette. "I grew up on a ranch."

"Alms to your teacher," he said. "You saved my life."

She smiled slightly. "Glad to be of service."

On the way back, he said little. The girl sat alongside him, and as he drove, he found himself growing curious about her. He looked over at her and decided that Henri was right, she was exceptionally pretty.

"What are you doing tonight?"

"Me?" She smiled. "Nothing."

"How would you like to go to a party?"

"In the jungle?"

"Hardly. There's going to be a reception at the German Embassy."

"Embassy? But that's in—"

"Mexico City. Yes."

"I don't have a plane ticket," she said.

"You don't need one," he said.

At three thousand feet, the jungle lay vast, dense, and impenetrable below them. Raynaud checked his compass and sat back in the seat. In the cockpit alongside him Jane Mitchell said, "How long have you had it?"

"Three years."

"It says 'Herpetology, Inc.' on the side panel. Is that your company?"

"That's it," he said.

"Snakes must pay well," she said.

"They do, they do."

She lit a cigarette and said, "Why did you ask me to come to the party?"

"Because you saved my life."

"I didn't."

"You did." He laughed. "Besides, you're very pretty. Have you got a dress, or do you want to buy one?"

"I have a black cocktail thing," she said. "It's mildly indecent."

"Perfect," Raynaud said. "The German ambassador is a dirty old man."

She looked out at the jungle. "But I don't have a hotel reservation," she said.

"You don't need one," he said.

The house was located in the *Marjunas* suburb of Mexico City, a modern, almost futuristic area of lava fields, the houses blending into the stark landscape. Raynaud's house had a pool and fountains in front, a lush garden in back. The house itself was glass and steel, harshly simple.

She looked at the living room, the Barcelona chairs and the native rugs, the careful use of heavy Spanish furniture, the white walls.

"Snakes may pay well," she said, "but not this well."

"You'd be surprised," he said.

His housekeeper, Margarita, a severe-looking woman of fifty, greeted them. She looked with distaste at Jane. "Will you have dinner, sir?"

"After the reception."

"For one?"

"For two."

When they were alone in the living room, Jane flopped onto a chair. "I'm exhausted."

"Drink first. There's plenty of time. The reception isn't until seven. What will you have?"

"Scotch on the rocks."

"Water?"

"No."

He mixed two Scotches. She was still wearing her boots and slacks and a man's shirt. She watched as he made drinks, and said, "I have a feeling about you."

"Oh?"

"Yes. I have a feeling that you are a liar."

He laughed. "I am."

"I mean, a *good* liar. A professional."

"I am. But I have a feeling about you, too."

"Oh?"

He gave her the drink. "I think," he said, "that you are running away, and not just from New York."

"His name was George," she said. "Does that explain anything?"

"Georges are awful," he said. They clicked glasses. Reddish afternoon sunlight streamed into the living room. "Would you like the guest room," he said, "or the master bedroom?"

"Which is preferable?"

"The master bedroom."

"Does it include the master?"

"Generally speaking," Raynaud said, "it does."

She looked at him steadily over her glass. "You were right about one thing," she said.

"What's that?"

"You're not very romantic."

He laughed. "No, I suppose I'm not."

"I think I would like a cold shower," she said, standing up. "I feel grubby."

"There's something better."

"Yes?"

He nodded to the outside. "The pool."

"I didn't bring a suit."

"Doesn't matter."

"It does to me."

"I mean," he said, "that I stock a supply."

*

He stood by the side of the pool in the fading light and watched as she swam. He toweled himself dry and sipped the Scotch and smiled as she turned at the poolside, and swam back in long, easy strokes. She had chosen the smallest bikini, a yellow one with red trim, and she wore it with grace and quiet confidence. She also didn't mind getting her hair wet: he disliked women who paddled about with their heads above the water.

He sat down in a deck chair and watched as she got out of the water and wrapped a towel around her. She sat next to him and said, "It feels marvelous. Stop staring."

"Wasn't."

"I have to lose three pounds."

"Where?"

She picked up her drink and combed her wet hair. As if suddenly remembering, she said, "How will I ever dry it? There won't be time."

"I have a hairdryer."

She paused then, and looked at him. "You come fully equipped."

"Just the usual," he said.

She sat back in the chair, closed her eyes, and faced the sun. "This is marvelous," she said. "I could stay here forever."

"You're invited."

Without opening her eyes: "Thanks anyway."

"Really," he said. "I'm going away on business. You'll have the house to yourself. You might as well stay."

"I couldn't."

"You certainly could."

She picked up her drink. "Where are you going?"

"To London. There's a convention of herpetologists."

She smiled.

"Is that funny?"

"No. It's just that I have to go to London as well."

"Oh?"

"On business," she said.

"I thought you were traveling around the world."

"Yes. But I have to stop in London." She looked at him. "When are you leaving?"

Feeling strangely guilty, he said, "Tomorrow morning."

She paused and sipped the drink, then set it down on the glass poolside table.

"I could go with you," she said.

"No."

"All right," she said quickly.

"I have to go to Paris first," he explained.

"Oh," she said. "I don't like Paris much."

"Neither do I."

She seemed depressed for a moment, then smiled. "Well, perhaps we'll meet in London."

"Yes." he said. "Perhaps we will."

"The Bronx," he said, standing in front of the mirror and tying his black silk tie. He looked at her reflected image as she stood in the doorway, watching him. She wore a black silk dress that was as scandalous as she promised: cut high to the hip and low over her breasts. "The Bronx. Ever been?"

"I've lived in New York."

"East Side, I bet."

She smiled. "Off and on."

He adjusted the ruffles of his shirt and shrugged into the dinner jacket. "Well, I was raised on the rough side of the Bronx."

"What made you decide to come to Mexico?"

He buttoned the jacket. "I went to Yale for a while. Six months, to be exact. Then I…left. Joined the Army. The Army discovered I was good at languages. They sent me to Monterey."

"But now you're going to the German Embassy reception."

"Yes. In Mexico, they think I am amusing. I had an aunt in Columbus who left me some money. Nobody knew she had it until she died." He laughed. "My parents were furious."

"That was how you started your business?"

"More or less."

He pulled his sleeves and adjusted the cufflinks. Then he turned away from the mirror.

"Shall we go?"

"You look quite foppish."

"An act," he said, taking her arm. They walked out of the bedroom to the living room. There he paused.

"Wait a bit. Forgot my cigarettes."

He left her and walked back to the bedroom. There he paused to look through the door; she was standing in the living room, admiring a Spanish chest, running her fingers over the carved surface.

He went to the bedroom dresser, took out the revolver, broke it open, and counted the shells. Then he jammed it into his belt.

He returned to the living room a moment later. "All set."

As they went to the door, she said, "You know, I don't believe you left your cigarettes behind at all. I think it was something else."

"Oh? Why?"

"Because there were three packs of cigarettes on the bar."

"Forgot they were there."

"Not likely," she said.

They walked down the steps cut into the lava to the garage.

The butler, dressed stiffly in white tie and tails, opened the door for Jane Mitchell and helped her out of the gray Imperial convertible. "Good evening, Madam," he said. "Good evening, Mr. Raynaud."

"Good evening, Luis."

"They are gathering upstairs, sir."

"Thank you."

Luis opened the door to the mansion and they entered the marble lobby. A curved staircase led up to the second floor; they heard the tinkle of glasses and laughter. As they walked up, Jane said, "Very impressive."

"The Germans are trying hard in Mexico. Making up for lost time."

"Or lost rebellions," she said.

At the head of the stairs, the man inquired after their names and announced loudly, "Señorita Mitchell and Señor Raynaud."

They moved down the receiving line.

"Charles," said the first in line, Mrs. Burkheit. "You have

brought another beauty with you. Wherever do you find them?"

"In the bush," Raynaud said.

"Charmed," Mrs. Burkheit said.

"Delighted," Jane said, extending a frosty hand.

"Do look after Charles," Mrs. Burkheit said. "He is so un-stable."

"He seems to look after himself," Jane said.

Charles smiled blandly.

The rest of the receiving line was the same: Mrs. Everson; Mrs. Spengler; Mr. Spengler; the wife of the Ambassador, Mrs. Kronkheit; and finally the ambassador himself.

"Delightful," the ambassador said.

"Wonderful to see you again," Raynaud said.

"She is quite delightful," the ambassador said, looking down Jane's dress.

"Thank you," Jane said, giving him a small curtsy and a large look.

At the end of the receiving line, as was the custom, stood a man with a large tray of drinks. Jane took a glass of champagne and said, "You were right."

"What?"

"He is a dirty old man."

"You chose the dress," Raynaud said.

"Still, he didn't have to stare that way."

"Anyone would stare."

"You haven't."

"Yes, I have," Raynaud said, staring.

"Stop it," she said, sipping champagne.

"Only if you tell me your decision," he said.

"About what?"

"About whether you want the master bedroom or the guest room."

They moved out among the guests at the reception. Raynaud walked to a corner and stood near the wall. In a sudden move-ment Jane pressed up against him and then stepped, back, smiling.

"So," she said.

"So?"

"You forgot cigarettes?"

"Yes."

"You forgot the gun which is stuck in your belt," she said. "I'd guess it is a thirty-eight Smith and Wesson."

"You have a very sensitive stomach."

"Trained."

She looked at him and sipped champagne. "I don't understand you," she said. "You won't take a gun snake-hunting, but you take one to a diplomatic reception."

"Actually, I have to leave soon."

"Oh?"

"Yes. A brief departure. For half an hour or so."

"Your business?"

"Yes."

"Snakes?"

"Of course," Raynaud said.

She stared at him evenly. "You're lying," she said.

"Of course."

The butler came up. "Señor Raynaud, you have a telephone call."

Raynaud moved away from her. "Excuse me for a while."

"I don't know anybody here."

"They'll introduce themselves. Don't worry." He moved off into the crowd. "Just watch out for the German ambassador. He's a whipper."

He moved to a corner and picked up the phone.

"Hello?"

"Señor Raynaud?" It was a deep and throaty voice.

"Speaking."

"I am ready."

"Fine."

He was about to hang up when the voice said, "But señor…"

He paused. "Yes."

"There is a small trouble."

"Oh?"

"Our friend. He has made preparations."

"Then we shall also make preparations," Raynaud said, and hung up.

He went downstairs and ducked back into the shadows beneath the curving marble stairway. There, he withdrew a penknife from his pocket and flicked open the blade. Deftly, he stabbed the tip of his finger and squeezed it until it was bleeding profusely. He wrapped the finger in a handkerchief and made certain that the blood stained through the white cloth.

Then he went to see the downstairs butler, Luis.

"Señor Raynaud, you have hurt yourself."

Raynaud shrugged. "A small cut. Broken glass."

"But you must attend it."

"No time," Raynaud said. "Call a taxi."

"There is a taxi outside, señor," Luis said. "It will take but a moment. If you will come with me to the first-aid kit…"

Raynaud hesitated, then followed him. They walked down a hallway to a small bathroom. A kit hung on the wall. Luis opened it and took out a bandage.

"I can take care of it myself," Raynaud said. "Just give me the tape."

Luis looked doubtful. Raynaud took the tape.

"Really, it is nothing. Very small. I can take care of it in the taxi."

"If you insist, señor…"

"I do."

Raynaud dropped the tape in his pocket, and with his other hand gave Luis fifty pesos.

"Now let's get a taxi."

In the taxi he applied a small strip of tape to the cut and put the rest of the roll in his pocket. He directed the taxi to a garage in the poor, Valdente section of town. There he got out and went in, tipping the attendant. He climbed into a battered, dusty Chevrolet sedan, inserted a key, and drove off. He was tired, gripping the wheel tensely. He knew it was the job, and the strain that was coming. He did not like to think about it, but it hung at the back of his mind. It was a big risk, with so much money involved.

For a moment, he wondered what Jane Mitchell would say if she saw him now.

He drove for several minutes, deep into the slums south of the city. At length he parked across from a modern high-rise structure. It was brightly lighted and freshly painted, but the laundry hanging out from the balconies gave it a dismal, depressing air.

He drove past the apartment house slowly, peering out of the car window. Around the building, someone had attempted to grow grass and small bushes, but the ground was too dry for the plants to take hold; they were blighted and scruffy.

He looked closely.

He saw one, crouching back from the door.

Two: a second, pulled back into the corners and deep shadows to the right.

And there was probably a third somewhere. Because Miguel could afford a third man, and because he would know it was necessary to handle Raynaud.

Damn Miguel.

He drove around the block and parked his car. He paused, blinked his lights, and doused them. Then he waited. After a moment Rico came up and slipped quietly into the back seat.

"What have you seen?" Raynaud said.

"Three," Rico said. "One in the front. Another to the side. A third upstairs."

"No more?"

"No more," Rico said.

"How long have you been watching?"

"Five hours, as you instructed," Rico said. He smiled, showing white teeth in the dark. "You do not trust Miguel, eh?"

"I trust no one," Raynaud said. "Not even you."

Rico seemed to accept this; he nodded. "Miguel has a new woman. She is a beauty."

"He cannot afford her."

"So he cuts the corners, eh?"

"If he can." Raynaud lit a cigarette and smoked in the silence. "Do you think they will try it before, or after?"

"After, I think."

"Did you see guns?"

"No. No guns."

Raynaud nodded, and puffed the cigarette. He stared at the apartment building. "You have done well, Rico."

"Thank you, Señor Raul."

"I shall go in now. If you hear gunshots, call the police. Understood?"

"Understood, Señor Raul."

Raynaud got out. He stripped off his dinner jacket and slipped it into the trunk; then he took out a long serape. It looked absurd, the brightly colored material against his dark trousers with the stripe. But in a fast situation, no one would notice.

He started to walk away, and Rico called, "Señor, shall I have him killed?"

"No. Not yet."

He moved forward toward the apartment house, watching the bushes from the corner of his eyes. Nothing moved. This, he knew, was the hardest part, to walk among the men as if he did not know they were there. But he had no choice; he must not alert Miguel. Otherwise all was lost.

Poor Miguel.

The last time Raynaud had visited the smuggler, he had noticed the woman. She was striking, a smoldering black-haired woman, but she was too expensive for Miguel. It was inevitable that he would try something like this.

Raynaud entered the building and took the elevator up to the ninth floor. His heart was pounding, thumping away inside his chest.

The elevator gave a musical chime and stopped. Raynaud walked down a long corridor to the door marked 12. He knocked, and stepped back.

Miguel answered, looking sleepy.

"Hello, Miguel."

"Señor Foxwell. I thought you would never come, my friend." Miguel smiled, stepped back, and gestured for Raynaud to enter.

The apartment inside was brightly lighted. Raynaud entered, his hand at his waist, beneath the serape.

"I am alone," Miguel said in a hurt voice. "Except, of course, for the woman."

"Of course." Raynaud grinned. "You think I don't trust you?"

"I know you don't trust me," Miguel said unhappily. He closed the door. "Brandy?"

"Small."

"This is a very special brandy," Miguel said. "Courvoisier."

"Where did you get it?" Raynaud asked, sitting down. He tried to appear casual; he knew it was important.

"It was borrowed from the British Embassy," Miguel said. "Five cases of it. The delivery truck had a flat tire, and while the driver went to telephone…" He shrugged, and poured a glass for Raynaud. "Excellent timing."

Raynaud raised his glass. "To you, Miguel."

"And you, Señor Foxwell."

Raynaud brought the glass to his lips and then set it aside as if a thought had come to him. "I am eager to be going."

"Ah. And I hoped you would stay."

"I cannot." Raynaud set the glass down. "The stuff," he said. "You have it?"

"Yes. Both. In superb condition. You wish to see?"

"No," Raynaud said.

"Ah." Miguel grinned. "Then you trust me after all."

Raynaud shook his head. "I will wait until I am in the hall to look," he said. "You know that."

Miguel laughed, not sure whether to believe it or not. He went to get the stuff and Raynaud waited on the couch. The girl came in, wearing a tight red knit dress that clung to her body.

"Señor Foxwell," she said.

"Señora." It was a polite term only; there were no illusions.

"It is nice to see you again," she said.

"Indeed, it is my pleasure." He watched her closely as she approached him.

"I cannot speak now," she whispered, "but be careful as you leave. There is a man and he may be armed."

"Just one?"

"Yes. One. But an evil man." She came close and brushed her breasts against his arm. "Be careful. And tomorrow you can find me at the Café Andaluz."

"All right," he said.

Miguel returned with the cardboard box under his arm. "Here it is," he said.

"Good." Raynaud took the box, feeling its weight, then set it on the chair. "Now the money."

"You will remember," Miguel said, "that we agreed upon one thousand dollars."

"That's right," Raynaud said. He opened his billfold and removed three crisp hundred-dollar bills. He set them on the table.

"But, señor—"

"Miguel," Raynaud said, sliding back his serape to show the gun, "I have received some bad news recently."

"But, señor, I do not know what you have heard. It cannot be true. We do business together for many years. We are old friends."

"That's right," Raynaud said, standing up. "But I trust my source."

"Your source?"

"Yes. Your friend there."

The girl looked at him in shocked surprise, and Miguel whirled on her.

At that moment, Raynaud brought the barrel of the gun down hard across the back of Miguel's head. It made an ugly crunching sound and the Mexican dropped silently.

The girl stared with wide eyes. "Señor," she began.

"Sorry," Raynaud said, "but you know how it is."

With a second blow, he caught her behind the ear, a careful blow so as to avoid the face. The girl's face was her livelihood and he did not want to ruin it with a jagged scar from the sight at the end of the barrel. If Miguel wanted to ruin her face later, that was his business.

Besides, the girl had lied to him. There were three men.

He watched as she fell to the carpet, her skirt sliding up to her hips. She was a sensual girl, even unconscious. Quickly, he bent over her and withdrew the tape from his pocket. In a few quick strokes he had taped her hands and legs behind her back, and fastened a strip across her mouth and eyes. He moved to Miguel and did the same. The tape over the eyes did nothing, except disorient them.

He slipped out of the apartment with the box firmly under his arm. The hallway was clear. He shut the door and walked down the hall to the elevator.

He paused at the elevator, then pressed the button. It lighted. He hesitated a moment, then hurried down the service stairs at the end of the corridor. He moved quickly but silently down eight flights of stairs, and halted at the ground floor.

Looking out through the small glass window in the door, he saw a Mexican in peasant costume—bright serape and drab, baggy pants—lounging next to the elevator. Another was just outside the door, and a third, near the street and Raynaud's car. They were obviously good men; they blended well, inconspicuous, average, retiring. Their bodies seemed perfectly relaxed though he knew they were not.

Good men.

He went back to the first floor, padded down the corridor, and pulled the fire alarm.

Racing back down, he saw the three men looking at each other, startled, confused. The alarm rang loudly, and above him he heard the shouts of frightened tenants. The men heard them too. Raynaud ran out toward the first man and caught him head on, knocking him to the ground. He kicked him hard in the head and stomach; the man vomited and was still.

Raynaud pushed through the doors with the box under his left arm. The second man crouched as he approached. Raynaud drew his gun and the man backed off; Raynaud swung and caught him in the face with the flat of the barrel and the bones of the nose cracked sickeningly. The man fell to the ground.

The third man, waiting by the car, drew a knife. Raynaud glanced back at the building; the alarm still sounded and the tenants were opening their windows, shouting, looking out, and running down the stairs. Raynaud fired his gun in the air and the third man, startled and afraid, turned and ran. He dropped his knife in the street.

Raynaud jumped in his car and roared off as the first police patrol car and fire engine arrived. As he drove away, he hoped that Miguel would have the sense to run for it. If Miguel was quick, he would break the tapes and cross the Guatemalan border before midnight, hiding out in a small village somewhere. If he did that, Angelo would never find him.

And Raynaud hoped to hell that Angelo would never find him.

The butler said, "Ah, Señor Raynaud, you are back."

"Luis, I must make a call."

"Of course. There is a private telephone in the drawing room."

The butler showed him the way to an empty room on the ground floor, decorated with heavy, Spanish-American furniture, but charming in its way. Luis retreated respectfully as Raynaud dialed.

An irritable, sleepy voice answered. "Hello."

"Angelo? This is Marcus."

The voice did not seem particularly pleased. "So? Business or pleasure, Señor Marcus?"

"Business. You know Miguel Santoz?"

"The little mestizo who smuggles?"

"That's right."

"What about him?"

"Kill him," Raynaud said.

The voice at the other end sighed, "Kill him, or scare him?"

"Kill him."

"How much?"

"One hundred dollars."

"For one hundred dollars," Angelo said, "I do not go into Guatemala. I am wanted there."

"Kill him in Mexico."

"If he is still here."

"Yes," Raynaud said. "If he is still here."

He hung up and went back to the lobby.

Jane Mitchell was in a corner, talking with a short man in a rented, baggy set of tails. It made him look rather like a turtle balancing on the edge of his shell. Jane introduced him and said, "Charles, this is Peter Manchester."

"How do," said Peter Manchester, with a small but firm hand-shake. "Import-export. What's your game?"

"I'm in the slave trade," Raynaud said.

"Oh," Manchester said. "That's related."

"Related to what?"

"Import-export," he said vaguely. He was quite drunk. "How long you been at it?"

"What?"

"The slave trade."

"Years," Raynaud said. "You see, my father was an Eskimo."

"Really? You don't look Eskimo."

"I know," Raynaud said, "but I have an Eskimo name."

"Personally, I hate the cold," Manchester said. "Hate it. That's why I came to Mexico."

"Understandable," Raynaud said.

"Quite," Manchester said, and wandered off for another glass of champagne.

Jane looked at him for a moment. "Everything all right? With your business."

"Fine," he said. "Just fine."

"No trouble?"

"Nothing much," he said.

"You seem in a good mood."

"I am," he said. He noticed again her abbreviated dress, and put his arm around her. "Won't you catch cold, in a dress like that?"

"Don't you know?" She laughed. "We Eskimos never catch cold."

They walked off, through the party.

"I'm glad you're back," she said.

"I'm glad to be back."

"Then take your hand off my ass."

"It was around your waist."

"Then it slipped."

"I guess it did."

"And it's rubbing right this minute."

"Feels nice."

"Stop it."

Benson came up. Benson was drunk as usual. Benson always got drunk on other people's liquor.

"Charles. What brings you in from the bush?"

He shrugged. "Business."

"Snakes again?" Benson shuddered. "Where are you off to now? Sweden? Canada? Rio?"

"Paris, actually. A delivery of three."

"Paris." Benson sighed. "And all he cares about is snakes. A tragedy." He winked at Jane. "Quite a looker you have there, snake man."

He wandered off.

"Snake man?" Jane said.

"That's what they call me."

"Why?"

"Because of my, ah, line of work."

"Somehow," Jane said, "I don't believe it. I don't believe you're only interested in snakes. Get your hand off my ass. People are watching."

"People aren't. And talk nicely."

"I'll scream." Pause. "That's better."

"You're very cruel," he said, his hand up around her waist again.

"And you're quite dexterous," she said.

"Quick hands. Useful in business."

"I'm not in business," she said, and spun lightly away from him.

They had dinner on the terrace, alongside the pool. He told her stories about his travels and avoided too much talk about his past. He disliked talking about his past, or thinking about it. Things were good now: he could sit by his pool beneath the stars and eat a candlelit dinner with a pretty girl. The present was enough.

After dinner they had coffee and cognac. She sat back in her chair and said, "I'm tired. All that champagne."

He glanced at his watch. It was late; he would have to pack. And for that, he would need to be alone.

"All right," he said. "Margarita will make up the guest room."

She smiled slightly. "I don't have to fight you off?"

"Probably not."

"I admit," she said, "I was expecting a battle."

"I never fight with women."

"Whom do you fight with?" she asked, looking again at the scar.

"Customs officials," he said, and rang the bell for the servant.

Margarita took Jane off to the guest wing, and he remained alone for a moment, staring up at the stars and planning the next morning. He considered the details, and small points, the minor facts. They would be crucial, as they always were.

Raynaud believed in details. You never got caught, if you attended to details, and did your homework.

He got up and went past the master bedroom to a small study. There he unlocked the lowest drawer of the desk and removed a strongbox, also locked. He opened this and took out the four passports.

Charles Foxwell, born Louisville, Kentucky, 1930. Middle-aged, white hair, horn-rim spectacles.

Barnaby Raymond, born Chicago, Illinois, 1928. Grinning all-American into the camera, a smooth unlined salesman's face.

Raymond Charles, born New York, New York, 1931. A drooping, jowly countenance with a dissatisfied scowl. Moustache.

Charles Raynaud, born New York, New York, 1932. His own picture, without changes.

He picked them up and examined them in turn. Then he looked at the other documents, the import and export licenses for Mexico, France, England, Germany...

"Am I disturbing you?"

He looked up. Jane was standing in the doorway, in a floor-length white nightgown. How long had she been there?

"No," he said calmly, pushing the passports aside, so that they were out of her view. "Not at all." He moved from behind the desk and walked over to her.

"I wanted to tell you," she said, "that the room is wonderful, and I'm going to bed."

She looked young and girlish in the nightgown.

"You want to be tucked in?"

"It's not necessary," she said. "Will I see you in the morning?"

"No. I leave early. But I hope you'll stay and use the house…"

"I may, for a day or two."

"Good."

"Will I see you in London?"

He shrugged. "Possibly."

"Then I'll say good night," she said.

She hesitated for a moment. He bent over and kissed her lightly on the forehead.

"Good night," he said.

He watched as she walked down to the other end of the house, then he turned back into the study and closed the door behind him, and locked it.

At the desk, he selected his own passport. It indicated he had not been to Paris in a year and a half, a respectable amount of time. His own passport would be fine.

But clothes…

He went to the closet and slid the doors open. He would need something tweedy and scholarly. It was summer, of course, but tweeds were still best. Then a heavy, woolen knit tie from England. And sensible cordovan shoes. It would all look right together.

He dropped his passport into the breast pocket, together with the French import license covering everything but unvaccinated primate animals and feathered birds. He put the Mexican export license in another pocket.

Then he walked out to the terrace. He took with him a red marker and a stencil. On the terrace was the perforated box. He set the stencil over it and wrote in French, Spanish, and English:

CAUTION: POISONOUS REPTILES

He lifted the stencil, surveyed the printing, and smiled. He set sawdust on the inside, then picked up the heavy canvas sack containing the snakes he had caught that morning, and transferred the snakes to the box.

They made rustling sounds on the sawdust. It was all mildly sinister.

He looked at the box while he had a final brandy and then, very tired, he went off to bed.

✿

At six in the morning he was showered, and dressed in his tweeds. He had the box under his arm and was slipping out the door when he saw Jane Mitchell.

She smiled at him. "I wanted to see you off."

"You shouldn't have bothered."

She nodded to the box. "Those are the snakes you are delivering?"

"Yes."

She was still wearing her nightgown; her face was creased prettily from sleep. "And why the get-up?"

"What get-up?"

"The tweedy clothes. You look like a college professor."

He shrugged noncommittally.

"I think," she said, "that you are very strange."

"I am."

"I hope we meet in London," she said. "Do try to make it."

"I will," he said.

"Do," she said, and came up and kissed him very hard on the mouth.

"That's quite an enticement," he said. "Is it a preview of coming attractions?"

"Maybe," she said. She looked at him steadily for a moment. "We have a lot to talk about in London."

"Oh?"

"Yes," she said. She kissed him again, lightly this time, her lips just brushing.

"Such as?"

"Such as why you have four passports," she said, and smiled.

"You were spying," he said.

"I was curious," she said.

"And now?"

"And now, I am even more curious," she said, and gave him a final, very long kiss, which bothered him and amused him and left him feeling a little dizzy, but altogether good.

The airplane cruised at thirty-five thousand feet over the blue water of the Gulf of Mexico. Seated forward in the economy class, looking rather timidly out the window, was Dr. Charles Raynaud, Assistant Professor of Zoology.

He had taken pains to be sure everyone knew his position; he announced it loudly to the ground crews and the girls on the plane. A stewardess came up and said, "Would you care for a drink, Doctor Raynaud?"

"I would adore it," Raynaud said. "Absolutely *adore* it. I'm parched: do you have any sherry?"

"I'm sorry. We don't."

"Dubonnet?"

"No. I'm sorry."

"Then ginger ale."

The stewardess nodded and left. Raynaud removed his wire-rimmed spectacles and wiped them on the end of his tie. He squinted and blinked myopically at the other passengers, then replaced his glasses and settled back in the seat.

Professor. He smiled to himself.

He had learned long ago that certain kinds of status went unchallenged by virtually anyone. Few people recognized this. For example, nobody ever called upon a man to prove he was married, except under the most extraordinary circumstances. Similarly, you could claim any number of academic degrees and professional qualifications—professor, doctor, lawyer— without the slightest trouble, so long as you fulfilled the expectations of the people around you. A doctor had a black bag and a serious demeanor. A lawyer had a briefcase and a rigidly conservative suit. And a professor...

He smiled as the stewardess came up with his drink. She saw the box on the seat alongside him, and read the label.

"What do you have there?"

"Three snakes," Raynaud said.

"Snakes?" She gave a girlish shudder.

"Very rare and valuable snakes," Raynaud said.

"I see," she said. "Are they really—"

"Poisonous? Very. Very, very, very." He sipped his ginger ale and smacked his lips. "Among the most poisonous known. They are members of the species *Xanthus*, indigenous to the Yucatán jungle."

"Fascinating," she said, looking down the aisle, as if she wished to leave.

"Oh, quite," Raynaud said. He rubbed his hands together.

"Are you aware that one ounce—one ounce, mind you—of their venom could kill all the inhabitants of a small city? That no more than one hundred molecules of venom can paralyze a healthy man for life?"

The stewardess nodded numbly.

"The venom," Raynaud explained, "does not work by the usual methods of depolarization of the neuromuscular junction or interruption of axonal coupling. Nor is there an oxidative-phosphorylation effect. Rather the venom contains an enzyme, phosphogluconase. It's important in intermediate metabolism. Carbohydrate entry into cell membranes. Shift of receptor sites, that kind of thing."

"You seem to know a lot about it," the stewardess said.

"Oh, yes," Raynaud said. "You see, snakes are my life."

2. PARIS

In the sterile, glass-and-steel confines of Orly Airport, he talked with the customs officer. He spoke French badly, as suited a zoology professor.

The customs officer glanced at Raynaud's bags and said, "You will be long in France, Monsieur?"

"Two months."

"On vacation?"

"Yes, but also business." He handed the man his import license. The customs officer scanned it quickly.

"It is for that?" he asked, pointing to the box.

"Yes."

"I must call." He went to a phone nearby. Raynaud looked down the line of other waiting passengers, talking with different customs officials. And then he recognized a familiar face.

Arriz.

It was incredible: he was certain Arriz was dead. There had been several reports, yet here he was, in the flesh, going through French customs.

Without a disguise, either, Raynaud saw. Christ, Arriz had guts.

And obviously a bad passport, because the customs man studying it was lingering, looking at each page. Finally he paused and held the page with the photograph up to the light.

"Monsieur," said the customs man, "I am afraid this passport is not—"

Raynaud did not wait. In a moment he had slit the tape which held his box closed, and allowed one of the snakes to fall out onto the floor. A woman saw it and screamed.

"Back, everyone," Raynaud said, making a great commotion. "Everyone back. They are very poisonous."

The snake slithered over the baggage and slipped down behind the customs area. There was great noise and confusion now.

Raynaud scrambled after his snake. A young girl began to cry loudly. A little boy chewing gum laughed and pointed to it; he tugged at his mother's skirts to get her attention. The mother saw it and fainted.

Several minutes passed before he was able to retrieve his snake and get it safely back into the box. When he looked up, Arriz was gone.

The customs man down the line realized it too. "Stop that man!" he shouted.

Raynaud looked over. Arriz was walking quickly out through the lobby, toward the waiting taxis.

"Stop him!"

The guards ran, and so did Arriz. He sprinted into a taxi, slammed the door, and roared off. Probably with a gun at the cabby's ear, Raynaud thought.

Raynaud's own customs man came back, after a lengthy conference on the phone. He had missed all the excitement. Meantime an airport official was berating Raynaud in rapid French about the dangers of animals improperly caged; how could Raynaud be so clumsy? Raynaud was trying to make apologies in his slow French with a bad accent when the customs man cut in.

"Monsieur Raynaud. Come with me, please."

There was a moment of silence.

"Is something wrong?" Raynaud said.

"Your animals," the customs man said. "They must be checked."

"But my license—"

"They must still be checked."

Raynaud sighed. The customs man said, "Bring your bags, and follow me."

Raynaud followed. He had not expected this; in theory the customs people were supposed to take one quick, horrified look and pass him by. He trailed behind the customs man as they moved down a corridor, away from the tourist arrival area. Finally they came to a door marked IMPORTATION. The man opened it without knocking, and waved Raynaud inside. The room contained a bare desk, and a chair. There was no one in the room.

"Please wait here, Monsieur Raynaud."

"Docteur," Raynaud corrected, in his best priggish style. He allowed himself to show some irritation over the proceedings.

The man was contrite. "Pardon, Docteur. If you would be so kind, have your import license and passport ready. It will be just a few moments."

The door closed. Raynaud was alone.

He smoked a cigarette and looked around the room for an ashtray. Finding none, he ground it out on the floor.

Another man entered the room. He was heavyset and jovial, wearing a gray uniform, not the tan uniform of customs officials.

"Docteur Raynaud. Sorry to inconvenience you."

"Not at all," Raynaud said, rather stiffly.

The man stepped behind the desk. "Your documents, please."

Raynaud handed them over. The man studied them briefly and tapped the import license with his finger. "Snakes, eh?"

Raynaud nodded.

"In the box?"

"Yes."

"It is unfortunate," said the man, "that one of them should have slipped out back there. It caused a great commotion."

"I apologize," Raynaud said. "You see, the tapes were weak. The Mexicans insisted on examining the contents."

"The Mexicans," the man said with a laugh. "They are so absurdly suspicious. May I ask why you are bringing these snakes to France?"

"I am a Professor of Zoology. I am delivering these to the Institut des Études Reptiliennes."

"I see," the man said.

He opened the desk drawer and removed a thick brown manual. He thumbed through it and for a moment Raynaud thought he was looking up the Institut. That would be a disaster, because the Institut des Études Reptiliennes did not exist.

But the man smiled and said, "Ah, here we are. Rules governing importation of reptiles. Category seven, snakes." He ran his finger down the page. "They are not intended as pets?"

"Good Lord, no. They are extremely poisonous. Purely scientific research."

"Yes. Here we are. Research purposes." He read for a moment, shrugged, and closed the book. "There is no problem."

This seemed to conclude the official business. He reached into his pocket. "Cigarette?"

Raynaud took it. The man lit it for him, and grinned. "Actually," he said, "this is all because of Artur."

"Artur?"

"The customs man. He hates snakes, can't bear the sight of them. That was why he had you sent here. Normally we handle other problems—dogs without the proper shots, that kind of thing. Monkeys with a virus."

Raynaud sucked back the harsh smoke from the Gauloise cigarette, savoring the taste. But he remembered at the last moment to cough convincingly.

"Too strong?" the man asked.

"Just not used to them," he said.

The official pointed to the box. "There remains a final formality," he said. "May I see them?"

"The snakes?"

"Please."

"Of course," Raynaud said. "But stand back, they are quite deadly."

He slipped the seals and opened the lid slowly. The customs man glanced inside quickly, then nodded.

"All right," he said, "that's fine."

Ten minutes later, after a short lecture on being careful not to let them loose again, Professor Charles Raynaud was in a taxi, headed toward Paris.

He found a room in the Hotel Villefranche, a modest pension on the Left Bank, which he judged suitable for a zoology professor. While signing in, the manager regarded the cardboard box with suspicion and gave Raynaud another lecture on the snakes. Raynaud promised he would guard them securely.

In his room, he placed the suitcase on the bed, and the box alongside it, then went to dinner. The manager recommended a café around the corner, and it was not bad. Raynaud had boeuf bourguignon, and looked at the flaking paint on the ceiling. It amused him to look at the ceiling and to think that in another few days he would be dining at La Tour d'Argent.

After dinner, he used the restaurant telephone to make a call.

"Monsieur Graham, please."

A neutral voice said, "Who is calling?"

"Doctor Raynaud."

"One moment, please."

There was a short pause, then, "Monsieur Graham requests your presence at lunch tomorrow. One o'clock for one-thirty. Is that satisfactory?"

"Perfectly," Raynaud said, and hung up. He waited a moment and then dialed another number.

It rang four times before an angry voice said, *"Merde, alors."*

In fluent Parisian French, Raynaud said, "Information, please."

"Who calls?"

"A friend."

"What price?"

"A thousand francs."

"New or old?" The voice laughed sarcastically.

"New."

"What information do you seek?"

"I want to find Arriz."

The voice laughed again. "Arriz is dead."

"Arriz is alive."

"You are mistaken; he is dead."

"Find him. A thousand francs. I will call again."

Raynaud hung up. He had put the call through to Vito Mantini, known locally as the answer man. Vito dealt in information; he knew everything about everybody. He did not, of course, know as much as Arriz, but he might be able to find Arriz. And Arriz was very important.

Whistling, Raynaud left the restaurant and returned to his hotel. It was now nearly midnight; he went to his room and stared at the cardboard box on the bed. It was a perfect time to finish the job. He opened the box and allowed the snakes to slither across the bedspread and across the carpet.

He patted one on its flat black head.

"You did well," he said.

The forked tongue, pink and smooth, flicked out. Looking at the snakes, he thought to himself that they were terribly, repulsively ugly. They were of the species *recanthus*, known to the Yucatán natives as humpsnakes, because of the way they raised part of the body just behind the head into a hump as they moved forward.

"I'll be sorry to see you go," he said.

He opened his shaving kit and removed a long, sharp razor. He felt the edge with the ball of his thumb, and looked at the snakes. Two were crawling over the carpet; the third remained in the box.

"Sorry," he said.

With his bare hands, he picked up one and carried it into the bathroom. The snake was nearly four feet long; it coiled around his wrist and forearm. He held it behind the head, and watched the slit eyes and flicking tongue.

He placed the neck on the edge of the washbasin, and then, with a swift movement, brought the razor down. The blade cut through the flesh, met crunching bone, and then the head dropped into the basin. The body, decapitated, writhed with considerable and frenzied power. Purple-blue blood spurted from the cut. He struggled for a moment to remove the coiled body of the snake from his arm. He let the remains twitch in the bathtub while he went out to get the next.

The second snake was more wary, but with a firm grasp, he caught it behind the head, and carried it to the bathroom. The procedure was repeated, the body left to writhe in the tub. He returned for the third, and then it happened.

The third snake, still in the box, sank its fangs into the back of his hand.

It hurt like a cigarette burn—a moment of stunning pain, an instant of heady dizziness. He dislodged the snake's head, and pulled it away from his bleeding hand.

"Bastard," he said. Angrily, he carried it into the bathroom, and cut off the head as he had the others. Then he returned to his suitcase and found a Band-Aid.

The snake had cut deep, but fortunately it was not poisonous. Though ugly, these snakes lacked the ability to produce sufficient venom to be harmful to man, though they were deadly to small rodents. He placed the Band-Aid over the symmetrical twin punctures in his hand, and sat down to wait.

Within minutes, the area around the punctures became swollen and inflamed. Then the numbness started—first locally, in the back of his hand, and then extending up his forearm to the elbow. He found he had trouble moving his swollen fingers.

He lit a cigarette, and relaxed. He was not frightened; this had happened to him before, in the jungle. The natives all believed that smoking a cigarette helped things. Raynaud had once mentioned it to a doctor, who said it was possible. Something about nicotine constricting vessels and slowing the spread of poison.

Half an hour passed. He smoked three cigarettes, and went in to look at the bodies. The bathroom was bloody; two of the bodies were still moving, twisting and coiling in the tub. He knew they might continue this spastic motion for as long as an hour after death, and he could do nothing until they stopped.

Sometime after one o'clock, the numbness in his arm began to recede, replaced by a tingling sensation. He went to check on the snakes and found them lifeless; he collected them quickly, slipping them into a paper bag. He closed it, and went outside.

In the cool Paris evening, it was a short walk to the Seine. After the heat of Mexico, the air seemed almost cold, and he shivered as he walked. He waited until he was alone, out of sight of lovers and wanderers. Then he dropped the bag into the water. It struck the surface, and sank instantly.

It was finished.

On the way back to his hotel, he bought a bottle of red wine in a cafe, and drank it as he cleaned up the mess in the bathroom. Then he went to the cardboard box, removed the stuffing, the sawdust, and the reptile droppings, and lifted up the false bottom.

No one had noticed that the bottom of the box was three inches shallower than the outside dimensions. They had been too interested in the snakes. Now Raynaud looked at two carefully packed artifacts of great value: a Mayan necklace of gold and jade, from the Classic period, and a figurine in the shape of a seated, blind man, from the Pre-Classic period.

He lifted out the treasures, and held them to the light. They were truly beautiful: flawless, perfect, marvelous.

He felt sure that Monsieur Graham would be pleased.

Raynaud finished his wine, undressed, and got into bed, but he was too excited to sleep. He lay on his back in the dark and stared at the cheap flowered wallpaper in the room. He wondered which hotel he should move to in the morning: the Ritz, or the George Cinq?

He finally decided on the George Cinq. It was more expensive. Besides, J. D. Barrett had once mentioned that he had stayed there.

Raynaud had mixed feelings about Barrett. Barrett was a friend, a tempter, an accomplice, and a customer all mixed into one odd package. Raynaud had met him shortly after his own arrival in Mexico at the age of twenty-three, fresh from flunking out of Yale and two years in the Army language school. At the time, Raynaud was working on the excavations as a translator and foreman; Barrett had come to Yucatán as a tourist.

He was a huge, hearty Texan with thick hands, a red face, and a bulging wallet. He was in oil, which he referred to as "the business," as if there were no other, and he had come on a tour from San Antonio to see the ruins. Barrett sweated profusely in the Yucatán heat, and was forced to change clothes several times a day; his friends joked about it, but he did not seem to care.

Late one afternoon, Raynaud had been in Henri's Valladolid hotel bar when a group of tourists arrived. Among them was Barrett. In his loud way, the Texan struck up a conversation.

"You work on the ruins," he said.

Raynaud nodded.

"Must be damned fascinating. Buy you a drink?"

Raynaud nodded.

"Tequila?"

"Tequila."

"Two tequilas," Barrett said. He turned to Raynaud. "You're young. What the hell you doing screwing around in Mexico?"

"Just a temporary job," Raynaud said.

"It goes nowhere," Barrett said.

"That's occurred to me," Raynaud said.

"Unless, of course, you have some angles."

The drinks came. They drank them with lime and salt.

"You know," Barrett said conversationally, "I collect art."

"Paintings?"

"Some. Mostly native art. I'm kind of a nut on it, always have been. I have a private collection."

"I see," Raynaud said.

"A private collection means that you don't have to show it to anybody—any authorities, or people like that."

"I'm not sure I follow you," Raynaud said.

Barrett reached into his wallet and withdrew a card with his home address and phone.

"We private collectors," he said, "pay good money for high quality merchandise."

"It's illegal to—"

"That," Barrett said heavily, "is why we pay such good money." He got up from the bar and scratched one drenched armpit. He reached into his wallet again. "Pay the bartender, would you? Keep the change."

He gave Raynaud a hundred-dollar bill.

"No, really, I couldn't—"

Barrett leaned close, and rested a powerful hand on Raynaud's shoulder.

"Don't be a damned fool," he said, and sauntered off. One year later, almost to the day, Raynaud crossed the border with a girl named Allison. She was an extremely pretty girl with a large chest and a small, tight sweater. The customs people were so interested in her that they never bothered to wonder if she might be sitting on a box containing a Pre-Classic figurine in the shape of a coiled serpent.

It was in excellent condition; Barrett paid four hundred dollars for it.

That was several years ago, and since then Raynaud had been doing a steady but small business. He quickly established safeguards: he sold nothing to tourists within the country, but transported everything out of Mexico himself. In doing this, he learned quite a lot about customs officials.

The worst customs officials were the young ones, new to their jobs, careful and meticulous, searching for the slightest irregularity. The older men were secure in their jobs, softened by many years of monotonous work, and geared to discover only minor infractions. They were looking for suspicious characters, and for suspects who might be smuggling out only a few commodities—money, diamonds, heroin, marijuana, cameras, and watches. But nothing more.

Certainly nothing big: that was the secret of Raynaud's success. The smuggling of large articles was a bygone craft. Mostly, it was done by sea. Nobody had the guts to carry something large through a major international airport, or a border crossing.

As a result, border officials did not expect large smuggled items. Certainly nothing so large as a woman, like the one Raynaud had taken from Switzerland to Montreal. That had been an unusual assignment; the girl was Austrian, blond, and very beautiful. She was the mistress of a Canadian aluminum processor who had met her one winter in Baden. Unfortunately the industrialist was married and could not bring the girl over openly; Raynaud had been hired, through a friend, to see that the girl got to Canada a naturalized citizen.

Raynaud accepted the assignment and considered various possible approaches; however, after meeting the girl he decided that marriage was the most reasonable solution. He married her for a period of twenty-four days, enjoyed himself thoroughly, and deposited her on the industrialist's doorstep after obtaining a rather unusual annulment. The industrialist was furious, but unfortunately he had paid in advance.

Raynaud made fifty thousand dollars on that transaction. He also contracted a painful illness and considered cabling the industrialist to that effect, but decided not to since the man had been so unpleasant.

At the time, fifty thousand dollars had seemed like a lot of money. Now it was routine: five or six times a year he took on jobs as large, or larger. He had met discriminating collectors, and demanding ones. It was no longer possible to deal in low-grade merchandise; these men wanted gold, silver, and jade pieces—and were willing to pay for them.

Men, for example, like Houghton Graham.

3. GRAHAM

"You're late," he said, in a disgruntled voice. "You've kept me waiting."

He sat like a small animal curled up in a leather chair at the far end of a vast library, which occupied nearly the entire floor of the mansion. His voice was muffled by the books that covered every wall, from floor to ceiling.

"Come closer," Houghton Graham said. "I can't see you from a distance."

Raynaud approached. Graham watched him with bright, intense eyes. He was an old man, past seventy, and very pale. He was short, with a delicate thin body and a long birdlike neck. His face was heavily creased; beneath his chin hung folds of loose flesh which made him look rather like a turkey. The folds quivered as Graham spoke.

"Please sit down. You look well." He smiled wanly. "I have been looking forward to your arrival; there is a party tonight."

Raynaud sat down. "In my honor?"

"Ostensibly." Graham chuckled. "In fact, it is to celebrate the demise of the Duchess of Wooster, who died one year ago today. A grand occasion. Did you know her?"

Raynaud shook his head.

"Nasty woman," Graham said. "Wouldn't let poor Edgar drink, while he was alive. Killed him off at an early age. At least, what seems to me an early age."

Graham sat forward. Though it was a hot May day, a fire blazed in the fireplace.

"Ah," Graham said, rubbing his hands. "You'll have to excuse me. I can't seem to keep warm any more. Did you say brandy?"

"Yes," Raynaud said. He had learned years before that Graham drank brandy, day and night, and disapproved of anyone who did not.

"Good. Excellent." The old man's voice was crisp and surprisingly strong. It was the voice of a man accustomed to giving orders, but then Houghton Graham was one of the most phenomenally successful authors of the twentieth century.

He watched as Graham poured from a crystal decanter into two snifters. The man had a delicate, almost feminine way of moving. He was graceful as only a small man can be.

"To your health," Graham said.

"To yours," Raynaud said.

They drank, and Graham walked to the window, where he could look out over the vineyards that surrounded his mansion. He had bought it twenty years ago, a cavernous house in the wine country south and west of Paris.

"No indeed," he said, "my health does not need toasting. I am sorry to say that my doctor visited me yesterday and informed me I would live to be a hundred." He allowed himself a slight smile. "Damn his black medical soul."

"I should think it's good news."

"Ummm," Graham said, swirling the brandy in his glass. "You're young, that's the reason. When you're young, you want to live forever, but you'll get over that." He smiled again, as if inwardly amused by something. "Where are you staying?"

"The George Cinq."

"Good God, Charles. You mustn't. Move out immediately. The only people who stay in the George Cinq are alcoholic dukes and internationally known, sexually depraved actresses." He snorted. "Move out at once. Did you have a good trip over?"

"Yes, fine."

"No trouble with customs?"

"None."

"It must be very dull, being a customs officer. Watching people come and go, moving about. And always you just standing there. Ghastly dull. I have always thought the most boring job in the universe is held by Saint Peter. Can you imagine being the customs officer of heaven? A hellish fate. You're much fatter, Charles."

"Not really." Raynaud smiled.

"You must be prospering."

"I think so," he said.

"Read any good books lately?"

"No."

"Neither have I," Graham said. "In desperation I have taken to reading labels of things: wine labels, catsup labels, directions for canned soups. It's the only interesting reading left."

Raynaud said, "Do you want to see what I've brought you?"

"Not now. First lunch. I am already hungry, and looking at anything beautiful always makes me famished. I suppose," he said with a frown, "that the psychiatrists could make something sexual of that. But then, psychiatrists always can."

They had lunch on the terrace at the rear of the house, looking out over the vineyards. The meal was simple, chicken with tarragon cooked in a cream sauce, but carefully done. They had two bottles of wine, and afterward, smoked cigars.

"You know," Graham said, "I've never asked you how you feel about smuggling."

"Dastardly business," Raynaud said.

"No, I'm serious."

Raynaud puffed the cigar and paused a moment. "Actually, I like it."

"You give that impression," Graham said, nodding. "Does it amuse you very much?"

"Yes, as a matter of fact."

"And what else do you do, Charles?"

Raynaud frowned. He sipped his wine and set the glass down. "I don't understand."

"I mean, what other kinds of work."

"Nothing." He shrugged.

"I know all about that absurd snake business you pretend in Mexico."

Raynaud was stunned, but he did not blink. "Oh?"

"A friend." Graham smiled. "He spoke of it."

"Oh? Who?"

Graham wagged a finger. "Secret."

He leaned back from the table and looked at Raynaud for a long moment.

"You see, Charles, I always had a rather simple view of you. A straightforward person. Smuggles a bit, makes a lot of money, has a bit of fun and adventure. Enjoys playing two roles. That sat quite comfortably with me for a long time."

"But now your view has changed?"

"Yes."

"Why?"

"The party tonight," Graham said.

"What about it?"

"I had the most frightful pressure put on me to have it. All sorts of queer people bothering me about it. And all suggesting that it be held tonight. By some queer coincidence, the very day you cabled me you were arriving."

Raynaud shook his head. "Coincidence."

"I don't believe in them."

"Then how do you account for it?"

"That's not the point," Graham said, laughing his high-pitched, chirping, birdlike laugh. "The point is, how do *you* account for it?"

"I don't," Raynaud said. "I haven't got the faintest idea."

"Charles," he said, "you are the most superb liar I have ever met. Shall we take coffee in the library and look over your things?"

It was late afternoon, and light was fading in the library. Graham switched on a lamp and peered at the necklace, running his hands over it.

"Exquisite," he said. "This is from Tikal?"

"Yes. Exceptionally well preserved, too, considering it is a thousand years old."

Graham nodded.

The first time Raynaud had visited the author, bringing him a small carved jade face, he had calmly told Graham a wild story about the discovery of the piece in the Sacred Well of Chichén. Vividly, he described the scene: a young girl painted yellow as were all sacrificial victims in the Mayan civilization; priests painted blue, flinging her off the cliff into the murky pool and allowing her to drown as a gift to the gods, while the warriors, young men painted black, stood and watched.

Graham had said nothing, but had poured himself more brandy. And Raynaud talked on, this time about jade. In all Mexican civilizations, jade was highly valued. There were no known deposits of jade in the country, and the stone was considered more precious than gold. The Aztecs used to believe they could find jade by climbing a hill on a misty morning and watching how the vapors rose from the stones. Because it was so valuable, jade could only be worn by priests or noblemen; farmers, if caught with jade, were killed.

Graham had listened with interest, then said, "Fascinating. But this piece didn't come from Chichén."

Raynaud had been confused, but Graham had merely laughed. "I like a good liar," he had said. "There are so few left."

And the two men had been good friends since. Raynaud had made three more trips to France, bringing artifacts for Graham. But he never again made the mistake of telling him a story about the pieces.

They were admiring the necklace when the butler came in to announce that there had been a mistake; a hundred cases of champagne had been ordered but only ten delivered.

"Damned fools," Graham said. "Order up another ninety. To be delivered before tonight."

"Sounds like quite a party."

"They usually are," Graham said.

"Will I be suitably dressed for the evening?" Raynaud asked, looking down at his blue suit.

"For these parties," Graham said, in a half-irritated, half-amused voice, "suitable dress is usually nudity."

The first guests began to arrive at eight, and Graham unaccountably disappeared to his room. Raynaud was left alone, but fortunately Alex, Graham's personal secretary, was there to introduce him around.

Raynaud was unprepared for the variety of people who came. There were distinguished-looking men with gray hair, wearing tuxedos; young girls in miniskirts; men in dungarees, sandals, and sportshirts. They were mostly French, and most seemed to know each other. After a while, Raynaud moved over to the bar.

Some of the younger girls were interested in him, and came over, one by one, to talk. One worked for Olivetti and loathed Italian men; another was a student and talked passionately about Reich; a third wanted to know all about the jungle, which she had heard was terribly hot.

Raynaud was beginning to wonder how he might make an unobtrusive exit when Graham appeared. He arrived without fanfare, slipping among his guests, shaking hands, talking briefly. Raynaud noticed that he was not always pleasant: to one middle-aged woman he said, "Celia, dear, how nice to see you. Is it true you're flat broke these days?"

The woman made a gurgling sound but did not reply. This seemed to delight Graham; he laughed and moved on.

He came up to Raynaud a few minutes later.

"So there you are. I might have suspected I'd find you at the bar. You look bored."

"No, actually, I—"

Graham cut him off with a wave of his hand. "Do you seriously think," he said, "that you can convince me these dreadful parties are worthwhile? Impossible." He leaned close and said quietly, "I only hold them so they won't sit about in Paris and say, 'Whatever happened to Houghton Graham? Is he dead yet?' I couldn't bear that, you see."

He took Raynaud's arm.

"Come along. There are one or two interesting people here."

Raynaud was led across the terrace.

"By the way," Graham said conversationally, "I take it you're heterosexual?"

"Yes," Raynaud said. He was startled.

"Then you might contrive to meet the young lady in the corner. The dark one. She's Vietnamese, or something. I'd introduce you myself, but I've forgotten her name. Besides, it's not my cup. Ah, here we are." He broke boldly into a group of six people clustered around a man who sat on the grass.

"Peter," Graham said to the seated man, "good of you to come. I want you to meet a special friend. Peter Loëve, Charles Raynaud."

Peter nodded briefly. He was a tall, thin man with black hair, cropped close, and large, moody dark eyes. His clothes hung loosely on him.

"Peter is a German, and we all know Germans are pigs, but Peter is an exception. He has a remarkable gift."

"Oh?"

"Yes," Graham said. "You wouldn't expect it in a German, actually: he can see the future."

Raynaud nodded politely. He had seen mystics and fortune-tellers before. There were several in Yucatán, strange old men who smoked hemp and went into muttering trances. Raynaud had never believed any of it.

"I am especially fond of Peter," Graham continued, "after he predicted that I would not live past eighty-five. That was a great relief to me. Peter, would you mind telling Charles his future?"

Raynaud was surprised: "Mine?"

"Yes," Graham said. "You're curious about it, aren't you?"

"I suppose so."

"Then have a go. Will you, Peter?"

Peter stared blankly at Raynaud for some moments, then nodded.

"Marvelous." Graham rubbed his hands together, and looked at the half-dozen people standing around, watching.

"One other thing, Peter," he said in English. "Speak English, so these turds watching can't figure it out."

Peter nodded again, slowly, and closed his eyes. Without opening them, he said, "Sit down, Charles. Close to me." He spoke English with a thick German accent.

Raynaud sat. Peter kept his eyes closed and swayed back and forth for some moments in silence. Then he looked up and fixed Raynaud in a cold, hard stare. His eyes did not blink or waver.

"I feel…that you are afraid of what I will say."

Raynaud shrugged.

"Yes, it is true. You are afraid because…because you have just made a lot of money, and you do not know what will happen next."

Raynaud glanced up at Graham. "Did you—"

Graham laughed. "Haven't seen him in months, dear boy."

"Not long ago," Peter continued, "you saw death. And you killed, but…I do not think it was a man. No it was not. You killed something else."

Raynaud began to feel uncomfortable. He fumbled in his pocket for cigarettes. The man was a hoax, of course. If you spoke in sufficiently general terms, the words could apply to anybody. A housewife swatting mosquitoes, anything.

"Snakes," Peter said. "That is what you killed."

Raynaud sat upright.

Graham tittered. "He's remarkable, isn't he?"

"And in the future," Peter continued, "there will be more killing. Very soon."

"When?" Raynaud said.

"Soon."

"What about women?" asked Graham in a sly voice. "Do you see any women for our Charles?"

"Yes," Peter said tonelessly.

"That dark one here tonight?"

"No, but others. Many others, and then just two. One is old. I cannot see the other one."

"Aha," Graham said. "An affair with an older woman. Peter, that's wonderful."

He clapped the German on the back.

Peter blinked and looked up irritably. The mood was broken, and Raynaud felt oddly and unaccountably released. He looked down at the cigarette in his hand and saw he had never lit it. He did now, and stood up.

"I am sorry I could not do more," Peter said, "but it is late, and I am tired."

"That's quite all right," Raynaud said. "I don't know how much more I could have stood."

"Did it amuse you?" Peter asked.

"I'm not sure. Should it have amused me?"

"Only you can say," Peter replied, and looked away.

Graham took Raynaud's arm and led him away. They walked back toward the bar.

"Take my advice," Graham said, "and don't believe a word of it. He uses little tricks, as you may have noticed. He's very perceptive, and something about your appearance or manner must have told him you'd been in the jungle. That would account for that hocus-pocus about snakes, eh? Complete rot, the whole thing. But he's diverting, don't you think?"

"Yes," Raynaud said. "Very."

As they walked, Graham stopped to pick up what looked like a handkerchief lying on the ground. It turned out to be a pair of women's panties.

"Dear me," Graham said, checking his watch. "Ten o'clock, and they've already started. It's one of the curses of having such soft lawns. You'd be astonished at what the gardeners find, the morning after these parties."

Raynaud grinned.

"Still," Graham said, "one can't blame them. It's been going on for centuries, and I certainly can't expect it to stop for one of my parties."

Raynaud was about to reply when, looking across the guests on the terrace, he spotted a familiar face. It belonged to a chunky, muscular man of medium height, who stood next to a stunning blond girl.

Raynaud had not seen that face for more than ten years.

"Excuse me a moment," he said to Graham. "There's somebody here I'd like you to introduce me to."

Graham did it perfectly. He walked up to the man and said, "Richard, I want you to meet a dear friend. Richard Pierce, Charles Raynaud."

Richard Pierce looked up absently and extended his hand, "How are you, Raynaud?" Almost immediately, he turned away.

Graham frowned. It was clear to Raynaud that Pierce and Graham were not very friendly.

A moment passed. Pierce sipped his drink and then turned slowly back to Raynaud.

"Did you say…"

Raynaud grinned.

"Son of a bitch! Charles Raynaud!" He smiled broadly and held out his hand again. "Charles Raynaud, Jesus Christ! Charles Raynaud! What the hell are you doing here?"

"Actually, I'm—"

"No, no. Stand back and let me get a look at you. Jesus Christ, of all people. You look good."

"So do you."

Pierce grabbed Raynaud's hand and pumped it a third time.

"Jesus, this is incredible. I'm a bugger's aunt."

Then he stopped and looked down at Graham.

"Sorry about that, Houghty."

Graham did not reply. He turned to Raynaud. "Where did you meet this ostensible human being?"

"At Yale," Raynaud said. "Years ago."

"Yale," Graham repeated. He spun back on Pierce. "You never told me you went to Yale, Richard. I take it you were sent down?"

Pierce stiffened. "It was a long time ago," he said.

"I have no doubt of that. Well, I shall leave you two to discuss fond memories."

He stomped off. Raynaud sensed that Graham was rather disappointed in him, but at the moment he did not care. He was immensely pleased to run into Pierce, particularly here.

Pierce looked at the blonde standing alongside him. He smacked her bottom. "Run along, sweets," he said. "I'll see you later."

He threw his arm around Raynaud's shoulder. "Come on, I'll buy you a drink."

"The liquor's free."

"Then I'll buy you a girl."

Raynaud smiled. "From what I can see, the girls are pretty free, too."

Pierce shook his head. "Not the best ones, lad. Not the best."

The use of the old term irritated Raynaud. Pierce had always called him lad, and apparently meant nothing by it, yet Raynaud found it condescending.

They came to the bar and got two glasses of champagne.

"So here you are," Pierce said, "chatting it up with faggot authors in Paris. And dressed very expensively." He touched Raynaud's lapel. "You've been moving right along, haven't you, lad? I always knew you would. Cheers."

They raised glasses and drank.

"Are you staying out here?" Pierce asked.

"No, in Paris."

"Where?"

"The George Cinq."

Pierce raised his eyebrows. "My, you *have* been moving along. Did you marry into it, or steal it, or what?"

"Stole it," Raynaud said.

"Good for you," Pierce said. He lit a cigarette. "It's marvelous to see you again. Staying long?"

"A while. I'm on business. First here, then London."

"And then what?"

"I'll go back to Mexico. Yucatán."

"Good lord, you're full of surprises tonight. Did you make your money in Yucatán?"

"In a sense."

Pierce laughed. "You're being very close about it. I suppose that's the difference between a man dedicated to making money and a man dedicated to spending it, like myself."

"You have trouble spending it?" Raynaud asked, grinning.

"Frankly," said Pierce, with mock gravity, "no." He sipped the champagne. "This is terrible stuff." He turned to the bartender. "What is it?"

"Piper-Heidseck sixty-four," said the bartender.

"Ah, well, no wonder. Terrible." He emptied his glass on the lawn. "Let's drink Scotch. Much safer."

"It's all right," Raynaud said. "I'll stick to champagne."

"You'll poison yourself," Pierce warned.

"I'll take my chances."

Pierce watched while the bartender made him a Scotch on

the rocks. "Houghty never did have any taste in champagne," he said.

"I haven't heard anyone call him by that name," Raynaud said.

"Not surprised. He hates it."

"You don't get along?"

"No." Pierce laughed. "For some reason, he considers me a lazy wastrel. Can't imagine why. But he once called me that, to my face, and I didn't appreciate it. We've been at knockers ever since."

"Where are you living now?" Raynaud asked.

"London. I feel London is currently the best place in the world to spend money, except, of course, for Beirut. The best women are in Beirut. Ever been?"

"Yes," Raynaud said.

Pierce shook his head in wonder. "You keep giving me these shocks," he said, "and I'll have a heart attack."

He laughed, but it was not entirely pleasant. Hearing the veiled irritation, Raynaud was happier than he had been in a long time.

Shortly after midnight, Pierce told Raynaud that a friend had borrowed his car to take a girl home. Pierce was stranded; could he ride back into Paris with Raynaud? It was logical, since Pierce was also staying at the George Cinq.

Raynaud agreed.

Pierce went off to collect his blonde, and Raynaud said good-bye to Graham.

"It was good of you to come," Graham said. "I hope you will visit me again. By the way, I have put in a draft at my Paris bank waiting for you in the sum of thirty thousand dollars. You need only present yourself with your passport to collect it in whatever form you wish. Is that satisfactory?"

"But we agreed on only twenty-five—"

"I won't hear of it," Graham said, holding up his hand. "But I do have a final word of advice."

"Yes?"

"Watch out for Richard Pierce."

"All right," Raynaud said.

"I can see by your face you don't take me seriously. I wish you would." Graham leaned close. "Richard Pierce is a complete, utter, slime-coated bastard."

4. PIERCE

The three of them—Raynaud, Pierce, and the girl—got into Raynaud's car. Raynaud drove, and Pierce sat beside him. The girl sat in the back seat.

"Speak English," Pierce said to Raynaud, as they set off down the long drive to the iron gate at the edge of the estate. "The snapper doesn't understand much English. Her talents, I fear, are not linguistic, though she has an ingenious tongue."

Raynaud glanced at the girl in the rear-view mirror. She was staring stonily forward, her pretty face bored.

Pierce lit a cigarette. "Now then," he said, "tell me about yourself. What have you been up to all these years?"

"Oh, nothing much," Raynaud said.

He had already decided to go slow with Richard, to play it very cool. His natural inclination, even in college, had been to treat Richard like a rich fool. But Richard was not a fool. Obnoxious, perhaps, but not a fool.

Pierce reached into his coat and withdrew a bottle.

"What's that?"

"Some of Houghton's crappy champagne. Better than nothing." He peeled the foil, pulled away the wire, aimed the neck out the window, and popped the cork with practiced smoothness.

"If you don't like Graham, why'd you go to his party?"

"My mother," Pierce said. "She and Houghton are good friends. When she heard he was having this party, she insisted I make an appearance. She was quite obnoxious about it, in fact. A bit odd."

He took a swig and passed the bottle.

"But anyhow," he said, "we're celebrating. Drink up, and tell me what you've been doing. And don't be so damnably offhand about it all. Infuriating."

"All right," Raynaud said.

He glanced over at Pierce, studying the features in the green light from the dashboard. His friend had aged: the handsome, almost delicate face was now brooding and dissipated, the features slack, the expression moody. But he still had his eyes: large, dark brown, with long lashes.

"Well, to begin with, I've made some money."

"Obviously," Pierce said.

"Doing various sorts of jobs, most of them easy. And I got married once. She was rich. Killed in an auto accident; her car went off a cliff."

"And you inherited her fortune?"

"Some of it."

Pierce laughed. "Charles, that's wonderful. Really wonderful. Tell me, was that before or after you got out of jail?"

Raynaud gripped the wheel tightly and stared forward at the road. For the first time he sensed that everything, the whole damned plan, might be more complicated than he had suspected before.

Pierce continued to laugh softly. "You see, I've followed your career more closely than you might think, Charles. It was six months, wasn't it?"

"Five and a half," Raynaud said.

"For playing a confidence game in New York. That's what the police thought it was."

"Yes," Raynaud said.

"But actually it was something else."

Raynaud said, "You really have been following things closely."

"And all for a reason," Pierce said, suddenly serious. He paused. "You were smuggling then. Is that what you're doing now? Artifacts?"

Raynaud shrugged.

"You needn't be modest. You're quite well known, in some circles. You supplied pieces for Sir Hugh Beckwith, and Lady Ashley Mountfort. Also Victor Seizel. Am I right?"

"You are."

"Very skillful, by all reports," Richard said. "Exceedingly clever. But one thing puzzles me, Charles."

"What's that?"

"Your other occupations."

Raynaud said, "I have none."

"I know all about your marriage," Richard said. "But that was just to get Whittington's whore into Canada. Have you been doing other jobs like, ah, that?"

"On occasion."

Richard smiled slightly. "When the price is right?"

"Only when the price is right."

Richard laughed. "You make it sound quite sinister, Charles. Have you ever killed anyone?"

"Not that I recall."

"Could you kill someone?"

Raynaud hesitated just a moment. "No."

"You're quite sure?"

"Quite. Sorry."

"Oh, don't apologize. I find it reassuring." Richard stared forward at the road, and then he laughed, a different hearty laugh, and Raynaud realized that he had changed his mood, with the same lightning facility he had shown ten years before. "Charles, this is really marvelous, seeing you again. Absolutely marvelous. My old drinking friend, an international smuggler. We must spend an evening together. When do you go to London?"

"Day after tomorrow, I think. It's not definite."

"Splendid! That's just when I'm going back. You'll stay at my flat, of course."

"I don't think—"

"Nonsense. I insist upon it."

Raynaud said, "We can discuss it later."

He had a brief mental image of all the long discussions they had had in the past, the endless hours in bars and restaurants and college haunts, where he had told stories of his youth in the slums, and how he had gotten the scar on his neck from Johnny Sloane, while Richard Pierce, the rich boy from England, bought the drinks and listened in silent fascination.

It was something he had not thought about for a long time.

"And you?" Raynaud said. "What've you been doing for ten years?"

"Spending money," Pierce said. "I went into that business

after I left Yale. It was where my natural aptitudes lay." He laughed. "Did you know I went to the University of Geneva after Yale?"

"No," Raynaud said. "How did you like it?"

"I was only there two weeks. Then my father died."

"I'm sorry."

"Don't be. I wasn't, particularly."

He stared forward at the road, illuminated in the yellow French headlamps.

"I went home for the funeral," Pierce said. "Bloody big affair. Dozens of MPs and ministers and so on. And I talked with my mother. You should meet her sometime. She's rather amusing, as a type. She's a nymphomaniac, you know." He snapped his fingers. "Come to think of it, you might have met her. She was in Mexico last year."

There was something wrong about the way Pierce said it, something that instantly alerted Raynaud. It was a casual, off-hand thought, but it did not come out that way.

Raynaud said, "I thought you knew all about me."

"Just a few snatches of business gossip."

"Well," Raynaud said, "I've never met your mother."

"Odd. I really thought you might have bumped into her at some point."

"Mexico's a big place."

"Ummm. Well, anyway, after the funeral, I got tired of hanging around that big house, so I left and bought a flat in Belgravia. And a Maserati. Super car, absolutely marvelous: I used to drive it for hours on end, in the middle of the night." He stopped and lit a cigarette, then said, "I suppose I was actually rather thrown off by my father's death. I didn't realize it then."

With a long swallow, he finished the champagne and threw the bottle out the window.

"Ever since, I've had an allowance. Quite a nice one. You see, I haven't come into the estate yet. There's another two months to wait. Father stipulated that I had to be thirty-four years and two months."

"Why that age?"

"He was sentimental. He was that old when he made his first million. Pounds."

"I see."

"He was always rather sentimental, even about my mother. Oh, by the bye, one thing: I've got myself engaged."

"Congratulations."

"Not exactly. I only did it to humor my mother. She thinks I'm unstable. Can't imagine why. I did it for her."

"Nice girl?"

"Gorgeous. She's Italian. Sandra Callarini. Comes from a good family and all; she's been working at Wentfield, in films. But not a monkey—quite the other way."

"Monkey?"

Pierce laughed. "A monkey is a girl who holds her jobs with her tail."

Raynaud laughed. Pierce had not changed. Not a bit.

"She has a maddeningly beautiful body," Pierce said, "which she absolutely will not share. I dated her for three months— can you imagine?—and got nowhere. It began to prey on my mind. I lost sleep. I lost weight. I was nervous and restless. Then my mother began on this marriage thing, so I decided to kill two birds with one stone. So to speak."

"When is the wedding?"

"There will not be a wedding," Pierce said, with flat finality. "Once I take over the estate I can tell my mother to go to hell, and the girl, too. Just a few months more."

"It's definite, then?"

"Oh, yes. It all reverts to me, automatically, unless I am either dead or in jail. I don't intend either. Also, I am supposed to demonstrate 'business acumen' or some damned thing to the trustees. But that's settled."

"Oh?"

"Yes. About five years ago I started a little project on the side. A friend had an idea for reducing costs in deep-water drilling. I got enough capital out of the estate—with Lucienne screaming bloody murder—to start a North Sea operation. It's done splendidly. We've just incorporated it: Shore Industries, Limited. In the black already, and I expect that within five or ten years, it will bring in more money than all the other Pierce holdings."

Raynaud shook his head. It was typical of Pierce. Things just seemed to fall his way. In college he had been a casual but lucky speculator on the stock market, and a lucky card player. He had never studied for exams but always seemed to do well. That was just the way he was. Mentally quick the way Raynaud was physically quick.

"Then you're spending a lot of time with this company?"

"Time? God, no. One or two mornings a week at most. I have other things to worry about."

"Then who runs the operation for you?"

"Nobody. I'm the president. But if one is organized…" He shrugged. They came into the outskirts of Paris, and Pierce glanced at his watch. "The night's young. It's barely two. Shall we go out on the town?"

Raynaud shook his head. He was very tired. "Not now. I just arrived yesterday, and I haven't adjusted to the time."

"Come on. I can get us a pair of marvelous girls. It's a beautiful night. Shame to waste it."

"No, really."

"This is in the nature of a last fling for me," Pierce said, "before I go back to England and become formally engaged. After that, I'll have to be discreet. Loathe discretion."

"Not tonight," Raynaud said.

"Then let me get you a tranquilizer."

"Thanks, I don't need one."

"A beautiful, redheaded tranquilizer. Help you to sleep. Rub your back, and so forth."

Raynaud shook his head. Pierce was still the same. He had always been impetuous, and always childishly irritable if he didn't get his own way.

They drove another few miles in silence, then Pierce said, "Stop a moment. I've got to make a call."

Raynaud pulled over to the curb. Pierce got out of the car and went into a café. Raynaud saw him walk to a telephone on the wall, drop in his jeton, and speak briefly.

He turned to the girl seated behind him and said in French, "Tired?"

"A little."

"What's your name?"

"Dominique."

She seemed bored. Her face was blank and expressionless. Pierce came back, got into the car, and said, "All right. Off we go."

Twenty minutes later, they arrived at the George Cinq. They got out, and Raynaud gave the doorman the keys. Walking into the lobby, Raynaud noticed that Pierce had a slight limp. "What happened?"

Pierce smiled. "An experience worthy of you," he said. "It was a girl with a knife, two years ago. Slashed my leg in bed." He smiled. "She wasn't going for the leg."

"Lucky," Raynaud said.

"I suppose."

They got into the elevator. Pierce said, "I'm in room one ninety-three. Why don't you call me in the morning? We must go out on the town together. We simply must," he said, patting Dominique's bottom. "There is so much to see and do here."

Raynaud nodded.

"Call," Pierce said, "any time after noon." The elevator stopped, and Raynaud got out. Pierce was staying one floor above.

"Sleep well," Pierce said, and grinned.

The doors closed.

Raynaud walked down the hall to his room, unlocked it, and went inside. A girl was there, sitting in a chair, smoking a cigarette.

"Who are you?" he said.

"Vivienne."

"What are you doing here?"

She was a beautiful girl with a slim, taut body and dark red hair.

"I bring you the compliments of—"

"I know," Raynaud said. In a sense, he had expected it. He held the door open. "You want room one ninety-three."

The girl frowned. "No, I was told—"

"Room one ninety-three," Raynaud repeated.

Looking confused and uncertain, she picked up her purse and sauntered to the door. There she stopped and put her hand over Raynaud's, giving him a questioning glance.

"Room one ninety-three," he said firmly.

She shrugged, and left.

When he was alone, he undressed and wondered if he had done the right thing. Pierce might be annoyed. On the other hand, it might be expected. The old Charles Raynaud of college days would be pleased but resentful at such a present. Perhaps Pierce was testing.

Testing what? he wondered.

He picked up the telephone and dialed swiftly. A voice answered on the tenth ring.

"Merde, alors."

"I am calling back about a dead man," Raynaud said, "who is not dead."

"Oh, yes. For a thousand francs."

"That's correct."

"The dead man has been located," the voice said. "Do you know me?"

"Yes. We have done business before."

"Then you will find me at Saint-Lazare tomorrow at ten. The café across from the Métro station. Bring the money."

The phone was dead. He smiled and replaced it in the cradle.

Then he lay down to sleep, feeling much, much better about everything.

Richard Pierce awoke irritably. He was cramped and cold. Looking over, he saw that the two girls had pulled all the blankets to their side; he was naked from the waist up.

Angrily, he pulled the blankets back. The girls stirred, and opened their eyes.

"Hello," said Dominique, the blonde. Her voice was soft and sleepy.

"I thought I told you to be gone when I woke up," Pierce said.

She said nothing, but pouted, looking hurt.

"Get out," Pierce said.

The girls stared at him. Particularly the redhead, Vivienne.

"Go on, don't just lie there. Get out!"

They were frightened now. They scrambled out of bed. Without pleasure, he watched their naked bodies as they dressed. His head was throbbing: champagne. Houghty's hideous, horse-piss champagne. Always gives you a head the morning after.

The girls finished dressing and began to comb their hair.

"Forget it," he said. "Get out."

They stopped and went to the door, where they paused.

"Well, what are you waiting for? The manager will pay you."

They left.

Damned girls. He had told them quite distinctly to be gone in the morning. He hated to wake up and find girls in his bed; it disgusted him. Especially girls like these. They looked fine in the evening, but the next day, with the makeup smeared, their faces pale…

Hideous. Like witches.

He reached for his watch on the bedtable. Eleven o'clock. Jesus Christ, eleven o'clock. No wonder he felt like hell. He rolled over and tried to sleep again, but he was too angry, and his head hurt too much. He swore, and got up.

He looked at the bed. Christ: stiff stains on the sheets, curly hair, streaks of mascara and makeup on the pillows. It looked like hell. He went to the phone and called room service. He wanted a maid to change his bed. The voice at the other end was soothing.

"Now! Change it now!" he shouted, and slammed the phone down.

Stupid frogs. No damned idea about running hotels. Did they think he wanted to come out of a shower and look at *that*? That lousy stinking, greasy bed.

They were dirty people. Everybody said it, the French were a dirty people. It was true.

Damn it. Eighty dollars a day for this suite. What was he paying for, anyway. The right to have his sheets changed when he wanted it. A little service, that was all.

He went into the bathroom, ran the sink full of cold water,

and dunked his face in. The water was a shock, but it cleared his head. He pulled it out, dripping, and stared into the mirror.

"You look like a piece of shit," he said.

Then he got into the shower.

At thirty-four Richard Pierce was worth almost as much as any single man in England. His father—his adopted father— was Herbert Edgar Pierce, the man who had built the Pierce empire of tea and rubber plantations in Burma and Malaya in the early part of the century. Most of that was now gone, of course, taken away in successive waves of nationalization. But there were still the copper mines in Australia; they now provided the major income from the estate. And, of course, all the other holdings.

Pierce remembered little of his true parents. They were named Trevor-Carter; his father had long been a friend of Herbert Pierce. When Trevor-Carter and his wife were killed in a German bombing raid on London in 1940, Richard was adopted by Herbert. At the time, Richard was six years old, and had been sent to the country to live while the war continued. He rarely saw his adopted father until he was ten, and the war ended.

He got along wonderfully with his father and spent several happy years, until the marriage with Lucienne. Almost overnight, that marriage changed everything.

Lucienne Ginoux was a French singer, living in London. She had become famous during the war, a favorite with the troops, particularly the thousands of Americans who had been massed in southern England before the Normandy invasion. She was tall, aristocratic, beautiful, and nearly forty. She was also a bitch.

For as long as Richard could remember, his father treated him well, and his stepmother treated him badly. As a young boy, he was conscious of an almost visible hate emanating from her, a hate which he did not understand, but soon responded to in kind.

He also hated her for what she did to his father. At the time of their marriage, Herbert was fifty-eight, a man in his prime, wealthy and successful. There were rumors of an impending knighthood, of a high government position. The marriage to

Lucienne abruptly ended those rumors. It was widely acknowledged that Herbert had married badly, and there was nothing to be done; the threat of scandal was too great.

Richard remembered that his adopted parents fought a great deal, because his mother kept having affairs, and his father didn't like it. When he was seventeen, Richard went up from Eton, where he was a mediocre student, to Queen's College, Cambridge. He was accepted only because the college needed money, and they hoped that Herbert Pierce might make a considerable donation.

Richard was unhappy at Queen's. He was sent down after two years, spent some time in London, and then went to Yale. Things were better there; he made several friends, and for the first time in his life, he felt at home. The separation from his family helped. However, eventually the rounds of parties and drinking bouts became too much. He flunked out after two years.

From America he went to Geneva. Soon after he arrived, his father died in an automobile accident, under rather mysterious circumstances. Richard immediately quit. He never did anything serious again in his life.

After the funeral, he made an arrangement with his mother. It was a polite arrangement, and the essence of it, though unspoken, was clear: Richard would be given a substantial allowance for the next ten years, until he inherited the estate. In return, he would avoid Lucienne as much as possible.

The arrangement worked well. Richard was able to travel, to indulge himself with fast cars, exotic food, and erotic women. Recently, however, his spending had increased. He had had several fights with his mother about money. To avoid the fights, and to humor her generally, he had agreed to marry. For him, it was purely a delaying maneuver. When he reached thirty-four years and two months, he would inherit the estate, and Lucienne would no longer be trustee.

Then he would dump the Italian girl and cut Lucienne off without a penny.

That prospect gave him considerable pleasure.

❖

After his shower, he came out to find that the bed was made, the room tidied. He looked around: his martini was not there.

Damn.

He called room service. "Why hasn't my martini been brought?"

"We have no record of an order, sir."

"Of course you have a record. Look around. And get a martini up here immediately."

He slammed down the phone. Incompetent frogs. The only decent thing about the country was the women. Without the women, France would be a desert.

Just a few crappy cathedrals.

Minutes later, a boy arrived with the martini.

"I've told you people before," Pierce said, "that I want a cold, very dry vodka martini here every day at noon. I want to wake up and find it waiting. Understand?"

"Yes," the boy said.

"Good."

He gave him twenty francs, dismissed him, and sat down with his drink. It was good; cold and burning. He lit a cigarette and wondered what he would do for the evening.

Then he remembered Raynaud.

Now there was a stroke of luck. Imagine, running into the lad again, after all these years. Such perfect timing. It was almost too good.

He picked up the phone and called Raynaud's room.

"Hello?" Raynaud said.

"Sorry if I woke you," Pierce said.

"No, no. I've been up awhile."

"Where've you been?" Pierce said.

"To the bank. A little business."

"Any plans for tonight?"

"No."

"How about this afternoon?"

"Well, actually, I thought I'd take a walk."

"You have a car, don't you?" Pierce said.

"Yes, but I feel like walking."

"In Paris? Your feet'll be covered in dogshit." He laughed. "How about tonight? Want to make an evening?"

"Sure."

"Drinks at six? In the bar, here?"

"You're on," Raynaud said.

"Good, good. See you then."

Pierce hung up and sipped his drink. He had a few arrangements to make. He picked up the phone again and made several
calls.

5. INFORMATION

Charles Raynaud had arisen early, gone to the bank, and transferred Houghton Graham's money to his own account, using a bank draft. It was a relatively simple transaction, even for a French bank, and it took just a few minutes. Then he had gone to Saint-Lazare and the Café Royal, opposite the steps leading down to the Métro station.

He had arrived at nine-thirty, intending to be early. He wanted to watch Mantini arrive. The old Italian had been, in his day, a superb thief, and he was not above a few sly moves in his old age.

Precisely at nine-fifty-five Mantini came strolling up the street. Wearing a blazer and carrying a cane, he looked like a cheap imitation of Chevalier, but his step was light and his eyes beneath the cap were darting and watchful as he surveyed the crowd sitting at the sidewalk tables.

He stopped when he saw Raynaud.

For a moment he looked puzzled, then he bowed slightly and sat down at the table with him.

"*Merde, alors,*" he said. "So it was you, after all."

"Yes."

Mantini smiled. "It has been a long time, Charles."

"Only four years."

Mantini had helped him once, in Rome. The Count Ramazzi had accepted a gold-inlaid Pre-Columbian piece from Guatemala and then, quite blandly, had refused to pay Raynaud. The Count had, in fact, offered to call the police if Raynaud did not leave immediately.

Four days later, it was Mantini, aged but agile, who had slipped into the villa north of Rome and taken the piece back, leaving behind a neatly wrapped sack of horse droppings. Then he had deftly picked the lock of the safe behind the Dufy on the west wall of the study, removing the two fifty million lire which the Count Ramazzi had failed to bank, and consequently, to pay taxes on. For this, Mantini had graciously accepted fifty percent of the take.

"Only four years?" Mantini said. "It seems longer."

"No."

"It seems like centuries," Mantini said. "How did you know I was living in Paris?"

"I heard," Raynaud said.

"And did you also hear about Arriz? I swear, I thought he was dead. There were rumors that the *guardia civil* had finally caught him. On the border, at Hendaye."

"I know. I heard the same rumors. But as it turned out, I saw Arriz."

"Oh? Where?"

"Orly."

Mantini chuckled. "So you were the one. I heard that someone had released some snakes, and caused a commotion...." He sighed. "I should have known it was you. Arriz will be grateful."

"He better be," Raynaud said.

"I have his address," Mantini said. "But it was difficult."

"We agreed on a thousand francs."

"It was difficult," Mantini repeated.

"A bargain. We are old friends."

"I am old, you are not. It was difficult and costly to obtain the information."

Raynaud sighed. "How much?"

"Five thousand."

"No."

"Ah, my friend. Then we cannot do business." Raynaud signaled to the waiter to bring coffee, then turned his attention to the street. He watched a pretty girl in a very short skirt stride past. In the current fashion, the girl wore a pale transparent blouse and no bra.

"Two thousand," he said.

"She is delightful," Mantini said. "If only I were younger. Four and a half."

"Her breasts are small. Two thousand five."

"But what do you think of the one coming? The redhead? Four thousand."

"Bitchy."

"Nonsense. She is an angel. She has gentle eyes. Four thousand."

"She would screw you if she could."

"Let us pray," sighed Mantini, lighting a cigar.

"Three thousand."

"You are very difficult, Charles. Do you not find her ass charming?"

"No. I said, three thousand."

"I heard you."

Mantini sat back in his chair and smiled slightly as he smoked the cigar. His eyes were on the street. "I am getting older each minute. Soon, I will no longer even watch."

"You'll watch until you die," Raynaud said.

"I fear the day I stop watching," Mantini said, "as I once feared the day…. Four thousand."

"You're stubborn. Three thousand."

"Three-eight."

"Three flat. My best offer."

"I had forgotten, Charles, how nasty you Americans are. Three-five. I barely cover expenses."

"Three flat," Raynaud repeated. "It cannot be more."

"Robber," Mantini said, puffing the cigar. "Bastard."

"Three flat."

"Three-five." He smiled. "Still in the same business?"

"No."

"Something different?"

"On occasion."

"Killing people?"

"No, as it happens."

"I always thought," Mantini said, "that you had the potential to kill. I mean it as a compliment."

"Three flat," Raynaud said.

"Do you like the blonde that is coming? She has a most delicate waist."

Raynaud sighed. "All right," he said. "I give in. I can't take any more. Three and a quarter."

"Three-five."

"Three-four."

Mantini set his cigar down in the Cinzano ashtray. "Sold," he said. Raynaud nodded, and watched the blonde.

"Rue Ambrose Bierce," Mantini said. "Apartment nineteen, third floor. Knock four times: one-two-three-pause, and then four. You understand?"

"I understand," Raynaud said, reaching into his pocket for the money.

The blonde sauntered past, aware of eyes upon her, swinging her hips in a saucy, delightful way.

"What is it?"

Raynaud stared at the man at the door. He was nothing much, unless your taste ran to pale young men with plucked eyebrows who were dressed in tight, black leather pants and a black leather shirt cut open to the waist.

"I want to see Arriz."

"Arriz is dead."

"Tell him it is Charles. He knows me."

"Arriz," the leather boy said, arching one delicate eyebrow, "is dead."

"Tell him," Raynaud repeated. "Or I will break your neck."

Leather-boy hesitated, so Raynaud stepped forward quickly, swinging his right arm stiffly, catching the boy in the neck just below the cartilages. He fell back and tumbled to the ground, clutching his neck and making choking sounds. Raynaud stepped into the room.

Arriz was there, wearing the same old red-and-silver smoking jacket he had worn for years. He looked calmly at Raynaud as he sat on the couch and smoked a thin cigarette.

"Now look what you've done. You've hurt André."

"André was being obnoxious," Raynaud said.

"Help the poor child to his feet," Arriz said.

Raynaud did not move. "Help him yourself."

Silently Arriz stood and walked over to leather-boy, bending over him and making small, soothing noises. Presently leather-boy seemed to recover, and staggered to his feet. He glared hatefully at Raynaud.

Arriz said, "You should apologize to André."

"I'd rather not."

"He'd feel much better if you explained it was a mistake."

"It wasn't," Raynaud said.

Inwardly, watching Arriz, he felt sad. The Spaniard was once proud and strong and fiercely intelligent; he had worked as a loyalist during the Civil War and then afterward; later he had slipped into smuggling.

Now this.

Arriz stuck his hands in his pockets and said, "I will tolerate your outrages only because—"

"I saved your skin."

"Not delicately said," Arriz nodded, "but accurate. Why are you here?"

"Information."

Arriz smiled blandly. "No," he said.

Raynaud looked at him for a moment, then shrugged. "The police will be glad to know where you are."

"By the time the police arrive, we would be gone."

"Not if you were unconscious." Raynaud shrugged.

Arriz moved his hand in his pocket. "Before you could reach me, I would have shot you twice through the chest."

"Perhaps not."

"You wish to try?" Arriz said.

"Not particularly."

Arriz smiled. "I am glad. Frankly I have no quarrel with you, Foxwell. And you are right, I owe you my, ah, skin."

He walked across the room and sat down again. To André he said, "Bring us two brandies."

André disappeared into another room, still rubbing his neck and glaring at Raynaud. When they were alone, Arriz said, "I am grateful for what you did."

"You should be."

"Were you in trouble for it?"

"Only a little."

"You thought very quickly," Arriz said. "But then, you always do."

"Information," Raynaud said, bringing him back.

"Yes, of course. It is always information. So many people seek information these days. I rarely smuggle anymore. How did you find me?"

"My mother told your mother," Raynaud said.

Arriz shrugged. "As you will. And the information you wish?"

"Richard Pierce," Raynaud said.

Arriz closed his eyes and leaned back. He gave a long sigh. "Richard Pierce," he said. "Richard Pierce. English. Thirty-four. Father a man of the old empire-building era. Mother a Parisian singer. Scandals about her, many, many scandals. She wears them like halos. Met her?"

"No. Go on."

"He is engaged to be married to some Italian starlet. Hasn't received his inheritance yet; he will, soon. The will is complicated. More?"

"More. Who wants to kill him?"

Arriz opened his eyes. "Kill him?"

"Yes."

"Has someone tried to kill him, Foxwell?"

Raynaud smiled. "You have the information, not me."

"Most interesting, if there has been an attempt," Arriz said. "Richard is in business now. Shore Industries, Limited, based in London. He is President, or Board Chairman, or whatever."

"And?"

"And his company is engaged in drilling operations in the North Sea. Searching for oil. It was recently started and is losing fabulous sums of money."

"Oh?"

"Yes. I heard nearly half a million pounds last year. No one can explain it adequately. But apparently it is not the consequence of poor business sense, as you might expect."

"Then what?"

"The company," Arriz said, "is only a front. Many people are convinced of this. It was formed to search for oil, and that is what it is presently doing, but that does not really justify its existence. Many believe it was formed for some other purpose. The precise purpose is unclear."

"But you have heard something," Raynaud said.

"Oh, yes. Rumors. Wild stories. You may believe them or not, as it suits you." Arriz took a deep breath. "The stories say that Shore Industries is bidding as prime contractor on the Channel Tunnel project, and that it expects to place the lowest bid, and thus get the contract for the major work. It will claim experience as a contractor for offshore operations, and it will claim experience in dealing with subcontractors who will do the actual dredging, drilling, and laying of the tunnel. The stories also say that Pierce expects to lose money on the contract bid, but that he will bargain for a high percentage of profits."

"So he'll make it back?"

"And more. That, at least, is the story."

"And how does Pierce know he'll place the lowest bid?"

"Because of his connections. You remember, half a million pounds last year. That is a great deal of money. It must have gone somewhere."

Raynaud said, "And you think it went into bribes?"

"Money well placed is money well spent," Arriz said.

"Who did he bribe?"

Arriz shook his head. "No idea."

"Who's paying the bill for the company?"

"His father's empire. Indirectly, through his mother, Lucienne. She is quite unhappy about the whole situation, as you might imagine. Strictly speaking, she doesn't have to support Shore Industries and allow Richard to spend all the money. There is speculation why she has done so."

"Yes?"

"The speculation suggests that she plans to humor Richard until she can get a large annual stipend guaranteed from him. And she plans to do this by putting Shore Industries into great jeopardy in the near future, just as Richard's plans begin to jell."

"How?"

"By putting the entire Pierce empire into jeopardy."

Raynaud said again, "How?"

"It is complicated. I do not have all the details. But apparently the Pierce empire is overextended. It is too widely diversified into new industries which have not yet paid off. Much of the collateral, and the working capital, comes from an Australian copper mine which the Pierce group now owns. But ownership could be lost if an American company that has seventeen percent of the stock sold out to the right party."

"Will the American company sell?"

"There are rumors."

"So Pierce will lose control of the mine?"

"That," Arriz said, "is what the rumors say."

"What is the American company?"

"It is called Mitchell Mining."

"Who owns it?"

"Formerly, an American named Mitchell. But he died last year. Now, it is in the hands of his daughter."

"What's she like?"

"Young. A fun-loving sort, from all accounts. Several scandals in New York."

"Her name?"

"Jane Mitchell," Arriz said. He looked up as André entered with the brandies. "Ah," he said, "here we are. Have one, Foxwell, and sit down. Let us talk over old times. Do you have more questions?"

"Just one. Who would want to kill Pierce?"

"Practically anybody who knows him well," Arriz said, and raised the brandy snifter in his hand. "Salud."

"The inner muscles of the thighs," Pierce said. "That is the key to everything."

Raynaud watched the girl on the stage, a slim, full-chested blonde who was removing her clothes in the manner that only French girls seem to learn.

They were sitting at the Crazy Horse, at a very good table, just a few feet from the girl. They could see the fine sheen of sweat on her body.

"A bit thin for my taste," Pierce went on, "but she has slim ankles. And such exquisite thigh muscles..." He laughed and poured more champagne. "What did you do today?"

"Business," Raynaud said.

"You make it sound very mysterious."

"I went to the bank."

"And afterward?"

Raynaud glanced quickly away from the girl to Pierce. For a moment he wondered if Pierce had had him followed. Raynaud had not checked, at the time, for a tail: that was an oversight. He cursed himself.

"Afterward, I did some checking up."

"Oh?"

"Yes."

"Checked up on me, did you?"

"Yes," Raynaud said.

"Why?"

The girl on stage was now completely naked, shaking her body in blue and green spotlights.

"I was returning a favor."

Pierce lit a cigarette. He did not take his eyes off the naked girl. "You were annoyed I had found out so much about you?"

"Let's say I was surprised."

"And you wanted to know why I had gone to the trouble."

"More or less."

"It's quite simple," Pierce said. "A few months ago, I was a little paranoid. Convinced they were out to get me."

"They?"

"Some business associates. I'm involved in some rather complex transactions at the moment."

"What sort of transactions?"

Pierce laughed. "Complex ones," he said.

Raynaud watched as the girl finished her dance and slipped away behind the curtains. He sipped his champagne and waited as Richard filled the glass again.

"You were afraid of being killed?"

"I was afraid someone would try."

"Business associates?"

"Possibly. In any case, that's all over now. And I'd rather not talk about it. It was all a bloody farce, from start to end." He glanced at his watch. "Which reminds me," he said. "We mustn't be late."

"Late for what?"

"Some people we have to meet. I think you'll like them. Gorgeous, both of them."

"Is that so?"

"That's so," Pierce grinned.

They left just as the comic came on, and went outside to catch a cab. They stood by the curb, watching the traffic. A dark blue Mercedes sedan pulled over toward them, very fast. Raynaud watched it come, expecting the driver to slow, but he did not. The car continued at full speed.

When it happened, it happened fast. Raynaud swung his arm around Pierce and threw him back, toward the club, onto the pavement. He let himself fall back just as the car rushed past them, tires squealing, and roared off down the street.

The doorman helped them up and brushed them off. He was talking very rapidly in French. "Drunkards! Fools! It is always the way. Do you know last year a man was killed? Here? Right at this club?"

Pierce straightened, tugged at his tie, and said to Raynaud, "Thanks for that."

"Any time."

"Maniacs! Sometimes I think that the world is crazy. Crazy. It is impossible—"

"Our thanks," Pierce said, and gave the man a hundred francs.

The doorman was silent, his stream of chatter interrupted by the money. "Monsieur, many—"

"That's all right."

"Did you get the license?" Raynaud asked him.

"No, monsieur, I am sorry."

"Was it a French license?"

The man shrugged and pocketed the money at the same time. "I am sorry. In the confusion…"

"Never mind," Pierce said. A cab had pulled up; he got in and beckoned to Raynaud. "Come on."

Astonished, Raynaud got in. "Never mind? When you nearly got—"

"Forget it."

"But—"

"I said, forget it. It was a mistake, that's all."

"Mistake, hell."

"Look," Pierce said, "let's just forget it."

Raynaud stopped, lit a cigarette, and glanced over at Pierce. Raynaud noticed that his own fingers were trembling slightly, but Pierce was quite calm.

"You're taking it well."

"Why not? It was just a mistake, a bloody mistake."

"How can you be sure?"

"I am, that's all," Pierce said. "I just am."

He stared out the window.

"Why are you so certain?" Raynaud said.

"Because I am," Pierce said. "I nearly got hit by a drunk. Plain and simple: no significance whatever. I refuse to let it ruin my evening."

"That was no drunk. The driver was in perfect control of his car. He knew exactly what he was doing."

"For Christ's sake, Charles."

The taxi pulled up in front of the Montaigne bar, near the Plaza-Athénée. Pierce got out and Raynaud followed him.

"Now look," Pierce said, paying the driver, "I want you to forget this. Just forget it. We're going to have a good time tonight and we're not going to think about this."

"You're out of your mind."

Pierce grinned. "Yes," he said, "I am."

"Ah, Caroline. You've come." Pierce kissed the dark girl on the cheek. "Meet Charles. Charles Raynaud, Caroline Versin."

Caroline took Raynaud's hand and smiled almost shyly, but her eyes were blatantly inquisitive.

They all sat down again to the drinks.

"Caroline," said Pierce, "is an actress. She played a pervert for Godard, didn't you, my dear?" He patted her hand.

She shrugged, and said to Raynaud, "You're French?"

"No," he said, speaking French. "American."

"You have a French name."

"My parents were French."

"Ah."

"Caroline was superb as a pervert," Pierce said. "You should tell Charles about it."

She shrugged. "There is nothing to tell. It was in the script. Jean-Luc—"

"Oh, it's Jean-Luc, is it?"

"Everyone calls him Jean-Luc," she said.

"What are you doing now?" Raynaud said. He thought to himself that she was very beautiful. Large eyes. He liked large eyes.

"Another film." She shrugged. "And after that, another for Roger and his fat wife. Ugh."

Raynaud smiled, thinking that all this might be amusing after all. Under the table, the girl's knees touched his. They ordered another round of drinks; he was feeling slightly high and very good.

It was the last coherent feeling he had.

Raynaud awoke with the sun on his face. He rolled over, squinted, and opened-his eyes. He was in his bed, in his room at the hotel. Soft sheets. Fleur-de-lis wallpaper in blue and silver.

He yawned and stretched. His foot touched something warm. He explored it tentatively with his toes. Another leg.

He looked over, and saw a girl lying next to him. She had red hair.

Red hair?

Surprised, he peered over her shoulder at her face. It was Vivienne, the girl he had ordered out of his room the first night.

What was she doing here?

Quietly, he got out of bed and walked around the room. It was a wreck: the mattress half off the bed, two empty champagne bottles on the floor, an unfinished bottle of Scotch on the mantel. Clothes strewn everywhere. Bra and panties hanging from the chandelier.

He went to the windows, feeling dizzy, and looked down on the Avenue George V. It was midday; elegant men and women hurried along, barely glancing at the shop windows.

He thought about the evening and slowly it began to come back to him. He glanced back at the redhead, Vivienne, curled up on the bed.

Then he heard a metallic clink from the other room.

Walking out of the bedroom, he saw a table with breakfast laid out on it. A girl was sitting at one chair reading the newspaper, legs crossed. She was naked. She put the paper down and smiled as he entered: Dominique, the girl he had met with Richard on the first night.

"Hello," she said. She seemed quite fresh and bright.

"Hello," he said.

"You look awful. How do you feel?"

"Awful," he said, sitting down at the breakfast table. As he did, he noticed the green alligator tattoo on Dominique's abdomen. He remembered what Richard had called her: the snapper.

There was coffee and orange juice and a small glass of clear liquid. He held it up. "What's this?"

"Martini. I thought it might help."

Quickly he poured it into the orange juice, and drank it down. It might not help, but it couldn't hurt. Dominique watched him in silence and scratched one breast absently.

"Tell me," Raynaud said. "There was a dark girl, named uh…"

"Caroline? She left."

"Why?"

Dominique smiled. "You don't remember?"

Raynaud frowned and poured coffee. "Not at the moment."

"She left, very angry, because you wanted to do this thing."

"What thing?"

"This sex thing. I don't know the English word."

"Then tell me in French."

She told him.

"Oh, yes," he said, slowly recalling.

"You wanted to do it, very much."

"So you arrived."

"Yes," Dominique said. "We like it, you see."

"Yes."

"You were wonderful," Dominique said. "Very wonderful. I hope we did not hurt you."

"I doubt it," he said, pouring sugar into the coffee.

"We probably did," Dominique said. "We usually do, when they are good ones. Turn around."

Dutifully, he twisted in his chair. She made sighing noises. "Does it hurt very much?"

"It doesn't hurt at all."

"I should cut them. My nails. They are too dangerous. But some of that is Vivienne. I always tell her, cut the nails, men do not appreciate it. But she never listens."

She sighed and rubbed her breasts again. "They are sore," she said. "Richard was biting them again. Such a beast."

She stood, the alligator on her abdomen wiggling as she moved. "It was much better," she said, "when he liked my backside. More padding."

She went off to the bathroom.

"Where is Richard?" he asked.

"Upstairs. With the others." She paused. "Oh, by the way, there was a telegram. It is on the tray."

She pointed, and continued on. When he was alone he opened it:

LONDON W1

CONFIRM ARRANGEMENTS FOR ARRIVAL
AGREE ANY DEMANDS

LILI MARLENE

He stared at the telegram, then lit it with a match and dropped it burning into an ashtray. It was still in flames when Dominique padded out of the bathroom.

"Why did you do that?"

"It was a secret," he said.

"Secret messages?"

"Yes." He smiled. "The very best kind."

The phone in the bedroom rang three times. They heard the redhead, Vivienne, groan and say, "Turn the damned thing off."

Raynaud went in to answer it.

"Christ. Charles. Is that you? My bloody head is killing me, absolutely killing me. How do you feel?"

"I've felt better," Raynaud said, looking at Vivienne, who had rolled over in bed, the sheets sliding away. She was snoring now.

"Christ. I feel half dead. I have to go back to London tomorrow. We must talk, Charles. Can you find the bar of this godforsaken hotel?"

"Probably."

"In about an hour?"

"All right," Raynaud said.

The bar was cool and quiet at midafternoon. Raynaud sat cradling a cold martini in his hands while Richard, looking red-eyed and exhausted, said, "We'll go together, of course. And you'll stay at my flat."

"Thanks," Raynaud said, "but no."

"I insist."

Raynaud shook his head.

"Why not?"

"This is a business trip," Raynaud said. "I've got things to do."

"London hotels are awful. You'll hate them."

"I rather like them."

Pierce lit a cigarette, striking the match feebly several times before it finally burst into flame. "Look here, Charles. I really must insist you stay at the flat. People would talk otherwise."

Raynaud raised his eyebrows. "Oh?"

"Yes. You see, you're the best man at my wedding."

"What wedding?"

"Well, at the party anyhow. You've got to be present at the party. And you've got to stay at the flat. We'll have a marvelous time together, really."

"No."

"Charles, you must. I'll be miserable if you don't."

Raynaud sipped his martini and stared at Pierce's reflected image in the bar mirror.

"You're very eager to have me around, Richard."

"You are my closest and dearest friend. Believe it or not."

"I don't. What's on your mind?"

Pierce sighed. "It's the party. I admit I can't stand the thought of it. And my dear mother. You've got to come along, for moral support."

Raynaud shook his head. "Try again."

"That's the truth, really."

"Bullshit."

Pierce waved to the bartender for more drinks. He said nothing for a long time. Finally, he said, "You're stubborn, Charles."

"Very."

Raynaud smoked his cigarette and waited until the drinks had come, and the bartender moved away. "All right," he said, "I'll tell you what. I'll come to London with you, and stay at your flat, and go to your party with you, and do whatever you want me to do. For five hundred dollars a day."

Pierce choked on the drink. "What?"

"I think it's reasonable," Raynaud said,

"Five hundred a day? Are you out of your mind?"

"That's the going rate," Raynaud said, "for a good bodyguard."

"You're being absurd. I don't need a bodyguard."

"Don't you?"

"No. Absolutely not. The very idea—"

"Okay," Raynaud said, shrugging. "Forget it."

Pierce hesitated, staring down at his glass, swirling the pale liquor. "Four hundred," he said.

"No. Flat rate: five hundred a day. Take it or leave it."

"Four hundred."

Raynaud shook his head.

"Christ," Pierce said. "All right, have it your way. Five hundred."

Raynaud sat back and smiled slightly. "How long will you need my, ah, services?"

"I don't know. At least a month."

"Then I'll want half in advance."

Pierce frowned.

"Half in advance," Raynaud repeated. "A check for, say, three thousand pounds would be adequate."

"Let's say two," Pierce said, taking out his checkbook.

"Let's say three."

Irritably Pierce wrote out the check, his pen scratching in the quiet of the bar. He tore the check off, waved it dry, and handed it to Raynaud.

"Satisfied?"

"Almost. Tell me who's trying to kill you."

"I don't know. Maybe I'm being paranoid about the whole thing."

"But you must fear someone."

"We can discuss it in London," Pierce said.

"We can discuss it now, just as well."

"London," Pierce said. "It's a long story. London."

They left in the morning.

6. LONDON

The rain fell from gray, dreary skies as they left the arrivals building of Heathrow Airport and got into the chauffeured Rolls-Royce. Richard slumped down in the back seat and nodded to Medgars, the driver.

"Welcome back, sir," Medgars said.

"Thanks for nothing," Pierce said. He closed the glass partition separating front and back seats.

Medgars gave a small shrug and started the car, driving smoothly down the ramp and through the tunnel, then turning right toward London.

Raynaud said, "Is this your car?"

"Christ no. Lucienne's."

"Nice."

"She likes it," Pierce said indifferently. He had a marked distaste for Rolls-Royces. For one thing, the sellers were such bastards. Lucienne bought a new one every second year, always in a different color. She alternated between Jack Barclay and Owen's. But they were both bastards. Stiff-upper-lip bastards.

Medgars drove smoothly; the sound of the motor was a low, well-bred purr.

"It drives well," Raynaud said.

"It's all right. Medgars has been to the school."

"The school?"

"Yes. Rolls runs it, for chauffeurs. Teaches the sons of bitches to drive. Smooth shifts, gentle stops, all that sort of thing. Very chi."

"I see."

Pierce stared out the window. They were coming in from the west, through a dreary, dismal industrial area. He sighed. Undoubtedly Violet would not have the flat in shape, and undoubtedly Lucienne would be in an evil mood. He had to get more money from her. A lot more: he owned a thousand quid to Lonny from that chemin game four weeks ago. And the new rugs in the living room would be several hundred more.

He opened the glass partition and leaned forward to speak to Medgars. "How is she these days?"

"She, sir?"

Medgars. Always the polite sod.

"Mrs. Pierce, damn it."

"Very well, sir."

"That's wonderful news," Pierce said dryly.

"Will you be seeing her, sir?"

"Later." Bloody sod.

"Yes, sir. Shall I tell her, sir?"

"No," Pierce said. "Let it be a surprise."

It was always a surprise for Lucienne, always a nasty shock. The minute he walked through the door she reached for a ciggie and a drink to help her through the trauma of a meeting. A cripple, she was, without a ciggie and a drink. And always nervous, with that pinched-up, bitchy look on her face the whole time. Any mention of money tied her lovely face into knots of agonized pain.

They came into Chelsea and continued north and east, past the Royal Hospital.

"Where are we going?"

"My flat."

Pierce anticipated Raynaud's reaction to the flat with some pleasure. He had bought it two years ago and had spent nearly a year fixing it up. He had put more than six thousand pounds into it, over Lucienne's wails of fiscal pain.

The flat was in Belgravia, not far from Sloane Square. It was a whitewashed building with a black wrought-iron railing in front; Pierce had the second floor. The ground floor was occupied by a retired MP and industrialist who was, fortunately, deaf as a bat, so there was no problem with parties.

Medgars carried the bags up and Pierce unlocked the front door, which was painted a cherry red—he had specifically insisted upon the color, cherry red—and had a burnished brass plate reading, "Now is the time for all good men to come."

Lucienne had objected violently to that plate, which made it all the more amusing.

Raynaud saw it and laughed. A simple, American sort of laugh, rather dumb and automatic.

Still, he was glad to have Raynaud with him. Bloody animal, Raynaud. Reflexes of a cat. No wonder he'd gone to the jungle, it suited him perfectly. It was reassuring to have him with you, going about with you, even if it cost three thousand quid.

He was coming into a crucial time. Crucial with Lucienne, crucial with Shore Industries. He had worked bloody hard with Shore Industries. He had great hopes for it. Nothing must be allowed to spoil that.

Soon, of course, Raynaud would begin asking questions, but Pierce could handle that. He could keep the answers vague and mysterious. Just enough truth to satisfy Raynaud.

"Why are we standing outside?" Raynaud asked.

Pierce laughed, shaking off his thoughts, and swung open the door. They went into the living room. It was very mod: a thick white rug and stark white walls; a minimum of furniture, all of it Meister, chairs and couches in black leather with stainless legs. The coffee table was inch-thick smoked glass on a stainless frame. On one wall was a giant painting of a hamburger, dripping catsup; on another was a large spiral in red and orange which made you dizzy if you looked long enough.

"Wow," Raynaud said.

"Like it?"

"Superb."

Along one wall was his Clairtone G, a rectangular teak box with two spheres at either end. He picked up a small hand-held box and pressed a button: music filled the room. Raynaud nodded, impressed, and he should have been: the whole thing had cost nearly five hundred pounds.

"This is rather neat," Pierce said. He went to the wall, and pressed the light switch, which was a round push button. The lights went on; he pressed again, and nothing happened.

"Something wrong?"

"No. It's a delay switch. Sixty seconds before the lights go out. The same everywhere in the house."

He pressed a second button, and the drapes slid closed over aluminum runners.

"Pretty clever, eh? The motors are specially silenced."

Pierce, enjoying Raynaud's expression, led him to the guest bedroom. It was luxuriously done, with an orange rug and a double bed.

"I think of everything. Durex in the second drawer of the night table. If you need it. Most of the birds take pills."

He showed him how the push-lock doors worked on the closet, and then led him to the guest bathroom, completely outfitted. It even had a bidet.

"Just in case," Pierce said. "One never knows."

They went back into the living room, and through to the kitchen.

"There was no second bathroom when I first arrived," Pierce said. "Had to be installed. And all the wiring had to be torn out and done over. Then the central heating ducts and the air conditioning and filters…"

"It must have been expensive."

"Worth it," Pierce said.

The kitchen was small but bright and modern; countertops of Formica and stainless steel. Pierce was proud of the kitchen. Birds liked it; they appreciated it. A small bar; six-burner electric stove; two ovens, one powered by infrared so it never got hot. A special charcoal broiler which he had imported from California. A large hooded duct and fan to carry away cooking smells. Electric can opener, mixer, blender: very good for frozen daiquiris.

On one wall, attached by a clip, was another hand-box. He picked it up and pressed a button; the music changed.

"Can do it from any room in the house. Also this."

He turned a round fixture that looked like a thermostat, and the lights dimmed.

"Rheostat. Works everywhere."

Raynaud pointed over the refrigerator at a small television screen. "Why do you keep that there?"

Pierce laughed. He pushed a button on the set and it lighted immediately—transistorized, no waiting for warm-up—to show the downstairs hall. Another button, and it showed the hall outside his front door. Another, and the screen showed Raynaud's room. Finally, the scene shifted to another, larger bedroom which Raynaud gathered was Pierce's.

"Concealed in the walls," Pierce said. "It's very small, a Japanese thing. One of these days, I'm going to buy a video tape unit, but that's another three hundred pounds and Lucienne has been difficult lately. Still, it'd be fun. Instant replay, blow by blow." He laughed. "So to speak."

Raynaud, the bastard, was not amused. Probably wondering who would be looking in on his own bedroom action.

"Come along," Pierce said. "I'll show you the workroom."

They went into the master bedroom. It was as large as the living room, styled in sharp contrast to the rest of the house. The walls were covered in red velvet, and the rug was one-and-a-half-inch red pile. And washable.

The bed was eight feet square, with a large headboard.

"Like it?" Pierce said.

"Very much."

"Rather like a Victorian bordello, don't you think?"

"A bit."

"They love it," Pierce said. He touched a concealed button and opened a closet door. The inside of the door was covered with neat scratches. "One hundred and seventy-four," he said, "by actual count. Not bad for a year and a half."

"Not bad at all."

"They love it. Feel the bed. It's soft, but not too soft."

Raynaud dutifully felt the bed. He was moving slowly, as if in a trance. Must be a bit hard to take, Pierce thought happily.

"Bought it at Harrods," Pierce said. "Gave them rather a shock, actually. I went in and asked them what bed was best for fucking. Funny little salesman hemmed and hawed before he came up with this one. It's stuffed with gnu hair, the mattress. Gives it that soft, springy resilience."

"Very nice."

"I'm fond of it. The bathroom is here."

Pierce led him into the bathroom, also carpeted in red. It was large, with a sunken tub, a built-in shower, bidet, and toilet with electrically heated seat. A small closet on one side was filled with small bathrobes, frilly nightgowns, colognes, and cosmetics.

"Completely equipped. Oh, I almost forgot. The headboard."

They returned to the bedroom, and he showed Raynaud the built-in bar, refrigerator, stereo speakers, and clock telly.

"Well, that's the lot. Drink?"

"Scotch."

"Good." As they left the bedroom, Pierce said, "It was that or ostrich feathers."

"What?"

"The mattress. I think I made a wise choice. I've been on an ostrich-feather mattress. Cynthia has one. Definitely inferior—though of course she likes it."

"Ummm."

In the living room, Pierce mixed two stiff drinks. Raynaud looked as if he needed one. He was doing his best to remain unimpressed, but he wasn't succeeding. In fact, he seemed a little green.

Well, there would be more to come. "I'm rather dreading the party day after tomorrow," Pierce said. "Shall we get some girls for tonight? A last bash?"

"Whatever you say."

"Good." He reached for the phone. "There's a marvelous thing you'll want to meet. She models and does credits for movies."

"Oh?"

"Yes. You know, they flash the titles across her tits. She has a super body. She's been in those spy things."

"I see."

"She's too big for me, but she'll be just right for you. I'll ring her up."

"Fine."

"Throws a wild one," Richard said. "You'll be exhausted."

As he reached for the telephone, it rang. He picked it up and said, "Hello?"

"Richard, my boy, how are you?"

Pierce recognized the deep, warm voice immediately. "Hello, Uncle John," he said.

"Just get back?"

"Yes, actually. Half an hour ago."

"Come over for dinner," Uncle John said. "If you feel up to it."

"Fine. I'm here with a friend."

"Bring her along," he said.

"It's a he, actually."

Uncle John laughed. "Switching, are you?"

"An old school friend."

"Oh?" He seemed surprised. He knew Richard wasn't much on old school friends.

"Yes," Pierce said. "Ran into him in Paris. Pure luck."

"Well, I'll look forward to meeting him. Drinks at seven, is that all right?"

"Yes, of course."

When he hung up, Raynaud said, "Who was that?"

"My uncle."

"What'd he want?"

"He's invited us to dinner. No girls for tonight, I'm afraid." He sighed. "And the engagement party is day after tomorrow. That leaves just one evening."

"Which reminds me," Raynaud said. "This weekend I'll have to leave you for a few hours."

"Your business?"

"For a few hours."

"Well, it doesn't matter," Pierce said. "I shall be away. I'm leaving with Sandra, right after the party. Be gone the whole weekend."

Raynaud raised his eyebrows. "You don't want me along?"

Richard laughed. "Rather not."

"Won't you be worried?"

"I only worry," Pierce said, "when I'm alone. Besides, we'll be in a quaint little hotel in Wales. Nobody could find us there." He glanced at his watch. "Anyway. We'd best dress now, if we're going to make drinks by seven."

"What do we wear?"

"Black tie, of course," Pierce said. "Uncle John is rather proper, in his own way."

*

Pierce grinned at himself in the mirror as he shaved. He felt good; Raynaud had been impressed as hell with the apartment. But then, everybody was. Damned fine flat. Everybody said it. And the nice thing about living in a chi place like Belgravia was that there was never any scandal. The cops were circumspect; they had to be, with the Danish ambassador right next door, and the German ambassador around the corner, and the German ambassador's mistress across the street. To say nothing about the mistress's girlfriend, who had once been very close to the Yugoslav cultural attaché.

Chelsea was raided all the time, and Battersea was too, now that it was getting up as a fashionable place. And Bloomsbury was impossible, the coppers practically lived there.

But not Belgravia. Not with all the important people and the big industrial firms and diplomatic immunity for every second town house.

Before moving to Belgravia, he had lived in Chelsea, in the rich part off King's Road. His parties were broken up five times in as many months, and finally he decided to be done with it. Lucienne, bless her frosty heart, had approved of the move. Thought it would be good for his manners, or his soul, or something. But then she knew a lot about the Belgravia crowd—she'd seen nearly every bedroom ceiling in the area.

Dear, dear Lucienne.

He glanced over to the toilet. Normally he kept a picture of her above the toilet; it wasn't there. Violet must have moved it. Violet was Richard's cleaning lady. She was a stiff old bird of seventy who seemed very proper until she got angry; then she poured out the language of her dead husband, a sailor in the merchant marine. But Violet liked Lucienne, and disapproved of Richard's keeping her over the toilet.

Just where she belonged. Dear Lucienne: all her life she had managed to make him feel like a worthless sod. Very skilled at making men feel worthless.

But soon, he thought, all that would change. Shore Industries would be an immense success; he would inherit the Pierce fortune.

And absolutely everything would change.

7. BLACK

In the guest room, Charles Raynaud sat on the bed and bounced experimentally. As he did so, he examined the room carefully, noticing every detail: including the television camera, located high up by the ceiling, imbedded in the wall with nothing but the barrel of the lens protruding.

That would have to be fixed.

He climbed up on a chair and quickly stuffed tissues into the barrel, blocking the lens. He smiled as he did so. Poor Richard with all his gadgets. He was like a child in an amusement park, with this apartment. A fabulous array of purring, whirring gadgets. Pierce obviously loved every one of them. They were possessions, shining devices to be pointed out, displayed, explained, and demonstrated. He treated women the same way. He would offer you a woman the way he offered you a chance to try his new pressurized cork-remover. The same childish delight in his face: "Try it out. Isn't it clever?"

He took a shower and reminded himself that he must be careful. It was a mistake to underestimate Richard. A serious mistake. He had made such mistakes in the past.

Like the Delaware business.

Six years before, he had taken a Middle Period Aztec water pitcher in the shape of a turtle to an industrial chemist living in Delaware. While he was there, he had taken a liking to the chemist's bored wife and transported her across state lines. Her husband, a fat and apparently lethargic man, was not amused and called the police; the motel was raided. Raynaud later discovered that the woman always took her men to the same motel. In the end, the chemist got his water pitcher for nothing, and Raynaud returned to Mexico shaken but wiser. He had learned something about people, particularly people who chose to appear foolish.

Pierce, he knew, was not a fool. He would have to be very, very careful.

He tied his bowtie and straightened it, looking into the mirror. He looked at his own face, and saw the boyish features which were, in a way, like Pierce's. For a moment the similarity disturbed him.

Pierce stuck his head around the door. "Ready to go? We mustn't keep Uncle John waiting."

The garage was located in the mews behind the house. It opened at the sound of an ultrasonic whistle, emitted from a gadget in Pierce's pocket, exposing a sleek, wine-red machine which stood barely four feet off the ground.

"Maserati," Pierce said. "Hop in."

It was a two-plus-two. Raynaud dropped into the comfortable bucket seat, feeling the real leather. He looked at the dashboard, which was covered in black leather, elegant and businesslike. The gearshift was mounted between the seats. In front were two chrome air vents.

"Air conditioning?"

Pierce laughed. "Of course."

He started the car. It came to life with a deep rumble exaggerated by the confines of the garage.

"Air conditioning in London?"

"Comes with the car," Pierce said. "These wops. Always hot."

He backed out.

"Ghia body," he said, "and a four-point-seven engine that will bring you bloody close to two hundred miles an hour. We'll have to take it out to the M1 some day and give the Jags something to think about."

He roared down the narrow alley and onto the street. The speedometer climbed quickly to sixty, though traffic was heavy.

"Learned to drive at Brands Hatch," Pierce said. "They have a little circuit there, give you lessons in speeding safely. Never fear."

He weaved expertly through the dense clutter of minis, black humpbacked taxis, and private cars.

"Where are we going?"

"Saint John's Wood. Very chi-chi part of Hampstead. Uncle John's quite a success, as doctors go."

"He's a doctor?"

"Psychiatrist. Psychoanalyst, actually. At one time he had a large Harley practice, but he's given all that up now. He's gone over to research."

"In psychiatry?"

"I don't know, exactly. It has to do with pigeons and monkeys and so forth. I never understood it. You'll have to ask him."

Raynaud nodded.

"Uncle John," Pierce said, with slight awe in his voice, "is frightfully intelligent."

The room was nearly square, and high-ceilinged, paneled in dark wood which gave it a close, almost stuffy atmosphere. Antiques were everywhere, mostly silver, and mostly in need of polishing. Several yellowing photographs were hung on the walls; Raynaud was looking at them when the butler, dressed formally in black, came in to say that Dr. Black was detained briefly at the laboratory and asked that they make themselves comfortable. What would they drink?

Scotch, they said. When they were alone, Pierce said, "Uncle John approves of Scotch."

"Oh? Why?"

"He's Scottish himself. From Edinburgh. He's from a family of doctors, all living in Edinburgh. He's the only one who came down to London. Because he was so dreadfully clever."

Pierce touched an antique drinking cup, wiping away the dust on the rim. "I'm afraid, though, that he doesn't keep the place up well. A bit tacky all around. He isn't here much, and I don't suppose it matters to him."

"He lives alone?"

"Yes. He was married, but his wife died. A long time ago."

"I see."

"Nobody knows quite what happened. It's all a bit mysterious, and Uncle John never talks about it. They say it was a heart attack."

"Is he actually your uncle, or just a family friend?" Raynaud was staring out through dusty curtain at the trees and rolling hills of Hampstead Heath.

"Oh, no. A true uncle. He was first cousin of my father. There's a picture here, somewhere. Wait a bit...yes. There it is. Over to the right."

Raynaud saw two men in hunting jackets, standing with shotguns in the crooks of their arms. One held a pheasant. They wore caps and their faces were partly in shadow; it was difficult to see their features. They stood rather stiffly for the photograph, but with them was a young woman who was standing casually, one hand on her hip, laughing, her head thrown back. She seemed to be very amused about something, but there was an exaggerated falseness to her pose.

But she was certainly sexy.

"Who's the girl?"

"Lucienne. My stepmother. Uncle John and my father had rather a falling out after my father married Lucienne. Uncle John got along well with Lucienne, you see—sometimes too well."

"Your stepmother? Was your father married before?"

Pierce looked surprised. "Didn't you know? I was adopted. Parents died during the war. Pierce isn't my real name; it's Trevor-Carter. I was adopted when I was six years old."

"No," Raynaud said, "I didn't know."

Pierce grinned. "You seem annoyed."

"Why should I be annoyed?" In fact, he felt a strange, deep sort of anger.

"Lucienne is annoyed," Pierce said. "For her, it is the final infuriating irony of the whole thing. That I will inherit the estate without even being the biologic heir. She has only herself to blame, you see."

"How do you mean?"

"She would never have a child by my father. Absolutely refused."

Raynaud noticed that Pierce always referred to Herbert as his father, but Lucienne as his stepmother.

"Your father and Doctor Black didn't get along, then?"

"No. There were rumors at the time. Personally, I never

believed any of them. Uncle John is a marvelous person, and he's been a great help to me."

"How?"

"Dealing with Lucienne," Pierce said. "He doesn't like her any more than I do, but he knows how to get round her, and I don't. So he's been a great help to me."

At that moment, a deep voice said, "Good evening, gentlemen."

Raynaud turned to face the ugliest man he had ever seen.

Jonathan Black was a huge man with a powerful physique, but it was the face that you noticed first: a hawk beak of a nose, curving to a blunted tip above a thick, fleshy mouth. A skull totally bald. Heavy, black, thick eyebrows. He looked like a strange, lumbering bird of prey as he advanced into the room.

And the eyes: a peculiar, washed-out gray, very cold, and constantly moving beneath heavy lids. He walked with his chin habitually tilted up, as if to compensate for the lids.

"Uncle John, meet Charles Raynaud."

"How do you do."

Black's grip was cold and firm, the fingers hard.

"Charles is in the snake business," Pierce said.

"Oh?" Black smiled slightly, and rang for the butler. "In what sense?"

"I supply animals and venom for research groups," Raynaud explained.

"Not Central Scientific in Cleveland, surely?"

"No. Mexico."

"Ah," Black said. "Herpetology, Incorporated. Is that it?"

Raynaud nodded, wondering how Black knew. The butler came and Black ordered a Scotch.

"I've had a few dealings with your organization," Black said. "In my own work, we occasionally use various venoms. Mostly the anticholinesterases. Of course, I'm off that for the moment. Are you here for the convention?"

Raynaud nodded.

"I hope to attend a few sessions myself," Black said. "It's this weekend, as I recall."

"Yes," Raynaud said.

"What convention?" Pierce said.

"The International Congress of Zoologists and Herpetologists," Black said. "They're having their annual meeting in London."

Pierce looked quickly at Raynaud, but said nothing.

Black sat down, not slowly and heavily as Raynaud expected, but lightly and swiftly.

"Well, now," he said, "and how long will you remain in London?"

"I'm not sure."

"At least a month," Pierce said.

"Oh?"

"He's going to be my best man, Uncle," Pierce said.

"That's wonderful," Black said, looking at Raynaud from beneath heavy lids. "Just wonderful. London is amusing at this time of year. You have, I gather, known Richard here for many years."

"We were in school together."

"Ah. Excellent. And you've kept in touch all this time."

"Not exactly," Raynaud said. "As a matter of fact, we met in Paris quite by chance."

"How extraordinary," Black said, in a voice which did not sound in the least surprised.

He did not continue the subject, and Raynaud found that odd. He wondered whether it was merely the bland acceptance of a psychiatrist, or whether it was something else. Because Raynaud had a brief, unsettling feeling that Jonathan Black had known all along that Pierce and Raynaud would meet. Almost as if he had planned it himself.

Dinner was served with a simple elegance that contrasted with the clutter of the living room. They began with cold cucumber soup, then crayfish in drawn butter.

"Are you still in practice?" Raynaud asked. "Richard tells me you've gone mostly to research."

"I've gone entirely to research," Black said. "In fact, you are eating it now."

He laughed as he saw Raynaud's startled look. "I mean the

crayfish," he said. "I began with the crayfish ten years ago. At the time I was tired of neurotic people telling me their fantasies for twenty pounds an hour. I wanted something more challenging. There is nothing, you know, very challenging about clinical psychiatry. I have often felt the most effective psychiatrist would be a man without vocal cords: all he could do is listen, and give no advice. Since the patients don't want advice, he'd be a rousing success."

He sighed. "Anyway, I tired of it, and turned to crayfish. There was a group working on them in Cambridge. Biochemical people, all involved with synapses and transmitter substances and end-plate potentials. All quite basic: learning what makes a nerve cell fire, learning how it carries its information, how it is propagated from cell to cell. The crayfish is good to study because it has large, simple nerve cells and simple ganglia. You need large cells so that you can stick your electrodes into a single cell and be assured you are measuring one cell, not two or five. We measured voltage potentials and changes and nerve-firing patterns. I found it interesting for a time. More wine?"

He nodded to the butler, who took the bottle around.

"But finally I tired of crayfish as well. Basically, crayfish are tiresome animals. They eat nothing but garbage. So I turned to drugs and psychopharmacology. I wanted a larger field, with broader implications for people. This was about six years ago: researchers were finding all sorts of new drugs that affected the mind. It was an exciting, restless field. I've been in it ever since then."

"What kinds of drugs are you working with?" Raynaud asked.

"Nothing very spectacular, I'm afraid." Black made a deprecating gesture. "Not lysergic acid or tryptamine derivatives. Nothing to expand the consciousness or warp the mind. No, I've been doing rather simple and straightforward work with anger."

"Anger?"

"Yes. Anger has always fascinated me. It is a common reaction, shared by man and many animals alike, but we understand practically nothing about it. We accept it. But we do not understand it. A man can become angry for a variety of reasons, and

can, while angry, perform a variety of acts he would not otherwise perform. He can kill, he can destroy, he can respond in
the most bizarre manner. And we say, 'it's because he's angry,'
as if that explained it."

Raynaud sipped his wine.

"But there must be physical reasons for anger," Black said,
"and there must be biochemical reasons. The brain must, in
some way, become altered. An angry man is different from a
calm man. How? That is what I have set out to discover."

"And what have you found?"

"That it is a very frustrating field," Black said. "Progress is slow.
In fact," he smiled, "on occasion, it makes me quite angry myself."

Driving home, Richard Pierce said, "What did you think of him?"

"Your uncle?"

"Yes."

"Interesting." In fact, Raynaud had been disturbed by him.
Everything about him—his manner, his voice, his dusty house
on Hampstead Heath—was strange and faintly bothersome.

"Yes," Richard said, "he's a fascinating man. To tell you the
truth, I don't know what I'd do without him. Since my father
died, he's been almost a substitute father to me. Strange, when
you think about him and Lucienne."

Pierce paused. "By the way, was it true what you said about
the International Congress of Whatever?"

"That I'm going?"

"Yes."

Raynaud nodded. "It's true."

"Why are you going?"

"It's expected. I'm in the snake business, remember."

Pierce laughed. "Speaking of snakes, wait until you meet
Lucienne."

"I'm looking forward to it."

"Don't," Pierce said.

When he was alone in the house, Dr. Jonathan Black dialed a
number and spoke quietly for several minutes. "I have met
Raynaud," he said. "He should be ideal."

When he hung up, he poured himself a brandy, then seemed to think better of it. He left the brandy on the arm of the chair in the living room and walked upstairs to his bedroom. There, in a drawer, he found a stethoscope and unbuttoned his shirt, sitting on the edge of the bed.

He took a deep breath, and placed the stethoscope bell against his chest.

He listened, in frowning silence, for a long time.

8. SHORE

The girl could not have been more than eighteen. She walked gracefully down Regent Street in the afternoon sunlight, her long legs bare beneath the miniskirt, a pocketbook swinging from her shoulder. The skirt was yellow velvet, and the ruffled blouse was stretched tight over enormous breasts.

Richard Pierce, hung over, seemed to revive. He pulled the car to the curb and leaned out the window. "Hey, Pet!" he called.

To Raynaud he said, "That's Petunia, the model I was telling you about. Film credits across the tits."

Pet came up, smiling, swinging the purse. Her hair was long, blond, straight, hanging over her shoulders.

"'Lo, Dickie."

"Give you a lift, Pet?"

She smiled. "I'm up now, thanks."

"What on?"

"Speed."

She leaned over, looked in, and saw Raynaud. "Who's the friend?"

"Charles Raynaud. You should meet him."

She gave Raynaud an appraising look. "Yes," she said. "I should."

"Then hop in." He opened the door.

"Where're you headed?"

"Anywhere."

She laughed and got into the back seat. Raynaud turned and said, "Hi."

"You're American."

"Yes."

She shifted on the seat, tugging at her miniskirt. "Here for the sights?"

"More or less." He grinned.

Richard pulled out into traffic, heading toward Piccadilly

Circus. Pet opened her purse, found a comb, and combed her long hair. She glanced at her face in a pocket mirror.

"I'm such a mess," she said. "I had an audition this morning."

"Oh?"

"Yes. Chubby Norton. You know him?"

"Sure." Richard explained to Raynaud. "Chubby Norton is one of the young geniuses. He makes films about dollies that get preggers. Message cinema."

"He's really quite nice," Pet said.

"Did you get the part?" Raynaud said.

"No," Pet said. "But he's really quite nice."

They drove around the statue of Eros, and down Whitehall toward Parliament.

"I'm showing Charles the town," Pierce said. "We were going to call you later."

"Oh?"

"Yes. We're up for a bit of fun tonight."

Still combing her hair, Pet said, "Sandra coming?"

"No. Can't make it."

"Oh."

"You free?" Richard said.

"Actually," Pet said, "I'm not. Date with a heavy."

"Young Chubby?"

"No. He's not like that."

"Really?"

"Quite the other way," she said, with a sigh. "Shame. I like his eyes."

"I didn't know you had a thing for eyes."

"Don't be crude, Dickie."

"Don't put on airs, Pet."

She finished combing her hair and snapped her purse shut. "I'll be at the party tomorrow," she said. To Raynaud: "Will you?"

"He's the best man." Pierce laughed.

"I see." The news seemed to annoy Pet. "You've known Dickie a long time?"

"More than ten years."

"How nice." She turned to Pierce. "I take it you'll be there, tomorrow night, Dickie?"

"Wouldn't miss it for the world."

"And Sandra will be there? She can make it?"

"Don't be nasty, Pet."

"Just asking."

"Yes, everyone will be there."

"Even your son?"

"Very nasty, Pet."

"They say he looks like you."

"Just because she didn't have your affinity for Doctor Winsten—"

"You can let me off," Pet said, "at the next corner."

"—doesn't mean—"

"The next corner, Dickie. Thanks for the ride."

Pierce pulled over and opened the door. Pet got out, showing lots of leg and frilly underpants.

She glanced back at Raynaud. "Perhaps we'll meet again," she said.

Then she shut the door and turned away without looking at Richard. He pulled out, and said, "Moody bird. Always has been. It's the success. She's forced to nob it with producers and directors who lust after her body. Quite incredible, did you notice? Practically the best body in England. When she was younger, she made a lot of money as a figure model."

Raynaud looked back and saw her standing on the corner as they drove off.

"What did she mean about—"

"A son? It's true, I have one. A little boy in Bristol or Manchester or somewhere. He's two or three now. I paid for the abortion, but the girl wouldn't have it. Simple dolly. She was a close friend of Pet's. Pet likes to play high and mighty, even though old Winsten has scraped her out three times that I know of, and maybe more."

Raynaud said nothing.

"Some day," Pierce said, "when I come into the money, I'll adopt that kid. And he'll have everything. Everything he could want. He'll be the happiest kid in the world."

"Didn't you have everything?"

"Yes," Pierce said. "But it was different." He spun the wheel sharply, making a U-turn.

"Now where?"

"My offices," Pierce said. "I want to see how my little project is coming." He laughed. "It's not much to look at, but you may be interested."

The gilded raised lettering on the mahogany paneling said: Shore Industries, Ltd. Beneath was an emblem, a modernistic representation of a drilling rig. The carpet beneath their feet was thick blue pile.

"Come along," Pierce said. "We'll catch them unawares."

He opened the door. Four secretaries, all attractive, stopped typing to greet him. Pierce waved to them and walked through a second door, into a smaller room. One girl sat there, at a teak desk.

"Good afternoon, Mr. Pierce. Are you in for the afternoon?"

"I am in," Pierce said, "for exactly one hour."

"Yes, sir. Shall I put calls through?"

"Yes."

The girl stood up behind the desk. "Here are the messages from last week. Did you have a good trip to Paris?"

"Excellent," Pierce said briskly. He walked through another door which said: PRESIDENT: R. PIERCE.

Raynaud watched him in astonishment. A few minutes before, he had been casual, almost sloppy, and badly hung over. Now he walked erectly and spoke in brisk, firm tones.

"Sit down," Pierce said, closing the office door behind him. His private office was starkly furnished: two Barcelona chairs, a glass-topped desk with chrome legs, a telephone, an intercom, and a dictating machine.

"What do you think?"

"Impressive. How much time do you spend here?"

"Practically none. But it doesn't matter. Business expense. And it's mostly for show. You see, this office does no real business. Our work is largely financing; we subcontract for the drilling and search operations, and skim off a percentage of any strikes.

Naturally, we also absorb losses. That's why we can command such a large percentage of any oil that's found. We act as a kind of buffer for subcontractors."

He sat down behind the desk and leafed through the stack of letters and telephone messages.

"You'll have to excuse me for a while," Pierce said. "Make yourself a drink. Push the second shelf over there."

Raynaud did; it slid back to reveal a bar.

"Want something?"

"No."

Pierce turned away and picked up the first telephone message. He flicked on the dictating machine.

"Reply to Mr. Angus Corford-Stone, of Worthingham, Limited. Please be advised that rates in excess of six and one quarter percent are unacceptable. Final decision from Worthingham, Limited, must be reached by the twentieth of this month. New message—"

He tossed one aside, and picked up the second.

"Reply to John Stack. Our west shore rig is tied up until late January of next year and hence is unobtainable. New message."

The third.

"Reply to Mr. Lewis Jackson's secretary. Please inform Mr. Jackson I do not bother with messages from secretaries. Mr. Jackson should communicate with me directly, or by letter. New message."

Raynaud made himself a Scotch, and watched Pierce work. He was like a different person, a whole new man, sitting there in the starkly modern room, snapping out decisions....

"Reply to Edgar Morain. Current stock options are due April thirteenth, with a five-day extension obtainable by written application, filed not later than April first."

"You're very efficient," Raynaud said.

Pierce did not seem to hear. He had picked up the next message, this one a letter, and was dictating a reply. Something about tanker deployment in the east fields and minimum tonnage per twenty-four hours. He went on to another letter concerning storage facilities in Dover and port fees and licenses.

Half an hour passed, and then the intercom buzzed. As he answered it, Pierce glanced at the now small stack of messages left.

"Mr. Pierce, Mr. Bryce has called to arrange an appointment."

"No time," Pierce said. "I'm leaving the country in the next twenty-four hours."

"He says it's urgent."

"Make an appointment for him a week from today at four."

He flicked the intercom off, finished the pile remaining, and stood up. He rubbed his eyes, sighed, and then seemed to notice Raynaud.

"How about a drink?" he said, with a grin.

"Finished?"

"Yes."

Raynaud made a drink. Over his shoulder, he said, "Sometimes I think you're schizophrenic."

"Sometimes," Pierce said, "I am."

Late in the afternoon, they remained in the office, sitting by the large glass window, looking out over the city. Pierce was smiling happily.

"You're very proud of all this, aren't you?" Raynaud said.

"I bloody well am," Pierce said. "Listen, all my life I've heard stories about how I got here because of luck. I was the lucky bastard, adopted by the millionaire. I was the worthless sod who came into the money. All my life I've heard that. And now I'm going to show them. Shore Industries will make a fortune. An absolute fortune."

He spoke with vehemence, then seemed to catch himself, and relaxed.

"Anyway," he smiled, "it's a dream." He glanced at his watch. "Ready for the evening?"

"What's on?"

"A reception for Cora Archer. You know her?"

"Only by photograph." Cora was the latest of the fashion models to make it big.

"In person, she is even worse." Pierce sighed. "But she is sexy enough. And it should be a kicky reception. Lots of grooves and lots of grass. It's that kind of circle. Which reminds me."

He picked up the phone and said, "Get me Sandra Callarini." He set it down and waited. "Have to tell her I'm busy," he said, and smiled.

A moment later, the phone rang. He picked it up. "Sandra? 'Lo, love. Dickie. I'm tied up, I'm afraid. Yes. Yes. Showing Charles around. Yes. You know how it is. Yes, of course. No, no, but it's very sweet of you. Of course. Right. Bye."

He replaced the receiver.

"Simple as that," he said, and grinned.

The flame of the torch hissed out, blue-tipped, cherry core, sizzling and crackling in the air. It touched the metal, spitting sparks and a white hot light

"I tell you your trouble," Carlos said. He wore welder's goggles and a T-shirt, and was bent over his newest creation, a three-foot-high sculpture of a nude woman. The model was a young, slim, blank-faced girl, standing on a crate nearby.

"I tell you your trouble," he said. "It is sex. All Americans worry about sex. Sex, sex, all the time. Darling, move your leg."

The model shifted her position. Raynaud smiled as he looked at her. She did not seem to mind standing nude in a corner of a room filled with people. On the other side of the room people were clustered around Cora Archer; here, only a few people stood to watch the sculptor work.

"You are in trouble because of sex," Carlos continued. "You are preoccupied, unable to release your inner energies. Straighten your back, darling, and stick them forward. That's the girl."

"I'm tired, Carlos," she said.

"I know it, darling. That's when you're best."

Raynaud said, "Do you always work in the middle of parties?"

"Always," Carlos said. "It stimulates the juices."

"What juices?" said the girl.

"The juices, darling," Carlos said, and shook the torch at her irritably.

Pierce wandered over. "Hey, lad, a bird wants to meet you."

Raynaud looked at him, at the eyes, and saw that he was very high.

"All right."

"Kinky bird."

"All right. Coming."

"No, just breathing hard," Pierce said, and drifted off again.

Carlos, bending over his work, said, "He a friend of yours?"

"Richard? Yes."

"That's funny," Carlos said. "You don't seem like a bastard."

It was not a very large room, but in crossing it, he somehow picked up a girl who linked her arm in his and began to talk rapidly of the Chichester art school, did he know it, it was really quite good, quite a good *reputation,* you know, and that counted in the art world. A number of Americans, some rather nice, she had become fond of Americans, generally speaking, most people weren't but she was, and she thought he was American, because he *looked* American, he just had that look, that wholesome look, that special nice look, he was really rather handsome, did he know it? Was he just visiting? Did he have a place to stay? Because she lived quite nearby, oh, it wasn't much, really, just a place, a flat, but comfortable in its way. Cindy had had it before she did, and Cindy was absolutely *mad* on Americans, particularly blacks, but personally she didn't care for blacks, it sounded terrible to say, but they *did* have a smell, after all, well, not a smell, but an odor, a distinctive odor, which you didn't get in Africans, she meant real Africans, like from Ghana or Nigeria or places, now why was that? Of course, she had heard that the American blacks were all intermixed, diluted out, even the best of them, from the slavery days, was that true? Never mind, she didn't care, where was he staying? Did he have a place...

Just as strangely, she was gone, wandering off across the room, until she came to rest with another boy, who smoked pink cigarettes from a holder, and wore a uniform from the battle of Waterloo.

"This is Cora Archer," Pierce said. "Cora is a dear friend of mine. She's grandniece of the Earl of Kent."

Cora Archer wore a high-waisted gown of white lace that

looked like a nightgown. She had a thin, cadaverous body with large eyes, heavily made up.

"Great-grandniece," Cora Archer said.

"All the same," Pierce said, throwing his arm around her. "She's still a dear."

Cora wriggled out of his arm and looked at Raynaud. "Do you work for a living, or what?"

"I work," Raynaud said. He was trying to guess her age. She looked young—sixteen or seventeen—but it was impossible to be certain.

"Glad somebody does."

"Cora is super, absolutely super."

"She is the summing up, the complete summing up," said a voice. Turning, Raynaud faced a smooth-cheeked young man in a dinner jacket

"She is turned-on, wired-in, with it. She is the next Twiggy, the final Shrimp, the successor to Verushka."

Raynaud said to Cora, "You model?"

"She does not model. She *is*."

Cora said, "This is Luke, my manager."

"Adviser, personal adviser," Luke said, with a slight bow. "I manage nothing: merely advise."

"He tells people how great I am," Cora said.

"You *are* great," Pierce said, putting his arm around her again.

Luke, the manager, looked at Pierce, then at the arm. Pierce took his arm away.

"You can see it in her face," Luke said. "In the luminosity of the eyes, the expression of the body. She has it, this one."

"See what I mean?" Cora said. "See the way he is?"

Pierce said, "Does he follow you everywhere?"

"She's busy tonight," Luke said.

"I wasn't asking you," Pierce said, glancing at Luke, then at Raynaud, as if for encouragement.

"I'm telling *you*," Luke said.

Cora said, "I'm busy tonight, Dickie. Serious."

"You're putting me on."

"No. Serious."

"There, she told you," Luke said.

Pierce said, "Why don't you get yourself a drink?"

Luke was short, no more than five-six or -seven, with the neatness of a small man. He smoothed the lapels of his jacket, and said, "Bugger off, Dickie."

"You think you own her, like you own your wristwatch? You think she's your *property*."

"She's not yours."

"I think," Pierce said evenly, "that Cora wants to spend the night with me. I think she wants you to go away."

"She doesn't."

Cora said in a flat voice, "I'm busy tonight, Dickie."

"You won't be, in a moment," Pierce said. He clenched his fists, and looked again at Raynaud.

Very deliberately, Raynaud stuck his hands in his pockets.

"All right," Pierce said. "All right."

And then, without warning, he swung. The blow caught Luke in the midsection, staggering him, doubling him over. Pierce jumped forward, swinging in short, vicious jabs. Luke fended the blows as best he could as he struggled to catch his breath. His face was red.

Suddenly, he caught Pierce's hand, and in a single swift move swung him, flipped him, and threw him to the floor. Raynaud smiled: so the little man knew judo.

Pierce got off the floor, his eyes on Luke, who was crouched, arms forward, feet spread, palms wide.

Pierce lunged.

Luke caught him, pulled him close, spun him, and tripped him. Pierce slammed down to the floor, very hard. He recovered with surprising speed, attacking again. Luke parried once more, delivering a flat punch to the kidneys and a shove that threw Pierce against the wall. He bounced off with blood running from his nose and his left eyebrow.

"Little fart," he snarled, and threw himself forward. Luke caught him with a blow to the ear and a second to the stomach; Pierce collapsed and got up slowly, still bleeding. He was winded. For a moment he stared at his crouched opponent.

Then he grabbed a steel sculpture, perched on a nearby pedestal. It was a statue of a man, and it seemed quite heavy.

Luke's eyes widened as he saw. His body tensed.

"Little fart," Pierce said again. He approached cautiously, holding the club in his left hand.

Raynaud stepped back. The girl said, "Stop them."

Raynaud shook his head.

"You must stop them."

"They wouldn't like it. Either of them."

Pierce moved closer, swinging the club slightly, getting the feel of the weight. Luke stepped back and Pierce seemed to gain confidence. He wiped the blood from his nose with the back of his hand, glanced at it, and smiled grimly.

Luke's face was expressionless. His eyes were fixed on Pierce's hands.

Pierce lunged

Luke stepped aside smartly, a maneuver that almost succeeded. As he fell, Pierce swung desperately, the hands flailing wildly, and he caught Luke on the forehead. Luke fell.

Pierce recovered, saw Luke on the ground, and threw himself on him. He raised the club, swung, raised it again, covered with blood.

Raynaud moved forward.

He caught the club in midswing and tore it away. Pierce looked startled, then angry.

"What the hell…"

"Leave him alone."

Luke was lying in a crumpled ball on the floor, not moving. He was unconscious; his hair was mixed and matted with blood.

"What the hell."

"It's over. It's all over."

Cora ran over and threw her hands over Luke protectively. Raynaud pulled Pierce away. Pierce was in a daze; he looked at his blood-covered hands.

"I hope I killed him," he said.

Cora was bent over Luke, sobbing.

"You don't," Raynaud said.

"I do. I hope I killed him, the little fart."

"Better get out of here." Raynaud steered him toward the door.

"The fuck. I want to see if he's dead."

"Better get out of here."

"The bastard," Pierce said, wiping his hands on his jacket. "Did you see? He knew karate."

"If he knew karate, you wouldn't be alive now."

"He knew karate."

"Judo," Raynaud said, with a sigh. "And not even that, very well."

As they went out through the door, stepping into the cool night, Pierce said, "So you're the expert on judo now, is that it?"

"They taught us in the Army," Raynaud said.

They walked to the end of the block, where there was a taxi rank. They climbed into the first one.

"Anyway," Pierce said, "it was no thanks to you."

Raynaud shrugged. "I was hired to protect you from other people, not from yourself."

"And if I had been losing? What would you have done then?"

"But you didn't lose."

"You're goddamned right," Pierce said. "I won. Didn't I?"

"Yes," Raynaud said. "You won."

Pierce chuckled. "I feel like having a woman."

"You look like hell," Raynaud said.

"I know where we can get a pair of beauties. Real beauties. And cheap, too."

In reply, Raynaud gently pushed Richard's nose with his finger. Pierce yelped in pain and fell back against the seat.

"All right," he said, frowning. "All right."

Raynaud gave directions and they returned to the flat.

9. ANTIDOTE

The next day, Pierce got slowly out of bed, surprised that his body was stiff and sore. For a while, he couldn't remember why, and then the evening came back to him. Scruffy Luke, with his scruffy bird. Putting on airs, when everyone knew she'd plumped her tail down for every guy around, and played the flipside for some of the dollies. Inventive, she was, very inventive.

He walked over to the dresser and saw three crumpled pound notes. They reminded him that he was running out, and would have to see Lucienne. He'd been putting it off, trying not to think about it. Bloody old Lucienne. Wonder if she still got her periods. Great convenience for the boyos if she didn't; open season, round the clock. Or maybe they didn't care.

Christ.

Head throbbing like an unhappy dangler. And that bitch Pet, slooping along in her frilly see-throughs, showing the crotch all around, and pretending it wasn't there. Talk about the son—the *son*, for Christ's sake, what the hell. All for Raynaud's benefit. Crafty little Pet. No fool.

He went into the kitchen and mixed himself a martini. Raynaud wasn't up yet; the clock on the wall said two in the afternoon. Pierce turned on the television over the fridge and switched it to Raynaud's room. Blank. Fucker must have blocked it. Better not have damaged the camera; they cost two hundred quid each. Japanese coming up in the world. Who said labor was cheap?

He poured the martini into a glass, swirled it, and gulped it down. Chilled piss, that's what it was. But necessary. It was the only thing that made any difference the morning after.

And it was always the morning after.

Back to the bathroom, stumbling twice, almost falling. Chilled piss sloshing around in his stomach, but going to work. He began to feel better. He knew he shouldn't drink so much, Uncle John always said so, but it was after noon, for Christ's sake. Everybody drank after noon, even the stuffy ones.

He turned on the shower and got in. As the water struck him, he realized he was still wearing pajamas. Shit. He climbed out and stripped them off, then got back in. The water felt good, steamy and clean; he breathed deeply.

Raynaud, that fucker. No fool. Imagine, blocking the camera. Dirty trick. Just what you'd expect. He had even liked what's-her-name, the phony redhead in Paris. You'd think if a girl was going to dye her hair in that line of work, she'd be thorough.

The frogs were a dirty race.

Old Raynaud, he was a frog. At least partly. But you had to hand it to him, he was quick. So damned quick. Hands like a flash.

Pierce grinned. He thought about Luke and laughed aloud. Raynaud had been impressed by the way he handled Luke, the dumb bastard. Pierce could tell Raynaud had been impressed. Raynaud had even worried that Pierce might kill him. Marvelous. The look on Raynaud's face when he had reached for the club. Marvelous.

And Raynaud was useful, a good sort to have around. Raynaud was well paid; the Americans expressed it directly: money talked. So long as Pierce was paying, Raynaud would stick around. And do what he was told.

Pierce smiled again. It might be amusing to really make Raynaud earn his money. Really make him put up with hell. It would be amusing to see how far he could push Raynaud. He suspected he could push him quite far indeed.

Still smiling, he climbed out of the shower and thought of Lucienne. Then he thought of his pills. He must not forget them. The daily schedule was crucial. He opened the medicine cabinet and took out the dispenser, removed the pill marked 8, and swallowed it. The taste was nothing special—rather flat and chalky, like aspirin. But Uncle John had assured him it was the real thing, real arsenic. Thank God for Uncle John.

Pierce had gone to Uncle John two months before, after an especially bad fight with Lucienne. At the end of the fight

Lucienne had been furious, purple with rage. It had scared Pierce to see her that way, though it had never scared him before. He suddenly realized that she was a desperate woman. She had only a few months left before he would inherit the estate and dump her.

She might try to prevent that.

He had gone home frowning, and thought things over. The more he thought, the more worried he became. He broke into a cold sweat, and went to see Uncle John. As usual, John was friendly, glad to see him. Pierce had said, "If you wanted to kill someone, how would you do it?"

John just laughed. "I wouldn't advise killing Lucienne."

Pierce shook his head. "No, I'm serious."

John mixed him a drink, watched as he sipped it, then said, "Why do you ask?"

"Curious."

"Tell me why."

"Answer the question first."

"How would I kill someone?" John shrugged. "Poison, I suppose."

"Why poison?"

"It's readily available, and difficult to trace. Much better than a knife or a gun."

That was exactly what Pierce had already decided. He said, "What kind of poison?"

"Arsenic, I imagine."

"Why?"

"Cheap. Readily available."

Pierce nodded. "In rat poison, things like that?"

"Yes," John said.

"Is there an antidote?"

"Not specifically, no."

"Fast acting?"

"Quite. A few minutes and it's finished."

"Does it have a taste, or an odor?"

"No, not really."

"Could you put it into a drink? Disguise it?"

"Probably."

"How about food?"

"Yes."

"Oh, Christ," Pierce said. "And there's no antidote?"

"No. Why?"

Pierce had then explained about his fears, and the argument with Lucienne. Black listened to it all, then said, "If you're really worried, there's one thing you can do."

"What's that?"

"Take graduated doses, to build up a tolerance."

"It won't hurt me?"

"No, not if it's correctly graduated. You start with very little, and then build up to larger doses."

"And that will protect me?"

"There are no guarantees. But it will help. Only, Richard..."

"Yes?"

"If I may say so, you're being very foolish. Lucienne may dislike you, but she wouldn't think of hurting you."

"She would."

"No, you're wrong."

"I tell you, she doesn't want me to inherit the estate. She'll do anything to stop me."

Uncle John had sighed. "Will you feel better if I write a prescription for graduated arsenic doses?"

"Yes."

"All right then, I'll do it." He sat down at his desk and wrote it out. Pierce found it absolutely illegible. "Now then," Black said, "the pills will be stamped from one to forty. They'll all be the same size, because they will contain different quantities of neutral packing. Don't let the size throw you. And be careful to take them serially. If you start with number forty, you're a dead man."

"I'll be careful."

"Let me know if you have any trouble," John had said. "And, uh..."

"Yes?"

"...I'd suggest you keep this private."

*

Pierce had kept it private, and he had been careful to take them in order. The first ones made him sick, but now, nothing. He was obviously building up tolerance. It gave him a good and secure feeling to know that Lucienne couldn't hurt him.

A very good feeling.

He dressed in slacks and a sweater and went into the kitchen to make another drink and eat a sandwich. His thoughts turned to the party tonight, and Sandra. Sandra was a queer bird, a real odd one. Her Italian background, no doubt. The way she kept shoving his hands away, just as they were touching softness, it was really quite maddening. She had Old World ideas about things, a sense of propriety that appealed to him, though it was maddening.

And she had promised. As soon as they were engaged…

Tonight.

He would take her away, away from her bitch friends, from everyone. That would clinch it.

But he needed money. That meant facing Lucienne. He glanced at his watch—he could probably buzz over and see her this afternoon. Or later, at the party.

He decided the party was better. There would be other people there, and she couldn't make a scene. The very idea of a scene terrified Lucienne. A scandal was all right—she almost seemed to enjoy a scandal—but never anything public, never a scene.

He'd talk to her at the party.

An hour later, Raynaud wandered in, looking sleepy.

"'Lo, lad. Good rest?"

"What time is it?" Raynaud asked, rubbing his eyes.

"Four. Want a drink?" He held out the pitcher of martinis. "They're good."

"No. Christ. Is there any coffee?"

"You'll have to make it yourself," Pierce said.

Raynaud put the water on to boil. He rubbed his eyes, then said, "Maybe I'll have a drink after all."

"Good man."

Pierce poured him a glass. Raynaud sipped it and winced. "What's in this, arsenic?"

"No. Just gin. But I soak the olives in vermouth first."

"Strong as hell," Raynaud said, gulping it back. "What time's the party tonight?"

"Nine. Plenty of time."

"Will I meet Sandra?"

"Indeed you will. And I'll thank you to keep your hands off her. It won't be easy, I assure you. One wants to touch."

"Is she so spectacular?"

"Wait and see."

"And your mother will be there?"

"Stepmother. Yes, I imagine so."

Raynaud watched Pierce carefully as they finished dinner. They ate in an excellent Hungarian restaurant on Frith Street, in Soho. The food and wine should have made Pierce expansive, but they did not; he tried vainly to tell amusing stories, but he was tense.

After dinner they walked along the dark streets, past the twenty-four-hour strip joints, the restaurants, the book stores, the theaters showing *Gay Lusts* and *Whip of Desire*. Pierce remained tense.

"Worried about the party?"

"No. Of course not."

"You seem jittery."

"Well, it is a bit unusual. Engagement."

"But you don't intend to stick to it."

"Still," Pierce said. He walked along, looking in the shop windows.

"I used to come down here a lot," he said.

"Not anymore?"

"No, not much."

"Why not?"

Pierce shrugged. Then he said, "Oh, have you seen these adverts?" He pointed to a tobacconist shop window. The window was filled with small, hand-printed ads. "The tarts have always advertised here. Cost you sixpence a week for a legitimate card, and a guinea for the usual."

Raynaud looked at them. Mostly, they advertised massage,

or Swedish and French treatments. A few for language lessons. Some were more original.

"YOUNG GIRL SEEKS EXCITING NEW POSITION." Bayswater phone number.

"OWNER wishes to sell or rent sports model, soft pink upholstery, convertible."

"FUR MUFFS for sale."

"Model offers accommodation in picturesque setting."

"Rear-view mirrors for sale. Easy attachment to all makes."

"TRAINED BEAVER for hire."

Pierce said, "Believe it or not, they're getting more subtle. You'll notice most of the numbers are in Bedford Hill. That's the new area. And Epping Wood."

They walked on, passing several girls lounging in doorways.

"Never fool with these," Pierce said. "Terrible, all of them. Cost you a fiver—that's because you're American—and she'll milk you in three minutes and toss you out the door. Bad show. And they all expect flag."

"What?"

"Flagellation. They expect it. Most of the customers come here specially. Clerks from the City, they're the worst, slinking about with their bowlers and umbrellas, and you know they're itching to get the whip into their hot little hands."

"You're joking."

"I'm not." Pierce lit a cigarette. "You want a decent girl, you've got to go through the proper channels. So to speak. But at least you'll have the satisfaction of knowing one of the service stations of the House of Parliament. One of the finer pumps, as they say."

He laughed. They came down to Shaftesbury Avenue but it was theater time, and all the cabs were taken. Pierce waited impatiently at the curb, smoking the cigarette quickly, then said, "Let's walk on a bit."

"What's the matter?"

"Nothing."

"Your hands are trembling."

"No, they're not. Well, yes they are. Look: this sounds foolish, but I think we're being followed."

"Followed? But why?"

"I don't know, but we are. We've gone along for four blocks, and there's a man still behind us. Tan mac and a brown hat."

Raynaud smiled. "And you think he's following us?"

"Yes." Pierce lit another cigarette, holding it tensely in his fingers. "I do."

"Why?"

"I tell you, I don't *know*."

"All right," Raynaud said. "Take it easy. We can handle it simply enough."

"Don't look back," Pierce said.

"I wasn't going to," Raynaud said. "You see that music shop up ahead? When we get there, stop and shake hands with me. Wave goodbye, and walk on. I'll wait there."

"All right. But remember. Tan mac and—"

"A brown hat. I know. Just take it easy."

They walked on a few yards, until they reached the music store. Guitars, sitars, and sheet music were displayed in the window. They shook hands, and Pierce walked on. Raynaud lit a cigarette, glancing back as he did so. He saw the man Pierce had described. A short fat man, trundling along, looking harmless. Raynaud waited until the man was quite close, then turned.

"Say, friend—"

The man looked up, startled.

Raynaud grabbed him by the collar and flung him into the doorway, out of sight.

"I say—"

"Shut up," Raynaud said. He frisked him quickly, felt a weight in the left pocket. He drew out the gun, a snub-nosed revolver, and saw Pierce coming back.

Raynaud dropped the gun into his own pocket and Pierce, coming to the doorway, said, "Who is he?"

"Don't know."

Raynaud lit his lighter and held it near the man's face. By the yellow, flickering light, they saw a chubby, ruddy, innocent-looking face.

"Please, please, there's been some mistake—"

"Why were you following us?" Pierce said.

"I wasn't following you. I was simply—"

Raynaud struck him, hard, across the cheeks. "Answer the question."

"Please, I wasn't, I don't know…"

Raynaud said to Pierce, "You recognize him?"

"No."

Raynaud slapped the fat man again. "What's your name, friend?"

Quite unexpectedly, the man began to shout for the police. He had a high, squeaking voice, but quite loud. Raynaud stepped back, and at that moment, the man twisted free and ran down the street, shouting for the police.

"Let's get out of here," Raynaud said.

They ran down the block, around the corner; then Pierce slipped into a pub, and Raynaud followed him.

They paused at the door to catch their breath, then sat at the bar. They each had a whisky, then Raynaud said, "All right. What's this about?"

"I don't know."

"Who was he?"

"I don't know."

"You're sure you didn't recognize him?"

"Positive."

There was a moment of silence.

"I'm going to have another Scotch," Pierce said. "Then I'll feel better." He motioned to the bartender. "By the way," he said, "that little man. Was he armed?"

"No," Raynaud said. "Why should he be?"

"I don't know."

Raynaud watched Pierce a moment. Something odd had happened: Pierce was no longer trembling. His hands were steady and calm.

And he genuinely did not appear worried. It was impossible to fake: Pierce was not worried.

Feeling strange, Raynaud said, "Richard, do you have any enemies?"

"That's all I have." Pierce laughed. "I seem to make enemies the way some people make friends."

"I'm serious."

"So am I."

Pierce frowned. "Then that man was armed, after all?"

"No. But he was definitely following us. I spotted him a while before you did."

"Then why didn't you say something?"

Raynaud smiled. "I wanted to see whether you'd spot him yourself."

"Goddamn it, I'm paying you—"

"Because," Raynaud said, "you were acting strangely all night. Almost as if you expected something like this."

"Expected it? What kind of nonsense are you talking?"

Raynaud shrugged. "Suit yourself."

"Well, look, he didn't look much like a paid assassin, did he?"

"No. But the next one might."

"For Christ's sake, Charles. Do you suspect me of something, or what?"

"I suspect everyone. Of everything."

"Listen," Pierce said. "I'll tell you what I think. I think it was nothing at all. I think it was my stepmother."

"Your stepmother?"

"Yes. She's done it before: had me followed. I know that, for sure."

"Why would she do that?"

"She's afraid I'll disgrace the family name, or something."

"She's actually had you followed?"

"Several times. Once, all the way to Cannes."

"What did you do about that?"

"Nothing. He was an innocuous little fellow. I left him alone."

"Then why—"

"Worry about this one? Because now I have you, and you're hired to look after such things."

He tossed money onto the bar top and stood up.

"Come on," he said. "We've got to be off, or we'll be late for the party."

Raynaud walked with him to the door and out onto the street. He said nothing more, but he was thinking furiously. It was all wrong, now. Nothing added up, nothing made sense. And he felt a strange, cold shivering chill for the first time in many years.

10. THE PARTY

Raynaud pretended to listen as the young man with curly hair and pimples said, "I have absolute proof. Absolute. Woodbines give you hemorrhoids. My grand-aunt and first cousin—both smoked Woodbines, and now look at them. Cheaper to buy, oh, yes, much cheaper, but they give you hemorrhoids because of poor draw. Few people judge their cigarettes by ease of draw, though they should. Take Player's Navy. Your more Establishment cigarette, yet it draws poorly. I much prefer Senior Service, do you smoke it?"

"No," Raynaud said. "I don't."

"More's the pity," said the young man, and he drifted off. "Just remember," he said, over his shoulder, "Woodbines are a *nasty* cigarette."

Raynaud sighed and looked over the party. Through the elegant rooms of the house, fifty or sixty people wandered. They were all brightly dressed, the girls in minidresses, the men in carefully cut suits and spectacular ties, but the talk was vacant and dull.

He had run into Pet, who was wearing pink polka-dot bell bottoms and a shimmering silver overblouse which was cut low to display her massive breasts. Pet talked endlessly of Sandra, and what a nice girl she was; she also talked about Chubby, the dear man.

Raynaud talked with her for a while, then he talked with another girl who was in rep at Chichester and had a crush on Larry; an architect who thought Sutherland had botched Coventry; an advertising man who worked for JWT and handled part of the CVP account; a forlorn medical student who wanted to become a consultant at St. Bot's; a girl who was mad on Edwardian loving cups; a middle-aged man who manufactured foundation garments; a girl, rangy and tough, who told him of the joys of shooting pheasant in northern Ireland; a sleepy-eyed literary agent who handled Ron Shaw, an absolute bastard of a man, but so talented, did you see his Claudius against Leighton's Hamlet on BBC?

Then there was an action painter who kept scratching his crotch as he talked about New York, which he wanted to visit; a girl who did figure studies for Ed, such a dear chap, really a sweetie; a flat-chested matron who announced in a funereal tone that Mirabelle was finished since they lost Jacques; a heavyset German in a dinner jacket who claimed that Dutch girls were the best in bed; a bespectacled Scotsman who wore a kilt and was doing classical research at the Ashmolean, numismatics mostly.

Among everyone present, there was a bored, desultory way of speaking, as if they were all waiting for something, marking time. Even Pierce seemed bored.

"Say," Raynaud said. "Where's Sandra?"

"Coming, coming. She likes a grand entrance."

Half an hour later, Sandra appeared. He coughed on his Scotch when he saw her.

She was not tall, but slender, and her face was delicately beautiful. Her hair was brown, with highlights of blond, and curved softly around her face and shoulders. Her eyes were large, a piercing clear green. Her nose was beautiful; her lips were soft; her chin was firm. Her body had a gentle, sensual quality, and her manner was cool, calm, understated.

There was a peacefully sexual look about her that was immediately arresting. Raynaud stared, until a girl impatiently tapped his arm.

"I'm still here," she said. She sounded both annoyed and amused.

"She's quite something," Raynaud said.

"Yes," the girl said. She was a well-built girl who danced in a West End discothèque, the Ancient Land. "But cold as ice. Can you see that?"

"No," Raynaud admitted.

"Well, she is. It's surprising, when you think she's Italian. After all, the Italians are supposed to be mother earth, aren't they?"

Beaming, showing her off like his latest and most expensive gadget, Pierce led Sandra around the room. When they came to Raynaud, Pierce made the introductions with a grin.

"Richard tells me you live in Mexico," Sandra said. "I should like to talk to you about it sometime. When I was at Naples University, you know, I studied archaeology."

Raynaud was surprised. "You did?"

"Yes," she said. "I intended to get a doctoral degree. Then I won a beauty contest."

She gave a peculiar smile, as if the memory did not entirely please her.

"I can understand why," Raynaud said.

Pierce tugged slightly at her arm, and they began to move off.

"I hope we shall meet again," Sandra said.

As they left, Pierce looked over his shoulder and winked.

Later, while Sandra was talking excitedly to a group of girls, Pierce came over to Raynaud.

"What did you think?"

"She's a nice girl."

"You sound unhappy."

"No. It's just that somebody should tell her."

Pierce laughed. "I will," he said. "I will lay bare all my faults. Later." He lit a cigarette. "We're going to Wales. Tonight. Be gone for the weekend."

"Enjoy yourself."

"Will you be here when I get back?"

"Probably."

"Well then," Pierce said. He extended his hand. "Have a good time," he said, "at the snake convention." They shook hands.

Soon afterward, Raynaud left the party.

As he unlocked the door to Richard's flat, Raynaud suddenly regretted not having picked up a girl. Pet had been after him, licking her lips as she talked; it would have been easy. Now, the prospect of being alone in the apartment, alone with his thoughts, depressed him.

He passed through the living room, into the kitchen, where he mixed himself a drink. He made it very stiff; it would be his last before retiring. Something to help him sleep.

As he drank it, he sniffed the air. Perfume. Still sniffing, he went into the bedroom, which was empty. Then back to the living room.

"Bon soir," said the husky voice.

She was seated in the corner, in darkness, smoking a cigarette. Her legs were tucked up under her in a rather girlish fashion. In the flare of her cigarette he saw the haughty face—high cheekbones, dark eyes, firm mouth. Her hair was glossy, dark blond, falling over her face. Impatiently she swept it back.

"Hello, Lucienne," he said.

She smiled. "How are you getting on?"

"Fine."

"Does he suspect?"

"No. He suspects nothing."

"Excellent," she said, puffing on the cigarette. "Now come and kiss me hello."

Part II:
The Snake Convention

1. NO PERVERSIONS

He made her a drink and she followed him into the kitchen, kicking off her shoes and moving barefoot across the carpet. He had forgotten her bare feet. Funny, he thought, what you remembered,

"Enjoy the party?" she asked. She had a soft, low, sexy voice, a singer's voice, even now.

"Not much. Scotch?"

"Vodka. On the rocks." She smiled. "You don't remember."

He looked back over his shoulder at her. "Hold it against me?"

"No. Don't be silly. You look well, Charles."

"So do you, Lucienne. But then it hasn't been long, has it?"

"It's been long for me," she said. "My nerves are shot."

He gave her the drink.

"Let's go back into the other room. The bright light hurts my eyes."

They returned to the living room. Raynaud noticed the way she moved. Restless, but with a smooth grace, an angular, tough-looking, controlled body. She sat down in a liquid, coiling motion.

"How is he?" she asked.

"Richard? All right."

"The chance meeting in Paris went smoothly?"

"Very smoothly."

"Then he truly does not know?"

"That you've hired me? No. He doesn't."

"Good," she said.

He waited for her to explain, but she did not. She had always been that way, always a little mysterious.

"By the way," she said. "What did you think of her?"

"Who?"

"Sandra."

"Very attractive."

"Yes. Much too good for Richard. Still, she's old enough to

know her way around. I expect she's after the money. Everyone is."

She puffed on her cigarette irritably. "Miss me?" she asked.

"Yes." It was true, in a way. He had missed her. When he had
first met her in Mexico she had been just another rich client who
could command the most exclusive tour, with the most private
guide. Charles was no longer giving tours, having quit to study
snakes and assume the role of gentleman scientist, but somehow she heard about him and insisted that he be retained as
tour guide, no matter what the price. He had finally agreed to
guide her.

He soon realized that she had come to Yucatán the way some
women went on African safaris, and she expected Raynaud to
play white hunter. He hadn't liked the idea at first; later, he
had. And something must have happened to him, because when
he went back to Mexico City, Allison took one look at his face
and said, "Who was she?"

He smiled at the recollection.

"Do I amuse you?"

"Just remembering," he said.

She looked at him across the room and patted the couch next
to her. "Come sit next to me."

He did; she took out another cigarette and he lit it for her.
There was the flare of the match, and then darkness again.

"I've always liked your face," Lucienne said. "It shows character. Not like Richard. He has a doughy face; it shows nothing
but alcohol and venereal disease. How are you getting on with
him?"

"It's difficult."

"You mean he's difficult. Can you bear up?"

"Probably. If you tell me what it's all about."

"Later," she said.

"Don't keep me in suspense too long."

"Don't keep me waiting too long."

He kissed her then and felt her cool fingers on his neck and
her body relaxed against him. Then she stopped.

"Not here."

"Why?"

"Not in this apartment."

"Then where?"

"Come," she said, standing up and taking his hand. "Come."

The room was dark, and warm, and close. She rubbed her nose against his shoulder and said, "I'm glad to see you are still the same."

He smiled in the darkness; she pulled away from him.

"Something wrong?"

"No," she said, getting out of bed. "But I have my rules, remember?"

He laughed. "Yes," he said. "I remember. Brandy and soda afterward."

"Yes," she said. She turned on a small bedside lamp, which glowed a soft pink. Everything in the room was pink. The sheets were pink satin, as was the bedspread and the canopy above. The rug was thick pink pile. A door led to a pink-tiled bathroom.

In the dim, soft light he watched her mix the drinks, thinking to himself that she was one of those rare women who seemed somehow more graceful and elegant when undressed.

She glanced over her shoulder. "What are you staring at?"

"Your legs."

"Do they please you?"

"Absolutely," he said. He lit a cigarette and lay on his back in the bed, feeling relaxed and pleasantly tired. He found himself staring at a mirror image of himself—he sat up, startled, and realized that a large mirror hung suspended over the bed, concealed in the draped folds of the canopy.

"Christ," he said, "how long has that been there?"

She gave a low laugh. "Since nineteen hundred and eight." She gave him the drink, took the cigarette from between his lips, puffed it, and gave it back. "This house was standing at the time of the funeral of Edward the Seventh. In fact, the Archduke Ferdinand stayed here. The historical people are very fussy about letting me make changes, so I left it. Besides," she said, "there are no perversions like old perversions."

"Do you, ah…watch?"

"Sometimes. When I get bored."

She laughed, and kissed him, and said, "It's nice to have you back."

"It's nice to have you, too."

She gave a mock frown. "Were you always so vulgar?"

"Yes," he said, and stubbed out his cigarette. "And I am going to be more vulgar and talk about money. Now tell me why you wrote me that letter."

She pouted. "Oh, Charles, must we now?"

"Yes."

She touched his cheek with a cool finger. "Your face has gotten hard and stern."

"The suspense is killing me."

She laughed. "Is it such a mystery?"

"It is to me," he said.

"Actually," she said, "it is quite simple. Richard needs looking after. That's all."

"Why? He seems to have gotten this far on his own."

"Yes, but we are approaching a rather crucial period in his life. He is about to inherit the estate. Next month, to be exact."

"So?"

She shrugged. "I am worried about him."

"Why?"

"You are full of questions," she said, "and it can all wait until morning."

"I'd rather—"

She put her hand over his mouth, very gently but firmly. "I insist," she said.

"All right," he said.

2. NEW DEBTS

Richard pulled the Maserati into the drive and parked next to the front steps. He looked up at the second floor; a light was on in the bedroom window. She was still awake.

Alongside him, Sandra said, "Where are we?"

"Lucienne's house."

"Why?" She looked at her watch. It was a heavy, masculine model, the latest thing for London girls to wear. "It is late, and we must catch the plane—"

"I'll only be a minute. Just saying goodbye."

He kissed her and she responded warmly, a kiss full of promises and anticipation.

He turned on the radio for her and patted her knee. "Sit tight. Be right back."

He climbed the steps to the door and rang the bell. Immediately, he began to feel nervous; his palms were sweating, and his tongue felt dry. It was always like this. Had been for years.

He remembered once overhearing an argument between Lucienne and Herbert over him. Lucienne had called him a runty little snot who did nothing but play with himself. Hearing that, he realized for the first time that she had been spying on him. He never forgot it. He knew that, even now, Lucienne managed to keep track of him.

There was no answer. He rang the bell again. From the car, Sandra said, "Perhaps she's asleep."

"No, no."

He rang a third time long and angrily. Finally a voice, muffled through the heavy oak, said, "Who is it?"

"Richard."

The door was opened. Lucienne stood there in a red velvet bathrobe.

"What do you want?"

"A little talk."

"Now? Come back tomorrow."

"I can't." He pushed past her, into the front hall.

"Get out of here," Lucienne said.

"What's the matter?" he asked mildly. "Anything wrong? You're alone here, aren't you?"

"Yes," she said.

"I should hope so. You wouldn't be dressed like that if there were a man here." He laughed.

She walked into the living room, mixed herself a drink, and lit a cigarette. Her movements were quick and nervous. She sat down on a chair, pulled her bathrobe tighter around her, and said, "What do you want?"

"A small loan."

"How much this time?"

"Three thousand."

She said, "Impossible," and sucked on the cigarette. "I haven't got it."

"Lucienne, dear, you've got it twenty times over."

"I just gave you two thousand," she said, "before you went to Paris. That was less than two weeks ago."

"I had debts."

"And now you have new debts?"

"I have debts."

She sighed and brushed her hair back from her face. She looked tired and old, but there was a flush to her cheeks. She had probably just gotten it.

"Enjoying yourself these days, Lucienne?"

She shrugged.

"You look well."

"Richard," she said, "you cannot have the money, and that's final."

"You have very good coloring tonight."

"You make me angry."

"I'm so sorry." He cocked his head and pretended to listen. "I hear something upstairs. It must be a burglar."

"It's nothing. Your imagination."

He stood. "No, I'm certain. A burglar. I'd better go investigate."

"Richard, stay here." Her voice was cold.

"I'm worried for you," Pierce said, "all alone here in this house. If it is a burglar, you might be raped or something."

"Your concern is touching."

"I'll just have a quick look." He started toward the stairs.

Before he had taken a dozen steps, Lucienne said, "Come back, and I will write the check."

"For three thousand?"

"For three."

Pierce grinned. "Just to be sure, better make it four."

"As you wish."

She began to write the check. Pierce went over and sipped her Scotch.

"Nasty of you not to offer me one."

"I assumed," she said, "that you were in a hurry."

"I am, but there's always time for a friendly drink." He leaned over her and watched as she filled in the amount. Four thousand pounds. Delightful.

She signed the check, tore it off the pad, and waved it dry. Then she gave it to him.

"Very nice," he said. He went to the door. "Such a pleasure to see you again, Lucienne."

"Goodbye, Richard."

He opened the door, and looked back at the living room. Suddenly he saw a coat, a tan raincoat, draped over one of the chairs. Thrown there, no doubt in the heat of passion. Still, it was a funny-looking coat. Familiar, somehow. Funny how something so commonplace as a raincoat could look familiar.

For a moment, he thought it was his. He almost went back to fetch it, and then he stopped.

He knew.

Lucienne was watching him. She had seen him notice the coat. She was wondering if he suspected....

"He must be very important," Richard said.

"Who?"

"The burglar. Is it that sod from the Westminster Bank again?"

He gave her his leer, the expression he knew she loathed. It worked: she slammed the door in his face, furiously.

Well done, he thought, as he went down the steps to the car. Well done. You've sized that one up beautifully. May save your life, even.

A life saved is a life earned.

And who could tell? Perhaps he could figure a way to screw Charles, really screw him. That would be enjoyable. Almost as enjoyable as screwing Lucienne.

As he got into the car, Sandra said, "Everything all right?"

"Everything," Pierce said, "is just fine."

In the morning, Raynaud awoke to find himself alone. He stared up at his image in the mirror, frowned, then laughed.

"You and the archduke, buddy," he said.

He felt good. He had slept well and was relaxed. The annoyance with himself that he had expected to feel was absent; he got up and went into the bathroom. A razor, soap, aftershave were neatly laid out for him, along with cigarettes—his brand—and an ashtray. Thoughtful, but practiced. A calculator, this one. He reminded himself for the hundredth time since he had first met Lucienne that he would have to be careful. She was one of those rare women who understood men better than they understood themselves. She could put you in the mood to do handstands in Hyde Park, or to fight a tiger, or, God help us, make love beneath a Victorian mirror.

Very sly, Lucienne. And studied: every gesture, every movement, every expression had its calculated effect. It had bothered him, when he had first met her. Later he understood that she could not help it. It was the way she was, or perhaps it was the result of long years on the stage. He had never seen her sing, but he had talked to men who had; everyone who had seen her remembered her, vividly, down to the color of the dress she had worn, the color of the nail polish she had used.

He would have liked to see her. He lit a cigarette and began to shave, whistling to himself.

A clever little girl. A minx. A fox. Funny, he thought, how often you described her as an animal. And never a cat. She had smooth, almost casually graceful movements, but she was not a cat. Something sharper and more predatory.

He finished shaving and went back to the bedroom. His clothes were draped over a chair. He reached into the pockets and withdrew the small card written in a fine hand:

> *My dear Charles:*
>
> *I write you on a matter of utmost urgency. I have reason to believe that Richard's life may be in danger, most of all from himself. A close companion at this time would be valuable. If you could contrive to be at Houghton Graham's villa on the 28 of this month, an accidental meeting between the two of you may be arranged.*
>
> *I recognize that my request is inconvenient and most sudden. I am prepared to pay you five hundred dollars a day if you can come.*
>
> *With fond love,*
Lucienne

Damned funny letter. So formal, and yet so purposely puzzling. That line about being in danger from himself—now what the hell was that supposed to mean?

As he stared at it, he had a strange sinking feeling. He could recall that feeling only once before, when he had been conned into smuggling two emeralds from Mexico to Canada. They were enormous things, large as hen's eggs, and they were stolen. He had suspected that, and had suspected trouble, but he had agreed to smuggle them anyway.

Then, when he got to the airport, he saw the customs officers going over all the outbound passengers carefully; they had been tipped off.

Raynaud, angry and afraid, had done the only thing he could —he turned and ran. A policeman stopped him at the doors, but he was able to say in a breathless voice that he had arrived at customs and suddenly realized he had left his passport at home and did not want to miss his flight.

The cop bought it, and Raynaud took a taxi home, his clothes drenched in sweat.

That evening, he had visited the man who had given him the

emeralds. The man was an engraver, specializing in stamps which he smuggled out to various countries and sold.

Raynaud confronted him and did the only sensible thing: he crushed the man's right hand in a press.

The memory of those agonized screams just before the engraver fainted was not pleasant, even now. Nor was the memory of the airport, when he suddenly realized, with an awful horror, that things were wrong, terribly, terribly wrong.

He had that same feeling now, looking at the letter.

After breakfast, over cigarettes, he said, "I give up."

"About what?"

"About Richard. Why you brought me here."

She smiled. "It really bothers you, doesn't it."

He shrugged. "You've made elaborate plans for my meeting with him. To be certain he does not know. And—" He began to tell her about the incident with the car in Paris, and then abruptly decided not to. He could not be sure why he hesitated.

"Yes?" she said.

"Nothing."

"Well," she said, "as I told you before, it's actually quite simple. I am afraid that Richard's life is in danger. He is not the most diplomatic of men, you know. In both his personal and business life, he has made enemies."

"Yes," Raynaud said. "But there are enemies and enemies."

"Do you know about his knife wound? The limp?"

"He told me how it happened."

"I wonder. It was a Greek girl, living in London last year. Her father was attached to the Embassy in some way. Richard managed to get her pregnant, but the girl didn't mind. She assumed it meant he would marry her. When she found out he had no intention of marrying her…"

"She went after him."

"Yes. Apparently she wished to eliminate the source of the trouble."

"Pleasant."

"But the point," Lucienne said, "is that this is always happening to Richard. And over the years it has gotten worse. Now, with his business, he has made many enemies. He is arrogant with men who are not amused by it, and he has ruined at least three previously wealthy men that I know of."

"So you want him protected."

"Yes."

"Motherly concern?"

"Don't be absurd," Lucienne said.

They had another cigarette in the living room. Lucienne nodded to a large oil portrait of a stern, solemn man dressed in a black suit with a black moustache. He looked like something out of another world, Raynaud thought—a master of commerce in the finest days of the Empire.

"My husband," Lucienne said. "Herbert. You can see for yourself what he was like."

"Lots of laughs," Raynaud said.

"He was a kind man, in his way, but strict. He was much more intelligent than most people gave him credit for. He knew that Richard and I were…not close. He also knew that Richard was a wastrel who needed time to mature. So he established the will, making me executor until Richard became thirty-four."

"I see."

"But he also did something else. I do not hold it against him, for it was prudent. But he did it: he wrote the will to state that if Richard did not live to reach thirty-four years, the estate would all go to charity"

Not a fool, Raynaud thought. Not a fool at all. He looked with new respect at the face glowering out from the painting.

"So you see my position. If anything happens to Richard in the next few weeks, the estate is lost. And so am I." She sighed. "I gave up a great deal to marry Herbert Pierce, Charles. I ended my career, and in some ways I ended my life, at least the life I loved. I did it because I was fond of Herbert, of course, but—"

"There was also the half billion dollars."

She shrugged. "I am the widow of a wealthy man. I have my expectations."

"Yes," Raynaud said, "but aren't you forgetting something?

When Richard inherits the estate, he may cut you off without a shilling to your name."

Lucienne laughed. "Is that what he told you?"

"He mentioned it."

She shook her head. "He can't. You see, Herbert was, if nothing else, fair. The will states that my income after Richard inherits the estate will be determined by him—but that it shall not be less than three thousand pounds a month."

That would be more than eighty thousand dollars a year, at the new exchange rate. Not bad, Raynaud thought, for an attractive widow with, no doubt, many wealthy male friends. Not bad in any case.

"So you want to be sure Richard inherits the estate."

"He *must* inherit it. He must."

"And you're willing to pay five hundred dollars a day?"

"If you can guarantee his safety."

"But I can't."

She looked up in surprise. "You can't?"

"Not for five hundred a day."

For a moment she was silent, and then she said in a low voice, "Charles, if you are putting the squeeze—"

"Look at it this way," he said. "If Richard lives through the next month to inherit the estate, over the next twenty years or so you will make about two million dollars. Give or take."

"So?"

"To protect such an income must be worth more than five hundred a day."

She lit a cigarette. "How much do you want?"

"A thousand a day."

"Impossible. It's far too much."

Raynaud shrugged.

Lucienne looked steadily at him and said, "You are as bad as Richard."

"Almost." He nodded.

She smoked her cigarette and stared out the window. Finally she said, "All right. As you wish: a thousand a day. How do you want it?"

"A check will do nicely. Uncrossed, of course."

She raised an eyebrow. "You have a Swiss account?"

"Doesn't everyone?"

She laughed, and wrote the check swiftly. "Five thousand on account," she said, "and the rest at the end. Is that all right?"

"Weekly is better, I think," Raynaud said. "We'll have another seven thousand next week."

She sighed and nodded.

"Meantime," he said, "tell me why you are worried about Richard."

"It's his business," she said. "You've seen Shore Industries? That shiny new office?"

"Yes."

"Well," she said, "it's all a front."

"For what?"

"I can't be sure. But there are rumors that Richard is planning something vast. Some say he's going to start a wholly submerged mining complex. Some say it's the Channel Tunnel project he's mixed up in. All I know is that he has poured money into it at a fantastic rate. An impossible rate. And it is money that does not appear on any ledger. Last year the sum of eight hundred thousand pounds simply disappeared."

"Disappeared?"

"Yes."

"That's a lot of money to have disappear."

"You can be certain," Lucienne said, "that it wasn't burned to provide heat."

"Any idea where it went?"

"I suspect it went for bribes. He is buying out people in order to arrange his project."

"Any idea who?"

"I've been trying to find out. Richard gets the financing for Shore directly from the estate trustees. A group of six connected with Barclays Bank. Presumably they have some idea what he's up to, but they won't say."

Raynaud nodded. The story sounded crazy enough to be true. It would be like Richard to move through the business world by buying businessmen. After all, he bought everyone else.

"Any idea who wants him dead?"

She shook her head. "None."

"That makes it difficult."

"I know." She grinned wryly. "But you're getting a thousand a day."

"I will need something more," he said.

"Yes?"

"A gun."

"A gun? Why?"

"We're talking about murder. People who commit murder don't try it with rubber bands and paper clips."

"But a gun…"

"Can you get one?"

"It is very difficult in England. The laws are strict."

"Yes, but can you get one?"

She frowned, thinking. After a moment she said, "I do not believe it is a good idea. You should not have a gun."

"I may need it."

"You must do without."

"It may make the difference—"

"No," Lucienne said. "No guns."

Raynaud found this very odd. He said, "What would happen if Richard did die?"

"The estate would go to charity. I told you."

"There is no way to break the will?"

"None."

"And if he died accidentally?"

"The same."

"And if he committed suicide?"

She hesitated. "I don't think that is covered in the will."

"Do you have a copy here?"

"Of the will? No."

"Why not?"

"Why should I?"

Raynaud shrugged. "It seems an important document. I would have thought you'd have a copy."

"No. My lawyers take care of all that. I'm not much of a businesswoman, I'm afraid."

"I see," Raynaud said.

They walked in the gardens behind the house, moving between rows of neatly trimmed hedges.

"What," he said, "do you think of Sandra?"

Lucienne shrugged.

"Do you want Richard to marry her?"

"Yes."

"Why?"

"She is a willful, headstrong girl, and she has a good future as a film actress. She knows it. She also knows—or will soon come to know—that I have friends who can make or break her career."

"You're looking forward to somewhat more than three thousand pounds a month."

"It sounds terrible, I know. But you understand Richard. You know how childish he is, how petty. One must meet him on his own terms."

"Blackmail through his wife?"

"Pressure," Lucienne said. "Pressure."

"You think it will work?"

"I have some hope."

"You seem to have thought it out very carefully," he said, "for a woman who has no business sense."

She shrugged. "Everything is different for me now," she said. "I have changed since Herbert died."

"When was that?"

"In nineteen fifty-eight. A long time now, though it seems only a few days ago. We were taking a motor trip to the south of France, on National Seven. We had a flat in our Citroën—it was a rented car—and my husband got out to look at the tire. The left front tire." Her voice went low. "Then a car came along and…struck him."

"I'm sorry."

"It was a terrible, terrible thing. We got him back into the car, and—

"We?"

"Jonathan. Doctor Black. He was with us. We got him back into the car, and Doctor Black administered first aid. But he was dead before we reached the hospital in Arles. My husband," she said, "was sixty-eight at the time."

"Did they ever catch the driver?"

"No," she said. "Never."

"And then Richard came home for the funeral?"

"Yes, he came home. He was more worried about the money than anything else. He was terrified that I might have gotten everything in the will. As it turned out, he was secure—he had only to wait a few years, and it all became his. But he begrudged me even the three thousand pounds."

She spoke bitterly.

"I'm sure Richard has filled you with terrible stories of his return home for the funeral. The fact is that Richard hated his father—his stepfather—almost as much as he hated me. Richard was a mean, irritable child and he grew into a mean, irritable adult, capricious and disgusting. I remember, at the funeral, sitting there and hearing his laughter. A low, obscene laughter like someone clearing his throat. Very soft, but it was there."

She paused and lit a cigarette. "I'm sorry," she said. "I don't mean to say all this."

Raynaud said nothing.

"But I must be honest," she continued. "Just because I have asked you to protect him, it does not mean I feel he is worth protecting. I would as soon see him dead tomorrow. Even with the scandal. Even with the newspapers and the courts. I would as soon see him dead."

"But you would lose the money."

"Yes," she said. "On the other hand, I would see my husband's efforts preserved. I want that, want it very badly. Herbert was a strange man. In many ways he was cold and unfeeling. But he had a dream, an ambition, a vision. He worked and sweated to make it come true: half a billion dollars in the largest single business empire in England to be ruled by a single man. I want to see that vision continue and grow. I want to see half a billion dollars used for something besides champagne, motor cars, and abortions for tarts. Is that so strange?"

"Richard may turn out—"

"Now you sound like my husband." She turned away from him angrily. "He watched Richard for years, and refused to believe the bad, refused to see the rot, the decay, the dissipated evil. He continued to hope and believe—right up to the day he died. He loved Richard: and Richard hated his guts."

She sighed and looked at her watch. "But we have talked long enough. You have things you must do, and so do I. You'll keep me informed of what is happening?"

He nodded.

"All right then," she said. "Good luck."

She kissed him lightly on the cheek, and they walked back from the gardens, toward the house.

On his way home he stopped to hire a rental car and drove it cautiously through the wrong-sided London traffic. It was an odd sensation, to drive a car with everything reversed; it seemed strangely appropriate, matching his thoughts.

Lucienne had put on a remarkable performance, truly skillful, but it did not come off quite right. She was ambiguous: first she wanted Richard protected, and then she wanted him dead. First she was looking out for her own interests, then she was ignoring them. And that final tirade against her adopted son, a viciously accurate catalogue of his faults...

Why?

And why had she been unwilling to discuss it the night before? He recalled an old Yucatán saying: "Never trust a woman who talks business in bed. And never trust a woman who talks bed in business."

For better or worse, he now realized he did not trust Lucienne. He was convinced Lucienne was pushing him toward something, guiding and directing him as subtly as she knew how.

Well, he thought, there were certain steps he could take to deal with that. Beginning with his little insurance policy. He always carried it with him to important meetings; it had proved invaluable in the past.

Reaching into his breast pocket, he removed the tiny tape

recorder and set it on the seat beside him. At the next spotlight, he flicked a switch and heard the tinny but still recognizable voice say, "He loved Richard, and Richard hated his guts."

He switched the recorder off.

Someday that tape might be very useful.

3. THE GAME OF AGE

It was going to be all right, she thought. It was going to be beautifully, gorgeously all right.

She stood in front of the mirror, wearing the leotard, going through her exercises with smooth precision. For as long as she could remember, she had done these same exercises, in the same order, feeling the sweat seep through the black knit of the leotard, feeling the burning ache in her muscles as she strained. But it had repaid her amply: at thirty-nine, her stomach was still flat and hard, her thighs firm, her calves slim and attractive. And her face was still good, the green eyes bright, the lashes long, the wrinkles slight and easily hidden by amphetamines and makeup.

She did not look her age. She knew it, and it pleased her. At parties, when she got tight, she defied men to guess her age, while she watched their faces carefully for signs of flattery and underestimation. Usually, they said thirty-two or -three; the liars said twenty-eight. But it didn't matter. What mattered was that no one cautiously ventured forty, or forty-two. What mattered was that they were pleased to talk to her, pleased to command her attention, at least for a moment, pleased to feel that she was interested in them. That was what mattered.

She lay down and did one hundred sit-ups, in quick succession. She did them easily, with barely a catch in her breath; she had good stomach muscles, no children, never, and anyone with her knew that, and that pleased her, too. She had never wanted children, but Herbert hadn't understood. He thought it had something to do with him, with her feeling toward him.

Perhaps it did. But she didn't think of it that way. When she thought of it at all, she thought of something pushing out—pushing *out*—and she thought of the size of the head, really gigantic when you considered it, a stretching, unnatural, painful thing, and for what purpose?

No, no children. Never. She hadn't the slightest desire for them. She knew men, and knew what they thought. She knew the way their minds worked. You could have a man and hold him in a thousand ways, keep his attention, his interest, his desire, but at the bottom of it all there was sex, raw sex, pure hot hard sex, or there was nothing at all. So funny: the English girls who insisted on displaying their minds, on attacking men with their minds, on raping their intellects. English girls understood nothing. Men were not excited by a woman's mind. It was nothing of interest.

She remembered the first time, when she had been just a girl, newly arrived to Paris from the country, but already making a name, *une petite célèbre.* She had been introduced to a wealthy banker and minister in the cabinet. He was an older, experienced man with wide contacts and influential friends; he knew everyone in Paris, was well educated, spoke wittily of things she had never heard of. She had been terrified to meet him, convinced he would find her dull and insipid. But it hadn't turned out that way; instead, he found her charming, installed her in a luxurious apartment, introduced her to his friends, and was very good to her for as long as it lasted. In the end, she threw him over, and she had the satisfaction of seeing the hurt, the sadness, and the fear in his face. She felt very strongly that she had triumphed, there was the pleasurable knowledge that she had ended it, not he.

And she had learned. She had learned how to trap a man, how to shift the balance of power and initiative from him to her, how to arrange a relationship to suit her needs. In any love affair, one person was insecure—she resolved that it would never be her. And it never had been.

Later, of course, it was easy. She was Lucienne Ginoux, a singer, a personality, a "creative force," whatever that was. She always read the papers and the critics with a kind of sad amusement. The critics were men, and like all men their judgment was, she discovered, flexible. It was her rule never to make an enemy of a critic—and never, precisely, a lover; she kept them hanging, dangling, hoping, and the reviews glowed.

Her affairs were numerous but, at first, discreet. She was young and uncertain and acted cautiously. Later, when she was an established artist and personality, she became bolder, taking what she wanted when she wanted it, ignoring the rest. Oddly, this seemed to please her audiences; they wished to believe that she was a hotly passionate woman, almost as if this fact increased her availability to them, to each man sitting in the darkened room, staring at the figure in the spotlight. It gave substance and hope to their dreams; the fantasies became more tangible, and she prospered.

By the late forties, her fame had spread all over Europe. She was wealthy, in a fashion, but she was also tired. The public eye, the perpetual scrutiny which had once been so exhilarating, began to pale. She was tired: tired of hotel rooms, late hours, interviews at dockside where she sat on her white leather suitcases and posed with her legs crossed, tired of interviews, of the popping flashbulbs, tired of the intimate dinner parties on two continents, where famous men she did not like kissed her hand and touched her leg experimentally under the table.

Tired of the rush, of the quick changes backstage, of the gowns to be fitted and the appointments to be kept. Tired, even, of the lovers who no longer saw her as a person, but rather grunted over an idol, isolated from her, wrapped not in her arms but in their private dreams.

Tired of too many cigarettes, too much Scotch, too many roses sent backstage, and too much bad air. She was drinking more—drinking too much—and bothered by the bad air. She went to see a doctor in Paris, feeling sick and disgusted and tired and bored.

She remembered the incident vividly, even twenty years later. God, was it twenty years? She shook her head: it was. He had been a famous physician, a patriarchal, white-haired man, lean and handsome, a man who ministered to Ministers, and even the Premier in those days: was it Mendès-France? No, he was later.

Anyway, she had gone to see him, in his expensive, subdued offices, and he talked to her for an hour about her life and work. Talking with him, she had the old feeling—he did not see her as a patient, or as a person, or even as a collection of sickened organs. He saw her as Lucienne Ginoux, hot-blooded singer of hot-blooded songs. Finally, irritated, she had cut him off and announced that she sought medical advice, not polite conversation.

He examined her briefly, saying nothing, and then he sat down again behind his desk.

"You know," he said, "what the problem is."

She shook her head.

"The liver," he said. "You are headed for disease of the liver. The early changes are already there."

"What should I do?" She was horrified by his words: she was only in her teens, still young and vibrant.

"You know that as well."

She stared at him steadily, then said, "I can't quit."

"You must."

"Impossible."

"You must."

Angrily, she had stormed out of his office. What did he know, anyway? He was just an old man, who treated old men, whose fingers probed the diseases of heads of state, government officials, weak old men who sat behind a desk. She went out and immediately arranged a full schedule for the coming months, trips to Germany, Italy, and England....

It was in England that the cough began. A bad, choking cough, and her weight began to fall. At first, she was pleased; the bones of her ribs showed, giving her a slim, taut look which she enjoyed. But later, she worried. So she saw an English doctor.

He was younger, handsome, but very businesslike. He examined her briskly and did an X-ray of her chest.

"Lung disease," he said.

She threw up her hands. The French said liver disease, the English said lung disease.

"Is it serious?"

"I'm afraid it is," he said. "You have tuberculosis."

She sagged back in the chair. This time, the words meant something. Her father, an army colonel from Lyon, had died of tuberculosis. She had been fourteen at the time. She remembered it vaguely—the hacking, gravelly cough, the changes from a vigorous man to a pale skeleton, the weakness, then the blue color toward the end....

"What can I do?"

The young doctor smiled reassuringly. "Ten years ago," he said, "it would have been difficult. Even two or three years ago, it would have been hard, because antibiotics were in short supply. Now, however, there are drugs."

"Drugs?"

"Yes. A new drug called streptomycin, and another called isoniazid. They seem to work well."

"Must I quit singing?"

"You must go to a hospital," he said.

"For how long?"

"As long as it takes. But with luck, you will be out in six months."

"Six months!" It had seemed an eternity. She was just nineteen. "But I have engagements, concerts, nightclub—"

"Cancel them," he said. "It is the only way."

She did, with a peculiar mixture of sadness and relief. And she spent only four months in the hospital, as it turned out. The drugs made her feel sicker, but she began to gain weight and strength. It was a pleasant hospital, in Switzerland. Because of the publicity, she had entered under an assumed name, Françoise Doreau. She liked life there. The nurses and the doctors did not realize they were dealing with the great and glamorous Lucienne Ginoux. To them, she was just a pretty, but sick, girl. At the very first, it annoyed her to be deprived of the attention and adulation, but soon after, she realized what she had been missing. The chance to talk to people, the acceptance. The freedom of conversation unencumbered by awe. Nobody after her autograph. No reporters, no photographs, no rigidly fixed smiles for the cameras.

That was where Herbert Edgar Pierce came in.

She had met him shortly after her return to the circuit. She was taking things easy, recuperating. When she left the hospital, she had had great plans for a new life, for a change. But she found herself falling back into the old pattern. A German actor was first, then an Italian auto manufacturer. Neither lasted more than six weeks. She was becoming depressed, and her voice was showing it—the old fire, the old confidence, was disappearing. She was drinking more than ever, and smoking three packs a day, though her doctors forbade it.

Then she met Herbert Pierce.

She knew, of course, what he meant. Half a billion dollars. Prestige. Acceptance. But she saw other things as well: he was a kind, mature, gentle man. She could imagine him as a stabilizing influence, a man to fix and hold her love, to freeze it forever and give her peace from restlessness.

So she had married him.

She was a happy, domestic wife for six months, and then she had met Jonathan Black at a dinner party. He was the first. Others came later, and still others...

Lucienne finished her exercises, stripped off the damp leotard, and walked into the bathroom to shower. She felt tired and rang for the maid, and asked for a vermouth. It was too early for a drink, but she needed something. Something to take away the sting of dead relationships, slaughtered hopes, lost faces. Something to keep her from looking too closely into the mirror.

A pretense, she thought. A fabulous and absurd game, to battle with age. One never won. All the exercises and diets and drugs and makeup did not cure age—only postponed the inevitable deterioration.

She remembered how it used to be. Once, she could do whatever she wished with her body—fill it with liquor, cover it with straining young men, keep it up late at parties, dance it until dawn. Her body never complained, never showed fatigue.

Then the sickness, and afterward, the slow decline. She saw the signs everywhere. That slight, telltale fatigue at the top of the stairs. The desire to leave a party at midnight. The dentist who told her she needed gum treatment. The ladies who worked in the lingerie shops who no longer complimented her on her figure, as they once had. The slow change in dress size: from a five, to a seven, and now an occasional nine.

She did not wear bikinis, anymore. She told herself it was propriety; a mature woman dressed more demurely. But she knew there was more. She had never worn makeup until ten years ago, not even lipstick or eyeshadow. She had never dieted until eight years ago. She had never taken amphetamines until five years ago.

And the men were changing. Once, it had been older men, patient, willing to help her, to wait. She was drawn by their wealth, their confidence, their self-assurance. Now it was younger men, who were no doubt attracted to her for the same reason. The tables were turning, the balance shifting.

Exercises, diets, makeup.

Damn.

All her life, she had lived by her wits, her voice, and her beauty. Her beauty now was fading; her voice was gone. She was left with her wits.

Well, she thought, that was something. Wits and experience, experience with men. That would be enough. She looked in the mirror, tugging at her face, her breasts, her stomach.

Not so old, she thought.

A brief flash of color caught her eye. Glancing out the window, she saw a girl in a shocking pink miniskirt. No, it was more: microskirt, they called it. Barely covering the buttocks. The girl was no more than sixteen or seventeen, her long legs bare, taking easy, loping strides.

Damn London. It was not, she thought, a pleasant place to grow old. Irritably, she stepped into the shower and turned the water on, hot and stinging. The maid brought the vermouth and Lucienne told her to leave it on the basin.

In the shower, she washed herself carefully and thought about what she must do. The plan: the plan was the thing. Richard must be foiled, and soon. Lucienne had worked too hard to allow anything else. She had given up her career, given up every-thing, for Herbert. Now that Herbert was gone, only the money remained.

Was it so bad to want the money?

No, she thought.

She deserved it.

And she would have it.

4. ANGRY CAT

Dr. Jonathan Black parked his Aston Martin in the parking lot next to the research wing of St. Catherine's Hospital. Briefcase in hand, he went into the lobby and took the elevator to the third floor. The elevators in the building were large, full-hospital size, with walls of stainless steel.

He went directly to his office, at one corner of the psycho-pharmacology section. He set his briefcase down and looked through his mail. As usual, it consisted mostly of reprints of articles by other scientists working in areas related to Black's own field.

His secretary came in, and said, "Doctor Black, the surgery is ready."

"All right," he said, shrugging out of his coat. "Tell them I'm coming shortly."

He hung up his coat on a hook by the door, removed his vest, and went down the corridor in shirtsleeves. The operating theater was at the end of the wing. The red light next to the doors was on, indicating that the theater was in use.

Black went in a side door and entered the scrub room. There was a row of lockers along one wall. He stripped to his undershorts, putting his clothes in his locker; then he put on a gown, mask, and cap. He pulled back the sleeves of his gown and stepped to the sink. The water was operated by a foot pedal. He washed his hands with hexachlorophene soap for ten minutes, then dried them under an air jet. Then he pushed through the swinging door with his shoulder, keeping his hands clean, and faced the operating team: three men in gowns and masks, leaning over a center table beneath a bright overhead lamp. The team straightened as he entered.

"All set?"

"Yes, doctor."

A nurse came up and slipped rubber gloves over his hands. Black flexed his fingers and said, "We'll check the charts first."

This would be a difficult operation, the most delicate he had ever performed. He had attempted three previous operations of the same type, and the results had been poor. In one case, death had resulted on the table.

He picked up the charts, which were laminated in plastic that could be sterilized. The charts consisted of a map of the brain, with coordinates and gyri laid out.

One of the team said, "It's the hypothalamus, doctor?"

"That's right," Black said. "We'll take the anterior nucleus this time. Bilaterally."

"Yes, sir."

"Is the cranium removed?"

"Yes."

He stepped forward and looked at the body on the table. It was a young cat, perhaps a year old. The animal was on its back, its four paws tied down carefully. The skull cap had been removed, exposing the pale pink surface of the brain.

"Grid," Black said.

The grid was brought. It was a cagelike affair, which fitted over the head and attached to it. By a series of gears, a probe could be positioned with the grid at any desired coordinates. This allowed a point within the three-dimensional substance of the brain to be fixed.

"What is the anaesthetic?" Black asked, as he screwed the grid onto the head.

"Cyclopropane and a local for the scalp, since we were removing bone and skin flap," said one man.

"And it was?"

"Procaine amide," the man said.

"All right" Black glanced at the chart "The coordinates for the anterior nucleus are A, twelve, seventy-one. Fix that." Those directions would locate the point in three planes. The anterior nucleus was a diffuse collection of nerve cells deep within the brain. It was felt to be involved with emotional responses in some poorly understood manner.

"Fixed, sir."

"Nitrogen probe," Black said.

A large cylindrical tank on wheels was brought over. At the top on the cylinder was a pressure gauge and a slim length of metal tubing, which ended in a long, needle-sharp probe. The probe was given to Black, who inserted it through the grid and lowered it until it almost touched the surface of the brain.

He paused. "All set?"

The others nodded tensely.

Black lowered the needle precisely seventy-one millimeters into the brain. The sharp probe penetrated the doughy substance easily. At the exact distance, he stopped.

"Nitrogen," he said. "We'll give it a two-second burst."

Someone pressed the button on the tank. A faint hissing sound as liquid nitrogen at minus two hundred ten degrees flowed through the tubing, down the probe, and out into the brain of the cat. Whatever that liquid touched, it would destroy instantly, freezing it, killing it.

"Two seconds, doctor," a man said.

"Very good." Black removed the probe, feeling the cold dampness of the metal after the nitrogen had flowed through it. When he pulled it free of the brain, the tip of the needle was still smoking.

"All right," he said, as the nitrogen bottle and probe were wheeled away. "Close it up."

The team went into action, replacing the cup of bone which covered the brain, then suturing the skin over that. Black watched for a while before he left the room.

As he passed through the swinging door, he said, "Keep it on amobarbital for forty-eight hours. Just in case."

They nodded. He stripped off his operating gown and mask in the scrub room and dropped them into a large laundry sack. He washed his hands again, and returned to his office, stopping by the laboratory to tell the assistants to expect a new cat, and to treat it gently: The cat would probably try to destroy itself.

In his office, he considered the implications of what he had just done. He had taken a cat, a perfectly normal, gentle cat, and turned it into a monster by destroying a few hundred crucial nerve cells. Without those cells, now frozen by nitrogen, the cat would be wholly changed: its personality, its mannerisms, the way it walked and acted. Everything changed.

A few hundred brain cells.

He shook his head slowly. In some ways, it was astonishing to think that a creature's personality could reside in so few cells, such a small amount of protoplasm. There were other parts of the brain, less significant than the anterior nucleus, which could be destroyed with no demonstrable effect on the animal.

It came down to a matter of delicacy. Every creature had its physiological weak point, its Achilles' heel. And every man had his psychological weak point. Black thought of Raynaud.

A straightforward man, Raynaud. He wore his feelings on his sleeve. He knew what he wanted, and he knew how to get it.

Raynaud was easy.

Raynaud would change, under the proper stimulus, as swiftly and as easily as the cat had changed. Raynaud wanted wealth, and he would do anything to get it.

Anything at all.

Walking down the corridor, Kemelman, research chief of the unit, said: "Apparently, you are being considered strongly. I might as well tell you I've been recommending you for several years."

"That's very good of you."

"You deserve it," Kemelman said flatly.

Black lit a cigarette. "My answer," he said, "is quite simple. I would be flattered and honored."

Kemelman got up. "Good. I'll let them know." He went to the door. "This isn't official, you understand, I don't want to raise false hopes."

"I understand."

"Something still might go wrong in the committee. But that's unlikely."

Black nodded.

Kemelman smiled. "We'll see what happens. Good luck, John."

"Thanks."

"See you."

Kemelman left. Black stood and walked around the small office, smiling to himself. F.R.S.: it was almost too good. He had wanted to be a Fellow of the Royal Society for years, and privately he had felt he had deserved it for the last five or six years. His research had been outstanding, with broad implications. The Americans had made use of some of his data for their space program; the British Army had used it in their training for brainwashing and interrogation techniques. A psychiatric group in Geneva used much of his experimental material in the treatment of recalcitrant human cases.

But still: to be elected to the Royal was a risky and uncertain business. Some of the most deserving scientists, like Fleming, discoverer of penicillin, had waited years before being accepted. It was absurdly exclusive, with only six hundred members out of the thousands of scientists in the country. The exclusivity meant that politics were important to membership, but it also meant that the F.R.S. was more prized than a knighthood.

Often, he had driven past the headquarters in Burlington House, across the street from the Society of Antiquaries. He had long since come to regard it as the most exclusive and desirable club in London. It was old, founded by King Charles II, and venerable, with Newton, Wren, Huxley, Kelvin, and Dale as past presidents. And it had its traditional avenues of entrance, the foremost being Cambridge, which was fortunate for Black.

He looked across the room at his diplomas. Most prominent was the parchment from Cambridge University. Black had gone there in 1939, obtaining a starred First in his Natural Sciences tripost three years later. Not many starred Firsts were given in the sciences, and his success immediately led him to St. Cat's, where he did three years of hospital before being licensed to practice. Black worked as a physician for several years; the war was on, and the beds were filled with wounded and maimed soldiers and civilians.

As time passed, however, he became increasingly interested in psychological injuries of wartime—men who had recovered yet felt they were still ill; men who had not been injured at all but remained fixed rigidly in a catatonic trance; men with slight wounds who were convinced they were going to die; hysterical

women who had lost husbands or boyfriends and acted almost
as if they had undergone amputation of a limb. When the war
was over he started in psychiatry and was practicing a few years
later. With his academic credentials and professional contacts,
and with the help of his cousin Herbert Pierce, who by then
was a millionaire many times over, Jonathan Black opened
plush offices near Harley Street, and began to treat the cream
of British society.

He accepted his success easily. As the only child of a prominent Scottish physician, and the descendant of a long line of
important scientists, it seemed only natural that he should
succeed. He was, for a six-year period, the most fashionable
psychiatrist in all London, even more fashionable than Sir
Lawrence Poole or Henry Carter-Wright. He made a good deal
of money, though never as much as Herbert Pierce, whose
personal wealth at that time was increasing by twenty million
pounds a year.

That always irritated Black, even though Herbert never made
a thing of it. They used to meet for lunch once or twice a month
at Le Camargue. Herbert usually spent the meal asking for personal advice, and Black did not discourage him. The personality
of Herbert—a rather stupid man, when all was said—fascinated
him. In particular, there was a peculiar blend of hard-nosed
business acumen mixed with astonishing personal naïveté. It
was remarkable that a man could be such a good judge of the
pound, and such a poor judge of flesh. Lucienne was a perfect
example: when Herbert announced that he wanted to marry a
restless tart of a girl who had a reputation as vast as all London,
Black was speechless. And then when Herbert explained his
theories about reforming her, making a proper woman of her...

Even now, Black smiled sadly at the recollection. Men lived
in a world of their own making, an unseen world of their illusions, hopes, and fears. In the case of Herbert, his illusions had
proved his undoing.

And, eventually, it would prove the same for Lucienne.

Black had never met her at the time Herbert first proposed
his intention of marriage. He knew of the French singer only

by reputation, from the endless lewd stories and jokes in circulation. He did not then know how charming and willful she was, how subtly she could play upon a man's emotions.

The secretary stuck her head in. "Doctor Black, the patient is recovering."

Black snapped out of his thoughts. "Right," he said. "I'll see to it."

When he arrived in the lab, the cat was lying on its side, asleep, breathing gently. Its shaved head was covered in bandages, then a layer of cotton wool, and finally a protective plastic helmet.

The assistant handed Black a hemostat, a large instrument shaped like a pair of pliers. Black opened the door to the cage, and squeezed the cat's paw. The animal stirred slightly.

"When was the last amobarb injection?"

"Immediately post-op, doctor."

"What did you give?"

"Point five milligrams per body kilo."

"Good."

The effects would wear off at any time. Even as he watched, the eyelids flickered and the paws moved. The whole body gave a slight shudder.

"Better step back," Black said to the assistant

The cat opened its eyes, blinked, and kept them open. Slowly, it got to its feet. Black stared impassively at it. The cat turned, licked itself, and turned again.

"Come on, kitty. Let's see your true self."

The cat did nothing. It licked itself. "Come on, kitty." He prodded it with the hemostat, reaching through the bars.

The effect was immediate. The cat bared its teeth, fur rising. It gave a hiss and a snarl and flung itself at the bars of the cage, growling, chomping down on the bars. It struck the cage hard, and fell back. It picked itself up and hurled itself forward a second time, mouth wide, rage showing in the eyes.

"A vicious, unthinking beast," Black said, with a slight smile. With its hypothalamus destroyed, the cat was a prisoner of emotion, unable to modify or control it.

The assistant was a young man from Manchester with a BS degree. His face was pale. The cat leapt forward, snarling, banging against the cage, again and again.

"Good Christ," said the assistant

"Now you see the need for the plastic helmet."

"What shall we do with her, sir?"

"Meprobamate, for the time being," Black said. "We will start shock treatment in the morning. Give her a full milligram per kilo for the next day. Administer it with heavy gloves. Right?"

"Right," said the assistant, a bit shaky.

In his office, Black made out a protocol for the following day's experiments with the enraged cat. He scribbled down the duration and power of the shocks, and the dosage of the various drugs to be used. He was immensely pleased that the surgery had gone well. Now they could begin duplicate testing.

The cat was to serve as a control for further experiments. The cat was angry; it responded with violent rage, for purely physical reasons—part of its brain was destroyed. They knew this. But suppose a drug existed which could duplicate the effects?

This cat would serve as a standard against which violent behavior could be examined. And, in fact, there existed a true violence-producing drug. It was highly experimental, very expensive, and difficult to obtain.

But with any luck, he would have a pure gram of it by this afternoon.

And the experiments could begin.

5. THE CONFERENCE

"Let us assume," said Charles Raynaud, "that I am about to be screwed."

He paced up and down Richard's apartment, smoking a cigarette. He was alone; he had been pacing for hours.

"And let us assume," he said, "that somebody stands to profit by a half a billion dollars." He continued pacing. "Who?"

All right, he thought. Good question: who?

"Beats me."

He stared at the large painting of the hamburger dripping catsup.

"Lucienne doesn't want Richard dead. She hired me. But she won't give me a gun. On the other hand, I already have a gun."

He reached over to the coffee table and picked up the gun he had retrieved from the guest room closet a few minutes before. The gun he had taken from the little man in Soho.

"In theory, nobody knows I have this gun."

But in fact?

He turned it over in his hand, a snub-nosed .38, black and heavy, mean. He broke it open and rolled the cartridges out into his hand. He examined them carefully, and determined that they had been home-loaded; there were scratches on the shell casings. Perhaps not surprising in a country like England. But then again...

He bent over to look closer at the bullets themselves. They were grayish, dull in the light streaming in through the window. He squeezed one, and a slight gray powder came off on his fingers. He hefted one bullet in his hand, frowning: it was light.

Too light.

Quickly, he walked to the window and glanced out. It was a quiet Saturday morning; the street was deserted.

Raynaud reloaded the gun and fired at the opposite wall. The report was deafening; the gun kicked up in his hand. So: at least there was powder in the casings. That was something.

But when he examined the wall, touching it with his fingers, he had a surprise: the bullet hadn't penetrated the plaster. It had hardly made a dent. Instead, there was a small gray smudge on the white surface, and a little heap of gray powder on the floor.

Clay.

Quite clever. The clay was gray and dull, and looked just like lead. It fired like a regular bullet, with just one difference.

These bullets wouldn't kill a turkey with a bad heart. Fired at a man, they would probably not even penetrate the skin. They might cause a scratch or a bruise, but nothing more.

Strange.

He looked at the gun and saw the identification number along the grip. Probably Longwood still worked for the police in London. Good old Longwood, a tall, thin bureaucrat who was the pride of the police force because he was the model of the reformed criminal.

Raynaud decided to call him. He jotted down the serial number on the gun and went to the phone. As he did so, he glanced at his watch and noted that it was time to change. The International Congress of Zoologists and Herpetologists would be opening in another hour.

"Friends, members of the committee, fellow students of zoology," said the voice. It echoed through the long hall, amplified by a dozen loudspeakers, ringing over the heads of the four hundred delegates seated at the long tables facing the podium.

"It is, ah, a great pleasure to welcome you here to our latest conference. I trust that it will be an exciting and profitable experience for us all."

The speaker cleared his throat, the sound resounding through the hall. In the back, Raynaud stood leaning against the wall, thumbing through the program. It looked ghastly dull. The afternoon sessions, for example, dealt with such fascinating topics as "Zoo Hygiene," "Mating Techniques of the Captive Lion,"

"Normal Variations in Rectal Temperature of the Crocodile," and "Kangaroo Psychosis: Report of Case." He flipped through until he found what he was looking for, the panel on herpetology. It met after dinner, and considered four papers on reptiles and snakes.

The main speaker rambled on, and Raynaud walked out. Ranged around the central auditorium were several corridors filled with exhibits and displays. Half the delegates, not bothering to attend the keynote address, were out here, moving from booth to booth.

As always, he was struck by the International Congress. It was largely a zookeeper's meeting, and zoos, though no one could suspect it, were big business. A large urban zoo might easily have an operating budget of two million dollars a year, and throughout the world many zoos were expanding. There was growing interest in "natural habitats," in infrared rooms for nocturnal animals, in complex aquaria. All this meant money.

But there was a scholarly side to the International Congress, since it served as a convention for veterinarians as well. Obscure diseases of obscure animals were debated and fussed over by eminent men, long into the night.

And finally, there was a purely commercial aspect to the Congress. Pet food companies, manufacturers of antiseptics, vitamins, and animal cages were all represented—as were the drug companies. About five years ago, a number of drug companies had begun to realize the market for large volume drugs which existed among zoologists.

For example, if one of your captive elephants was acting up, he would require a quart or two of tranquilizer to calm him down. A lethargic gorilla might need several bottles of amphetamine before he perked up.

There was also the business of venoms and antivenom. Drug companies here were both buying and selling; buying from the snake farms, producing their antivenom, and selling it once again after processing.

Antivenom. Purified extracts. And a variety of research compounds used in pure biochemistry, neurology, and so on.

Raynaud walked among the booths, casually looking over the

displays and products offered for sale. He stopped to talk with a salesgirl wearing a microskirt about a new snake-noose with a spring-loaded attachment.

And then, looking up, he saw Jonathan Black.

The bald head, the beak nose, and fleshy face were unmistakable. Black was discussing something with a salesman at Valdez Chemicals' booth. Raynaud frowned. Valdez was a new company, based in Chile. It had been in business only a few years, but it had a reputation for aggressive research, and even more aggressive marketing. A variety of products had come from the Valdez labs, some of them good, some of them bad. A vaccine against the monkey SV-38 virus, for example, had killed dozens of monkeys before it was learned the vaccine was impure, and contained live virus.

He waited, looking at Black, wondering whether he should go over and say hello. He decided not to; after another five minutes Black finished talking, reached into his wallet, and gave the salesman some money. The salesman, smiling, gave Black a small vial of chemical, and Black walked off.

Raynaud went over to the booth.

"I say," he said, in his best English accent, "have you seen a tall fellow, heavyset, a bit balding?" Raynaud gestured, describing with his hands.

"There was one just here."

"Oh? Was there? Then he must have already bought it."

The salesman said, "Yes, he—"

"It was the Viliran, I take it?"

Viliran was Valdez' most widely sold product, an antiseptic for cleaning monkey cages. Many research groups used it.

"Viliran? No." The salesman looked confused.

"You must be thinking of the wrong man," Raynaud said. "I mean Doctor Jonathan Black, the neurophysiologist. He said he was coming here to try Viliran. We hear it's marvelous stuff." Raynaud said, "You see, I work in Doctor Black's lab with him."

"Ah." The salesman nodded. "Well actually, I was describing several of our products to him, and he became quite interested in another of them."

"Oh?"

"Yes. A new experimental compound called Dezisen."

Raynaud frowned. "Dezisen? I don't think I know it. Has it been reported in the literature?"

"Only preliminary work," the salesman said, "but allow me to give you these reprints."

He handed Raynaud several journal articles.

"Dezisen," he said, "is our name for the compound beta-amino-three-five-caphrophane. It is the form with the amide at the meta-position, and it possesses several interesting properties. Originally, we extracted the compound from the venom of *tarus kernictus*, the African peddle viper, but we have recently synthesized it *de novo* and can offer a purified extract."

"I see," Raynaud said.

"Furthermore, by moving the amide to meta-position from the para-position, which we do by a process of low-pressure acetylation, we have made the drug active p.o."

"Excellent."

"This offers a number of advantages over the injectable form, in terms of ease of administration. Any laboratory technician can now give the drug on a regular schedule. And none of the potency is lost. All the thalamic inhibitory effects described in those papers there"—he tapped the articles he had given Raynaud—"are retained, and to a degree which is quite striking. We at Valdez have little doubt that Dezisen will open whole new areas of neurological research. We are now working, naturally, on a drug which will counteract Dezisen. A drug which has the opposite effects. Such a drug would be, of course, a great benefit to mankind."

"Absolutely," Raynaud said.

"Your friend has already purchased two grams," the salesman said, "so I don't suppose you'll want more. But if you do, you can reach me here, at this address. Call any time." He gave Raynaud his business card.

As he was leaving, he ran into Porton Lewis, who was wearing a red flannel shirt and dirty khaki pants. Porton Lewis was an Englishman who had left home at an early age, after deciding he did not want to be a barrister after all, and had settled in

Nicaragua. He always wore flannel shirts and khaki trousers, as nearly as Raynaud could tell.

"Hullo, Charles," Lewis said. "Fancy you here."

"Fancy you," Raynaud said. "Visiting the old country?"

"I thought it would be amusing," Lewis said. "Besides, I'm selling."

"What?"

"Fifty grams of venom from the *trichus licanthus*. Very rare, that. Nobody has an antivenom for it yet, and the drug companies are mad for me. Buy you a drink?"

"Of course."

They went to a nearby pub. Lewis saw the reprints under Raynaud's arm.

"What've you got there?"

"Stuff from Valdez."

"Yes. They're still aggressive as ever. Very pushy, for a drug firm. What's it on?"

"This stuff Dezisen."

"Christ." Lewis sipped his drink. "I heard about that. It'll make Valdez rich, it seems."

"Why?"

"Every chemical and biological warfare group in the world wants it. The early bids are already ranging in the millions of dollars."

"Why?"

"Because Valdez now has an oral form. That's the key, you see. Everybody has known about this venom extract for a couple of years. But nobody figured out how to make it in an oral form. Now, you can just spray it into the air, and let it hit an army. Wham! End of war."

"You think so?"

"It's logical," Lewis said. "Considering the effects. In animals, it's pretty clear. One dose and you get uncontrollable rage. A pure, blind reaction. Turns a normal man into a vicious beast: at least everyone assumes it does."

"It hasn't been tried yet?"

"No. Not yet."

"Apparently it's available," Raynaud said, "to research groups."

"Yes. In limited doses. For animal experimentation, of course."

"Of course," Raynaud said.

When he returned home to the apartment, the telephone rang. It was his friend Longwood, calling from the police.

"I traced that gun for you," Longwood said.

"And?"

"It belongs to someone named Richard Pierce. Do you want the address?"

"No," Raynaud said. "Never mind."

6. A MEETING OF TRUE MINDS

Poor Charles, Lucienne thought. He deserved better. She hated to use him, really hated to do it, but there was no other way. She had examined the alternatives before, running over them in her mind, and always she reached the same conclusion.

The poor, poor son of a bitch. She did not like to think of him in prison, or dead. Whereas she rather liked the idea of Jonathan Black in prison.

Or dead.

Jonathan was better off dead. He deserved death, and it saddened her to think that she could not arrange death for him. The best she could do would be twenty years in prison. For Jonathan, of course, that amounted to a life sentence—and a bitter sentence, since he expected to inherit her estate—but still, it was not death.

Jonathan: such a funny man. Always playing such a fierce, intellectual, calculating game. Didn't he realize he was transparent? Hopelessly transparent? All his petty ruses, his sly little hints meant nothing. She saw right through them.

She lit a cigarette and had taken two puffs when Jonathan strode into the room.

"Lucienne, my dear."

He bent over her, and kissed her softly on the cheek. She accepted it, then waited.

"Lovely perfume," he said.

And he kissed her hard on the mouth. She accepted this, too, not rejecting or responding.

After a moment he broke away and looked at her. "A shame," he said. "It's gone, isn't it?"

"Yes," she said. "It is."

He sighed, and dropped into a chair across from her. "How have you been?"

"All right."

"And our friend?"

"Fine."

"Have you, ah, re-established…?"

"Yes."

"Marvelous," he said. "It couldn't be better."

She said nothing. She continued to smoke her cigarette. There are times, she thought, when I loathe this man. When I detest his very presence in the same room with me. A big, fat, ugly, detestable man.

Seeing him now, she could not imagine why she had ever found him attractive.

"And you gave him the story about protecting Richard?"

"Yes."

"What was his reaction?"

"He is suspicious," she said. "I tried to allay his doubts, but the suspicion remains."

"Perhaps it is just as well. He is not a fool, you know."

"I know."

"How much are you paying him?"

"A thousand dollars a day."

Jonathan's eyebrows went up. "Rather much."

"He insisted on it."

Black laughed. "Good for him."

"He'll earn it."

"Of course," Black said. "And then, you do not expect ever to pay him."

Lucienne nodded.

"You know, of course, that he will think of ways to increase his income."

"Yes," she said.

"That means Richard."

"Yes."

"Excellent. I am certain Richard will pay whatever Charles asks."

She shrugged. "It does not matter, in any event."

"I am not sure. It may be a great advantage. I watched Charles closely at dinner. He is a careful, hard man. Out for himself, uncommitted to anything except, I think, money. Richard is not his friend. Richard is in some ways a model and a goal. But they are not friends. Actually, he hates and resents Richard deeply. That should be useful," Black said.

"How are your other preparations?"

"Proceeding smoothly. All arrangements have been made. Within two weeks, the scandal will break."

"The women?" she asked.

"Arriving on schedule."

"And the stock sale? Is it proceeding according to our information?"

"Apparently."

"Then there are no problems," she said.

"None. I am considering certain refinements, subtle touches, fine points to make everything more poignant and lascivious. To increase the press coverage."

"Excellent."

She smiled. He came over and kissed her again. "Goodbye, Lucienne," he said. "Be careful."

"I will."

"He's a handsome one…"

She looked at Black and laughed.

7. THE RETURN

"Charles, lad! Good to see you!"

Richard held out his hand as he came into the flat. Raynaud got up slowly, setting aside the Sunday newspapers.

"Just arrived, ten minutes ago," Richard said. He clapped Raynaud on the back. "How have you been?"

"Fine."

"Fix us a drink, will you?"

Sandra came in, wearing a pale blue shift, looking cool and very beautiful. But she seemed tired and subdued.

"Hello, Charles. How are you?"

"Fine. Good trip?"

"Yes, very interesting."

Pierce was walking ahead with the bags, going into the bedroom. "Come on with me, would you, love? Charles is going to make drinks."

She sighed, and glanced quickly at Charles. "All right," she said.

Raynaud went to the kitchen and made a pitcher of martinis, pouring straight gin over the ice cubes, not bothering with the vermouth. A moment later Pierce reappeared from the bedroom.

"Hey lad. Did you see her? Doesn't she look super?"

"She looks great," Raynaud said, stirring. He poured drinks and handed one to Pierce.

"Hey, lad, you just believe it. That little girl really does the job. Really does it. You know what they say: French girls know all the tricks, and Italian girls know none of them, but Italian girls are better anyway. That little girl gives you the wildest—"

"Keep your voice down," Raynaud said, looking toward the bedroom.

"Doesn't matter, she can't hear. Besides, what does she expect me to talk about? It's all we did for two days, for Christ's sake. Meals in the room. Never went out." He laughed. "By the way, speaking of French girls, guess who's coming into town? The snapper. I just heard. Remember Dominique? She got a tourist visa—don't ask me how, but she got one, and she's coming to London. Ah." He looked at the ceiling and smacked his lips. "Going to enjoy that."

"What about Sandra?"

Pierce shrugged. "They needn't meet. Besides, two days with one bird, night and day, it gets on your nerves."

"You didn't enjoy yourself?"

"Enjoy myself? Listen, I got rubbed raw. I was on speed just to keep up with her. I'll probably sleep forty-eight hours once she leaves."

He smiled.

"And you, Charles. How did you spend the weekend?"

"With snakes."

"The convention?"

Raynaud nodded.

Pierce lit a cigarette. He did not look at Raynaud. "And did you meet my stepmother?"

"Yes, as a matter of fact."

"When? I didn't see her at the party."

"She arrived," Raynaud said, "after you left."

"Ah." Pierce nodded and sucked on the cigarette. "You found her interesting?"

"Somewhat."

"Did you sleep with her?" He flicked the ash on the floor. "You needn't act surprised. Everyone else has."

Raynaud hesitated. "It's none of your business."

Pierce laughed. "Whatever you say, lad. Did she give you the full treatment?"

"What's that?"

"About me. About how I'm a disgrace to the family and all that rot. About how I've soiled my father's image."

"She never mentioned it."

"Bloody hell. She can't talk about anything for ten minutes without coming round to me."

"Don't flatter yourself."

"I don't," Pierce said. "But I know she's filled you neck-high with stories about me. About her oh-so-good reasons for hating me."

"She didn't say anything at all."

"Charles, Charles. I know her. I know how she is."

"I need another drink."

"We both do. I'll tell you one thing," Pierce said. "Any time you want to hear some real stories, just ask. I'll tell you who's besmirched the family name. I'll tell you the whole thing. Frankly, I even think that she killed him."

"Who?"

"My father. My stepfather."

"Who did?"

"Lucienne."

Raynaud said nothing.

Pierce gave him the drink and lit a cigarette. "You think she couldn't have arranged it?"

"It's very unlikely."

"I'm not so sure. They never caught the driver, you know."

"So?"

"It's just a feeling."

"Listen, your friend Doctor Black was in the car the whole time."

"That's right," Pierce said, "but he's only intelligent. Lucienne is cunning."

8. THE DUPLICATE

"And this, gentlemen, is our prize possession. This cat you see before you has had its anterior hypothalamic nucleus removed cryogenically. Inhibitory influences on rage are thus eliminated. Our attempts to induce a secondary inhibition by shock treatment have been wholly unsuccessful."

The psychology students, all down from Cambridge, all doing their Part Threes, gaped as the cat snarled and flung itself at the bars of the cage.

"Observe carefully," Dr. Black said. "This animal is totally beyond its own control. Further, it cannot be conditioned, even by our strongest stimulus—electroshock. However, there are approaches: gloves, please."

His assistant provided a pair of heavy canvas gloves with broad cuffs that extended up his forearm. As Dr. Black pulled on the gloves, he said to the assistant, "We'll use twenty milligrams this time."

"Yes, sir."

The assistant filled a syringe.

"The cat will be injected with meprobamate, a so-called minor tranquilizer. It is the active principle in Miltown and Equanil. Chemically, it is a propanediol derivative, and its mode of action is still wholly unexplained."

The syringe was passed to him.

"Stand back, please, gentlemen."

The students backed off as Black opened the door to the cage. He reached in with his gloved hand, and the cat attacked viciously, sinking teeth and claws into the canvas. With his free hand, Black maneuvered the syringe in, and with a swift jab, injected the contents.

The cat gave a scream of pure rage as the needle went in. It continued to scream for several seconds after Black withdrew his hands and closed the cage door. It howled in uncontrolled fury, rolled on the floor, clawed at the bars.

And then it stopped.

Quite suddenly, quite dramatically, it relaxed, the muscles loosening. The cat sat quietly and purred. It yawned, licked its forepaws, and looked placidly at the students.

Dr. Black removed his heavy gloves and opened the door. He reached in with his bare hands and stroked the cat.

"Nice kitty."

The cat closed its eyes and purred.

"You see, gentlemen? The cat has responded to a chemical. It is reacting in a way which cannot be duplicated by conditioning. It is producing a manner of behavior which it can no longer produce of its own will. In six hours, when the drug wears off, it will revert to a raging beast."

The students gawked in silence.

"Come along, gentlemen."

Black was giving them a visitor's tour, just the highlights, the most dramatic examples and the most unusual cases. He spared them the endless succession of tedious experiments with limited scope and narrow aims.

"Next, I would like to show you the reverse of the coin, so to speak. In one case, a neuroanatomical deficit, with a presumed biochemical deficit, produced a given behavior pattern— that of uncontrolled rage. Now, however, I would like to duplicate the behavior by purely biochemical means."

He reached into a cage and withdrew a calm, gentle cat. He held it in his arms and stroked the fur soothingly.

"This is Harold," he said.

Some of the students tittered at the name. Actually, the cat had no name at all, but Black always called it Harold for the tours. The students found it amusing.

"Harold is a perfectly normal cat, who occasionally goes into rages. We can arrange this by a simple injection of the drug Dezisen, which is a purified synthetic extract of South American snake venom. It is known to have a variety of neurophysiological effects."

As he held the cat, an assistant handed him a syringe and he injected a milliliter into the animal. Nothing happened; he continued to stroke it and replaced it in the cage.

For several minutes, the students watched breathlessly. The animal lay on the floor of the cage and purred in contentment.

And then, with a frightening sudden fury, it lashed out. It became precisely the same as the first cat, snarling in rage, banging against the bars of the cage.

"As you can see, Harold is now responding to the drug. He will do so for another fifteen or twenty minutes. With higher doses, the response can be sustained for as long as an hour. I should advise you that we have no explanation for the effect at this time; all we can say is that it happens, and that there is very little variation in response from animal to animal. It seems to be quite specific as a trigger to the rage reaction."

One student said, "Does it work only in cats?"

"No. We have tested it in mice, dogs, and monkeys. The effect is the same."

Someone laughed and said, "People?"

"No one knows," Black said, "the human response. But we assume it is similar."

He returned to his office at four o'clock, smiling slightly. Everything had gone well; the students were impressed. In a simple, petty way he enjoyed impressing young minds.

And the early tests of the drug were working out well. They had gotten to the point of taking blood and urine samples from an animal during and after the acute rage reaction. They could find no abnormalities, no excreted end-products, nothing. It seemed to vanish without a trace.

All in all, it appeared to be the ideal drug.

He wondered what would happen when it was given to Richard Pierce.

Personally, Black disliked Pierce. He knew that the boy was fond of him, and he was careful not to disturb the illusion. Their friendship was important; trust was a blind emotion. And it was particularly valuable since Richard was by nature hostile and suspicious.

The matter of the arsenic pills was a perfect example. Richard had come to him quaking with fear, convinced that Lucienne wanted to kill him by poisoning. After a lengthy discussion, Black had said that arsenic was the most likely thing, though in fact arsenic would never be used—the police were alerted to it, and most arsenic victims were discovered. Much better would be an organic phosphate, like an insecticide, or a barbiturate, which would look like a suicide. But Black did not explain that to Richard.

Then there was the business of the tolerance doses. Patently absurd, of course—arsenic had a cumulative effect in the body; repeated small doses would lead to a chronic poisoning and eventual death. Black had been sorely tempted to prescribe real arsenic in the pills, but if Richard died he might have a nasty time with the police. In the end, he settled on plain Librium, a tranquilizer. The chemist made up special pills with numbers on them, and Richard never suspected.

He had even gotten sick on the early doses. Very amusing.

Well, no matter. The Librium couldn't hurt him, and it might keep him relaxed, make him drop his guard. That would help Raynaud.

At five, Black left the research building and picked up his Aston Martin. He was proud of the car, though it rankled him to think he had bought it secondhand. And whenever he saw it next to Pierce's Maserati, it seemed insignificant and tawdry.

He smiled to himself as he turned the key in the ignition. Black liked the Maserati, and it would soon be up for grabs; it would go cheaply.

Certainly Raynaud would not be around to buy it. Raynaud would shortly have problems of his own, major problems. They would have nothing to do with the purchase of a dead man's car.

Burgess, the butler, was on the second-floor hall phone in Black's house, speaking in a low voice. "Yes, madam. No, nothing else. Of course, madam. I will."

He hung up and walked briskly down the hall.

Black peered around the corner and smiled. Poor Lucienne. So suspicious in her old age—but so obvious about it. And to choose Burgess, a doddering old fool who nipped the Teacher's in the evening and then remarked in the morning that the maid must have been at it again. Burgess was as subtle as a water buffalo.

Black had known about Burgess and his daily calls for almost a year. He had made the discovery by chance, but it had not surprised him. Considering Lucienne, it was almost predictable. She was paranoid about men, convinced that they were all out to ruin and destroy her.

Which was true, in a sense, but only in a sense. The interesting thing was her attitude toward Black. Even with the evidence staring her in the face, she refused to believe, to make the final step toward acceptance. She had deluded herself for years.

It had begun with the moment her husband was killed. The passing Citroën had only knocked him unconscious; he was not badly injured, and a few brisk slaps on the face would have brought him round good as new. But Black had pretended the injury was serious, and she had accepted the judgment though her eyes must have told her the truth. And then driving, with Black in the back seat holding his hand over Pierce's mouth and pinching the nose shut with his fingers, until the last heartbeat had died away....

Lucienne had known all along. She must have known.

Actually, Black had not planned the accident. It had been in the back of his mind, but he had not planned it, and when it had happened and the Citroën sped away, he had reacted quickly and smoothly. In a matter of minutes, Pierce was dead and Black could begin the tiresome charade of mouth-to-mouth respiration and rubbing the limbs. The ministrations served another purpose as well: they kept the corpse fresh-looking for the half-hour ride to the hospital.

A fresh-looking corpse, he knew from experience, was important.

9. A FURTHER ADVANCE

"It's a bad idea," Raynaud said.

"Bloody hell," Pierce said.

"Too many people. Too hard to keep track of you."

"Bloody hell," Pierce said.

"Anyone would have a dozen opportunities. I would be powerless to stop them."

"Listen," Pierce said. "You were hired to protect me, not ruin my life."

"I'm just telling you, is all. It's a bad idea."

"And I'm paying you five hundred a day to look after me. Anywhere I go."

Raynaud sighed. "How many will be there?"

"Fifty. A hundred. I don't know."

"Many people know you're going?"

"Some."

"No," Raynaud said.

"Now look, lad, you can carry this thing too far. I intend to go to the party. Susan Locke is a dear friend."

Susan Locke was the owner of a new boutique, The Chastity Belt, which was opening on King's Road in Chelsea. Pierce had been fiddling with the invitation all day, playing with it, staring at it.

"No," Raynaud said.

"Not only that," Pierce said, "but I intend that you should have some fun. I want you to take a girl yourself."

"No. Impossible."

"It will improve your spirits."

"It will decrease your chances of survival."

"Charles, for Christ's sake, be human."

"You've paid me to do a job."

"And you'll do it my way."

Raynaud said, "I'd feel terrible if something happened to you."

"Bloody hell. Only because I wouldn't pay you the rest of the—"

He broke off, snapped his fingers, and wrote a check quickly.

"One thousand pounds," he said. "A further advance. *Now* will you go to the party?"

Raynaud took the check. "Yes."

"And take Pet?"

"Pet?"

"Yes. I think she's the logical one for you. You'll adore her. Such a firm pair."

He grinned and dialed her number.

"Pet? Hello, love, how are you? Yes, I know…Did it go all right? Good…Listen, you free tonight? No, not me. Charles. You remember him? Yes, that's the one…Right…No, no, he's not that way at *all* …Yes, he has one. A Sunbeam, I think. Yes, super. All right…."

He cupped his hand over the phone.

"Listen, Charles. She's not free for dinner. Can you pick her up at nine?"

"Sure, I suppose so."

"Good." He returned to the phone. "It's all set, love. Nine. Right? See you there."

He hung up and began to laugh. "You'd better watch yourself, lad. She thought you were a fag."

"Maybe I am."

Pierce just laughed, and went into the other room to dress. It was only five in the afternoon; Raynaud said, "Changing already?"

"Yes. I have to go out early."

"Why?"

"Dominique's coming in at six-thirty."

"Dominique? Listen, you're not thinking of—"

"Of course, lad. She's come all this way to see swinging London. It's my duty to show her around. Besides, she needs the money."

"What about Sandra?"

"What about her?" Pierce said, and laughed. "By the way, it won't bother you if Dominique stays here, will it? She'll be in my bedroom."

"You're going to keep her here?"

"Sure. Cheaper than a hotel, and more convenient."

"How will you explain that to—"

"I won't. She won't ask, and I won't tell her. She need never know, eh, lad? I've got to be at the airport at seven. I'd better change."

At nine, when he arrived at Pet's flat in South Ken, she was not ready. She answered the door in her robe, smoking a pipe.

"Come on in. I'll just be a minute."

She handed the pipe to him. "Have a drag if you want. I don't drink, you see. Tried it?"

"Drinking?"

"No. Smoking."

He nodded.

"Oh, I forgot. You're from Mexico."

He sat down and put the pipe on a table. "I think I'll wait."

She gave him a quizzical look: "Straight?"

"No. Just tired. It'll knock me out."

"Okay. Whatever you say." She went into the bedroom and he heard her opening drawers. "By the way," she said, "where did you meet Richard?"

"We're old friends. From college."

"Know him well?"

"I don't know. I suppose. Why?"

"He doesn't really seem your type, somehow."

"We get along."

"Ummm. Was this his idea, or your idea?"

"What?"

"Me, tonight."

"My idea."

"That's good. I was worried."

"Why?"

"Because I thought he might be planning something with me."

"That worries you?"

"Yes," she said. "Come in here and zip me up, would you? And bring the pipe."

He took the pipe into the bedroom. She was struggling with a short dress in vivid purple trimmed in hot pink. She was staring into the mirror and tugging at the zipper behind.

"Damn," she said. "I knew I shouldn't have had lunch today."

He gave her the pipe and she sucked on it, inhaling deeply. He worked on the zipper.

"I gain weight," she said, "if I even look at food. Ah. Thank you."

He pulled the zipper up, and did the snap at the neck.

"Thanks awfully."

She took another drag of the pipe, and set it on the bureau. Then she started to comb her long, straight blond hair.

"Yes," she said, looking at him in the mirror, "I was worried. Two years ago, I had a flatmate. Name of Jennifer: Jennifer Olive, her real name, I swear it. She was a secretary at the Swedish Trade Board. A nice girl from Bristol, fresh in from the country. She met Richard and was swept off her feet. Madly in love with him for six months. All she got out of it was three hundred pounds for the abortion, and a goodbye peck on the cheek. He wouldn't even see her off on the train back to Bristol. I had to do that."

Pet finished combing her hair, and began collecting lipstick and tissues for her purse.

"She was a very trusting girl, Jennifer. Everybody knew it and tried to watch out for her. She was only bloody seventeen. Richard didn't care. He got her into that big car of his and she melted. What'd I do with my shoes?"

"Over by the bed."

"Oh, yes. Christ, this damned stuff's taking hold. We'd better leave."

She sat on the bed and pulled on her heels, black patent, T-strap. She stood and twirled for him. "Good?"

"Very good."

"I always thought I was top-heavy, myself. I've had these since I was twelve. Shall we go?"

"My car's in front."

They got in. He started the car, and they drove in silence for a while. Then she leaned back and sighed. "I always feel amorous," she said, "when I'm high. Liquor makes me sick, but this stuff... Do you like me?"

"Yes, I do."

"I'm glad. I like you, too. By the way, is it true Richard isn't coming to the party?"

"Who said that?"

"A friend of a friend, who had talked to Sandra. She's coming, I think. I imagine she wants to see all her friends after a weekend in Wales."

"Oh."

"Something wrong?"

"No, no. Nothing."

She smiled and touched his hand as he drove. "You know what I like about you?"

"What?"

"You didn't pinch my bottom while you zipped up my dress."

"Proves nothing," Raynaud said. "Maybe I'll pinch it later."

"Yes," she said. "Maybe you will."

10. THE INTERLUDE

Richard Pierce swirled the martini in his glass and stared around the room. Question: could you concentrate on the alcohol while unspeakable things went on down below?

He sipped it tentatively. Tasted nothing.

Answer: no.

Dominique, kneeling at his feet, paused and laughed softly.

"You find something funny?"

"No," she said. "Enchanting."

"Carry on," he said, and sipped the drink. Still nothing to taste. Sensation centered elsewhere. Natural enough. She was skilled, this one, the best they came.

So to speak.

Getting blotted, that was the trouble. Blasted and blotted. Five drinks at the airport, waiting for the plane from Paris. Immoderate. What the hell, everybody said so. Image to maintain.

But there was something else. He had planned it carefully; Charles was gone now, involved with Pet and her huge tits. Now was the time.

He moved away.

Dominique said, "Wait! Where are you going?"

"Change," he said. "Put on a party dress. I'll be back."

"A party?"

"Yes," he said, and walked off to the guest room. It took him only a few minutes to find the gun. His own gun. It was hidden —rather amateurishly—in the lowest drawer of the bureau, underneath some shirts. Hardly a clever place to hide it, if he said so himself. Old Raynaud not up to snuff.

He broke open the gun and counted the cartridges. Only five—that was odd. Very odd. He wondered what it meant. He sniffed the barrel, trying to determine if it had been fired recently, but it was impossible to tell. The gun smelled like a gun; it had a cold, metallic, oily smell, nothing more.

Ah well.

He shook out one of the cartridges and stared at it for a moment. Then he touched the bullet head with his fingers, feeling the consistency. Must be careful in such things.

He sipped his martini and decided everything was all right. He returned the gun to its hiding place, then turned his attention to a rather more complex problem: the tape recorder lying next to the gun. What the hell was Raynaud doing with a tape recorder? It didn't make sense at all. It was small, compact model, perfectly suited to carrying in your jacket pocket. From the worn edges, he determined that it had seen lots of use.

Clever, Raynaud.

But what the hell was he using it for?

He sat down on the bed to think about it and to finish his martini. At that moment Dominique walked in, wearing a short yellow dress.

"How do you like?"

"Extremely," he said.

She turned for him; he caught a glimpse of yellow panties.

"But you must take those off."

"What?"

"The panties. Take them off."

"Why?"

"They are forbidden," Pierce said, "at the party we are going to."

11. THE OPENING

The party was held in an immense, high-ceilinged room which had once been a Quaker meetinghouse. Now it was bare, except for racks of clothes and stacks of accessories: shirts, sweaters, belts, ties. The entire room was bathed in blue light and an acid rock group blared sound through the walls and corners.

Raynaud got a Scotch while Pet lit a cigarette and puffed it slowly, holding the smoke in her lungs. She refused a drink. When he came back from the bar he saw her staring moodily across the room. He followed her gaze and saw Sandra, talking with a group of six or seven girls.

"Bad," Pet said. "Very bad."

"What?"

"The whole scene. Look at her."

"I am. She looks fine."

"Then you should have some of this," She waved the cigarette. "You'd see it differently. Look at her face, she's afraid."

"That's silly. Why should she be afraid?"

"She is," Pet said. "Are you sure Richard isn't coming to-night?"

"Of course." Raynaud checked his watch. It was already ten-thirty.

"I hope you're right," Pet said.

A few minutes later, he was introduced to the owner. Susan Locke. She turned out to be a heavily endowed blonde wearing a military-cut jacket which reached barely to her thighs.

"Gorgeous to have you," Susan Locke said.

"Thank you," Raynaud said.

"Don't thank me," Susan said. "Not yet."

She wandered off. Pet stared after her. "Poor Susan. Such a lost soul. But a good business sense."

Raynaud looked at her legs. "Yes."

All the girls at the opening wore short skirts; if they showed more leg they'd be arrested for obscenity—or catch a cold. "Wrong climate for clothes like this," he said.

"You complaining?"

"Never," he said.

Above the dressing rooms was a large, purple sign: UNDER-WEAR IS IMMORAL.

Half an hour later, Pet had wandered over to join a small group passing the cigarettes in a corner. Raynaud got hooked into a conversation with an intense Indian reading PPE at Oxford. He was grateful when Sandra came over.

"Charles." She took his arm. "I didn't expect you to be here. Come, we must talk."

She steered him away from the Indian.

"I thought you needed help," she said.

"I did, I did." He smiled. "Very expertly done."

"Oh, he's a crashing bore. Well known. He comes to all the parties and searches for a new face, then grabs him. He always says the same thing to everybody. Was he talking about Chandrigar again tonight?"

"Yes, as a matter of fact, he was."

"Terrible person. These Commonwealth students can be deadly. Will you get me another drink?"

"Certainly."

"Cinzano."

They walked to the bar. He made it for her. In a far corner, he heard a loud voice say, "And I think he's a *ghastly* writer, and a bugger besides."

Sandra took the drink with a smile. She was wearing a simple linen A-line with a low bodice.

"You look rested," he said.

She paused, then said: "Where is Richard?"

"I don't know. At the flat, I suppose."

"I just called there."

"Perhaps he's sleeping."

She shook her head. "I wish you'd tell me."

"I would, if I knew. Maybe he went down to his local for a drink."

At that moment, with a drunken shout of greeting, Richard

burst stumbling into the room. Cradled under his arm was Dominique, laughing and clutching him as he almost fell.

Sandra looked over. Her eyes turned cold. "I see," she said.

At the door, Richard was leaning against the wall, drinking from a flask. A thin yellow stream trickled down his chin, staining his collar. Dominique was laughing. She wore a yellow, lasciviously tight dress with a ruffled skirt.

"Whose side are you on?" Sandra asked Raynaud.

"Hey, everybody," Richard was shouting. "Here she is, the sexiest bit in creation. And she has a *tattoo,* to prove it!"

Raynaud turned away and looked at Sandra. "Yours," he said.

"I may need your help later." Her voice was steely calm. He marveled at her self-control. There was no trembling, no cracking of her voice, no outward display at all.

Richard saw them and staggered over. "Well, well, well," he said, looking from one to the other. "Well, well, well."

"Hello, Richard," Sandra said.

"If this isn't a pretty sight. My best man and my fiancée. My lovely little wop fiancée. Having a quiet drink together. And she says to me, 'Hello, Richard.' Isn't that lovely? What's the matter, sweets? I remember when it used to be Dickie-bird. I remember all the other things you used to say when you were kissing it. I distinctly remember, in fact—*distinctly*, I tell you— I distinctly remember one particular little word you used. Do you remember?"

"Be quiet, Richard. You're drunk."

"What do you say, San? Should I tell my best man here what the word was? Or have you already whispered it into his ruggedly masculine ear?"

"Richard, go away. You're drunk."

"Drunk? *Drunk?* Me? Don't be absurd. I'm not drunk. I am pleasantly high. I am on top of the world....Oh, I say. I'm sorry. I haven't introduced you. Dominique, meet my fiancée. Miss Sandra Callarini. She had a word for me, you know. And I had a word for her. It was a French word, and it fitted perfectly."

He laughed, leaned over, and kissed Dominique wetly on the mouth.

Raynaud said, "All right, Richard. Take it easy."

"Take it easy? Lad, I couldn't do anything else. A few minutes ago, I could have gotten down on this nice rug here, this beautiful Persian rug, and given you a dazzling spectacle. But in the meantime—in the *mean*time—I have been temporarily discharged. I can do nothing but take it easy."

Raynaud glanced at Sandra. She was pale, staring straight forward, her body tense. He wanted to hit Pierce, and felt his fists clenching.

"Oh, say, look at that. Our friend is all worked up. I do believe he's going to strike me." Pierce released Dominique and walked up to Raynaud. "I do believe it. He'd like nothing better than to strike me. He's wanted to for years, for years and years. But he won't. You know that? He won't touch me. And you know why? He can't afford it. That's why."

Raynaud smelled whisky. He looked at Richard's red, sweating face.

"Go away."

"Dismissing me, eh? Ordering me about, eh? Pretty big man. Pretty big man."

He turned from Raynaud to Sandra. His face softened in a drunken parody of tenderness. "Oh, Sandra dear. You look so hurt, so shocked. Can't you understand? Isn't it quite simple? I simply couldn't bear to spend another day with you. Not one more day, not one more lay. No indeed. I had had my fill of you. Sweet, *sweet* Sandra."

Richard burped, and then laughed.

Raynaud suddenly became aware of the party around him, which had turned silent. Everyone was watching. Raynaud said, "That's enough, Richard. Get yourself a drink."

"A drink? You want to get me drunk? You son of a bitch, I'm going to teach you a lesson. I'm going to whip you here and now—"

He started to unbuckle his belt, but Dominique, standing back, had been watching Raynaud and sensed the seriousness of the situation. She grabbed Richard's arm. "Come on, Richard."

"No, leave me alone. I'm going to beat that son of a bitch—"

"Richard, come."

She tugged. Richard lost his balance and fell heavily on the floor. He sat for a moment and stared stupidly at the carpet, tracing the pattern with his fingers.

Dominique said, "I'm sorry for this." To Sandra, she said, "I didn't know. I'm sorry."

Richard struggled to his feet. He was still angry, but the fall seemed to have subdued him. He glared at Raynaud, and brushed off his jacket, and walked away.

The party became noisy again, supplied with a new topic of discussion.

Sandra said, "Do you have a cigarette? A straight one?"

"Yes." He lit it for her. Her hands were trembling. "You all right?"

"I will be. I think I need a drink."

"I'll get you one."

"No. Not here."

"All right. Let's go somewhere else." He looked around for Pet, to tell her, but he could not see her anywhere. The hell with it. "Let's go," he said. "Did you bring a coat?"

"No."

They slipped out of the party. He thought they did it unobtrusively, but just as he stepped out the door, he looked back and saw Richard, leaning against the bar, watching.

There was a slight misty rain outside. They got in the car and he started the windshield wipers, and said, "Where to?"

"I don't care. Some place quiet."

He put the car in gear. "You have anywhere in particular in mind?"

"We could go to my flat." Her voice was calm.

He glanced over. She was staring directly forward, watching the rain on the windshield.

"Let's go somewhere else."

"My flat is logical. It's quiet. We can relax there."

"Are you sure you want to?"

"Yes. I'm sure."

"All right. Where is it?"

"In South Ken. Off Gloucester Road."

As he started up Euston Road, she said, "You don't mind, do you?"

"No," he said.

"I have a terrible headache." And she said nothing more until they arrived.

To the right was Sandra Callarini, biting her thumb with even, sharp white teeth. To the left was Sandra Callarini in a bikini, laughing in the sunlight. Straight ahead was Sandra Callarini with her hair elegantly coiffed, her lips pouting. Alongside was Sandra Callarini looking surprised and amused, her mouth forming an *o*.

"Well," he said, looking at the pictures. They were all two feet by three feet, matte black-and-white enlargements. "How long have you had these?"

"A year. The studio made me: I'm supposed to be a narcissist or something. Part of the whole thing. I hardly notice them anymore."

She stood beside a giant head portrait of herself biting her thumb. In the flesh she seemed small and fragile.

"You photograph well."

"So they say. But I act badly. You take Scotch, if I remember."

"Yes. On ice, if you have it."

"Coming up." She tried a smile, a brave one, and went into the next room to make the drinks. He wandered from one photograph to the next, examining them.

"I'm sorry about tonight," he said.

"It's all right. In a way, I expected it."

She gave him his drink, and put her own on the table while she set a stack of records on the phonograph in the corner. A moment later, the music clicked on. Romantic violins, muted.

"Sandra—"

She sat on the sofa and said, "Sit over there, so I can see you. Talk to me."

"About what?"

"About Mexico. I've never been."

Mexico seemed very far away. He said so. He watched her and saw that she was still calm, still controlling herself.

"It's not so far," she said. "Tell me."

He told her a little bit about what he did, about the expeditions and the natives. For a while she seemed to be paying attention as she sipped her drink. Later, she looked away toward a corner of the room and frowned.

He stopped. "Still with me?"

"That bastard," she said. "That rotten bastard."

"I'm sorry."

"It wasn't your fault," she said. "I blame myself. Another drink?"

"I should be going."

"No, you shouldn't. I'll never forgive you if you leave me now."

She took his glass and mixed him another, and a second for herself. She did not seem drunk, or even slightly high.

"You may not believe this," she said, "but at one time I really loved Richard. Or thought I did. He can be considerate and gentle when he wants to. And although he had occasional... outbursts I felt it was because of his family. He's had an unhappy family life, you know."

"I've heard."

"Enough to make anyone peculiar at times. I disregarded all the signs, all the evidence..."

"You can't blame yourself."

"That bastard," she said. She lapsed into Italian, and swore fluently for several minutes. Finally she stopped, out of breath. "I hope you didn't understand that."

He smiled. *"Tutto."*

"You speak Italian?"

"Si. Scusi."

She laughed, and said in Italian, "That's really very funny."

"I learned a long time ago," he said in Italian.

"Where? Your accent is good."

"Florence. Rome. Naples."

"You have been to Naples?"

He nodded.

"I was born there," she said. "Or did I tell you? I went to

school and was studying physics—do you believe it?—when I won a beauty contest. It was a joke. And then there was a screen test…"

"Very lucky."

"Perhaps. But I have been in England now two years, with the films. I would like to go back."

"Will you?"

"I doubt it." She frowned. "That bastard doesn't speak a word of Italian. I tried to teach him, but he pays no attention."

"He's not a student."

"And you look like less of a student. It's odd, isn't it? The way people look, and the way they are. Most people see me, and they think one thing. Bed."

"You resent that?"

"Sometimes. The trouble is a man can see your body, and not your mind."

"Most women would willingly trade bodies with you."

She snorted. "Look at those photographs. Is that a sexy body? That's plucked eyebrows and shaved legs and makeup and beauty parlors. There isn't a person there at all. You know," she said, "sometimes I walk into a room, and I see the men stare, and I am pleased. In my heart I am pleased because I am Italian and I love the stares. But sometimes I want to scream at them: talk to me, I am a person, I am alive."

He smiled.

"I sound stupid, I know. But I cannot help it. It is a cliché, the actress who wants to talk, not make love. But it is true, too."

"I know," he said.

"My mother thought I was going to hell, to live in sin. My father thought the same thing, but he was glad, because he knew I would make a lot of money and buy him a new house, and clothes…"

He let her talk, not interrupting.

"And it is so cold here, the climate, the people, everything so cold."

"Why don't you go back? For a vacation, at least."

"You're sweet." She gave him a direct look, her eyes steady, the meaning unmistakable.

"Look, Sandra, it's late and I really should be going." He
started to rise, but she got up and pushed him back.

She stood over him, holding the empty glass in her hand.
Her hair fell softly over her face. "I won't beg you."

"All right. I'll stay: for one more drink."

"Thank you."

When she gave him his third drink, she sat on the arm of his
chair and stroked his hair.

"Sandra, this is foolish."

She leaned over and kissed him. He was unprepared for the
shock, the softness, gentleness of her mouth. It took him a moment to find the energy to break away.

"Please, sit over there."

Silently, she did as he asked. She smoothed out her skirt
over her legs and said, "Are you trying to be virtuous?"

"No. Just avoiding something messy."

She threw her head back defiantly. "I never regret anything.
Not even Richard: I do not regret him. I knew all along, and I
think I learned from him."

He was feeling uncomfortable; he finished his drink hurriedly,
and stood to go. It was then that she reached out and kissed him,
and he stood very still.

"Charles," she said, "you cannot help it. I am seducing you."

"I know," he said, with a nervous laugh.

"Then do not fight me. I cannot bear to be humiliated twice
in one night."

Afterward she looked away from him. The rain had stopped, but
the window was covered with a fine mist which scattered the
light from the streetlamp. He looked at her strong profile and
her soft hair. He bit her earlobe.

"Unhappy?"

"No. Thinking."

"About what?"

"About men, and what you can tell. You cannot hide anything
here. It all comes out. He was such a bastard to me."

"Forget about him."

"I'm trying," she said, "but you only made it worse. You were too nice."

"Maybe I should slap you around," he said.

"That's what he did," she said. "And the biting. He bites everything. Breasts, bottom, your legs. He even bit my toes until I screamed."

"But you didn't leave."

"No," she said. "Instead, I made excuses in my mind. His mother, his father, his uncle."

"Have you met him?"

"Oh, yes. I met them all."

"What did you think of Uncle John?"

"He frightens me. The eyes, especially. There is no warmth to them, no feeling, no sense of humanity."

"Richard likes him."

"Richard would. They are two of a kind, with women."

"Why do you say that?"

"It is a long story," she said. "And you must be tired."

In fact, he was not. He felt relaxed and good, but awake.

"No. A little hungry, maybe."

"Would you like some food?"

"I'll settle for a sandwich," he said, "if you will tell me about Uncle John."

"A sandwich? I am insulted. Veal piccante."

"Too much work."

"No, it is easy." She got out of bed, lightly, and stretched "Besides you have made me happy. I owe you something."

"You owe me nothing."

She looked at him for a moment. "I think you believe that."

"I do."

"Then be careful," she said, "or I will fall in love with you." She went to the closet and pulled on a simple dress, not bothering with underwear. Then she padded in bare feet out to the kitchen. She moved with a simple, comfortable grace.

"I could get used to it," he said.

"No," she said. "It would never work."

While she cooked, he sat at the kitchen table. She was relaxed with him; he felt as if he had known her for years. There was a strangely appealing quality about it, sitting there in nothing and watching her cook. He felt close to her, and warm toward her. And then he looked at her face and saw the fine features, the beauty, the eyes that were made to stare into a camera, and knew that she was right: it would never work. And a part of him was astonished that she had known this so instinctively.

"Uncle John," she said, "is a psychiatrist, but he is very peculiar."

"He does research."

"I don't mean that. I mean he has strange tastes. There is a rumor that he has syphilis which cannot be cured. It is in his brain, they say. And he is famous in Bayswater and Shepherd's Market, with the girls. Though he has money, he goes only to cheap girls."

"How do you know this?"

"His car. Many people have seen it."

"He's not married?"

"Not now. He was, a long time ago. His wife had money— not a lot, but some. She died under unusual circumstances."

"Oh?"

"The official story is that she had a heart attack. She died a day later. It seemed reasonable; she was in the hospital when she died, and there would have been no question except for one thing."

"What's that?"

"Her age. She was thirty."

"People can have heart attacks at thirty."

She shrugged. "Anything is possible. Aren't you cold, sitting there?"

"Are you saying she was killed?"

"No. But people who know Doctor Black seem to die quite frequently. He was there in the car when Herbert Pierce died."

"I heard about that."

"Doctor Black gave Herbert first aid on the way to the hospital, after he was hit by the car. Only Lucienne, who was driving, did not go to the nearest hospital, in Avignon. She went all the way to Arles."

"Maybe she didn't know the nearest hospital."

"Shouldn't she have asked?"

"She was probably upset, confused."

"Probably. And then there was another rumor. You see, according to the inquest—which was held in France—the car had broken Herbert Pierce's right leg and left arm and cracked five ribs. Yet he was dead on arrival in the hospital."

Raynaud shrugged.

"There was a rumor here, at the time, that he had probably suffocated along the way. As if somebody had held an unconscious man, and pinched the nose and covered the mouth. A very nasty rumor."

"Any proof?"

"None."

"Just a rumor," Raynaud said.

Whenever half a billion dollars died, he thought, there could be rumors. Sly rumors, amused rumors, vicious rumors. No man, even one so apparently outstanding as Herbert Pierce, could amass a fortune of half a billion dollars without making enemies who would pounce on him after death.

"Yes," she said. "There are always vicious rumors."

"You sound as if you believe it."

She shrugged. "I didn't, until three years ago. There was a scandal here. I was not in London at the time; I was shooting on location in Rome, but I heard about it. A prostitute, a call girl, very beautiful, specializing in unusual things. She was strangled in Mayfair. She was seeing a Minister, which was why there was a scandal. But then she was also seeing Doctor Black."

"And probably a dozen others."

"Probably."

Raynaud shook his head. "Sandra," he said, "I agree with you that Black is an unpleasant character, but you can't condemn him on this kind of evidence."

"Looking at his face, I could believe it. All of it. He despised Herbert Pierce, you know."

"Really? Why?"

"Because Black was always poor."

This surprised Raynaud. He had somehow assumed that Black was as rich as everyone else in the Pierce family.

"His whole side of the family was poor, though well educated. Pierce was poorly educated but wealthy. He was lucky in business. Black always thought of his cousin as a lout who had gained a fortune he did not deserve."

"Are you sure?"

"Yes. Black was intensely jealous—rather odd, in a psychiatrist —but that is why, I think, he had the affair with Lucienne."

"Black?"

"It was a slight scandal at the time. Another of your rumors. But people were interested, because he was related to Lucienne's husband."

"When?"

"It began shortly after the marriage, and it continued, on and off, for years."

"After she became a widow?"

"Yes, even then. It lasted for nearly ten years, I think."

"And now?"

"Nothing. They are friends. Lucienne's old lovers are always friends. She has the knack."

"I see."

"Have you met her?"

"Yes," Raynaud said. He did not explain more.

"Then perhaps you can see why. She is still beautiful, and still very French. Her list of lovers is endless—she has learned to handle men."

"I imagine so."

"You can be sure of it. She can get a man to do anything she wants."

The veal was finished, and she served it sizzling to him on the table.

"She has endless lovers," Sandra said. "There is something wrong with her, I think. She has had so many. All the famous actors, all the famous politicians, all the famous artists. She has had them all, for a time. Richard hates her, you know."

"I gathered."

"He talked to me about her quite often. He thinks she ruined Herbert's chances of becoming knighted, and receiving a Ministerial position."

Raynaud shrugged.

"I can believe it," Sandra said. "Even now, you will occasionally meet a middle-aged woman who can talk of nothing but Lucienne's shocking affairs."

"Do they bother you?"

"Me? No. But for Richard it was different. It was something to live with. He was always close to his father."

Raynaud almost said, "He hated his father," but caught himself in time.

"Richard used to tell me about her constantly," Sandra said, "in the old days. He would get very excited, very angry. Once, he even said he made love to her himself, but I did not believe him."

"Why not?"

"I don't know. Something about the way he said it. He is upset about her, now especially. He thinks she is trying to have him killed."

"Oh? Why?"

"I don't know. But he is convinced she wants to kill him. He has even seen Black about some poison-antidote pills."

"Richard likes Black."

"Yes. Black helped him, in fights with Lucienne. Straightened things out, smoothed the way. Richard appreciated that, since the fights were usually about money, and since he usually got his way in the end."

"Black interceded?"

"I think so."

Raynaud was slowly beginning to see that things were not so simple as he had once believed. These people and their motives, their drives, were all intertwined in a very complex way.

"How did you meet Richard?" he asked.

"At a party." She finished the veal, and wiped the sauce with a piece of bread. The peasantlike simplicity of the gesture contrasted oddly with the aristocratic beauty of her face. "Everyone meets everyone else at parties. Richard liked me, took me home, and practically raped me before I could beat him away. After that, he was fascinated; he dated me constantly, and I continued to refuse. I was quite astonished when he asked me to marry him."

"Why did you accept?"

She shrugged. "I come from Naples. The poor part of Naples."

She gave him a shy, questioning smile.

"I understand," he said.

They both arose early. Sandra had to get to the studio, and Raynaud was eager to be off as well. He had slept little during the night, but had lain awake, tossing and turning, thinking about what she had said. At breakfast, they were awkward and formal until he got up and kissed her on the cheek.

A car honked outside.

"That's the studio limousine," she said. "I must run."

"Okay," he said.

She grabbed a raincoat, then stopped. "What will you tell Richard?" she said.

"About last night? Whatever you want."

"What would you prefer to tell him?" she asked.

"That I slept on the couch, in the living room."

She smiled. "As I thought: you are too kind. All right."

The car honked again.

"I wish," she said, "that I was still a student at Naples, and I had just met you. You would sweep me off my feet, and take me to Mexico…"

"You wouldn't like it."

"I would have," she said. "Then."

He kissed her, but it was brief and impersonal.

"Thank you for listening to me," she said.

"Don't be silly."

"And come see me again."

"I will."

She kissed him on the cheek and held him for a moment. The studio car outside honked a third time, long and irritably.

"Sometimes," she said, "I feel all alone."

Then she ran for the door, and was gone.

12. POLICE

It was eleven in the morning when he unlocked the door to Pierce's apartment and let himself in. The living room was dark, the shades drawn, the room quiet.

The first gunshot startled him.

Raynaud dived behind the couch, seeing the bright yellow-white light from the barrel of the gun, and catching a glimpse of two figures sitting on a couch in the far corner: Pierce, with a shotgun in his hand, and Dominique, standing in a nightgown.

He dropped to the ground, and heard the sound of the gun being cocked.

"Hey," he said, "listen to me—"

The second shot roared within the confines of the room. There was now dense, acrid smoke.

"Hey, Richard, listen—"

Raynaud stuck his head up over the couch.

The third blast sent him ducking again.

"You son of a bitch," Pierce said, "I ought to kill you. Maybe I *will* kill you."

Still another shot, and then a metallic snap as the breech was broken open.

Raynaud leapt for the door. It would take Pierce a few moments to reload, and perhaps…

To his surprise, the stock of the gun struck him on the shoulder, knocking him against the wall. Pierce had thrown it. The gun clattered to the floor and Raynaud stopped, pausing at the door.

Pierce was laughing, and Dominique tittered girlishly.

"What the hell?"

Pierce continued to laugh, clutching his stomach. He walked to the couch and collapsed on it, doubled over in mirth.

Then Raynaud noticed. No bullet holes. No buckshot scatter.

Nothing. The apartment was unmarked. With the laughter
ringing in his ears, he picked up the gun and ejected the shells.

Blanks.

"Did I scare you?" Pierce said, still laughing. "Did I?"

"You scared me," Raynaud said.

"You poor bastard, you ran like a rabbit."

Pierce's eyes were filled with tears. He continued to laugh.

"You jumped like you'd been goosed. Jesus. Jesus."

Raynaud held the gun in his hands. "It wasn't funny."

"*Funny?* Christ, it was hilarious. If only you could have
seen…" Pierce sat up and wiped his eyes with his sleeve. "Jesus,
if only you could have seen yourself."

"It wasn't funny."

Pierce stopped laughing and sulked. "It was."

"No, it wasn't."

"But they were only blanks, for Christ's sake."

"It wasn't funny."

"You've been too long in the jungle, lad."

"Don't call me lad."

Pierce got up. He walked over to Raynaud, and took the shotgun out of his hands.

"All right," he said. "I won't." He hefted the gun in his hands,
feeling the weight. "Like it?"

"Beautiful," Raynaud said.

"I got it from Harrods. On sale."

"That's nice."

"Did you have a good time last night, Charles boy?"

"Don't call me boy."

"Did you have a good time last night?"

"Not very."

"How strange," Pierce said. "She's usually very good in bed.
Was she tired?"

"She was upset."

"Oh, that's too bad."

"She didn't care for your little display."

"A shame. Bloody shame." He smiled. "And did you comfort
her?"

"Some," Raynaud said.

There was a knock at the door. Pierce opened it and said, "Come in, officer."

A bobby stepped hesitantly into the room, and looked around at the thick blue smoke.

"Sorry, sir, but we heard shots…"

"That's quite all right," Pierce said. "You were right to investigate."

The bobby stared at Pierce, then Raynaud, and finally Dominique curled up on the couch. Nobody said anything.

"Is there, ah, something wrong, sir?"

"Not at all," Pierce said. "I was merely shooting at my good friend, Charles Raynaud. You see, he spent the night with my fiancée."

Raynaud said nothing. His early, furious anger was cooling; he watched Pierce, trying to understand what he was doing.

"Shooting at him, sir?" the bobby said.

"Yes. Blanks, of course."

"That's illegal, sir," the bobby said. "You should be aware that any use of a deadly weapon—"

"Oh, I know that," Pierce said. "But in this case nobody is going to press charges. Mr. Raynaud is my house guest. He is visiting here from Mexico for a few days. We are old friends, you see."

The bobby frowned and sniffed the smoke. He continued to stand hesitantly by the door, not really stepping into the room. He was being circumspect; this was, after all, Belgravia. One couldn't treat Belgravia residents like Cheapside riffraff.

"Do you mind, sir, if I ask the gentleman about that?"

Pierce stepped back. "Not at all."

"Sir," the bobby said to Raynaud, "if you wish to press charges on this matter, you will have to—"

"No charges," Raynaud said grimly.

"You're quite certain, sir?"

"Quite certain."

The bobby nodded and shook his head, bewildered. "Very good, sir. Sorry to disturb you all."

He touched his cap and left. Pierce closed the door behind him, leaned back, and smiled at Raynaud.

"Expertly done," Raynaud said.

"I thought so."

"What was the point?"

"No point," Pierce said.

Raynaud said nothing. He realized quite clearly that Pierce had used the incident to make certain the police knew a lot about Raynaud. It was a bizarre incident; there would be talk among the police; everyone would soon know that there was a strange American friend of Richard Pierce who had allegedly slept with Pierce's fiancée and at whom shots had been fired from a shotgun.

The police would keep that in the back of their minds. Pierce had seen to that.

Why?

Raynaud said, "I have a business meeting this morning. You'll have to do without me."

"Charles, I'm paying you to be at my side."

"You're also shooting at me," Raynaud said. He walked to the door and left, while Richard stood there and watched. As he walked down the stairs he paused for a moment to listen. Quite distinctly, he heard Richard and Dominique laughing.

Laughing about what? he wondered, and continued on down.

Lucienne was wearing a blue silk jumpsuit. Her feet were bare as she paced up and down in the living room beneath the glowering portrait of Herbert.

"You shouldn't have left him alone," she said.

"It was important."

"I'm paying you to watch him."

Raynaud shrugged. "I'm unreliable."

"Charles, for a thousand a day…"

"Listen," he said, "what does Richard know about you and me?"

"Know? He knows nothing."

"Are you sure?"

"Of course, Charles. Why?"

"He is acting strangely."

"How do you mean?"

He shrugged. He was not going to tell her about the incident with the gun. He was not going to tell Lucienne any more than he had to.

"Tell me, Charles."

"It's hard to explain."

She said, "Was he very drunk last night?"

"Yes. Very."

"I heard there was a scene," she said.

He wondered briefly how she had heard. "There was."

"What happened?"

"Nothing much. He made a fool of himself."

She sighed. "As usual. You were with him all night?"

"No," Raynaud said. "I wasn't with him all night. He had a girl and he didn't want me with him all night."

"I see." She puffed on a cigarette, and stubbed it out nervously. "A thousand dollars a day is a lot of money."

"I'm earning it."

"You seem to spend a lot of time away from him."

"Not much," Raynaud said.

"Where were you last night?"

"I spent most of the evening reading."

"Reading what?"

"War and Peace," he said.

"Enjoy it?"

"Too complicated," he said, "for my taste."

The maid came in and said, "It's eleven, madam."

She nodded, and said to Raynaud, "Come with me."

They went to a room painted bright yellow. It was not large, and the ceiling was low; in the center was a padded leather couch, and overhead was a bank of a dozen sunlamps. Lucienne flicked on a switch and glaring light poured down on the couch.

"We don't all live in the jungle, you know," she said, as she began to undress. She did it slowly and gracefully, knowing he would watch. "London is very low on that vitamin, what is it?"

"D," Raynaud said.

"Yes. Vitamin D."

She lay down on the couch and relaxed. At her side was a timer, which she set. A quiet ticking could be heard.

"Ten minutes on a side," she said. "It is like cooking a steak." She smiled. "I loathe being pale."

Her skin was the color of burnt honey. "You're not pale," he said. And then he remembered Sandra's skin, a natural olive, and smooth.

"When I was younger, I would lie on the beach at Menton until I was almost black. And my hair was lighter then."

"You miss France?"

"I miss the sun. Not France. France is a nation tied to the past, still dreaming of Napoleon. When I think of my father…"

She lapsed into silence.

"In Lyon?"

"Yes. He was a military man, a colonel. Very strict. He did not smoke or drink, and when he was angry, he would beat us. With his brass-tipped cane. Sometimes he even beat my mother."

"When did you leave home?"

"When I was fourteen. I met a nice boy and stayed with him. Not all night, just until midnight. Then I went home, feeling strange and happy and womanly. My father—he was very sick then—was waiting with his cane. I took one look and ran away."

"Have you gone back?"

"No. Never. Sometimes I write to my mother, and sometimes I send her money. But I have no desire to go back to Lyon."

Raynaud leaned against the wall. He was silent, thinking about Sandra and what she had said.

A buzzer sounded. Lucienne reset the timer and turned on her stomach.

"They say it gives you cancer," she said, "but I am not worried."

He said nothing, still thinking.

"You're very quiet, Charles."

"Thinking."

"About what?"

"Richard."

She arched her back into a hard, sensual curve beneath the hot white light of the sunlamps. "Charles," she said, "I have an itch. Would you scratch it?"

13. TRUSTED MEN

When he was gone she sat in the living room and brushed her hair and thought about what had happened. Charles was not a fool, not a fool at all. He had come back to her because he smelled a rat. A dozen rats.

Perhaps she had made a mistake, bringing him to England. He was too clever for this job; she needed someone slow and simple, someone who did not think too much, or too clearly.

And yet she knew he was perfect. Basically, he was the ideal man. If he were alive at the end of it all—and she was certain he would see to that—then it was important that he should be intelligent. The police would not believe it otherwise. It would look too arranged, too much like a gaudy still life. The police would be suspicious. But with a man like Charles, a clever, elusive, intelligent man—and an alien on top—the whole business would become reasonable.

Sordid and reasonable.

Well, she thought, it was rapidly becoming sordid. The girl, Sandra, was a stroke of luck. She knew that he had slept with her, and was amused that he would not tell her. Was it caution, or a sense of honor? Amusing in either case.

But it was good, because there would be tension between Richard and Charles over the girl. Real tension.

And the reports of the other scenes she had received were equally encouraging. The party where Richard had made a proper ninny of himself, fighting with that agent. A lovely scene; all London was talking about it.

Yes, she thought, things were progressing well. If only she could keep Charles on the string for a few weeks longer. Until everything was arranged, and the whole thing blew up.

She sighed. Poor Charles, he really did deserve better. In his own way he was a friendly sort, rather sweet at bottom, and gentle. The toughness was all superficial; it could be melted away. Poor man: for a thousand dollars a day—it was absurd, absolutely absurd.

He didn't even need the money.

She mixed herself a stinger, lit a cigarette, took a deep breath, and called Jonathan. While she waited for him to answer the phone, she realized that she was gripping the receiver tightly, her knuckles white. That was foolish. Jonathan had nothing on her, and she had everything on him. He was in the ideal position —believing that he was controlling her, manipulating her, while in reality it was the other way around.

She didn't need Jonathan. Didn't need his advice, or his help, or his sly, coaxing counsel. All she needed was his drugs.

And, she thought, his friendship with Richard.

When he answered the phone, his voice was soothing. Such an ugly man, and such a soothing voice. It never failed to surprise her.

"How did it go today?"

"All right. But he suspects something is going on."

"We anticipated that," Black said. "Charles is not a fool."

"I know that."

Black chuckled. "He was probably just tired."

That annoyed her. He didn't have to bring that up, to remind her.

"I am well aware," she said.

"And angry?"

"No. I consider it good fortune."

"Yes," Black said, laughing again.

"Damn it, I do!"

"I'm sure," Black said smoothly. "By the way, do you think the girl told him anything?"

"Sandra? No. She knows nothing."

"I think you are right," Black said. "Shall I proceed with the next step?"

She had to smile, listening to him talk. "Shall *I* proceed?" as if he had planned it all, arranged it all. God, what an ego.

"Yes," she said. "I think so."

"When is she arriving?"

"I don't know. Tomorrow, or the next day."

"Then the stock sale will be made late this week."

"Yes," she said. "What did you discover about the Board?"

"Richard is up to his usual tricks. The eight hundred thousand dollars went to private commitments, all right."

"To whom?"

"Three men. Including Sanderson of ITI. He's in for half a million, himself."

"How?"

"Cash, my dear. Transferred in Switzerland, bank to bank."

"Then Richard suspects nothing?"

"Nothing at all. He still believes that Shore Industries is an impenetrable ruse—that nobody has figured out its true purpose."

"Good," she said. "And you're sure the stock sale will settle everything?"

"Oh, yes," Black said. "The Board will advise immediate liquidation."

"Of Shore Industries?"

"Yes."

"Richard will be furious."

"Absolutely," Black said.

"Lovely," Lucienne said.

She hung up and stared at the phone as she finished the stinger. She thought about Richard, and then Charles, and finally the girl, Sandra. It must have given him considerable satisfaction, to have Richard's fiancée. It must have pleased him no end. And she was beautiful enough.

Lucienne sighed. The kind of beauty a girl found at seventeen, and lost forever at twenty-five. A beauty mixed with hope and young dreams and mindless confidence. She would be attractive to him, vibrant and energetic and confident.

Damn.

She had a sudden helpless feeling: there was nobody she could rely on, nobody she could trust. For a time she had hoped she could trust Charles, that he would be direct enough, simple enough to be truthful with her. But no longer. She was back where she had started, alone in a world of scheming men.

Including, she thought grimly, the good Dr. Black.

Once Lucienne had loved Black with a kind of desperate fierceness. He controlled her utterly, and she adored him for it. She was so completely in love that nothing else mattered: the rumors, the sly jokes, even the fights with Herbert. There had been bitter fights, violent, snarling, animal. But it didn't matter to her; it seemed a fair price to pay for her few hours at his side. Those were the days when she still had her young, optimistic beauty. When she still believed in men.

When Herbert finally died, she had been relieved. The manner of his death was a shock, of course—so sudden, so unexpected and brutal. She remembered the swiftness and the way his body had been flung against the fender of the car, and then slid off, leaving a smear of blood on the metal.

And then driving to the hospital. She had wanted to ask directions, but Black, in the back seat with her husband, had said no, go directly to Arles. He had been quite calm as he administered first aid. She supposed the calmness came from his medical training.

They told her gently at the hospital, but it was still a shock. She had sobbed, and later, was grateful for the suddenness. No one would guess her inner feelings.

If she had any regrets, it was what Herbert's death had done to her relationship with Black. Afterward, Black had become more distant, more difficult to reach, and the sex between them went sour. They fought once or twice and decided the affair was over. It had been over for ten years.

She still saw him, because he was related to Herbert, and because she needed a man to lean on. He was strong, you could say that about him. And he gave her good advice on the management of the estate—much better advice than the trustees at Barclays Bank, a board of six grim little men she had never liked.

She could not recall exactly when she had no longer trusted Black. It was around the time when Richard began his business ventures. Jonathan had recognized what that meant long before she did; he had a better business sense, and was more perceptive about people. It was Jonathan who first predicted what would happen when Richard took over the estate: that he would summarily cut Lucienne off without a penny. Under the terms of the will he could do precisely that.

She sighed. How often she had wished that Herbert had put in a clause for three thousand a month—even three thousand a year. But he had stipulated nothing for her. It was all to be left to Richard's discretion.

And Jonathan was right: Richard would be brutal and final in his disavowal of her. At the age of forty, she would find herself without a penny to her name—and she had grown accustomed to money, lots of it, an acquired taste, but easily acquired.

Jonathan had come to her one afternoon and pointed to the house and told her that nothing, not even this house, would be left to her. He was chilling and cold as he talked. He said he was worried about her, thinking of her future. And he began to suggest things.

At first he was subtle. Slight hints, little dropped comments and unfinished sentences.

Later he became blunter. He talked about the will, and the provisions of the will. He talked about the legal problems of breaking the will. On one thing he was firm: Richard must remain alive. Herbert had been quite clear in that. If Richard died in questionable circumstances before the age of thirty-four, all the money went to charities. That clause could not be broken.

She listened to Black quietly, hiding her inner amusement. She did not bother to point out that she had considered the problem months and years before, and had come to several conclusions. She had even drawn up a tentative plan of action.

That was before she heard, quite by chance, from a lady acquaintance in Brussels, that there was a marvelous guide in Mexico named Charles Raynaud. The name instantly struck a chord—and why not? For years after leaving America, Richard had talked of no one except Charles Raynaud. Charles Raynaud was so witty, so strong, so daring, so criminal.

She had decided to visit Charles Raynaud. And she had. Seducing him proved to be even easier than she had anticipated. When she left Mexico, she knew that she had him in her grasp and could call upon him at any time. All she had to do was offer him sex and money. A winning combination, every time.

Charles: she wondered if he suspected, anywhere in the far recesses of his heart, that she had made a trip to the crummy jungles of Mexico precisely to meet him. To plan, two years in advance, this grand show with Richard.

And a grand show it would be. The newspapers would kick it around for months. Two dead women, a smuggler, and a millionaire heir.

Lovely stuff for the *News of the World*. They'd have a field day.

In the end, she would win. That was the important thing. But equally important was the fact that Richard would be finished. And so would Jonathan. Jonathan she loathed with a quiet, steady hate, but Richard was different. Richard was a full-blown bastard.

The telephone rang. It was four o'clock. That would be Carter Burgess.

"Yes?"

"Good afternoon, madam." The proper, well-trained voice was hushed. "I have my report."

"Go ahead."

"Yesterday afternoon, he was with a girl named Julia, on King's Road. In the evening, he had a late supper and retired early. This morning he arose at seven, breakfasted alone, and read the papers. Then he went to the dispensary, where he shut the door—"

"Listening to his heart again?"

"I expect so, madam. He called the doctor."

"And?"

"He has an appointment tomorrow, for ten."

"I see. Anything else?"

"Three calls, one from his laboratory on technical matters. Another from a girl named Dominique, who urgently wanted to see him. And a call from Richard, who told him that a friend spent the night with Sandra. Richard was quite upset."

So that was how Black knew, she thought.

"All right, Burgess. Thank you."

"Thank you, madam."

She hung up, and smiled to herself, wondering what Jonathan would say if he knew she was paying his butler to spy on him.

14. A PUZZLING MURDER

"Where did you go?" Richard Pierce said. He was sitting rigidly upright in the Jacobsen egg chair set in a corner of his apartment. Across the room a girl with dark hair, wearing dungarees, had set up an easel and was painting his portrait. She stopped at intervals to wipe the paint from her hands onto the seat of her pants.

"Out," Raynaud said. He walked over and looked at the painting.

"This is Michele," Pierce said. "She's doing my picture."

"I want to catch his essence," Michele said, frowning and bending over the painting.

"Then just open your mouth, love," Richard said, and laughed.

Michele wrinkled her nose. "You want a portrait of that?"

"It might be amusing," Richard said. He turned back to Charles. "Where *did* you go, old buddy?"

"Out," Raynaud repeated.

"Don't move your head," Michele said.

Richard Pierce held his neck stiffly. He said to Raynaud, "You can tell me about last night, if you want."

"There's nothing to tell."

"I don't mind," Richard said. "Frankly, I'd be interested to hear your reactions. To Sandra."

"She's a nice girl."

"Hell, yes, she's a nice girl. Do you think I'd get engaged to a pig?" He laughed shrilly, enjoying his own joke.

Raynaud said, "Where's Dominique?"

"She went out. Wouldn't tell me where. I'm surrounded by sneaky people, it seems."

Raynaud said nothing. He watched as the girl changed the line of the eyebrows on the portrait.

"Something bothers me about that girl," Pierce said.

"What's that?"

"Her visa. She got a three-month visa. That's not easy for a single girl who, uh, looks like Dominique. They usually catch hell at customs and immigration. Sometimes they don't get in at all, unless they have contacts."

"So? She has you."

Pierce sighed. "Yes. She has me. But she didn't use me. Didn't need me."

"So?"

"I wonder how she did it."

"Ask her," Raynaud said.

Pierce glanced at his watch. "I did. Michele, this is enough. Any more and I'll have a stiff neck."

"But Dickie, it's only been an hour."

"I'm getting a stiff neck already."

"But, Dickie—"

"Call you early next," Pierce said, standing up from the chair and stretching. "Really."

She paused, and dropped her arms. "All right," she said. "If that's what you want." She turned to Raynaud. "I've been trying to get this finished for weeks. Richard never lets me finish it."

"That's just the way Richard is," Raynaud said.

She nodded and packed up her paints.

When they were alone, Richard said, "Nice girl, Michele. Keeps it warm for you. About once a month, we have a time together. Very artistic, that girl."

Pierce glanced at his watch and walked to the window. He stood there, staring out across the street, at the whitewashed houses of Belgravia, set back behind wrought-iron fences.

"Shitty view from here," he said. "Ought to move. Seriously, I'm worried about Dominique."

"Why?"

"I keep wondering where she gets her stuff."

"What stuff?"

"She's an addict," Richard said. "Heroin. She must have a supply somewhere."

"Not you?"

"Hell, no." He frowned, looking out the window. "And how does an addict and a prostitute get into England from France? I keep wondering about that, too."

"You asked her," Raynaud reminded him.

"Yes. She gave me a queer story about some powerful friend in Paris, who arranged it. Very mysterious story."

"Maybe it's true."

"Maybe," Pierce said doubtfully. "But I'd believe her more if she said she'd given a bit to the customs man at Heathrow. Hello. What's this?"

"What?"

Pierce was pointing out the window. Raynaud, sitting on a couch across the room, could not see. He stood and came over.

"Funny bloke in a car across the street," Pierce said. "Looks like he has a—"

The first gunshot shattered the glass in front of them. Raynaud grabbed Richard and pulled him down as the second and third shots crashed into the room. Broken glass fell down over their heads.

"Son of a bitch!"

Pierce started to get up.

"Don't move!"

Raynaud held him down. They waited.

"Son of a bitch!"

"Don't get up. That's what he's waiting for."

They lay on the floor for a long time. Then Raynaud said, "Where was the car? I didn't see it."

"Blue car. Across the street. Looked foreign: a Fiat or Renault or something."

"All right. You stay here. I'll check from the bathroom."

"Son of a —"

"*Don't move.* Whatever you do, stay right here on the floor. Understand?"

Richard was beginning to tremble. "All right."

Raynaud crawled out of the living room to the kitchen, then debated standing up. Not wise, he decided: there might be more than one. The rear of the house faced an alleyway; another man might be there. He crawled into the bedroom, and then the bathroom. Cautiously, he got up just as he heard the sound of an engine coming to life. He looked out and saw a blue car on the street below driving away. He squinted, and saw the license: XJ 1189.

The car drove away without stopping. That meant it was probably one man. Just to be sure, he crawled back to the kitchen and peered cautiously out the window at the mews behind. Empty.

He stood, stretched, and walked back into the living room. Richard was standing among the broken glass, brushing it off his sleeves.

"Christ, what a mess," he said. "You see who it was?"

"No."

"Christ." He bent over and gingerly rubbed his hair. Small bright flecks of glass fell to the floor. "Man could get hurt."

"Apparently that was the idea," Raynaud said. He walked to the window and examined the shattered glass still in the frames. Three bullets had passed through; one of the holes was clean. He touched the cone-shaped depression and shook his head. A high-powered rifle, probably with a telescopic sight.

"Where did the shots come from? Show me."

Pierce went to the window. "Down there," he said, pointing across the street. "The car was parked there and there was a bloke leaning out with a brownish stick in his hands. At least, it looked like a stick."

"The man saw you?"

"Obviously. I was staring at him for several seconds. It was strange, you see…a man in a car with a stick. Very odd."

"Yes," Raynaud said, frowning.

"You seem puzzled."

"I am."

"Come on, I need a drink. A big one. What puzzles you?"

"I'm wondering," Raynaud said, "why he missed."

"Thank you," Pierce said. "Thanks very much."

"What I mean is that fellow had a high-powered rifle, and plenty of time to get off his shots. Also, he was cool—he didn't take off as soon as he'd squeezed the trigger. He waited awhile."

"So what? Maybe he was stupid."

Raynaud shook his head and watched Richard pour the drinks. "No," Raynaud said. "He wasn't stupid."

He was thinking back over the incident. Richard had been standing by the window for several seconds. The first shot was fired, and there was a pause. Quite a long pause—long enough for Raynaud to cross the room and pull Richard down. How long would that be? Perhaps as long as three seconds, perhaps four.

Then there had been two more shots in rapid succession, *after* Richard was down.

Why had the man waited?

There was only one logical answer: the man wasn't really trying to kill Richard. Just to scare him. Or, to convince Raynaud...

Raynaud watched Richard as he gulped back three fingers of Scotch without ice, and shudder as the liquid hit his stomach.

"Jesus," Pierce said. "What a mess."

"You know who it was?"

"Who?"

"The man in the car."

"No. Never seen him before."

"Was he the same man who followed us the other night?"

"No. At least, I don't think so." He poured himself more Scotch. Raynaud watched him. "Who's after you, Richard?"

"After me? Why should anybody be after me?" He laughed. "I don't know."

"Well, neither do I."

"What are you going to do about it?" Raynaud said.

Pierce laughed. "Have another drink, that's what I'm going to do."

Raynaud shook his head. "Call the police."

Pierce put his glass down sharply. "The police? Why?"

"Because," Raynaud said, "someone has just tried to murder you, that's why."

"I don't think it's serious," Pierce said, turning away and lighting a cigarette. "The police aren't necessary."

"Is there any reason why you don't want the police called in?"

"Don't be absurd."

"Then call them."

"And have a bunch of muddy coppers tramping through the flat, acting very busy as they measure and take photographs? And have the reporters as well. The *News of the World* speculating on which of my lady friends planned it all?"

"You think it was a woman?"

"No. But other people might."

"Then it's the publicity you're worried about?"

"I'm not *worried*," Pierce said, "about anything. I just don't want to be bothered, is all."

"If you'll pardon my saying so, you've never been worried about a scandal before."

Pierce sucked on his cigarette. "This is different."

"Why?"

"Because it is, that's all."

"But why?"

"Look," Pierce said, "I can't explain it to you now. But there are very good reasons for avoiding the police and the publicity. Very important and immediate reasons."

Raynaud said, "Your business."

"Uh-huh."

"What about your business?"

"I don't want to discuss it."

Raynaud sat down and said, "If you don't call the police, I will."

"Why, Charles?"

"Because someone has tried to murder you. It's unnatural—"

"For Christ's sake," Pierce said. "If you want to call the police so fucking much—"

He stopped, picked up the phone, and dialed swiftly.

Strike one, Raynaud thought: for playing the song and dance about your business, for hesitating, for beating around the bush, and for not showing the slightest distress—not the least tremor of the hands holding the drink—at the attempted murder. Most people are terrified for hours after a murder attempt. They tremble; they can hardly talk; they mutter and mumble and move in a daze.

And strike two, for knowing the telephone number of the police without looking it up or asking the operator. Nobody knew the number of the police. People simply didn't carry that information around in their heads.

Unless they expected the call.

"Hello," Richard said, "my name is Richard Pierce and I live at…"

Raynaud turned away. This was getting crazier and crazier. Nothing made sense, anymore. Nothing at all.

When the police came, Pierce seemed to lose all reluctance and hesitation to discuss the shooting. He described it vividly, with a wealth of detail—the kind of logical, clear detail that the average man cannot summon up after someone has shot at him.

He also managed to make Raynaud a witness to the proceedings. He made certain the police got Raynaud's name, age, passport number—the whole works. He did it in a casual way, but he did it effectively. The police grilled Raynaud for fifteen or twenty minutes, asking him what he had seen and what he had done. Raynaud told them everything, as it had happened.

Except for the license number. That he held back.

There were four policemen, who spoke in brisk, clipped accents. One was a photographer, who took several pictures. They departed in half an hour, after agreeing with Richard that there should be no publicity, that this was a matter for delicacy and tact.

When they were gone, Pierce said, "Well now. Satisfied?"

"Yes," Raynaud said. There was nothing else to say.

"How about a drink?"

"I could use one."

"You know," Richard said, "I got to thinking, while the police were here…"

"Yes?"

"I've been thinking that you were underpaid."

Raynaud shrugged. But in the back of his mind, a warning bell rang.

"I was thinking that there might be considerable danger to yourself, as well. You are taking a risk. You should be well paid."

"What did you have in mind?"

"Two thousand a day," Pierce said.

"Why?"

"Because."

Raynaud said nothing. Pierce looked at the broken glass, the shattered window.

"All right," he said. "I'm afraid, Charles. Really afraid. I need help."

"Business?"

"Yes."

"You'd better explain."

Pierce continued to stare at the window.

"All right," he said. "I've kept information from you for too long. You deserve to know. But serious talk demands serious drinking. Are you game for a pub crawl?"

"If you insist."

Pierce grinned. "I do," he said.

Pierce informed him before they started, with the air of a man about to climb Everest, that there were seven thousand pubs in London. They began at his local, a pub around the corner called the Monkey's Paw. It was new inside, the decor modern and nondescript. Pierce mourned the passing of the old, dark-wood interior over a pint of best bitter. When they finished the drinks, they moved on, driving in Pierce's Maserati.

Raynaud let Pierce do the talking. He was being very oblique, choosing his words carefully. But Raynaud knew that later, with more liquor, Pierce would loosen up.

"Let me ask you," Pierce said, as he drove. "Why should I be interested in oil mining in the North Sea?"

"Profit?"

Pierce shook his head. "Not a chance. The big American combines are moving in there, along with the major English and Continental corporations. A small company like mine, even managed well, wouldn't stand a chance."

"Then why?"

"Preparations," Pierce said. "Groundwork. I am building a reputation. As a matter of fact, the company is losing money at a fabulous rate. People don't know that, of course. On the surface we are phenomenally successful. But I've poured more than a million pounds into Shore Industries in the last year alone."

"Expensive groundwork."

"Yes, expensive. But worth it."

"Why?"

"All in good time," Pierce said.

He was obviously enjoying himself, spilling out details in bits and snatches, between drinks. At each pub, Pierce insisted they try a different drink, and Raynaud bravely drank them all: bitter, pale ale, brown ale, stout, half-and-half, Russian stout (the strongest beer in the world), a black-and-tan, a tot of straight, a lager and lime, a whisky mac, hard cider, Merrydown, a vodka lean.

"There is an enterprise on the horizon," Pierce said. "An enterprise which none of the American corporations can touch. It will be wholly English, very ambitious, and fabulously profitable. If it can be arranged."

"What kind of an enterprise?"

"It is related to Shore Industries."

"I gathered."

"And the work Shore is doing. Drilling, testing, offshore siting. Logistics to isolated stations."

"I don't follow you."

"That is the beauty of it," Pierce said. "Nobody has followed me—so far."

They moved on, from pub to pub, long into the night. In the end, Raynaud remembered only the names: the Black Friar, the Cheshire Cheese, the King's Head, the Hoop and Grapes, the Printer's Devil, the Griffin, the Magpie and Stump.

"You see," Pierce said, "my father's empire was based on rubber and tea. And the British Empire—it was all contingent on political stability. There has been no stability in Burma and Malaya; most of what he had and built up has been nationalized. The major profit-making enterprises are now mining operations in Commonwealth countries, particularly Australia. There's a copper complex in Darwin which is highly lucrative."

"I see."

"But that was the old way," Pierce said. "Very unimaginative. Simple exploitation of cheap labor and raw materials was fine in nineteen hundred, and even nineteen thirty. But it is not so good now, with all the bloody emerging nations. Not so good at all. Now, it is a question of manipulation of capital already accumulated. Manipulation to new and greater ends."

"Such as?"

"Major, highly expensive, vastly complex technical feats which require organization, planning, and money."

"You are going to provide that?"

"Yes."

"And the technical feats?"

Pierce looked around. "This pub bores me. Shall we move on?"

There were others: Six Bells, Wellington's, the Black Lion, the Prospect of Whitby, the Nag's Head. They lingered at a few, like the Chelsea Potter, which claimed the largest variety of liqueurs and spirits, and the Admiral Codrington, which had more than one hundred kinds of whisky.

"Charles," Richard said, "a little while ago, I offered you two thousand dollars a day."

"Yes. You did."

"Have you reached a decision?"

"No," Raynaud said.

"Well," Pierce said, "the offer still stands. You can have the money in cash, or in stock."

"Stock? In what?"

"The corporation," Pierce said, "that will build and operate the tunnel under the English Channel."

Raynaud said nothing. He permitted himself to show surprise, since Pierce seemed to expect it. He looked at Pierce and saw that Arriz had been correct, and Lucienne, in her sly way, had been correct. It made sense in an absurd sort of way; it was the kind of wild scheme that would appeal to Richard.

"You're kidding," Raynaud said.

"I'm not."

"A tunnel under the Channel? They've been trying to build one for two hundred years."

"And now they will."

"Beginning when?"

"Work will start in July nineteen seventy-two. Completion twenty months later. Carrying automobiles and railroad cars. Transit time forty minutes, as compared to the current sea time of ninety minutes."

"It's all arranged?"

"Virtually."

"What does that mean?"

"That means," Pierce said, "that I began laying the groundwork two years ago. I established a company, built personnel, and made a reputation for myself in an allied field. Shore Industries is geared to shift over to construction of a Channel tunnel at a moment's notice. We have experience, and we have subcontracting skill. We are in a perfect position to manage the entire operation."

"But you're only a small—"

"And we have capital."

"So?"

He shook his head. "Dear boy, we can underbid anyone in the world. I am personally prepared to lose fifty million dollars on the enterprise, if necessary."

"For a piece of the action."

"For a very large piece of the action."

"How large?"

"Twelve percent of corporation stock."

"What makes you think you can get it?"

"When the time comes," Pierce said, "only a few key people will be involved. A half-dozen corporations and their board chairmen. A handful of ministers on both sides of the Atlantic. Such men are, of course, beyond reproach in their judgment."

He smiled.

"But not beyond purchase. I have already spent eight hundred thousand dollars in, uh, private transactions. I consider it money well spent."

"I see."

"But there are many rivals. Many who would like to see me die before I inherit the estate of my father. Many who recognize that I am a threat to them."

"And these men would kill you?"

Pierce nodded. "We are talking of fabulous stakes," he said. "Conservative estimates of cost for building the tunnel range from half a billion to a billion dollars. But once completed, the tunnel will carry five million passengers, one million cars, and two million tons of freight a year. The income from passengers and cars alone will be at least thirty-five million dollars. By nineteen ninety that figure will be doubled or tripled. Of course, long before that the cost of the tunnel will have been repaid. Even with maintenance, it will be a staggeringly profitable operation."

"And you plan to get in on the ground floor."

"Precisely."

Raynaud sat back. "Who's trying to kill you?"

"I can't be sure. It could be any of ten or fifteen different parties—including, if you will excuse me, the French government. The French would like to see the prime contracts go to French companies."

"You want me to protect you against ten or fifteen parties?"

"Yes."

"Do you seriously think it's possible?"

"Yes."

"I don't," Raynaud said.

"Shall we give it a try?"

Raynaud shrugged. "If I'm paid in advance."

"I'm afraid that won't be possible," Richard said. "Unless, of course, you tell me who you're working for."

"Working for?"

"Yes," Pierce said.

"Nobody. You."

"I have reason to doubt that," Pierce said.

"Oh?"

"For example, the tape recorder in your room."

Raynaud hesitated. He did not know how to answer. He wondered whether Richard had found the tape, though he knew it was unlikely; the tape had been hidden in another part of the house, far back in a cabinet over the refrigerator. Still…

"What about the tape recorder? I've had it for years."

"It looks it. But why?"

"I use it in business."

"And the gun?"

Raynaud frowned. "You've made a very thorough search of my room."

"In the line of duty, old buddy." Pierce smiled. "By the way, do you know whose gun it is?"

"It's yours."

"Very good," Pierce said nodding. "Now tell me how you got it, old buddy."

"I took it from the man who was following us that night."

"And you neglected to mention it to me."

"Yes."

"Rather strange behavior."

"I didn't see any reason to disturb you."

"How thoughtful." He sighed. "And what do you intend to do with the gun?"

"Nothing."

"You're quite sure about that?"

"Quite sure," Raynaud said.

Something happened then. Pierce seemed to accept what Raynaud had told him, and he began to get very drunk very fast. He talked wildly and improbably of the tunnel plan, of his schemes and payoffs. Raynaud listened, getting drunk too, but not believing any of it

It was possible, of course, that Richard was involved in negotiations to build a Channel tunnel. It was also possible that he was slipping money to various people to smooth his way.

But it was not possible that anyone would kill him for it.

Businessmen retaliated in kind. There might be a response from rival firms—there almost certainly would be—but murder was simply impossible. Large corporations did not murder anybody. They didn't have to. Instead, they would use lawyers and researchers to find a crack, a flaw, a chink in Richard's plan. And they would set out to widen the crack, wedge it, and split it up the middle. Other people could ruin Shore Industries without much trouble, and they would, the moment they felt threatened.

Which meant that Richard was projecting, puffing himself up to a vast self-importance, to the point of ultimate egotism, where he believed himself worthy of someone's homicidal intentions.

No, Raynaud thought, impossible. If he were the head of a large firm, he would destroy Richard but not kill him. He would apply pressure, would shift funds, would perhaps arrange a scandal for Richard.

But nothing so crude as killing him.

On the other hand, someone had followed Richard, and someone had shot at him. There was no disputing that, though both attempts had been failures, amateurish in their way.

They had more to drink. Raynaud pretended to listen to Richard talk. And all the time, he considered the events of the past two weeks. He had the distinct feeling that something was missing, some vital connection hidden from him.

Caution. It would take caution.

But if he was cautious, he could come away in a few weeks with nearly a hundred thousand dollars.

And smelling like a rose.

When the last pub had closed, they stumbled back to the car, both drunk, both tired. A card was stuck beneath the windshield wiper.

"Damn," Pierce muttered. "A ticket."

As it turned out, it was not. Instead, a small printed card: "LONDON'S FINEST SPECIALTY SHOP/Yvonne, prop." And a number.

"What is it?" Raynaud said.

Pierce laughed. "Want to see the best whorehouse in London?"

"I don't know," Raynaud said, standing alongside the car, swaying. He felt very, very drunk.

"I think we should," Pierce said.

"Maybe we should take a taxi."

"A taxi? Nonsense. I say…nonsense." Pierce bent over the

door and tried to insert the key. He fumbled, making scratching sounds. "Damn lock. Keeps moving."

"Let's take a taxi."

"Taxi, schmaxi. Ah. There it is. Right down the slot." Pierce giggled and belched.

Raynaud got into the car and rolled down his window. He breathed the misty night air, trying to clear his head.

"Now," Pierce said, starting the engine, "you will see Yvonne's stable at work. Lovely girl, Yvonne. About eighty-five and ugly as a wart. But her girls. Ah. You want one, or two, or three, or what?"

"What?"

"What?" Pierce said, and giggled again. He put the car in gear, grinding noisily, and roared off. "Don't worry about a thing. Just sit back and relax."

"We should take a tax," Raynaud said.

"No tax. Taxi. Tax-*ee*. And we shouldn't."

"Why not?"

"'Cause you can't. Not to Yvonne's. It's a secret."

"Oh," Raynaud said. "But she advertises?"

"It pays to ad-ver-tise," Pierce said. "She does it for expensive cars. You know?"

"No," Raynaud said.

"Well, she does," Pierce said. "We'll get there in a minute. See for yourself."

He drove very fast, swerving around corners, tires squealing. He ground the gears with every shift, but did not seem to notice. His eyes had a dead, drunken look, and he laughed a lot.

"Where do you drive in Mexico?"

"All over," Raynaud said. "All over."

"I mean, where—on the right or left."

"On the right."

"Okay, then, I'll drive on the right."

The streets were almost deserted, but there were still a lot of taxis out. Raynaud said, "Hey!"

"Don' worry. We're in Mexico."

"Hey!" Raynaud said. The Maserati had moved to the right side of the road.

"We're in Mex'co. Olé!"

They screamed around a corner and saw the lights of another car approaching them.

"Stupid bastard. Wha's he doing on the wrong side of the road?"

Pierce increased his speed and the other car honked. They came closer and closer, Raynaud seeing it all through a soft, drunken haze. Then at the last moment, Pierce gave a shout and spun the wheel, and there was a lamppost coming right toward them, and a house and a fence, and then nothing.

Blackness.

15. HEAVEN

"Just put him down anywhere. It doesn't matter." Raynaud felt himself carried, and then set down on something warm and damp. He was sure he was dreaming.

"Bit of an accident is all," said a voice which sounded like Pierce. "He was in the death seat, you see. Alongside me."

"Doesn't matter, sir," said a gruff voice. "He goes as a double extra."

"Double extra! My good man!"

"That's it, gov. Take it or leave it."

"Why double, you scoundrel?"

"As luggage," said the man. "It was on the meter, plain as day."

"You regard this man as luggage?"

"That's it, gov. One bob extra."

Raynaud opened his eyes to see a man in a leather jacket talking to a man wearing a towel. The man in the towel was paying the other man. There were clouds of smoke everywhere.

"I must be dreaming," Raynaud said.

"Christ, no," said Pierce irritably. He finished paying the man in the jacket, then tightened the towel around his waist. "Not dreaming at all. That bastard just robbed me of a shilling. Charged you as luggage."

"Me?"

"That's right. You were out, you know."

"Who was he?"

"A taxi driver."

"Oh."

Raynaud tried to sit up, but his head throbbed. Pierce pushed him back.

"Steady now. There's a lump on your forehead. You cracked my windscreen, you know. With your bloody head."

Raynaud looked around at the clouds of misty hot air. In far corners were other men in towels.

"Where am I?"

"The Savoy Steam Turkish Baths," Pierce said, and laughed. "Did you think it was heaven?"

"No," Raynaud said, coughing. "It's too hot for that."

"Better relax," Pierce said. "You've had quite a jolt."

Raynaud lay back and breathed the hot moist air. "What happened?"

"We seem to have met up with a telephone pole. We clearly had the right of way, but these things can be so stubborn…"

"How's the car?"

"Left fender dented, and a crimp in the bonnet. Nothing that won't be set right in a day or so."

"That's good," Raynaud said.

"How do you feel, old buddy?"

"Nothing," said Raynaud, "that won't be set right in a month or so."

After the bath, he found he was able to walk. They had a shower, then a rubdown, and then were shown to private beds. He fell immediately asleep, and was only awakened by the redolent smell of eggs and bacon.

"Breakfast, sir," said a boy, leaving the tray by the door. Raynaud looked around, and the boy's eyes widened in horror. "I say, sir…"

"Yes?"

"Have you hurt yourself? Your head…" He touched his own forehead.

Raynaud got up and looked in a mirror standing over a washbasin. In the center of his forehead was a large, puffed, purple bruise.

"Don't mind that," he said. "I swallowed an egg, and it went down the wrong way."

"Yes, sir," said the boy, not cracking a smile. He left the room.

Raynaud turned to his breakfast and discovered that he was starved. Though his joints were stiff and his head ached, the rest of his body seemed all right. Lucky, he thought. Damned lucky. He might have been killed, or in the hospital for months.

Pierce came in, smiling. "Feel better, old buddy?"

"Just great," Raynaud said.

"That's good. I was worried about you, for a while."

"Were you?"

"Hell, yes," Pierce said. "Of course, I was."

Later in the day Raynaud went to the repair shop where the Maserati stood, a twisted, wrinkled heap of metal. He walked all around the car, trying to remember exactly what had happened.

One thing was clear: the car had struck a telephone pole. The front end was deeply indented, the hood telescoped back, the paint flaking away from the bruised metal.

But the telephone pole had struck on the left side.

Raynaud's side. The death seat.

He walked around the car a second time, trying to make himself believe the evidence before his eyes. There were no ways to hedge, no ways to avoid the obvious fact:

Richard had tried to kill him.

At great risk to himself. Richard had rammed his car into a telephone pole in such a way as to kill Raynaud.

By accident.

He stared at the sheets of twisted metal and shook his head. Why should Richard want him dead?

He searched for an answer, but found none. And when he left the repair shop, he was more afraid than he had been in years.

16. CHEERS, HELL

Jonathan Black lay tensely on his back as the doctor strapped on the electrodes. The doctor was a thin, severe-looking man, but he was known as an excellent cardiologist. Black had seen him monthly for five years, since his first myocardial infarction. Yet he somehow had never adjusted to the visits. They always made him tense,

"Just relax," the doctor said. He was applying white paste to Black's chest, and pushing on the suction electrodes. "You've certainly had this before."

He finished, and stepped back. "There we go. Just breathe easily."

He turned on the small machine, and watched as the paper began to roll out toward the floor. Black could see the black ink squiggles of the electrocardiogram. The doctor pressed buttons and turned dials on the machine. Then he stopped it, adjusted the electrodes, and started it again. He repeated this until he had covered all six V leads, and had a tracing on paper that was several feet long.

"Hmmm," he said, studying the paper.

Black sat up, pulled off the electrodes, and picked up a gauze pad. He sponged off the paste.

"Something wrong?"

"No, nothing."

Black held out his hand. "May I see it?"

The doctor turned away. "Something wrong with this damned machine," he said. "I thought so all along. I've got to have it looked at. Come back next week?"

Black kept his hand out. "May I see the tracing?"

"It's meaningless," the doctor said, with a shrug. He folded it and slipped it into his desk. "Absolutely meaningless. Shows right ventricular hypertrophy and left axis deviation. No sense at all."

Black sighed. "I'd like to see it anyway."

"Jonathan," said the doctor sternly, "you and I both know that it would just upset you. And you yourself have told me there are no symptoms."

"Symptoms of what?"

"Right heart failure. Edema, epigastric impulse, distended neck veins."

"No," Black said. "None."

"Well then? You've answered your own question." He smiled reassuringly. "But while I've got you here, let's do a chest film."

"Why?"

"Just to complete the picture, of course," the doctor said, consulting his file. "You haven't had one in a year."

"I haven't needed one."

"And you don't need one now," the doctor said, "strictly speaking. But you know the value of a yearly film. Especially in a smoker. You haven't given it up, I take it?"

Black shook his head.

"They never do. Especially doctors. Think they're invincible. How's your angina been?"

"Not bad. I get it once or twice a month, with exertion."

"Dyspnea? Orthopnea? PND?"

"No," Black said.

"Good. You've been following your heart closely?"

"Very."

"Any change?"

"No. Still grade two or thereabouts."

"As long as you're here, why don't I have a listen," he said, taking out his stethoscope. He clipped it around his neck and applied the bell to Black's chest. He had a characteristic gesture, peculiar to cardiologists: whenever he shifted the bell on the chest, he made a little nod with his head, and closed his eyes.

After a moment he straightened, "No change, I think. I shouldn't worry. Do the film now?"

"All right."

They went into another room. A technician was there, a plain girl in a lead apron, standing beside her machine.

"I want an AP and lateral for Doctor Black, Cynthia," the doctor said. He turned to Black and shook hands. "Call me in a week and we'll do another EKG. And we can discuss the film at that time, though frankly I don't expect any change from last year."

"All right," Black said.

"Cheers," the doctor said, and returned to his office.

Cheers, hell, Black thought, as he got into his Aston and drove off. Nothing cheery about that bastard and his little games. Hiding the EKG, throwing off some cock and bull story about a broken machine. That was crap; he would have noticed it immediately, before he had finished the first three lead readings.

Black knew what was happening. The angina was getting worse, the pain coming more often, more sharply. It struck him once or twice a day now, and often so severely that he had to sit down and rest. He carried nitro with him wherever he went, in a small metal box, handy at his side.

He had noticed the changes. Before, he had carried the nitro with him, but had never bothered to take it into the operating room when he was doing experiments. Now, it went with him everywhere, even there.

One severe attack, doubling him over, forcing him to drop the scalpel to the floor, had been enough to change that.

He sighed and lit a cigarette, feeling guilty. He knew he shouldn't smoke, just as he knew he should cut down on the rich foods. But he could not—denial, pure and simple, a classic denial reaction. But hell, he thought, half of England had suffered MIs worse than his and were walking around into their eighties and nineties. His heart attack of a year ago had been relatively minor, so minor that he had not bothered to tell anyone about it. And it had damaged the papillary muscle, giving him a grade-two murmur, but a grade-two murmur was often unimportant. Functional. Lots of people had them.

Black shook his head. He disliked being sick, disliked thinking of himself as a sick man. He regarded it, despite his training and his rationalizations, as a sign of weakness and inferiority, and he had only contempt for the weak and the inferior. He had often thought he should have been born in an older, more ruthless age; he would have succeeded there. Modern man was too overlaid with rules and habits which disguised his essentially bestial nature.

He recognized that nature, and allowed it to express itself. The weak pretended that man was good; only the strong could face the truth.

Lucienne, for instance. She was weak, deluding herself, playing elaborate games to disguise her own thoughts and fears. In many ways she reminded him of Evelyn, his first wife.

Dear Evelyn. She had become so boorish after a time. So infantile, nagging, irritating. She had made it easy for him to give her the rauwolfia alkaloid, dropping her blood pressure to practically zero in a matter of moments. The diagnosis, of course, had been a heart attack. No question of it. A bit unusual in a woman of thirty, but not impossible.

There had been no autopsy.

He smiled. And Lucienne was the same way. Only now there were new and better methods. Air guns, and unusual compounds, complex drugs that could not be traced after death.

It would be almost absurdly simple to dispose of Lucienne when it was all over. And it would, he knew, soon be over. First Richard—an easy mark, a problem so straightforward as to be almost tedious and boring.

And after Richard, a few changes in the will, and then Lucienne. Perhaps five or six years later. Something discreet and logical.

It was all going to be very, very simple.

When he arrived home, the butler said, "There was a call for you, sir. A Mr. Benton-Jones."

"Oh?"

"He said it was urgent, sir, and asked that you phone up when you arrived."

"All right. I'll see to it."

He went directly to his study and dialed the number, trying

to control the excited, nervous flutter in his stomach. Benton-Jones was a member of the board of trustees at Barclays which administered the Pierce estate. He and Black were old friends, and Benton-Jones usually tried to notify Black if something was going on with the estate. Naturally, until Richard took over, the trustees were directly responsible to Lucienne. But Black, through Benton-Jones, managed to keep informed as well, and Benton-Jones, a primly proper man, found it agreeable because he knew Black advised Lucienne on nearly all financial matters, and because he knew that Lucienne without Black's advice was often uncertain, hesitant, and difficult.

It was one of those peculiar relationships Black so enjoyed. Benton-Jones firmly believed that he was using Black to sway Lucienne around to the viewpoint of the board of trustees. That was why he did not mind reporting privately to Black the affairs of the estate—indeed, he felt it was his duty to do so. Black did everything he could to encourage Benton-Jones. He frequently backed the board, particularly on inconsequential matters. This pleased Benton-Jones, and cemented the relationship. And when Lucienne disagreed with the board, well, that was simply an occasional failure of Black's powers of persuasion.

Benton-Jones accepted that.

He dialed the number swiftly. "Mr. Benton-Jones' office."

"This is Doctor Black calling."

"Oh, yes, Doctor Black. I'll put you through."

A click, and then: "John?"

"Speaking."

"Bad news, I'm afraid." He sucked in his breath. "We've just received notification that Mitchell Mining, Incorporated, is selling its shares."

"In the mines?"

"Yes."

"How much do they have?"

"About a hundred thousand shares. That's seventeen percent."

"And they're selling all of it?"

"So we are told."

Black lit another cigarette. He was frowning, preparing his voice to be surprised. "This is dreadful. When?"

"Within the week. A lawyer is flying over to arrange it."

"Christ," Black said. "We can't do anything in a week."

"But there it is," Benton-Jones said.

"What is the current price?"

"For the lot? It's up to eight and a fraction a share, which works out to roughly eight hundred thousand, four hundred pounds."

"Impossible," Black said. "We couldn't come near that figure."

"Yes, but you wouldn't need to. According to our calculations, Pierce Limited needs only five percent. That works out to about twenty-nine thousand shares."

"How much money?"

"Two hundred and eighty thousand pounds," Benton-Jones said.

"What about Horsten, Vaals, and Meister?"

"Our information is that they're eager to buy all they can. We've suspected that, of course. In fact, there's speculation that they initiated all this."

"And they're willing to buy at a higher price?"

"Presumably."

"How much higher?"

"Well, they may drive it up as high as ten a share. Perhaps more, though we doubt that. Of course, there's no way of knowing for sure."

"How much have the Belgians got now?"

"Thirteen percent. They won't buy, but they'll throw in with the Dutch if they're able to pick up controlling interest."

"So in fact, we need at least three hundred and forty thousand pounds. Is that what you're telling me?"

"Yes," Benton-Jones said.

"And what is the advice of the board?"

"We met today to discuss the situation," he said. "It is our feeling that the Darwin mines are a primary asset of Pierce Limited, and that controlling interest should be maintained, if this can be done without sacrificing diversity in other areas."

Black frowned at the phone. "What, specifically, is the advice of the board?"

"Sale of minor holdings in four corporations that may be

safely sacrificed, including the Fiat shares. These sales will amount to something under two hundred thousand pounds."

"And the rest? Borrowed?"

"Frankly, we feel this is a time for liquidation and consolidation, not extension. Interest rates are not favorable."

"But there's another hundred thousand pounds needed."

"Exactly. One has the alternative of releasing all holdings in Pierce Plastics or of liquidating Shore Industries."

"I see. Pierce Plastics—"

"Is doing very well, yes. Extremely well. Projection figures are most promising."

"So that leaves Shore Industries."

"Yes," Benton-Jones said. "It has not done well, but assets for the last fiscal year were listed in excess of seven hundred thousand pounds."

"Debits?"

"Four hundred thousand. Perhaps a bit more by now."

"All right," Black said. He sighed, loudly, so Benton-Jones would hear. "What is the legal situation?"

"The corporation is entirely owned by Pierce Limited and may therefore be dealt with by the board as we see fit. Mrs. Pierce, of course—"

"I will discuss it with her."

"And Mr. Richard Pierce—"

"I'll discuss it with him, too." He lit another cigarette. "I'll call you back later. By the way, any idea why the Americans are selling?"

"Not the foggiest," Benton-Jones said, and rang off.

Black asked his butler for a triple Scotch and sat down, frowning at the phone. Everything was going perfectly, just according to schedule. The people at Mitchell had taken the bait brilliantly.

And they had acted brilliantly.

Normally, a company that planned to sell two million dollars' worth of stock on short notice managed to leak rumors, premonitions, grumblings of dissatisfaction. But this was swift as a lightning bolt. Which only meant that word had been leaked elsewhere.

No doubt, Black thought, to Horsten, Vaals. They could be counted on to drive up the price. Without question, the trustees of Mitchell, Inc., believed that they were acting soundly. They could have no idea that the original impetus for the sale had come from Jonathan Black himself.

It was a peculiar situation, Black thought, and remarkable in its way. For the past five years, the Pierce empire had been regrouping and extending itself, pulling back from the earlier sources of income—rubber and tea—which had been nationalized, investing in plastics, machine tools, cosmetics, and electronics. Much of this had been financed, directly or indirectly, by the copper mines in Darwin, Australia. The mines had been a late acquisition of Herbert Pierce in the last years of his life; the company now owned 46 percent of the stock.

The Amsterdam holding company of Horsten, Vaals, and Meister had been eyeing the Darwin mine for several months. Loosely speaking, they could count on 21 percent of the stock, and the Belgian group would back them with an additional 13 percent. It was well known that Horsten, Vaals wanted to cut dividends and reinvest profits within the subsidiary company itself, Pierce Copper and Brass, Ltd. It was a reasonable idea, but it would sabotage the new and still-insecure Pierce expansion into new areas.

Until now, there had been no danger from the Dutch. The American mining company started by a Montana rancher named Jackson Mitchell had shown no interest in the Dutch plans, and apparently had been content to take dividends from the Darwin mine stock.

That is, until they heard from a discreet and confidential source that the impact of such a sale on Pierce finances would be disastrous. The Pierce empire was overextended, precarious, and dependent on the mines. Anything would be sacrificed to preserve those mines, and the income from them.

Which meant that, however high the Dutch bid, Pierce would bid higher. Pierce would *have* to bid higher.

With the Dutch wanting the controlling shares so badly, and with Pierce dependent on retaining control, the price of stocks would skyrocket. It would amount to a vast profit to Mitchell.

For that reason, Black had leaked his information through a New York law firm. He had no doubt that the trustees of the Mitchell fortune would recognize the implications of a sale at this time.

But it was not the implications of their sale that interested Black. It was the implications for the Pierce empire—with a half-dozen new, burgeoning companies, all doing well. Except for one: Shore Industries.

The logical sacrifice.

To make capital, to preserve the more successful subsidiaries of the Pierce empire.

Quite logical—Shore Industries had to go.

Black smiled as he considered the situation. Everything had gone perfectly. Mitchell had acted according to plan. The board of Pierce, Ltd., had acted according to plan. The Dutch could be counted on to follow through.

Lovely.

Richard was screwed. His dreams of a contract for the English Channel tunnel were ended.

And Richard would be furious.

There was only one last question, and that concerned the girl. It was imperative that the American girl show up for the transaction. That was, he knew, the weakest link in his plan. For any of a million reasons, she might not bother to come.

But if his information was correct, if she were really an unhappy, rich girl living in New York...

He called Lucienne and explained developments.

"What about the American girl?" Lucienne said. "Is she coming?"

"No information yet. But I will bet on it."

"Good. I understand she's quite attractive."

"Yes," Black said, "but one never knows."

"Can you get Richard to kill her?"

"Probably."

"Good," Lucienne said. "What about Charles?"

"He will, of course, be involved."

"Excellent. Proceed with the plan."

Black hung up and called Benton-Jones. He told him to go through with the liquidation of Shore Industries, Ltd. Benton-Jones asked politely if this was agreeable to Mr. Richard Pierce.

Black said in a calm voice that Mr. Richard Pierce was not a consideration.

17. LICENSE

George Longwood, looking slim and proper, pulled the bowler hat down over his forehead and cupped his hands around his pint of bitter.

"Rather like it, actually," he said.

"What?" Raynaud asked.

"The Establishment life. Much nicer than the old days. But it doesn't pay as well, Charlie. Not at all."

"And it's not as exciting," Raynaud said.

"No, but that doesn't bother me. What bothers me is the pay, Charlie. The pay. A man's got to struggle along." He touched his bowler lightly. "Know what this sets you back? Bloody twelve quid, and it's a cheap one. Establishment life is frightfully dear."

"All right," Raynaud said, sighing. "How much?"

"Well, look," Longwood said. "The first time, checking out the gun. That was all right, for old times' sake. A friendly favor. But now, with the license. That was a bit sticky, what with everyone snooping about in the vehicle bureau. Bit sticky."

"Name your price."

"Fifty quid?"

"Done," Raynaud said. He reached into his pocket.

"Not *here*," Longwood hissed, in a horrified voice. "Not in public. I'm a civil servant, you know."

Raynaud took his hand out of his pocket. "I'll send it to you."

"No, you'll give it to me outside. Up the street and around the corner."

"And the information?"

"Then," Longwood said. "And only then."

Raynaud finished his drink, pushed two shillings across the counter, and stood. "See you."

"Right."

He walked outside, into the noon sun, suppressing a smile.

When he got to the corner, he paused and lit a cigarette. Long-wood joined him a moment later.

"Well, then," Longwood said.

"Here's your fifty." Raynaud handed him the bills.

"Well, then," Longwood said, slipping them into his pocket. "Take a walk?"

"Certainly."

They walked through the back streets east of Trafalgar Square. It was an area of drab government buildings, the headquarters of all the civil service agencies.

"That shooting at the Pierce flat," Longwood said. "It's gotten high priority. Don't ask me how. But it's being investigated like hell."

"Interesting."

"If I were you, I'd be careful."

"Oh?"

"Yes, Charlie. Because you're being investigated as well."

"Doesn't matter," Raynaud said. "I'm clean."

"Let's hope so," Longwood said. "Now, then. The car: XJ one-one-eight-nine."

"Start with the owner," Raynaud said.

"Woman," Longwood said. "Name of Shelia Ferguson. She's a flash tart. And very chi. Hundred quid for a night's sweat. Never been nicked, far as I know. Anyhow, she hangs out with a guy named Norman. Don't know his last name. Seedy little bloke. Did a bit for burglary, a while back."

"Where do I find him?"

"Battersea, most likely. Try the Cock and Hen. Work it through Shelia, eh? Everyone calls her Kitty."

"All right," Raynaud said.

"Good luck, Charlie," Longwood said.

He touched his bowler brim and strolled away.

Driving back to Richard's flat, he had that sinking feeling again. He felt like a blind man in a circus—things were happening all around him, but he couldn't see them. All he knew was that nothing added up. Lucienne wanted to protect a man she de-tested. Richard was subjected to repeated and ineffectual murder attempts, which did not really disturb him. Indeed, he practically ignored them.

The worst thing was that nobody would tell him anything. Lucienne was vague. Richard was vague. Black was impenetrable, and Sandra didn't know anything. He wondered, then, about Dominique. Perhaps she was involved in all this; he had not considered that before.

He would have to speak to her, alone, very soon.

Because Raynaud was certain, somehow, that it was all going to be over very soon.

When he got back, Richard was looking grim. "Charles," he said, "I think we'd better have a little talk."

"What kind of a talk?" Raynaud said.

"A talk about you," Pierce said.

"I'd rather talk about you," Raynaud growled, "and why you tried to kill me."

"Kill you?"

"Yes. You did a very neat job, with the car. By all rights it ought to have worked."

Pierce laughed. "You're paranoid, old buddy."

"Am I?" Raynaud poured two fingers of Scotch into a glass.

"Of course. You have it backwards—or is that part of the game?"

"What game?"

"You see," Pierce said, "I know all about it. About you and Lucienne. And your plans."

Part III:
The Venom Business

1. THE BEST OFFER

In a dim, vague sort of way, Raynaud began to see the light. The first small pieces of the puzzle began to fit together, the first minor explanations of minor facts. He was still uncertain about the rest, of course—but that would come.

Particularly if he stayed cool.

He said, "Plans?"

"Charles, Charles. Let's not dance about. I *know.*"

Raynaud sipped his Scotch and sat down on the couch. "Perhaps you'd better tell me," he said, "exactly what you know."

Pierce grinned, reaching for the back of Dominique's neck. "Item," he said. "Lucienne has been acting differently for over a year. Indulging me in Shore Industries. Bitching about the money—but still authorizing expenditures."

He poured himself a tall Scotch, and dropped one ice cube in.

"Item," he said, "Lucienne, who hates to travel, goes off to the wilds of Mexico quite abruptly. Why? To visit the ruins of Yucatán. Quite absurd: Lucienne doesn't know a pyramid from a penis."

He shook his head. "Item," he continued. "Lucienne urges me to go to Paris, and then is frantically insistent that I attend a party given by her dear friend Houghton Graham. Lucienne hasn't exchanged a civil word with Graham for ten years; nobody has, of course, but that's beside the point. The point is that she desperately wanted me to attend that party."

He took a long swallow of Scotch, and set the glass down. "Item," he said. "Who should appear at the party but Charles Raynaud, fresh from Mexico, and a touching reunion of old chaps takes place. Suddenly, quite naturally, you are at my side."

Pierce sighed, squeezing Dominique's neck tighter. "I knew, of course, that you were coming, Charles. That was why I had you investigated. I wanted to know everything about you that I could learn. About you and your venom business. I prepared myself as best I could."

"Item," Raynaud said, "you're not making any sense."

"Oh, but I am, Charles. Excellent sense. Lucienne has hired you, has taken pains to see that you accompany me, without my knowledge. That makes very, very good sense. And I am prepared, old buddy, to double her best offer."

"What offer?"

"Come, come, Charles. Lucienne's offer to have me killed. That's why you're here."

"Is it?"

Pierce sighed. "It is."

"You really believe that?"

"I know it, Charles."

"As a matter of fact," Raynaud said, choosing his words carefully, "she is eager to see you alive."

"Bullshit."

"Think about it."

"Bullshit. She's wanted me dead as long as she can remember."

Raynaud shook his head. "No."

"Then what?"

Raynaud said nothing. He stared in silence at Pierce, who held Dominique's neck in one hand and a drink in his other.

"What is it, damn it?"

Raynaud said nothing.

"Tell me."

Raynaud was thinking swiftly. He planned moves and countermoves, letting them flash through his mind. How much did Richard know? How much did Raynaud know?

"I can't tell you," Raynaud said.

"The hell you can't. I'm paying you two thousand dollars a day—"

"And frankly," Raynaud said, "I don't trust you as far as I can spit."

Pierce stared at his drink, swirling it in the glass. "How much did she offer you?"

"To do what?"

"Kill me."

"One hundred thousand dollars," Raynaud said.

"The bitch. I'll double it."

Raynaud hesitated. "You haven't got the money."

"I will."

"When?"

"When I inherit the estate. And that," Richard said, "will happen if I remain alive."

"And in the meantime?"

"In the meantime, you will have two hundred thousand reasons to keep me alive."

"No guarantee I'll ever see the money."

"That's right."

"Hardly satisfactory," Raynaud said.

Pierce smiled wryly. "If I don't pay up," he said, "you can always kill me."

"Not very lucrative."

"But satisfying, I'm sure. Tell the truth: haven't you wanted to kill me for a long time?"

"Off and on," Raynaud said.

"You see?" Pierce laughed.

Raynaud got up and made himself another drink. He suddenly felt tired; things were too complicated. "There's only one problem," he said. "Lucienne didn't hire me to kill you."

"No?"

"No. She hired me to keep you alive."

Pierce laughed. "That's absurd. You believed her?"

"She wants to assure her guaranteed income of thirty-six thousand pounds a year."

Pierce was stunned. He stared in silence, and finally said, "*What* guaranteed income?"

"The guaranteed income specified by the will."

"There is none," Pierce said.

"Yes. Three thousand pounds a month."

"No," Pierce said. "Look, I'll show you. I have a copy of the will right here."

He released Dominique, disappeared into the bedroom, and

returned minutes later with a gray, cardboard-bound folder in his hand. Across the cover was typed: "Last Will and Testament of Herbert Edgar Pierce."

Pierce flipped through the pages quickly, then stopped. "There are only two important passages. This is the first. It lists all the charities to which the estate will go in the event that the sole heir, Richard Albert Pierce, shall die as a consequence of unforeseen circumstance, medical or emotional illness, civil disaster, national emergency, accidents either on foot, or traveling in any motor vehicle, or by foul play."

He paused. "Very clear on that."

He continued on, turning pages. "The second passage is this one, which says that when Richard Albert Pierce shall inherit the estate, Lucienne Pierce née Ginoux shall relinquish all claims and rights to the estate, or any part thereof, including all properties, interests, royalties, leasing rights, stocks, bonds, common issues..."

He snapped the folder shut and handed it to Raynaud.

"Help yourself," he said. "It's slow reading, but fascinating in its way."

Raynaud slipped the will under his arm, determined to read it slowly and carefully from beginning to end.

"But the point, old buddy," Richard said, "is that she lied to you. And Lucienne never does anything without a reason."

"But why?"

Pierce shrugged. "She wants me dead."

"That wouldn't help her."

"It might," Pierce said, "give her a moment of satisfaction. Think about it." He glanced at his watch. "But don't be too late in dressing. We have a party tonight."

"Another one?"

"This is important. An opening at the Wheatstone Galleries for Julian Weiss."

"Never heard of him."

"Nobody has. But everyone will be there, positively everyone. An opening at the Wheatstone Galleries is not to be missed. Right?"

"Whatever you say."

"That's the boy," Pierce said. He patted Dominique on the head. "I never go anywhere without my bodyguard," he said.

"Tonight," Dominique said. "Do I come?"

"You come every night." Pierce laughed.

"I mean, to the party."

"Sorry, love. This is the boys' night out."

She pouted.

"Sorry, love. That's the way it is."

Raynaud sat in his room, smoking and reading the will. He did it slowly, going over several passages three and four times. As he read, he found himself feeling great respect for Herbert Pierce.

No fool, that man.

For example, Richard would not inherit full control of the estate, but rather would be given provisional control for a five-year period, subject to review by the board which could, however, only overrule him by unanimous decision.

There were other, equally cautious and astute clauses. In fact, the whole will was an elaborate system of checks and balances.

Yet there was nothing about Lucienne's guaranteed income. Pierce was right: nothing at all.

Why had she lied to him?

What did she hope to gain by keeping Richard alive?

He went back over the will and read it more carefully. It was eight in the evening before he found the paragraph he was looking for. The one logical paragraph which made sense of everything.

Or, at least, nearly everything.

It was a long and cautiously worded paragraph, but it was clear enough in its intent. Richard could not inherit the estate if he were incarcerated in an institution of criminal correction, if he were hospitalized for serious medical illness, if he were hospitalized for emotional disturbances or disorders.

Under such circumstances, the estate would remain in the hands of Lucienne and the board, until such time as Richard were released from said institution, or until such time as he died, in which case the estate would go to charity.

In other words, if Richard were in the hospital, or in jail, things would continue as they always had.

That was Lucienne's only way out.

And he was sure she was going to use it.

But how?

As he thought about it, he became convinced that the murder attempts were crucial to the whole business. The sideswiping in Paris; the little man in Soho; the gunshots in Belgravia.

He had to find out about them.

Now.

"What? Not coming with us?"

"I'll join you there," Raynaud said.

"But I might be killed," Pierce grinned, "on the way."

"Doubt it."

"Charles, I really must—I say, you're not going to run back to Lucienne, are you?"

"No," Raynaud said. "I'm not."

"When will it be?" Lucienne said, holding the phone tightly in her hand.

"In two days," Black said. "The girl has just arrived. She is definitely quite lovely. Richard will be certain to seek her out."

"And the death?"

"In two days."

"You'll tell Richard about the girl before?"

"Oh, yes. I'm arranging that."

"Make certain he is furious."

"Oh." Black laughed. "He will be. Don't worry."

When she had rung off, she smiled. She was not worried. Not about Black, not about Richard, not about anything.

Think of it: a vast scandal. Richard, about to lose his little project, because of a stock sale—a stock sale Lucienne had gone to great pains to engineer.

When Dominique died, and the police arrived, it would be a pretty little scene. Richard in financial trouble, and with a dead whore on his hands. His only companion, a smuggler from Mexico. The police would be investigating it for months.

And it would all come out. The bribes, the business, the sly moves, the illegal bank transfers.

She smiled, Richard would be lucky if he got away with twenty years. And Charles—poor Charles, sitting in the dock trying to convince the jury that Lucienne had hired him to keep Richard alive. Such an absurd idea! No one would ever believe him, and he hadn't a shred of proof. She had been quite careful about that.

At the very least, he would be deported. It would be that, or a jail sentence.

And that left only Jonathan. Fat old Jonathan, scheming away. She was certain he had some untimely end planned for her. But it wouldn't work, because she would see that he was implicated in the scandal. It shouldn't be hard. After all, he was the one who would kill Dominique.

She laughed: child's play, all these men. Mere child's play.

2. MITCHELL

Jane Mitchell stood before the mirror in her room at the Connaught and combed her long, straight blond hair. She decided as she combed that she was tired of it, and ready for a change. After all, that was why she had come to London: for a change.

There was a knock on the door. That would be room service. "Come in."

A small, dark fellow, rather timid-looking, peered around the door. "Lait grenadine?"

"Yes," she said. "Put it on the table."

He did, and brought over the bill. She signed it, adding a three-shilling tip. She wondered if that would be all right; she was never sure how much to tip in foreign countries. And the natives always complained that American tourists overtipped.

Jane did not want to be thought of as an American tourist, or even a tourist at all. She wanted to blend into the scene, to merge, to lose herself. And to forget. Forget New York, forget the whole bit.

And particularly to forget Cooper.

She continued brushing. The telephone rang, and she picked it up with her free hand. "Hello?"

"Jane? Peter Dickerson."

She smiled. He would never say simply "Peter"; he would be stuffy and formal until the day he died. Maybe even afterward.

"Yes, Peter."

"How's your room?"

"Fine. Great."

"That's good. The hotel is crowded this time of year, and I was worried—"

"It's a fine room, Peter." Looking out the window, she could see the quaint poulterer across the street, and Grosvenor Square farther down the block.

"Good," he said. There was an uncomfortable pause.

"Anything else on your mind?" she asked, hoping that he would cancel out of dinner. She couldn't take him at dinner, not after six hours next to him on the plane, listening while he made polite, stuffy conversation with his briefcase set primly on his knees.

"Look, I don't think I'm going to be able to make dinner. There are some last-minute things to check before the meetings in the morning. Which reminds me: do you want to be present?"

"For what?"

"The meetings."

"God, no."

"All right, then. I'll call you late tomorrow. Is there anything I can do in the meantime?"

"No, Peter. Thanks."

She hung up and continued brushing. Poor Peter. So polite around the clients, so proper. And he really wasn't bad looking, all things considered. But dull. Dull as hell.

God, Jane thought, what did Mrs. Dickerson do? Or was she used to it by now, after twenty years of solid suburban marriage to a solid New York lawyer.

Well, at least she was free for the evening, and the next day as well. Jane Mitchell did not want to spend her two weeks in London with Peter Dickerson. She was perfectly content to let him handle the business, so long as he left her alone. Anyway, she was useless in discussions of stocks and money; she neither understood nor cared about it. The New York firm of Whitman, Lockhardt and Dickerson acted as trustees of her estate. They were paid to take care of her money.

In theory, they were also paid to take care of her. There was a clause in the will about "moral and personal advice" which Daddy had inserted, and for a time it had caused her no end of hell. When she had been involved with number three, Carter James, old man Whitman had taken it upon himself to drive up to Poughkeepsie and advise her to break it off. Not good for a Vassar girl to be messing around with a producer. Did she know what kind of man he was? How many office secretaries he was seeing, along with her?

She had been furious with old Whitman. Only much later

was he proven correct: Carter was a skunk, a handsome lousy skunk, just as Whitman had said.

But it was to Whitman's credit that he never mentioned Carter to her again, never held it over her head. Obviously, Whitman was smarter than he looked. And Dickerson, too, was probably smarter than he looked. At least, Jane hoped so.

On the plane, she had toyed with the idea of seducing him. He was so proper he infuriated her. He had gone to Harvard and to Yale Law School and had married a Smith girl and had three nice little blond girls that he was fond of, but not too much because he didn't want to give them complexes. Dickerson was so damned logical. He was thought-out. He probably didn't even go to the john without considering the pros and cons first. He weighed everything, including himself. Once a day, he hopped onto the scale. She had been told that fact somewhere after the third martini, and the image of middle-aged Dickerson stepping onto the scale each morning before stepping onto the 8:03 from Darien was so absurd to her, so hideous and so ludicrous, that she began to think of seducing him. It might jar him into becoming a human being.

But she didn't, of course. She had resisted the impulse and had listened to him quietly and properly, with her hands folded in her lap. And she thought about her own father, who had had a high opinion of Whitman, Lockhardt. Her father had once explained that just because everybody in the firm acted as if they'd had a curtain rod shoved up their ass didn't mean they weren't clever and perceptive. It had taken Jane a long time to decide that he had been right.

A year after her parents died, Whitman had recommended selling a lot of stock in oil and buying into some damned firm that made copying machines. It had seemed absurd to Jane, but she went along. Now she had fifty thousand shares of Xerox, one of the fastest-growing assets in her holdings. The other recommendations of the trustees had been equally astute, so that a month ago, when they advised her to sell her stock in Pierce Copper and Brass, Ltd., she had readily agreed.

And when she heard that the stock sale required a trip to London, she had gone along, though it was not strictly necessary.

She could have signed over power of attorney for the transaction. But she wanted to see London, and she wanted to get
out of New York.

She sighed, licked her eyebrow pencil, and started to do her
eyes. No false lashes, she decided. Everything was going to be
different. New eyeshadow color, new lipstick, new dress, everything.

When she finished with the makeup, she stared at her face
in the mirror. She looked good, though tired: still on New York
time, she reminded herself. At least her eyes were not bloodshot.
That usually happened when she was tired.

She went to the closet and selected a dress. She wanted
something outrageous, and finally chose a sheer dress of black
and white checks. She slipped into it and looked in the mirror.
Christ, she thought, it barely covers it. If I sit down, I'm finished.

George would have liked this dress. It would have appealed
to him. But then George was a skunk, a real prick of a human
being. Handsome, to be sure, but underneath a complete louse.
George had been number five. She'd broken off with him two
months ago.

Thinking of George depressed her slightly. She remembered
numbers one, two, three, and four—they were no better. Skunks,
the whole bunch. Handsome, charming, smooth-talking skunks.
Number one had been in advertising, number two and three
were television people—producers—and number four was an
actor. George had been independently wealthy, and didn't do
anything. Except louse up girls.

A real prick.

She hoped to hell she met some decent men in London.

At twenty-seven, Jane Mitchell was a startlingly attractive young
woman. She was very American-looking, tall, blond, and leggy
the way only American girls could be leggy. With a straight
nose and fine eyebrows, her face had an understated, regal look,
marred only by a slight tic in her left eye which became exaggerated when she was upset or drunk.

She was born in Washington, the daughter of a rough Montana
miner and a Boston socialite intrigued by blood more red than

blue. As a young girl, Jane was subjected to conflicting influences
—the social correctness of her mother, and the earthy directness
of her father—and managed to find a happy medium. She was a
good student, attending Concord Academy and Vassar College,
from which she graduated Phi Beta Kappa in French history.

A year after she left college, her parents were killed in a
small-plane crash in Jamaica. To get her mind off the tragedy,
she took up modeling, and rapidly became one of the most successful models in New York. Most Americans had seen her as the
girl who claimed new Cold-Power Whiz made clothes "Brighter
than white, whiter than bright." Still others had seen her demon-
strating the advantages of Creamy Delight, a pushbutton whipped
cream with less than one calorie per serving ("Slims you down…
down…down…").

Then there was a little summer stock, playing the part of Julie
in *Windsong*, at Westport. That was where she had met number
four, and the experience had permanently soured her on theater;
she had refused all offers for the next year.

She preferred commercials, and it amused her that they were
all successful, making her a good deal of money. Just before
leaving New York, she had shot one for Trend ("For the taste
that's clean as mountain air") and for Easy-Stretch bras ("Lifts
here, firms here"). It was fun. A bit mindless, perhaps, but fun.

Like the party, she thought, turning the invitation over in
her hands. It had been waiting for her when she arrived in the
hotel—a carefully engraved card, silver on linen, which said:

YOU ARE CORDIALLY INVITED TO ATTEND

AN OPENING

AT

WHEATSTONE GALLERIES

FOR

MR. JULIAN WEISS

PAINTER

8:30 TO MIDNIGHT

Improprieties encouraged

She flicked the card with her thumb. What the hell, she thought. It would be amusing; she would go. But she wondered who had sent it to her. Nobody knew she was going to be in London.

Except for one person.

Charles Raynaud.

She smiled: it would be amusing.

3. INFORMATION

Raynaud waited until he had finished his second beer before he spoke to the girl next to him. He had wanted to watch the pub for a time. The Cock and Hen, a battered place in the worst part of Battersea. Filled mostly with laborers and young, pimply-faced kids in outrageous clothes. One or two tarts. A strange group.

There was a tart sitting next to him. A tough, long, lean creature with long black hair and a short black dress. She had very large, hostile eyes and a sneering mouth. He could guess her specialty.

She noticed him looking at her and cocked her eyebrow. "Want a bit, love?"

"Maybe."

"It's ever so nice."

He nodded and bought her a drink.

"Just round the corner, love. Right conven'nt, it is. Interested?" She put her hand in his lap.

"What's your name?" he said.

"Cor, you're not a name one, are you? Call me Jackie, love."

"You know a girl named Shelia?"

The girl took her hand away. "Sheila? Here now. You ent got the scrub for her, ducks. Too flash, is Shelia."

"That's who I want."

"Put you back a sweet lump."

"Where can I find her?"

At that moment, another girl swept into the pub, wearing a glittering silver dress and silver mesh stockings. She was greeted with shouts and cheers from the men there, and she waved gaily.

"There 'tis, love," the tart said to Raynaud.

He bought her another drink, then got up and moved down the bar. Shelia was sitting at the bar, elbows on the counter, lighting a cigarette.

"Hello," he said.

She glanced over at him, then away. "Yah?"

"You free tonight?"

She smiled slightly, lit the cigarette, and shook out the match. "In real need, are you? Cor, these Yanks don't wait until you've had a drink. Bloody inconvenient."

He shrugged.

Still not looking at him, but staring straight ahead, she said, "This here's Friday night. Special night."

"And?"

"Cost you a one'er."

"What?"

"A hundred quid, lovey," she said irritably. "Take it or leave it."

"All right," he said.

She glanced over at him lazily. "Got a car?"

"Yes."

"Got a place?"

"No."

"Cost you another twenty."

"All right."

"Then that's it, then. Wait until I get me drink, and we're off."

The drink came, she gulped it back, and they left. She took his arm. She walked gracefully, with a kind of strong, physical confidence.

Outside it was dark and chilly. They got into the car and he turned on the heater.

She sat back, took out a mirror from her purse, and fluffed her hair. "Go up the block and turn right," she said, finishing with her hair and applying lipstick. "I'll direct you from there."

They drove for perhaps ten minutes, down dark, grim streets with depressing row houses. She did not attempt to make conversation. Finally, they pulled up in front of one house, no different from any of the others on either side, and she said, "This is it."

She held out her hand.

"Now?" he said.

"Right, lovey. Now."

He reached into his pocket, gave her the money, and waited

while she counted it. She did it slowly, obviously relishing the feel of the crisp bills.

"Very nice," she said, at last. "Out you go."

He got out and climbed the steps to the front door, waited while she unlocked it, and went inside. He was looking around.

"Not to worry," she said. "Quite safe here."

They came into a depressingly tawdry living room. The furniture was caving, tattered, the material worn threadbare in many spots.

"Action up there," she said, pointing to the stairs.

They climbed. He listened intently for other sounds in the house, but heard nothing.

They came to a bedroom, bare except for a single bed in the center of the room. On the walls were mirrors. The room was lighted by a single small lamp with a red shade.

"How do you like it, then?" she asked. She unzipped her dress and stepped out of it; she was wearing nothing underneath. She went to a closet and opened it. Inside, there were boots and leather clothing and whips.

"Eh? How do you like it?"

Raynaud leaned against the wall, watched her, and lit a cigarette. He said nothing. "Something wrong, lovey?"

"No," he said. "Nothing's wrong. I'm looking for Norman."

"Who?"

"Norman."

"I don't know no Norman, lovey."

"Think hard," Raynaud said.

She shook her head. "Don't know Norman, lovey."

"Sure you do," he said. "Just think about it." And he took out his gun.

"Here, now—"

"Where is he?"

"I swear I don't—"

"Shelia," he said. "I haven't got all night."

"Cor," she said. "What a mess we're in now. Here I bring you up for a little bit—"

She was moving into the closet, reaching up…

"Hold it."

She froze.

"That's not smart, Shelia."

He moved to her quickly, then, and slapped her hard across the face. "Not smart at all."

She took it well. She had had beatings before; she knew how to handle it. She let her head swing loosely on her neck, absorbing the blow. "Go on," she said bitterly. "It doesn't matter. Go on."

"I'm not going to hurt him or you," Raynaud said. "I just want a little information. But I want it now."

"Go on," she said. "I've heard that one before."

He had been expecting this, or something like it. He took out his wallet, removed five hundred-pound notes, and dropped them on the bed.

"That change things?"

"No," she said, staring at the money.

"Sure?"

"Get out of here," she said.

He shrugged. "Have it your way." He bent over, scooped up the money, and turned to leave.

"Wait a bit."

He paused.

"Why do you want to see him, eh?"

"Just a few questions."

"And that's all?"

"That's all."

"Give us the money, then."

"When you take me to him."

She pulled on the silver dress. "He's just downstairs," she said. "Now give us the money."

"Where?"

"Out back. In the garage."

He put the gun in his pocket. "Let's go."

She led him down the stairs, to the rear of the house, and through a door to the garage. A light was on, above a blue sedan, license XJ1189. A man was working, his head down under the car.

"Norman," she said. "We got company."

He came out slowly from beneath the car. The shock of recognition was immediate: the little man who had followed Raynaud and Pierce that night. The frightened, chubby little man.

"Hello, Norman," Raynaud said.

"What do you want?" Norman said, wiping his hands on his trousers. "Eh?"

He glanced up angrily at Shelia. "You brought *him* here?"

She looked helpless and frightened.

"Norman," Raynaud said. "Is this your car?"

"Yes," he said.

He was beginning to tremble.

"I won't hurt you," Raynaud said, "if you tell me a few things."

"Such as?"

"Such as who's paying you."

"Eh?" He cocked his head, trying to look confused.

"Yes. Who's paying you?"

"I don't follow yer, gov."

Raynaud swung swiftly and viciously, catching him just beneath the ribs. He felt his fist sink into soft flesh. Norman gave a little cough and doubled over, falling to his knees.

Shelia gasped.

"All right, Norman. The party's over. Who is paying you?"

Even as he asked, Raynaud was almost certain he knew the answer. There was only one person who stood to gain from any of this, and that was Lucienne. But how did she come to know a man like Norman?

"I don't know what you're talking about."

Raynaud had a moment of pure, hot anger. He didn't want to hurt the little man. It wasn't necessary, none of this was necessary. But if necessary…

He kicked hard, catching Norman just under the arm, knocking him back.

"Quickly, Norman. Tell me."

The little man glared stubbornly at him.

"You have nothing to gain by silence."

Norman said nothing.

Raynaud took out his gun. Norman saw it, recognized it.

"You...you wouldn't..."

"Why not?" Raynaud said. "What do I have to lose?"

Norman got off the floor. "Here," he said. "Perhaps we can work out—"

Raynaud swung with the barrel, catching Norman across the side of the face, knocking him down again.

"Just answer the question. Who's paying you?"

Norman was vomiting on the floor. Raynaud waited a moment. When Norman looked up at him, his face was pale.

"Mr. Pierce, it was," he said. "He was paying me."

"Mr. Pierce?"

"Richard Pierce. That's who it was."

Raynaud was stunned.

"You're lying," he said.

"No, I'm not, I swear it."

"You are."

"No, I swear it. He's had me working for him, ages now. Ages. Ever since the job I tried."

"What job?"

"Last year," Norman said, his eyes wide with fear. "Last year it was. I tried a job on his flat. Seemed a good idea; he was off with Shelia, here. Only he found me out."

"Oh?"

"Yah. He was going to have me nicked, but he didn't."

"In exchange for services."

"Yah. I don't hear from him for a year, and then he sends me to Paris. With instructions, money, everything."

"You were driving the car? The blue Mercedes? In Paris?"

"Yah."

"And your orders were to make it look good."

He nodded.

"And when you followed us?"

"Mr. Pierce, he said to me to follow you and see that you got the gun from me. *That* gun."

"I see. And the shooting in the apartment?"

"The same. He comes to me and says he has a little job for

me. When I heard it, I didn't want no part of it, but he says it's the last thing. He says that if I do it, she'll be screwed for sure. So I—"

"Wait a minute. She?"

"Yah. That's what he says. She."

"Who?"

"I don't know. It was just what he said. Not for me to pry. So I did the job, just as he says."

"Making sure to miss."

"Yah."

"And he said this was the last thing?"

"Yah. The last job. And he said he'd never call me again. I don't believe that, of course. I'm moving out, so he can't find me. I don't want no part of this. No part."

Raynaud took a deep breath.

"All right, Norman. I'll leave you alone now." He went back to the rear door, where Shelia was standing, her face cold and set. He opened the rear door, and turned back.

"Just one other thing, Norman. Don't say a word about this to anyone."

"No, I swear—"

"Especially not Mr. Pierce."

"Cor, I wouldn't call *him,* that's for—"

"Because, Norman," Raynaud said, "if you do, you're a dead man."

He went through the door and back down the hallway toward the front of the house. Shelia seemed to revive, then. She ran after him.

"Just a minute, lovey." She came up and caught his arm. "There's still the money."

"Money?"

"The five hundred quid, lovey. I took you to him, remember?"

"Yes," Raynaud said. "But on the other hand, you have a hundred and twenty pounds which, if I remember, you didn't earn."

She stared at him for one furious instant, and then spat in his face.

"Goodbye, Shelia," he said, and walked out to his car, wiping his face clean.

❋

As he drove to the party, he considered Richard's game and decided it was exactly like Lucienne's game, but in reverse. A mirror image, revolving around the fixed point of Charles Raynaud.

Richard had engineered a series of phony murders. He had arranged for Raynaud to get a gun which was filled with semi-blanks. Richard was prepared to have Raynaud attempt to kill him with that gun and those blanks. At that point, Richard could accuse Raynaud and Lucienne.

Bingo.

Raynaud vowed that he would not kill Richard, but that he would take the next opportunity to beat him to a small and featureless pulp. He could take care of Lucienne later.

If he could only understand her game.

Somewhere, a scandal was coming. A complex thing, intricate, delicate, dangerous.

But what?

As he moved through the damp London streets, weaving among the cars, he tried to guess. He would have been surprised to know that he would have his answer within ten minutes.

4. FELLOW TRAVELER

All in all, she found it a rather dull party. The men were plumpish and balding and mostly gay. Swish—the whole lot of them. She had forgotten about London men. She stood in a corner and wished she could meet someone terribly attractive and virile and interesting who would sweep her off her feet and carry her away from all this crap.

And then she saw Raynaud.

He was standing with a short man with dark hair and very large eyes; the short man was wearing a wine-colored blazer, pink shirt, yellow ascot, and gray glen-plaid slacks. He looked a little like a decorator's nightmare. Charles wore a blue suit and looked tired. He had a bruise on his forehead.

She was about to go over and introduce herself when he caught her eye and stared at her in the most astonished way. She could not tell what it meant: she had expected him to be glad to see her, but he didn't seem glad. He seemed astonished and a little horrified.

She started over, and then Charles did something odd.

He raised his finger to his lips, and shook his head.

Meantime the short man had caught sight of her and had hurried up. "You're new," he said.

"Yes," she said.

"And you are alone," the man said, in a mock-disapproving tone.

"I'm afraid so."

"There is nothing to be afraid of. We have come to the rescue. Allow me to introduce myself. I am Richard Pierce, and this is my fellow traveler, Charles Raynaud."

"How do you do. Jane Mitchell."

Charles took her hand gravely. "Miss Mitchell."

"Enchanté," said Richard Pierce, lifting her hand with an

exaggerated gesture and kissing it with a loud smack. She had to laugh. He dropped her hand immediately.

"Some zing iss funny? You zink it is funny?"

"No, no," she said.

"Then we must celebrate, eh, Gaston?" With a wink, Richard Pierce jabbed Charles in the ribs. Charles smiled patiently. She wondered what he was doing here, with this creepy little man.

"Come, come, my dear," Richard said. "As a visitor to the decadent old world, you will be gobbled alive without a proper guide. This is a jungle, a veritable jungle, and young girls should not brave it alone."

He held out his arm with a funny grin. She took it.

"Allow me to show you the sights and sins. Name your blackest wish, and it shall be granted."

She laughed. "I don't have any black wishes."

"No? I thought everybody had a black wish, somewhere inside them."

"Not me."

Richard was steering her out the door, clutching her arm tightly. Charles was following behind; she glanced back and saw a rather sad look on his face, as if he was forced into something unpleasant. She wondered why he acted like Richard's servant.

"I am sorry to report," Richard said, "that my auto is out of whack. It is at the Maserati repair shop now. But we shall manage."

At first she thought he was kidding about the Maserati, and then she decided he wasn't. A warning bell in her mind: she did not like people who identified themselves by their possessions. It was no points to her that he owned a Maserati. She had had three of them, at various times, and considered them bad cars. A Lotus was far superior.

"Taxi! Taxi!" Richard was shouting. He grinned at her. "They usually stop right away, if the girl is pretty."

"Oh, dear, what will you think if one doesn't come?"

"I will think that they are fag taxi drivers," Richard said sternly. "And I will dismiss them from my mind."

As it turned out, a cab stopped for them almost immediately.

They climbed into the back seat, Richard first, then her. As Charles started to get in, Richard said, "If you'd rather stay at the party, old buddy…"

"No, no," Charles said. "It was boring."

Charles got in and shut the door. The taxi driver looked back through the open glass partition. "Sir?"

"The Grouse," Richard said. The driver nodded. Richard reached forward and closed the partition.

"Perhaps," he said, "you find the London taxi ungainly. However, you will notice the room inside, the partition which makes conversation private, and the fact that the driver is forbidden —by law, mind you—to have an inside rear-view mirror. Thus he cannot see back into this compartment without boorishly turning and looking. So you see, the London taxi is actually the most civilized thing in the city."

She found herself laughing. "What's the Grouse?" she said.

"A club. It is owned by several London film people and backed by Brighton gangsters who keep it very clean. No riffraff, and every wheel weighted, every dice loaded."

"Die," Charles said, speaking for the first time. His voice sounded distant, mechanical.

"Quite right. You know, my friend Charles is far better educated than I. Far better. Aren't you, old buddy?"

"Yes."

Jane looked at him curiously. "You're American?"

"Indeed he is," Richard said. "An American living in Mexico, where he makes money doing queer things he won't explain to me. A mysterious figure, is Charles."

"You live in Mexico?"

"He does, he does," Richard said. "And you, my dear? What do you do?"

She shrugged. "Model," she said. "Act, sometimes."

"Marvelous," Richard said. "I can see why."

"Can you?" She disliked bald compliments.

"Absolutely."

"Tell me, Mr. Pierce—"

"Richard. Please."

"All right, Richard. What do *you* do?"

"Alas, I am a member of the vast ranks of the unemployed."

"He's a millionaire," Charles said, with a slight grin. A funny grin, sly, foxy.

"Really? A real millionaire?"

Richard looked at his shoes. "Well, actually—"

"You really are a millionaire?"

"Yes, I'm afraid so."

"That's very exciting. I've never met a millionaire before."

"Then this is your first opportunity. Gaze your fill."

She paused, then said, "I'm impressed."

"Don't be," Richard said, with a grin. "We millionaires are no different from other people."

"I'd heard that, but I never believed it."

Indeed, she found it hard to believe he was a millionaire. He seemed so childish, so aimlessly gay and frivolously amusing. Perhaps, like her, his fortune was managed by old men.

"And how did you make your money?" she asked.

"My father did."

"Stepfather," Charles said.

She saw Richard give him a quick glance; he hadn't appreciated that comment. "Yes, stepfather."

They arrived at the Grouse Club, which occupied the second floor of a mansion in Mayfair, looking out on a verdant park.

"Watch out for that park," Richard said, as they climbed out of the cab. "It's filled with buggers at night."

They went inside, into a lobby of ornate Victorian splendor, up broad marble stairs to cool green gaming rooms. Most of the clientele was young, but obviously wealthy. By and large, dress was conservative—men in dark suits or dinner jackets, the women in floor-length gowns.

"My dress," she said, in mild dismay, aware of the seven inches of bare leg above the knee.

"Marvelous," Richard said calmly. "Come along," He steered her toward the cashier. "What will you play? Blackjack? Chemin? Roulette?"

"Anything," she said. "Whatever you like."

"I like you," he said.

"Roulette," she said.

＊

"Red twelve," Richard said, and put a ten-pound chip on the marker. He had his arm around her waist, and was holding her quite close as he watched the ball slide down the curve of the spinning, polished wood wheel. When he had first put his arm around her, she hadn't liked it; he was too quick, assuming her interest in a matter-of-fact, almost bored way. Later, charmed by his humor and madcap manner, she no longer cared.

Richard was losing heavily. She guessed that he had dropped two hundred pounds already, with no end in sight. Although she knew it was intended to impress her, she did her best not to be impressed. This caused Richard to bet more heavily, and lose more consistently. She felt bad about that, but not very. It was his money, and he could throw it away if he liked.

He was rather a strange person, actually. At first she had thought him stupid, but he was not stupid. He was perceptive and accurate when he wanted to be, when he stopped his little patter of jokes and sly comments. She wondered why he was so intent on playing the clown.

Charles, to her annoyance, had drifted away and played twenty-one. He was not giving her a chance to talk to him, and she was immensely curious to know what was going on.

She watched Richard play, and said, "Your friend is quiet."

"Who? Charles?"

"Yes."

"He has women trouble," Richard said. "Black nine."

"Sorry to hear that."

"Don't be. Charles is making it with my stepmother, you see. Frightful bitch. Rots the masculine soul."

His stepmother? Very strange, she thought. She could not imagine Charles making love with anybody's stepmother.

"She collects men, you see," Richard said. "All shapes and sizes. Now she has Charles."

"He doesn't seem very happy."

"No, he never does."

After an hour, Charles came back with an armful of chips. He had obviously done well for himself. He walked up to Jane and said, "You picked the wrong game," and dropped the chips into her lap.

Richard said, "How much did you make, old buddy?"

"Not much. Fifty pounds or so. How much did you lose?"

"I never keep track," Richard said.

Charles said to her, "I'll buy you a drink. Richard had better stay here and try to win back his stake."

Before she could answer, Richard had said, "No, no, I'm finished."

Charles said, "But you still have some chips left."

"No, I'm bored. A drink sounds wonderful." He grinned. "Now that you've won all this money, you can buy us all drinks."

The bar was on the third floor, dark, lit softly by pink lights. There were oil paintings of demure nudes on the wall, chubby women reclining amid cherubs and little fat angels.

Charles bought three rounds of drinks, and she began to get tight. Richard became talkative, and Charles, seated alongside him, became very quiet.

By two in the morning, they were all quite drunk. At least she was, and so was Richard; it was impossible to say with Charles. He said nothing at all, but stared morosely around the room.

Richard said, "Aren't you tired, Charles? It's been a long night."

"No, I'm not tired."

"Jane, doesn't he look tired? Look at his eyes. Bloodshot. Drooping. Tired."

Jane shrugged. She wished Richard would go away.

"You look tired to me," Richard said.

"I don't feel tired."

"Yes, but you *look* tired."

"I don't care how I look."

"Well, you should. You look like hell."

Jane thought Charles would be angry, but he was not. He gave a slight smile, and said, "You can't see anything right now. Old buddy."

"Don't call me old buddy."

"I'll call you anything I like," Charles said.

"No, you won't," Richard said. He turned to Jane. "You know why not? Because he's my servant. My hired employee. My servant. Specifically, Charles is—"

Something happened. She didn't see exactly how it happened, because she was too drunk to pay attention, but Charles somehow managed to spill his drink all over Richard.

"Damn," Richard said. "Why the hell did you do that?"

"Do what?" Charles said.

"Spill my drink, you sod."

"I didn't spill your drink. Your drink is on the bar."

"I don't care whose drink you spilled, you sod."

Charles looked at him evenly and said, "Shut up and go clean yourself. You've mussed your trousers."

Richard looked shocked, almost as if he had been struck. Then, without a word, he got off the bar stool and walked off to the washroom.

Watching him go, she said, "That was mean."

"Possibly."

"Why did you do it?"

"I wanted to talk to you."

"Listen," she said, "what's going on with you two? The last I saw you, you were sneaking out of your house at six in the morning with snakes under your arm—"

He shook his head. "Long story. I can't explain now. You're here in London on business?"

"Yes."

"Selling stock?"

She frowned. How did he know that?

"Yes."

"Then you may be in some danger."

"Danger? But that's absurd—"

"It's not. Just be careful, will you?"

"But, Charles—"

At that moment, Richard came back. He had found paper towels and was drying his trousers. She expected him to say something to Charles, but he did not. Instead he sat down, ordered another drink, and said, "I'm tired of this place. Let's do something unusual tonight."

"Yes," Jane said. She glanced at Charles.

"Let's do something special," Richard said.

"Yes," she said.

"Something a bit risky."

"By all means," she said, "but what?"

"Hunting," Richard said.

"Hunting?"

"Yes. Duck hunting."

"But where?"

"Hyde Park, of course. It's the *only* place to go duck hunting, you know."

5. DUCK HUNTING

She was drunk, so damned drunk she could hardly see this Charles-person in front of her. He was talking to her while what's-his-face was inside getting the gun. God, what a wild pair they were. And Charles so damned handsome. She felt like grabbing him and kissing him, she felt like devouring him. She should have done it before. In Mexico. Devoured him.

Drunk? Jesus.

He was talking to her but she couldn't pay attention to the words. Except that he was being earnest, in a funny way. He didn't seem like the earnest type.

Moments later, what's-his-face, Richard, came back. He had a .22. For Christ's sake, a .22. For duck hunting.

"You can't hit anything with a twenty-two," she said.

"Oh, yes," Richard said. "Dead easy."

"You mean…"

"Of course." Richard laughed. "You shoot them on the ground. Preferably while they're sleeping."

"Not sportsmanlike," Jane said.

"Yeah, but it makes them easier to clean."

Charles was driving. She was in the back seat. Richard was sitting next to Charles with the gun between his legs, sticking up toward the ceiling like a giant thing. God, drunk, to be thinking this way. About giant things.

"What we are about to do," Richard said, laughing slightly, "is terribly illegal. In fact, we are breaking the law on five counts. At least."

"Oh." She was so drunk, she did not really care.

"Yes. We are in possession of an unregistered firearm. We are transporting it by automobile without a license. We are within a city of more than twenty thousand. We are using it for an illegal purpose. We are shooting ducks out of season. And finally, we are damning the Queen's property."

"We are?"

"Yes. Ducks in parks are the property of the Queen. Also geese and swans. They are her most loyal subjects."

"What about the Queen? Can she shoot them?" Jane asked.

"Yes. But Her Majesty is a notoriously poor shot."

They drove around Hyde Park and pulled off the road into a glade of trees. The park was dark and silent. They looked at each other.

"Now what?" Jane said.

"Now," Richard said, "we hunt."

"But won't somebody hear the shots?"

"Yes. But we will run like hell."

Charles said, "Isn't the park patrolled at night?"

"Yes. But we will run like hell."

"Oh," Jane said.

"Oh," Charles said

They got out of the car. Richard put on a raincoat and carried the rifle tucked up under his armpit, the barrel protruding down below the coat

"Careful you don't shoot yourself in the leg," Charles said.

"Never fear, old buddy."

They walked in silence, breathing the night air. They passed several couples necking in the grass. One or two couples in evening clothes strolled by, laughing gaily. No one noticed the gun under Pierce's coat.

Jane said, "Have you ever done this before?"

"Many times."

"Do other people do it?"

"Half of London," Richard said. "You forget that poaching is a venerable English art."

"But in Hyde Park?"

"We must make no concessions to urban living."

Up ahead, they saw a single figure approaching.

"Oops," Richard said. "Close one." He put his arm around her, holding her against him. She felt the gun in her ribs. They walked on, and she saw it was a bobby.

"Evening," Richard said.

"Evening," the bobby said.

They walked on.

Richard began to laugh.

"I don't like it," Charles said.

"If you don't like it, go home."

"We could be thrown in jail for this."

"What? A rough and tumble fellow like you, afraid of police?"

Jane, feeling drunk, said to Charles, "Are you rough and tumble?"

"He's very rough and tumble."

"He looks pretty rough and tumble."

"He is," Richard said. "Aren't you, old buddy?"

"Yes."

"See? He's the roughest and tumblest there is."

They left the paved pathway and set off across the grass. It was damp underfoot; she dimly realized that her shoes would be ruined.

"Where are we going?"

"To a nice little pond."

"And then what?"

"We're going to get dinner for tomorrow."

Charles said, "What about the car?"

"That's why we have to move quickly. They'll tow it away soon. And we need it for the getaway. All right: steady now."

They crept forward, through a low mist that hung over the grass near the water. Bullfrogs croaked in the night. Ahead, they saw a dozen ducks sleeping in the water and on the grass near the shore, their heads tucked under their wings.

"This is it," Richard whispered. "Everybody ready?"

They nodded. He brought the gun out from under his coat, and prepared to take aim.

"No, wait," he whispered. He reached into his pocket, withdrawing a flask. "A final drink."

He drank. They all drank. Jane hardly tasted the liquor. It could have been Scotch, or vodka, or anything. The park was silent around them, except for the frogs. Very faintly, they could hear the far-off sound of traffic.

Charles said, "I don't think we should shoot them on the ground."

"Shit, it's the only way," Richard said.

"Not sportsmanlike," Jane said. Looking at the poor ducks, peacefully sleeping, she felt sorry for them. They deserved a fighting chance.

"All right, then," Richard said. He turned to Charles, "You go forward and scare them. When they fly up, I'll shoot."

"No. You go forward, and I'll shoot."

"Bloody hell. You might miss and hit me."

The two men stared at each other for a long time.

"I might," Charles said. "But I won't."

"Bloody hell. I'm not risking it."

Jane said, "I'll go forward."

"No, you won't," Charles said. "He's too drunk."

"I'm too drunk. Look at you, old buddy, you can hardly stand."

"I can, too."

"Look at you."

Charles said, "Don't you trust me, Richard?"

"Hell, no."

Richard became excited. He waved the gun in the air. "You expect me to trust you? You think that I will—"

The gun went off, the report echoing.

"That tears it."

Whistles began to blow.

"Jesus. Fuzz."

Pierce stood frozen. Charles said, "Let's get out of here."

He grabbed Jane's hand. They started to run.

"Hold it right there!"

They stopped, and looked back. Richard was standing, the gun raised, pointing at them.

"You leaving me here?"

"Put the gun down."

"You taking my girl away, old buddy?"

"Put the gun down," Charles said, "before somebody gets hurt." He released Jane's hand, and whispered, "Move away." She moved off to the right.

Richard was laughing as he sighted down the gun. "I could plug you right there, old buddy."

A whistle blew, closer this time.

"Come on, Richard. Cut it out."

"You think I'm worried?"

"Come on, Richard."

Another whistle, from another direction, quite close. Richard laughed, and with a sudden movement, threw the gun into the pond. It splashed loudly; the ducks squawked and scattered. Still laughing, Richard ran to join them. They sprinted for the car.

Minutes later, they climbed into the car and sped off. They drove west, past the Albert Memorial, then out back through South Kensington. Jane, in the aftermath of tension, was laughing; it was all funny, all crazy.

Richard said, "You can let us off here, old buddy." He pointed to the taxi rank up ahead. "I'll see that Jane gets home."

"I'll drive her."

"No, it's all right."

Silently, Charles pulled over. He was almost meek as he sat by the curb and waited for her to get out with Richard. She was astonished by his behavior. It was so unlike him she thought he must be drugged. Or perhaps this Richard-person had some hold over him.

But damn him, anyway.

She paused as she got out and said, "Mr. Raynaud, I hope we meet again sometime."

"Call me Charles," he said, and gave her a slight, brief smile that was gone almost before it had come.

In the taxi, Richard did the damnedest thing. He gave her a flask and told her to take a drink, and then he moved away and did nothing at all. She had been prepared, in a drunken sort of way, to fight him off. But he wasn't having any. Son of a bitch, he didn't even like her.

When they finally came to the hotel, she was beginning to realize that Richard had been putting on an act for Charles. She didn't know why, and she didn't understand, and she didn't like it.

And Charles: "You may be in danger." Wasn't that what he had said? It was comic-book stuff. Intrigue. Fantasy. Danger from what?

Richard said, "In a day or so, my car will be fixed. Then I can really show you around."

"I'd like that," she said, thinking she would detest it.

"I'll call you."

"Do," she said. "Do."

6. THE FIX

Driving home, Charles Raynaud tried to control himself. He was totally, blindly furious. He would willingly have throttled Pierce a dozen times over during the evening.

Which was, of course, the object of the game.

Things were now much clearer, and for that he was grateful. Pierce had a strategy which was simple enough: to goad Raynaud into a murder attempt. Pierce had provided the weapon, and now he was providing the motive, the provocation.

Humiliation.

As he drove, Raynaud smiled. If Richard wanted Raynaud to kill him, Raynaud would oblige him. Raynaud would give him one hell of a murder attempt.

And, of course, fail.

But not quite the way Richard expected.

Back at Richard's flat, he found Dominique sitting alone in the living room, smoking a cigarette and rubbing her shoulders as if she were cold.

"He back yet?"

She nodded, and jerked her thumb toward the kitchen. She gave a slight shiver.

Raynaud said, "Are you all right?"

"Yes," she said. "Of course."

She needs a fix, he thought. She needs it very badly. He leaned over her and gave her a reassuring smile, but was careful to notice her eyes. The pupils were dilated. Yes, he thought, she needs a fix.

Raynaud walked out into the kitchen, remembering what Richard had said about Dominique and her heroin supply. Dominique had no money, and apparently no contacts. Yet she was getting stuff. Regularly.

Richard was in the kitchen, his jacket off, his shirtsleeves rolled up, mixing a drink.

"You were a bloody bore tonight," Richard said.

"I imagine you thought so."

"Bloody right I thought so. I'm paying you to keep me alive, not to be a bore."

"You don't look dead yet."

"No thanks to you." Richard poured two drinks and nodded to Raynaud to take one. "By the way, what did you think of her?"

"I liked her well enough."

"Did you," Richard said. "I hadn't noticed. I thought you were indifferent to her." He lit a cigarette, and said, "The poor girl, all alone in London, such a big city. We're meeting for lunch, you know."

"That's nice."

"Yes. Just the two of us."

"That's nice."

"I'd invite you along," Pierce said, "but you know how it is."

"Yes, I do."

Pierce laughed. "Why the long face, old buddy? I'll be good to her."

"I'm sure you will."

Richard appeared surprised "You don't mind?"

"Frankly," Raynaud said, "I couldn't give less of a damn."

7. FACE CHANGE

Jane Mitchell sat in the pink vinyl chair, wearing a pink smock, with a fluffy pink towel around her neck. She looked at her image in the pink-tinted mirror and thought: My God, I look like some kind of poodle.

Standing behind her was Godfrey, caressing her hair with his eyes closed.

He did it for a very long time. Finally, when she got tired of staring at herself in the mirror, she said, "What are you doing?"

"I am *listening*," Godfrey said, wrinkling his brow in concentration. "Listening to the message of your hair. Hair speaks to me. It is an organic, living, vital thing. It has a message for me and I want to hear it."

"I want it cut," Jane said. She was irritable today, hung over and irritable. She had called Richard and broken her luncheon date. She didn't really want to see him anyway. She could have been interested in seeing Charles, but not Richard.

Besides, she had other things to do today. Things to buy, and things to change.

"It is not so simple to cut hair," Godfrey said. He opened his eyes and examined the cut ends of her blond hair. "Who did this to you?"

"Kenneth," she said.

"Oh," Godfrey said, dropping her hair. "Him."

"He's a good friend."

"No doubt, no doubt. And I must say he is *adequate*, for an American dresser." He sighed. "I understand he has his own place, now that he's left Lilly Daché. I'm told it's all done in yellow."

"Yellow is his favorite color."

"Mine," said Godfrey firmly, "is pink."

"I noticed."

"Flattering."

"Yes," she said.

Godfrey was a funny little man, barely five feet tall. He worked while standing on a small vinyl-covered box. He was immaculately dressed in a pinstripe, mod-cut suit. His hair was long, combed straight forward, and cut in bangs just below his eyebrows.

"I must tell you that I do not hold with Kenneth's artiness," Godfrey said. "He claims simplicity, but he is really too mannered."

"I see."

"Your hair, for example. These cut ends—like corded hemp. Arty."

"Just cut it," Jane said.

"Yes, yes, but the crucial question still stands—cut it *how*. We must cut it as the hair demands, as the message speaks forth. Otherwise it will be all wrong. Your color is lovely."

"Thank you."

"Real, too," Godfrey said, in mild surprise, poking amid her roots.

"So they tell me."

Jane was feeling impatient. Godfrey had been recommended to her by several friends as an absolute wizard, the finest in London. But she had little patience with hairdressers, especially the good ones. They were too damned gay, that was the trouble. Porsche dealers, poodle clippers, and hairdressers—hopelessly gay, the whole batch of them.

"You must have a manicure and pedicure," Godfrey said. "At once. I cannot *think* while I look at those hands of yours. What do you *do* to them?"

"I walk on them, of course."

"Dear me," he said, with a little tittering giggle.

Oh, Christ, Jane thought. Another one. But she had to go through with it—she was here, and draped in all this pink crap, and Godfrey's healing hands had already touched her unworthy locks. Besides, it was true that everyone said Godfrey was worth it. A pain in the ass, but worth it. Even Givenchy, whom she had seen the last time he was in New York, even Givenchy towering over her had announced that Godfrey was the *only* hairdresser in London.

A smiling, rather apologetic girl appeared and began to work on her nails. Jane sat back and Godfrey continued to stroke her hair. If he didn't stop it soon, she'd go out of her mind.

"We must be decisive," he said. "Strong, decisive lines. Nothing frilly. Oh, no, that would be a disaster."

"But I feel very frilly today," Jane said, just to annoy him.

"No matter. In your heart, you are not frilly."

"That's very uncomplimentary."

"Artists must speak the truth."

"Oh." She could barely contain a giggle.

"Now, then. Janice."

Another girl appeared, holding a tray of scissors and instruments. She stood alongside him, handing him the instruments one by one as he called for them, like a surgeon.

Godfrey worked in silence for several minutes. Jane looked down and saw her hair falling to the floor.

"Don't move your head!"

"Sorry," she said meekly.

"Don't ever move your head while I am working!"

She sat rigidly, staring forward into the mirror as her hair was cut off. As he had promised, Godfrey worked decisively, pausing before each cut, then lunging forward with scissors gaping. The hair fell away in long clumps.

"It's taking shape," Godfrey announced. Jane looked at her hair, which was ragged and formless. She looked like a refugee from a fire or a bombing raid. "Taking shape nicely. Very nicely," Godfrey said. He patted her head reassuringly.

"Glad to hear it."

He continued to work, and she lapsed into her own thoughts. Peter Dickerson had called her earlier in the day, to keep her abreast, as he said, of the developments. Peter Dickerson was very pleased with the developments, and obviously very pleased with himself. He had been full of mumbo-jumbo about that stocksy-bondsy crap. Something about the Dutch wanting this, and the English wanting that.

Jane understood none of it. And she didn't want to understand. It had always seemed odd to her that anyone could get very excited about money. True, you got excited when you had a lot, or when you had very little. But in between, who gave a damn?

There were people, she knew, who really liked money. Not what it could buy, or even what it could do—what power it could give you. They just liked money. Plain and simple. They liked to play with it, to invest it, to buy and to sell and to make it grow.

Rather like gardening, she thought. Watering your money every day, tending it, feeding it, pruning it.

Gardening was also dull, she thought.

"Ah," Godfrey said. "Beautiful. Can you see it happening? I always find this exciting, these changes, this living sculpture, right before your eyes. Exciting!"

"Yes," she said.

Godfrey chattered on, still cutting, his tongue working as fast as his scissors. But in the end, when all the sprays and goos and lotions were finished, she had to admit it was astonishing.

She stared in the mirror for a long time, unable to speak. She looked *different*. Her hair was short, curled tight, falling to just below her jawline. It somehow made her look hard and tough and self-sufficient

Godfrey paused, then said, "You like it?"

She grinned, trying the grin on her new face, her new self. It was a tough, confident grin. A good grin.

"I like it," she said.

On King's Road, in the endless boutiques, she searched out what she wanted, and finally settled on half a dozen dresses. She had to have new dresses; hers were all New York length, too long for London.

She bought them as short as she possibly could. She realized that if your cheeks didn't peep out underneath, it just didn't count. One of the salesgirls tried to dissuade her from one purchase.

As Jane turned in front of the mirror, the girl said, "Well, frankly..."

"I like it," Jane said.

"Yes, but the cut is wrong. It's made for a less busty girl. You pull it up too far, if you see what I mean."

"I like it."

The girl looked quizzical. "Makes sitting a bit drafty, ducks."

"Then sell me some pants."

They showed her pants. All kinds of pants. Frilly pants and silvered pants and rubber pants and bikini pants. They were all pretty bloody awful. Finally they showed her a pair of white lace panties with LOVE written in vertical letters right down the front. And another with an embroidered cherry.

God, they were awful. The most vulgar things she had ever seen.

"I'll take them," she said. There were other things to buy. Purses—you had to have the sling-over-the-shoulder, drawstring type. Or you were nothing. A watchband as thick and bulky as you could find. Kinky shoes.

She did the complete thing, head to toe, top to bottom. And finally she stopped off in the salesroom and ordered the last straw. The man said they could deliver in two days' time, and she gave him a check.

Walking out, back into the sun, with the cool air on her legs and that delicious sense of half-nakedness, and her hair short, she felt better. Much better than she had felt in a long time.

As she went back to the hotel she found herself wondering if Charles had called and left a message for her. She asked at the desk.

He hadn't.

Well, what the hell, she thought. No point getting uptight. Not about him. Not about anything. And swinging her new purse, she went to the elevator and up to her room.

8. DEAD CATS

Jonathan Black bent down for a closer look. The bars of the cage were thick and sticky with red, drying blood. The cat lay on the sandy floor; across its head was a large gash.

"We found it this way," the assistant said, "an hour ago. Apparently the meprobamate wore off."

"Dashed itself to pieces," Black said, frowning. He unlocked the door and reached in to touch the cool, lifeless body. Dead of an overdose of anger, he thought. Amusing in a way—and also frightening.

"Clean it up," he said to the assistant, and left the room. He returned to his office, frowning, and his secretary gave him a sympathetic smile. She assumed he was bothered by the loss of the cat, but in fact his mind was on other matters.

He was making the final plans, and it required great delicacy. There was the stock sale—that had to be handled carefully. And then, of course, Richard had to be informed in such a way as to anger him. That would require care. And then the business with Dominique: another touchy problem.

Not, of course, that he did not believe he could deal with it. There was too much at stake now to permit a mistake. And too many things going for him.

Like Jane Mitchell, he thought. That was really too beautiful to be true. When he had sent the invitation to her hotel, he had merely hoped that Richard might meet her. Instead, he seemed to have got entangled with her and Charles in some tense triangle.

That was delightful.

Because it would provide the final stimulus for the Dezisen, the ultimate direction for the drug's action.

He lit a cigarette and thought about it. As he sucked back

the first puff, he felt a slight twinge of pain in his left chest, and a little tickle in his left arm down to the wrist.

Damn.

He stubbed the cigarette out quickly. And relaxed, breathing easily, closing his eyes for a moment. The pain went away.

He was all right, so long as the pain went away.

9. NIGHTMARES

Charles Raynaud sat in his car, parked across the street from Richard's Belgravia flat. He was annoyed with himself; it had been a wasted day. He had waited until Richard went off to lunch with Jane, and then had decided to follow Dominique, who had told him she was going shopping. Something about the way she said it struck him wrong. He remembered Richard's comments about Dominique and how she had gotten into the country. To say nothing of how she was getting her heroin.

So Charles had followed her. All day long. Dominique had spent most of the day in Harrods, and she had, indeed, gone shopping. He had watched her closely, because for a long time he had suspected that she would make her pick-up at one of the sales counters. Who would suspect a drug pick-up at Harrods? But it hadn't happened, obviously.

She had simply gone shopping. And she had bought a cigarette lighter, and a cigarette case covered in black Morocco leather, and a coin purse. And she had looked at fur coats.

For a very long time.

Jesus, what a waste. He could have spent the afternoon sleeping and learned as much.

When he returned to the flat he found Richard in the living room, seated on the couch, with Dominique lying naked across him. They were laughing; the new Stones album was on the record player.

"Welcome." Richard laughed. He was not drunk, though he had a drink in his hand. His face was flushed: sex, Raynaud thought.

"I have wonderful news," Pierce said. "My car is coming back tomorrow. I've called Jane and asked her if she wants to go for a ride; she said yes. We'll all leave at ten tomorrow morning."

"We?"

"Certainly. You're coming."

"I don't think so," Raynaud said. "How was your luncheon?"

"Excellent. Charming girl. And of course you are coming, Charles. I insist upon it. Besides," he said softly, "you are being paid to go with me, wherever I go."

"And that includes dates?"

"It's not precisely a date," Richard said. "We're going north. On M1. They haven't put a speed limit there yet. All the other M roads have them: seventy. Bloody seventy miles an hour. But M1 is still wide open. How about it? You can drive, if you want."

"All right," Raynaud said.

"You'll come?"

"I'll come."

The world was snowy-white, glaring and bright. They were whistling down a narrow track, banked on one side, and the toboggan hissed as it sped over the snow. Raynaud was in front; behind him was Jane, who held his waist tightly; next was Richard and then Lucienne.

"We're going too fast," Jane said.

"We're going too slow," Lucienne said.

"We're going," Richard said, and laughed.

The toboggan screamed through a curve, then shot down a straight track. The wind tore at his face and goggles, burned his cheeks.

"Why do you stare at me?" Jane said.

"He likes you," Lucienne said.

"He wants to get laid," Richard said.

Raynaud could not speak. He opened his mouth, but it filled with chilling, blistering wind.

"I'm afraid of you," Jane said.

"He loves me," Lucienne said.

"Old buddy, old buddy," Richard chanted.

The toboggan careened through another curve, sliding up the embankment, and Raynaud felt that it was going to pull loose, that it would pull loose, and then it did, flinging them high, up toward the clouds, at a tremendous speed, with the wind still in his ears, carrying the voices.

"You disappoint me," Lucienne said.

"How *do* you make your money?" Pierce asked.

"Stop staring at me," Jane said.

They were in the clouds, flying, floating. And always at a breathtaking speed.

"I had him first," Lucienne said.

"But I'm younger."

"Shut up, girls," Richard said. "I've had you both, and mother's better."

Below them lay the earth, the fields of England, verdant and rolling. For some reason, there was no snow. The ground was warm and moist.

"He scares me," Jane said.

"Richard is a prick," Lucienne said.

"I am a prick," Richard said. "I agree."

Raynaud wanted to talk. He wanted to say his last words, his final comments before he struck the ground, which rushed up.

"I have money," Lucienne said.

"I have love," Jane said.

"You have nothing," Richard said. "Either of you. Just stupid broads."

As they fell, Dominique appeared, and calmly passed out parachutes. They all struggled into them, their eyes on the on-rushing ground....

"You take one, too," Dominique said.

Raynaud shook his head.

"But if you do not take one, you will be killed."

Raynaud shook his head. He tried to speak; but there were no words. His lips worked soundlessly.

"Take one!" Dominique stamped her foot impatiently on a cloud.

"No!" he bellowed. It echoed through the sky like a thunder-clap.

"When I land," Richard said, "I'm going to take Jane."

"Yes," Jane said, panting. "Yes, oh yes, oh yes, yes, yes..."

Harold Wilson passed by in a helicopter. He leaned out, smoking his pipe, and surveyed the falling people.

"You don't like my shoe polish?" he said.

And then, quite suddenly, the sky was filled with planes. Kenneth Tynan circled in a private jet, screaming "Fuck, fuck, fuck" over a loudspeaker. A woman's voice from a Piper Cub said, "Keep America Bea-u-ti-ful. Plant a buush, or a shruuub, or ah tree..."

"Ve shall bury you!" snapped another voice.

The air was thick with voices.

"Don't pay any attention," said Lucienne.

"There will be a scandal," snapped Harold Wilson. "I warn you..."

"I am the Lord Mayor of London. I am the Lord Mayor of London!" shouted another man, who fell to the earth more rapidly than anyone else, and died immediately.

"I love you," Jane said, as her parachute opened into a pure white dome, curved like a breast.

"I love you, love," said Richard, kissing her.

"Pay no attention," Lucienne said.

Raynaud floated through an air filled with aircraft, shrieking voices, and billowing white parachutes.

"We are falling too fast," Jane said.

"We are falling too slow," said Lucienne.

"We are falling," Richard said.

Raynaud awoke and felt himself covered with the white parachute. He opened his eyes and saw the sheet. He was sweating and shivering. Cold moonlight poured in through the window.

"Are you all right?"

He looked over. Dominique, naked, stood in the doorway.

"I guess so."

"Here." She gave him a glass. "Drink this."

"What is it?"

"Cold water. You were having a nightmare."

"I guess I was."

He drank it. It tasted good; his mouth was dry and thick.

"Are you all right now?"

"Yes."

"Not falling anymore?"

He was startled. "Did I say anything?"

"Just words."

"Where is Richard?"

"Asleep. I woke and heard you. Are you all right now?"

"Yes," he said.

He lay down again, and slept soundlessly.

10. A DRIVE IN THE COUNTRY

Richard said, "Rise and shine, Charles."

Raynaud got up, blinking his eyes in the morning light. Pierce stood over him with a drink in his hand.

"That for me?"

"Right."

"What is it?"

"A martini."

"Christ, no."

Raynaud got out of bed and headed for the bathroom. Pierce said, "The car's here. You've got to see it."

"When I'm dressed."

As he showered and shaved, he thought about Richard. It was unusual for Richard to drink before noon; he usually waited ritualistically for twelve before pouring the first drink of the day. Yet today he was drinking, and offering one to Raynaud.

Why?

He sighed. Such a lot of whys, and so early in the morning. He wondered how Jane would act toward him, and toward Richard. He wondered what the hell he thought about her, and if he liked her. He decided he did like her, but he didn't know why. Something about her. She held back something, and it made her interesting. And she had a kind of tough but wounded quality, like a limping soldier. That made her interesting, too.

He smiled. Besides, she was sexy as hell.

Ah, he thought, there we are, back to essentials. He finished dressing and went out to the garage to join Richard. The car was there. Richard beamed proudly.

"Like it?"

The car had been repainted, from a deep red to a bright, mustard yellow. The color went well with the black seats.

"Very much."

Pierce gave Raynaud his drink. "Cheers. We pick up Jane in an hour."

Raynaud glanced at his watch. It was ten. He waited until Pierce was not looking, then poured his drink on the concrete floor of the garage.

"I think it's a perfect color," Pierce said. "Just perfect. And they did a good job on the body."

They went back into the flat. Pierce looked at Raynaud's glass. "Finished already? Make yourself another. I've got to dress."

When Pierce came back, Raynaud saw that he was dressed casually but elegantly. Blue blazer, red foulard kerchief, tattersall check shirt, and dark gray flannels.

"What's the occasion?" he asked.

"Occasion? No occasion," Pierce said, touching his foulard and straightening it. "Though I must admit I'm rather struck by the girl. Quite a stunner, isn't she? And such very soft breasts. We had a lovely lunch together. Shall we go?"

Jane finally showed up at noon, an hour later than planned. Richard had waited for her impatiently, smoking cigarettes and swearing under his breath. But when she arrived, he could not speak for several moments.

"Good Lord," he finally managed to say. "Good Lord."

She stood in front of the car and turned around. She was wearing a simple pink and yellow dress made of some fabric that clung tenaciously to obscene places and came to an abrupt stop just below her ass. Raynaud liked it immediately. He also liked her hair, which was short and simple and direct. He was amused to see how she moved and acted. It was different, as different as she looked.

"The new me," she announced.

"Marvelous," Richard said. He got into the car and held the door open for her. Raynaud said nothing.

"By the way," Richard said, "where have you been?"

"I had some business."

"What kind of business?"

"Oh," she said lightly, getting into the car, "agents and models, that sort."

"Ummm."

Pierce put the car in gear. Jane sat in the front seat, next to Richard. Raynaud sat in the back and looked at her neck, which was slim but somehow strong-looking, a very interesting neck. He slid over in the rear seat until he was sitting behind Richard. That way, he could look at her profile. Very nice profile. True, the nose was a little too long, and she had a slight tic in her left eye which was exaggerated when she was drunk, but still and all, a nice profile.

She glanced back at him. "Still staring?" She gave him a be-mused smile.

"Just my tourist's gawk."

She laughed.

They drove north toward Edgeware, and then west to pick up the first of England's high-speed thruways, the M1.

With three early-morning Scotches under his belt, Pierce drove badly. He ground his gears and allowed the car to shift all over the road. Once or twice, Raynaud saw concern in Jane's eyes, but for the most part she seemed very calm. As they pulled onto the motorway, Pierce said, "All right. Here we go."

He stepped on the accelerator. The car shot forward with incredible, startling speed, the engine growing from a low whine to a deep growl. They passed 70 before Pierce put the car into fifth, and from there they moved smoothly to 120, 130, and finally 150 miles an hour. The wind shrieked through the open windows. They closed them.

"Like it?" Pierce asked. "Bet you've never gone this fast before."

"Never," Jane said.

The car rushed down the road. In the right lane were Volks-wagens and lorries. In the left were Jags and Porsches, which hurriedly got out of the way as they approached. Far ahead was a blue Porsche 911.

"We'll catch it," Pierce said. He held the wheel at nine and three; good racing form, arms locked in front of him. "That car's top speed is only one thirty."

They approached the Porsche swiftly; like the others, it ducked into the right lane. Pierce laughed.

"This is the fastest car on the road," he said. "Absolutely the fastest. The Lamborghini may do better, but not much. Not bloody much."

They screamed down the motorway.

"Where are we going?" Jane asked.

"North. To a little inn I know."

Richard was chuckling as he spoke. Clearly, the power and speed were affecting him, on top of the Scotch.

"Charles has never seen this inn. Not surprising: I only take girls there."

Raynaud said nothing. So, he thought, the goading begins already. Well, let it start. Richard was going to be a very surprised fellow. Very soon.

"Eh, Charles, old buddy?"

"That's right," Raynaud said.

"Actually," Pierce said, honking as he approached a Ferrari, "actually, Charles hasn't seen a hell of a lot. He's still a hick at heart."

"That's right," Raynaud said. "Now you'd better slow down."

"Jane," said Pierce. "You may be wondering why I brought Charles along in the back seat. It was for appearances. Actually, when we get to this inn, we will drive Charles to the train station, and send him home to mother. If he doesn't have any money—which he won't, since he never has any money—I will lend him enough to get back to London. Then you and I—"

"Watch the road," Raynaud said.

He looked quickly at Jane. She said nothing. Her face was blank, expressionless.

Pierce honked at a lorry passing another, slammed on his brakes, and barely missed a collision as the slow-moving truck lumbered over into the right lane.

"As I was saying, we will rapidly dispose of my old buddy here, and be by ourselves at last. You'll adore this inn. It has a thatched roof, and whitewashed walls, and an adorable little garden. And, of course, the beds. Most excellent beds, with those thick feather fluffy quilts to put over you."

Jane said nothing.

Raynaud said, "Maybe she doesn't want to go."

"Are you deciding for her, old buddy?"

"No," Raynaud said. "But don't you think you ought to ask her?"

The Maserati tore down the road, streaking past the other cars, its engine screaming.

"Jane wants to be with me," Pierce said flatly.

Jane said nothing. Her eyes were on the road. She seemed fascinated, mesmerized, by the pavement rushing up toward them.

"She doesn't."

"She does," Pierce said. "She does." He laughed a harsh, sarcastic laugh. "You're deluding yourself, old buddy. Jane is a young model, and she digs money. I have money. And you? You've got the Mexican jungle. Nothing else: just the jungle. It's not for her, believe me. Her beautiful skin would be chewed by mosquitoes." Richard sighed.

"No, the jungle is not for her. All the snakes and natives and stinking swamps—not for her. This is a young woman of breeding and refinement."

He reached over and caressed her knee.

"Take your hands off me," Jane said coldly.

Raynaud felt an instant of pure, deep pleasure. "You heard the lady."

"Lady?" Richard laughed.

"You heard the lady," Raynaud said.

Jane, sensing the rising tension in the car, said, "Let's take it easy, fellas."

"That's right," Richard said. "You heard the lady, Charles. Take it easy."

"Take your hand off her knee."

"She likes it."

"She doesn't."

Jane was watching the road. Raynaud glanced at the speedometer. It was up to 170, and the engine sounded capable of much more.

"Richard," Jane said, "please drive with both hands. We're going very fast."

Richard immediately took his hand off her knee. He held the wheel and stepped on the accelerator. The needle moved forward, nudging 200 miles an hour.

"If you touch her again, old buddy," Raynaud said, "I'll beat your brains in."

Richard laughed.

The car streaked down the road at a flat 200 miles.

"I'm serious, old buddy," Raynaud said.

Jane turned back to him. "Please stop," she said. "Just forget it."

Raynaud said, "This is between us. Just the two of us."

"He'll kill us all," Jane said.

Richard laughed. "Me? A superb driver like me?"

Up ahead was an Aston Martin, doing 150. They approached it with frightening speed, as if it was standing still.

"Whee!" shouted Richard, as he honked the Martin into the right lane, between two slow-moving lorries. "Isn't this fun?"

"Please be careful," Jane said.

Raynaud said nothing.

"What's the matter, Charles? Scared?"

"No," Raynaud said.

"Afraid I'll walk away with your girl?"

"She's not my girl."

"You'd like her to be, though, wouldn't you?"

"No," Raynaud said. "I just don't want her hurt."

"In that case," Richard said, "better leave me alone. We're doing two hundred."

Raynaud watched the traffic in the right lane. It was a continuous stream of Minis, Volks, lorries, and slow MG's.

"Worried, old buddy?"

"Of course I'm worried."

"That's good."

Pierce put his hand very deliberately on Jane's knee. He caressed it, and pushed back the skirt to touch her thigh.

"She feels good, old buddy."

Jane stared forward. "Better watch the driving, Richard."

"I am."

His hand continued to stroke her skin.

"Very, very good, old buddy."

Raynaud sat back in his seat. He was thinking hard, trying to remember the Mexican trick, the thing they did with the neck. There was something...

"Deep in thought, old buddy?"

"Maybe."

"You touch me, and we go off the road at two hundred. Curtains for everyone."

"Maybe."

The neck. The carotids, arteries to the brain.

"Forget it, old buddy. Fate has willed it. You will be taken to the train station and deposited. You'll ride back to London, and Jane and I—"

There was a break in the traffic. Up ahead, a clear stretch of road, two lanes for three miles, and then a bridge overhead.

Raynaud grabbed Pierce around the neck. His fingers squeezed.

"Hey!"

The car swerved crazily.

"Let him go! Let him go!" Jane screamed.

Raynaud maintained his grip. He leaned forward, took the wheel, and steered them into the right-hand lane.

"Charles! We'll all be killed!"

They went off the road, into the dirt, then back on. Pierce and Raynaud fought for control of the car. They swerved back and forth; the speedometer dropped to 170.

The bridge came closer.

Jane screamed.

Pierce made choking sounds and tried to steer deliberately for the bridge. Raynaud shifted his grip, moving forward and catching Pierce in a hammerlock; with his free hand he tried to maneuver the wheel.

"For God's sake," whimpered Jane. "For God's sake, stop it, both of you."

The speedometer was down to 150. The bridge came closer by the second. At the last moment, Raynaud spun the wheel and they moved away, down the road. Pierce suddenly let go and swung with his fists back over his head. Raynaud took a blow to the back of the neck and the face.

Down to 100. Raynaud was now the only person holding the wheel. He released it, counting on the balance of the Maserati to run straight, and punched Pierce viciously in the jaw. Jane grabbed the wheel and tried to steer them off the road as Pierce and Raynaud swung at each other within the narrow confines of the car.

Suddenly they were off the road, onto the muddy shoulder, bouncing and jouncing. Raynaud landed a solid right to Pierce's ear; Pierce gouged Raynaud's eye with his thumb.

Jane managed to swing her foot over the gearbox and stamp on the brake. The car came to an abrupt halt, throwing them all forward. For a moment, they were stunned, and then Pierce, bleeding from his lower lip, leapt out of the car and stood glowering.

"Come on out, you son of a bitch, I'll kill you."

Raynaud started to get out, pushing the bucket seat forward. When he was halfway out, Pierce slammed the door shut, pushing his whole weight against it, catching Raynaud's neck and ankle. Raynaud saw gray for a moment, a wave of dizziness. He tried to push the door open. Pierce swung, hard, and caught Raynaud in the throat beneath the jaw. Raynaud felt a wave of blinding pain.

Pierce, holding Raynaud pinned by the door, swung again, hitting Raynaud in the nose. And then, with a mighty effort, Raynaud forced the door open, throwing Pierce back to the ground. Raynaud got out and stood over him.

"Get up, you little bastard."

Pierce looked at Raynaud and got to his feet slowly, warily.

"I've wanted to do this for a long time," Raynaud said.

"You've got your chance, old buddy," Pierce said. He stood, and flung a handful of dirt at Raynaud.

It missed his eyes. Raynaud stepped forward.

"Nice try."

Pierce began to look frightened. He took a nervous step back.

"Going somewhere?" Raynaud said. He grinned. "I'll tell you

a secret. I threw that gun away. The one with the phony bullets. So I'll have to kill you with my bare hands."

Behind him, Raynaud was aware that Jane was calling to him, telling him to cut it out, to stop everything. But he paid no attention; he saw only Pierce, and felt only the blood trickling down from his nose and oozing into his sock from the cut on his ankle.

"Come on," Raynaud said. "Stand and fight. Old buddy."

Pierce took another step back, then stopped. He seemed to gather courage and sprang forward. His foot came up, going for the crotch.

Raynaud caught it easily in his hand, and spun the heel. Pierce tumbled to the ground.

Raynaud picked him up, held him by the collar, and swung at his face. Hard. As hard as he could, hoping he would break something.

Pierce fell backward, clutching his face, covering it with his hands. Raynaud picked him up again, feeling fury now, a blood-thirsty sense, as all the rage, the taunts, the torments of the past week came back to him.

He punched him in the stomach, sinking his fist into soft flesh. Pierce gave a gasping grunt, and his knees buckled. Raynaud did not let him fall, but punched again. Pierce vomited.

Raynaud dropped him.

"You've soiled my hand. Old buddy."

Pierce, rolling on the ground in pain, made gasping noises.

Raynaud said, "You've got a lot of money, Dickie. But no guts." He wiped his bleeding knuckle reflectively. "Pretty good with the broads, as long as you pay them enough. But otherwise, nothing. And no brains. Short on brains, Dickie. Did you really think I was going to kill you? I'm not going to kill you. Get up."

Pierce moaned and tried to roll away.

"Get up!"

Pierce made no move, so Raynaud kicked him as hard as he could, just above the left kidney.

"Didn't you hear me, old buddy? You think I'm talking just to amuse you, like the old days? You think I'm waiting for you to buy the next drink? Get up."

Pierce, grimacing, tried to get to his feet, fell once, and tried again. He made it the second time. His eyes were wide with terror. His mouth was purple and swollen. He spit out a tooth and said, "I'll get you for this, Raynaud. I swear I will."

"No, old buddy. You won't. Because you haven't got the guts."

In a final, desperate lunge, Pierce attacked, butting Raynaud with his head, falling on him, his hands going to the eyes and the groin, tugging, pulling...

Raynaud struck. The blow caught Pierce on the side of the head and knocked him sideways. Feeling spikes of pain in his body, seeing flashing spots in his eyes, Raynaud got up, dusted himself off, and said, "You shouldn't fight dirty, old buddy."

He kicked Pierce twice more in the stomach and walked away. He did not look back at the body, and he did not hear the moans. He was afraid to look back, afraid he might change his mind.

Jane was standing next to the car. Raynaud looked at the door, at his blood on it.

Jane said, "Are you proud of yourself?"

"Yeah," he said. "It makes me feel good all over."

"I thought you were going to kill him, for a minute there."

"It occurred to me," Raynaud said. He felt suddenly tired, his body pained, his limbs heavy. He realized for the first time that he was gasping for breath, panting. He got into the passenger seat and said, "Let's go. You drive."

"You're going to leave him?"

"That's right. I'm going to leave him."

She got behind the wheel and closed the door. "Are you insane?"

"Sure."

"You must be. He'll have the police—"

"No, he won't. Drive."

She stuck out her chin defiantly and said, "I'm going to stay with him."

"The hell you are. Drive the car." Her little game annoyed him. Showing all this concern for Richard, all of a sudden. Hell, she didn't like Richard. Nobody liked Richard.

"If only you weren't so damned big," she said, but she started the car and pulled onto the road.

"Drive to the nearest petrol station, and stop there. We'll leave the car, and send someone back for him. Then you and I will get a taxi."

"A taxi?"

"That's right."

"To where?"

Raynaud sighed and closed his eyes. With his tongue he felt one of his front teeth; it was loose and bleeding. The pain in his head and his ankle was getting worse.

"Some place romantic," he said.

11. GENTLE CONVERSATION

Everything was wrong. He expected to feel cleansed. He expected to feel good. But he didn't; he felt like hell and everything hurt. Then there was the gas-station attendant, who was stunned when he saw Raynaud. He asked no questions and did as he was told with quick, nervous gestures. They left the car there, and took a taxi back to London.

"This will cost you a fortune," Jane said.

She seemed angry. Now why the hell was she angry? She could be anything, anything at all, but why angry?

"I'm the last of the big spenders," Raynaud said. He licked his lips and tasted salty blood. "You have a Kleenex?"

She gave him one. He wiped his bruised nose and face. One eye was swelling up, and the pain in his throat was severe.

"Why did you do that?" Jane said.

"Do what?"

"That fight, back there. Was it for me?"

"No."

"Because I don't appreciate the Neanderthal act. Dragging women away by their hair went out a million years ago."

"Don't flatter yourself. It wasn't for you."

"Then why?"

"It's a long story."

"It's a long ride into London."

She watched him for a moment, then said, "Here, give me that." She took the Kleenex away from him and licked it with the tip of her tongue. She cleaned his face; he winced as she touched the sore spots. But still, he liked the way she touched him. She had a good touch.

"Hurt much?"

"Hell, yes," he said. "It hurts a lot."

"I was just asking," she said.

She was silent then, wiping the blood away. She saw his ankle and took off his shoe and sock; the gash was deep and bleeding heavily. She cleaned it very efficiently and stopped the flow with more Kleenex. She seemed to regard the wound very matter-of-factly; most women would have fainted at the sight of it.

Finally she said, "I wish you hadn't done it."

"Oh?"

"Yes," she said.

After that, they said nothing at all. A dead and irritating silence fell. Raynaud reached into his pocket for cigarettes and came out with a mangled pack. He glared at it and tossed it out the window.

"Got a cigarette?"

She gave him one and watched as he lit it. His hands felt thick and sore and clumsy; the match wouldn't strike. Finally he got it lit. He found himself suddenly very angry. He was angry with himself, and angry with her. He was angry with Pierce, with the boy in the gas station, even with the cab driver and the traffic on the road.

Jane was staring out the window, doing a very good job of ignoring him. Finally, she said, "Are you really as brutal as you act?"

"Yeah."

"Because it's frightening, sometimes."

"Yeah."

She spoke without looking at him. Like he wasn't there; like she was holding a telephone conversation.

"Why," she said, "did you stare at me all the time?"

"When?"

"The last few days. Ever since we met at that party."

"I always stare at women. I'm brutal."

She sighed. "All right, I'm sorry I said that."

"Don't be."

She turned to look at him, and said, "Go to hell, you stupid bastard."

At the next town, some shitty little London suburban town, he told the taxi driver to go to the railroad station. There he got out and gave the driver a ten-pound note, directing him to take Jane to her hotel in London.

She frowned at him. "Where are you going?"

"I'm going back by train."

"Why?"

"I can't stand the company."

"Oh?"

She hesitated then, clearly angry, her face turning red. On her, it was rather attractive, but he was not in the mood to see her as attractive.

"I'm going with you," she said.

She got out of the taxi and slammed the door.

"You're not," he said.

"I am."

"I can take care of myself," he said.

She said nothing at all, but strode forward to the ticket booth and bought two tickets. He insisted on paying for his own, and she told him, very softly and sweetly, to go to hell.

"Pleasant."

"Think what you want," she said.

There was a twenty-minute wait until the next London train to King's Cross; they went out to the platform. Raynaud was limping badly because of his ankle.

"You ought to see a doctor about that," she said.

"I'll try to remember."

He was getting strange looks from the other people on the platform. Jane noticed and said, "Why are they staring?"

"I look funny."

"You do not." She said it with vehemence; he glanced quickly at her.

"No worse than any other beat-up gorilla," she added.

They went into the British Railways canteen, a dilapidated cafeteria, and got two cups of tea. They sat at a corner table; Raynaud sipped the tea and winced as the hot liquid burned around his loose teeth. She offered him a cigarette and he took it.

"I just don't understand you," she said. "I don't understand you at all."

"Well, I don't understand you, either."

"Did you *have* to beat him up, for Christ's sake?"

"Yes," Raynaud said. "I did."

"Why?"

"Because."

"Because what?"

"Just because," he said.

She was obviously annoyed by his answer, and she started looking in her purse for lipstick.

He looked around the room at the other people in the canteen, and then out the window at the people on the platform. They were middle-aged, middle-class, nondescript people. Then he looked back at her as she pursed her lips and ran the lipstick over them. She was very beautiful. Startlingly beautiful.

"I like that shade of lipstick," he said, feeling like a fool.

"So do I," she said, not smiling.

The loudspeaker announced the train to London, and they went out to board. They were traveling second class, in a small compartment, but it was an afternoon local, and not crowded. They had the compartment to themselves. The train started, and he felt the gentle rocking. He must have drifted off to sleep for a while; when he opened his eyes she was looking at him.

"Tired?"

He yawned. "I guess." He started to stretch and felt the pain and stiffness in his body. He winced and sat still.

"I'm sorry you hurt," she said.

"Kiss it and make it go away."

To his surprise, she leaned over and kissed him softly on the cheek, then moved back.

"Why'd you do that?"

"I wanted to see what I thought," she said.

"And?"

"I don't know," she said. She dropped her eyes and made nervous movements with her hands. Finally she opened her purse.

"You can't put on lipstick again," he said. "It wasn't that much of a kiss."

She hesitated, then closed her purse. She folded her hands in her lap and sat quite still for a long time, her eyes moving over his face, noticing the cuts and the bruises, the slowly swelling eye.

"You look like hell," she said, and she kissed him. Very hard, very long, very nicely.

When she stopped, she sat back with an odd expression on her face. She looked confused, afraid, and somehow pleased with herself.

"Now can I put on lipstick?" she said.

"No," he said.

He reached out and drew her to him and kissed her. He felt awkward at first, and then it was easy.

For a while, holding her in his arms, he was aware of the rhythmic clicking of the train, and then after that, he was aware of nothing at all.

She rested her head on his shoulder and said, "Are you a bastard?"

"Sort of."

"All I've ever known is bastards. I don't want another one."

"Reform me," he said, and kissed her again.

She turned her head slightly, so that he kissed her cheek. "Do I have a chance?"

"Better than average," he said.

After that he slept, and when he awoke the train was rumbling into the cavernous spaces of King's Cross station. She stroked his head and said, "You know, you haven't been very fair."

"Why?"

"The first night I got to London you had me in suspense."

"How's that?"

"You didn't want Richard to know we had met in Mexico. You said I was in danger."

"You are."

"What kind of danger?"

"A scandal," he said, "and a murder."

"How do you know?"

"Meet me tonight," he said. "We'll discuss it."

"Why should I meet you tonight?"

"Because I'm in the scandal, too."

12. PROMISES

"Six ball in the side pocket," Jane said, and leaned over the cue. She hesitated a moment, then shot; with a click the ball dropped. She straightened and rubbed the cue with the resin block. "Why are we here?"

"Good place to talk," Raynaud said.

"About scandals?" she said. "Two ball to the center."

She shot: clean, perfect.

"Among other things."

"You're being very mysterious. As usual. Why will I be involved in a scandal?"

"Because you are Jane Mitchell."

"I have been, for quite some time. Five into the left."

Raynaud watched as she shot. "Yes," he said, "but Jane Mitchell is the sole heir to the Mitchell Mining fortune. Conservative estimate of twenty million dollars. Holdings throughout the world. Including some shares in copper mines at Darwin, Australia."

She stopped and set her cue down. She stared at him in astonishment. "How the hell did you know that?"

"A tired old man told me," Raynaud said. "In Paris."

"It so happens I'm selling that stock," she said. "Very soon."

"I know. Do you know who owns controlling interest in the mines?"

She frowned and shook her head. "No."

"Pierce Industries, Limited."

"You mean…"

Raynaud nodded. "None other."

She regained her composure quickly. She brushed the blond hair back from her face and said, "What does that have to do with scandals?"

"I'm not certain. But I have an idea."

"It's funny you should mention that stock business," she said. "It's really quite peculiar. My guardians got some kind of tip, telling them to sell. Apparently some Dutchmen want the stock badly and will drive up the price. We stand to make a great profit."

Raynaud frowned. The pieces did not fit, at least, not yet. They were falling together, but not interlocking.

"That's why you're selling now?"

"Yes. Apparently this tip was really good."

"Where did it come from? The tip."

"No idea. Three to the right side."

She shot.

"I think," he said, "that you should be very careful in the next few days."

"I'm always careful," she said. "And you seem to forget Mexico."

"What about it?"

She opened her purse, and allowed him to look inside. The black revolver was there, among Kleenex, notepads, pens, make-up.

"You always carry it with you?"

"Always," she said. "Four ball to the side pocket." She shot, clearing the table.

"The game's over," she said, "and you've lost."

He smiled.

As it turned out, she did not go home directly. Instead, they went to a private club after the closing time for the pubs; it was a jazz place with an occasional stripper who attempted, unsuccessfully, to enliven things. Jane didn't mind the place because she had always been interested in strippers. Most women were, she felt. It was a kind of challenge, six different ways. Much more of a challenge for women to watch a stripper than for men.

They had several drinks, too many, really. She began to get tight, and the slight tic in her eye began to get bad, as it always did when she was tight, but she didn't give a damn, because she trusted the guy, somehow. She wasn't sure how she trusted him, or why, but she trusted him. And it had a bad effect: loosened the tongue.

"You're staring at me again," she said.

"Sorry. It's your hair."

"You're always staring at me. Why is that?"

"Maybe I like you."

"Do you *lust* after me?" she asked, giggling. Oops: drunk. Mustn't say things like that.

"A little."

"Just for the record," she said, raising her glass, "I am thirty-seven—twenty-one—thirty-six. Much better than *her.*" She nodded to the stripper.

"Yes."

"I have a very small waist."

"I noticed."

"I noticed you noticed." She giggled again.

"Tell me about yourself," he said.

"You wouldn't want to hear."

"I would."

"Well," she said, "then we need another drink."

"You sure?"

"I keep telling you," she said, "that I can look out for myself."

He got her another drink. He had a sort of concerned look on his face, very sweet.

"Well," she said. "I'll tell you. There were these five guys, see? Five. One, two, three…" She counted them on her fingers. "All the way up to five."

"Yes?"

"And they were all bastards."

She told herself she shouldn't be talking about this, not about any of it. There wasn't any sense, any point to talking about it.

"I've known a lot of bastards, men-wise."

"Ever been married?"

"No. And I never will be. I hate marrys."

"Marriage."

"Yes. You said it."

"Why do you hate it?"

"Just because. It's a bad idea. And all the men, all they really want is your mon—your body."

"That's not true."

"Yeah, so they say."

He seemed unhappy to hear her talk like this. He was frowning, concerned. Really sweet. A sweet bruiser, that's what he was.

"You're cute."

He smiled. "So they say."

She sipped her drink, spilling some. "Oops. Must have been drinking." She wiped her chin with her finger. "You know what else is cute?"

"What?"

"Diapers. They're very cute."

"Diapers?"

"Yes. You know, like for baby bottoms."

He nodded.

"Baby bottoms, they're cute, too. Small and round and nice. When I have a baby, I'm going to change the diapers myself and the hell with the maid. And that's the truth."

"Sounds good," he said.

"You are humoring me," she said sternly. "You are humoring me because I am potted. A potted plant. That's me. Right?"

"You're okay," he said. "Don't worry."

"I am not okay. I am potted. Admit it."

"I admit it. You're potted."

She giggled. "I like honest men." She sipped the drink again, this time without spilling it. She set the glass down with a small grin of triumph. "Tell you a secret."

"What."

"I almost had a baby, once."

"You did?"

"Stop prying," she said, pulling away from him on the bar. "You expect me to tell you everything about myself? I hardly know you."

She paused, and looked at him, cocking one eyebrow. She could not really see him well, because of the damn tic in her eye. But she pretended she could see him. Pretending was almost as good as the real thing.

"Are you a nice person?"

He shrugged.

"Because, you *seem* like a nice person. But you can never tell. What do you do for a living, with those snakes and everything?"

"I'm a smuggler."

"You're supposed to be serious. We are having a serious discussion. Very intellectual. What do you do for a living?"

"I'm a smuggler," he repeated.

"You know," she said, "you sound as if you believed that."

"I do," he said. "In fact, I'm convinced of it."

"A smuggler?"

"Not so loud," he said, looking around. Christ, he was cute when he looked around.

"You know what else is cute?" she said. "Pregnant women. They are very cute."

"You think so?"

"I do. I definitely do. I'll tell you a secret." She frowned. "No, I won't. Never mind."

"Go ahead."

"There you are, prying again." She finished her drink. "You know what? I think you are up to no good. No good at all. I think you're a bastard and a liar and a thief. And I know you're a smuggler. Though you're sweet to tell me."

"Any time."

"But why are you hanging around with Richard Pierce?"

"Damned if I know," Raynaud said.

"He's not nice."

"He is," Raynaud said, "much worse than that."

In front of the hotel, he opened the door to the car and said, "Can you make it all right?"

"Sure," she said. "It's always easy for me." And she thought, for Christ's sake, shut your mouth. You're asking for it.

Charles said, "That's good to know."

"It doesn't matter," she said, "one way or the other."

"You're right," he said, and kissed her lightly.

As she walked up the steps to the hotel, watching as the doorman weaved in front of her, drunken doorman, a real disgrace, she thought to herself that Charles Raynaud was an evil and unprincipled man, and very, very exciting.

13. MEDICINAL PURPOSES

"*Shit!* Shit, shit, shit, shit!"

"Take it easy," Black said, as he swabbed the cuts on Richard's face. "You'll be all right."

"The hell I will. What is that stuff, anyway?"

"Alcohol."

"Shit, it stings like hell."

"Just relax," Black said mildly.

He surveyed Richard's battered body. Charles had done quite a thorough job. Richard's left eye was closed; there were cuts and bruises around his jaw and dark purple blotches on his abdomen and back.

Black finished cleaning the cuts and applied bandages. Richard groaned and swore whenever the alcohol touched him.

"I'd like to kill her," he said.

"Her?"

"That fucking girl. I'd like to kill her."

"Why the girl?"

"It's all her fault. Charles and I were friends, before this. Before she showed up. He was the only real friend I had. Then she got in the way, with her coy prancing, her… her…" He trailed off, wincing as Black applied bandages.

"You're angry with her?" Black said.

"Stop psychoanalyzing me," Richard said. "I'm not in the mood."

"I wasn't psychoanalyzing you. Just asking."

"The hell. You were psychoanalyzing."

Black shrugged. He finished with the bandages and stepped back. "There," he said. "All done." He glanced at his watch, "I want you to go to the hospital now and have some X-rays."

"I don't want X-rays."

"And then, you can come back here."

"I don't want any bleeding X-rays."

"It's a precaution," Black said. "You might have a concussion. We'd better check it—after all, you wouldn't want to die just before you inherited your fortune, would you?"

"Lucienne'd love it."

"Forget Lucienne."

"Yah. I'd like to."

Black picked up the phone. "I'll just call a taxi," he said, "and they'll take you over to the hospital."

Pierce touched his bruised eye gingerly. "Like to kill that stupid Yank bitch," he said.

A marvelously blatant example of displacement, Black thought, when he was alone in his study. Totally irrational, and fully complete. Richard was angry, consumed with self-pity and hatred for Charles. But he could not fight Charles again, so he shifted his anger to the girl, a more vulnerable target.

Interesting. And useful.

Black tapped his pencil on the desk. This development could be put to use, particularly if he employed his trump card. For Black had a way to put pressure on Richard, the kind of pressure he would now be extremely vulnerable to.

It was all a matter of timing, of presentation. If the situation were presented artfully, Richard would react with an irrepressible fury. And if there were an extra touch...

An hour and a half passed before Richard returned.

"I think they sterilized me."

Interesting imagery, Black thought. "Oh?"

"Fucking X-rays," Richard said, entering the room. "You didn't tell me they were going to take so many. Sprayed my gonies a dozen times over."

"It was for the best," Black said. "But, Richard—"

"How about a drink?" Pierce said. "For medicinal purposes."

"All right."

They walked downstairs to the living room. On the stairs, Black felt a slight twinge of anginal pain in his chest. He ignored it, expecting it to go away, and fortunately it did.

They came into the living room. "What will you have?"

"Vodka. Straight."

"Ice?"

"No. This is medicinal, remember?"

Black poured it and handed it to him.

"Not joining me?"

"No. Bit too early."

"I haven't seen you take a drink for a long time," Pierce said. "And you've cut out smoking, too."

"No, just cut down."

"Something wrong?"

"No. Just trying to ease off on my vices."

Pierce laughed. "I'm the one that should be doing that."

Black sat down and motioned Pierce to a chair. Richard sat slowly, grimacing in pain as he settled himself. "Jesus, I hurt all over."

"I can imagine."

"Jesus, all over." He sipped the drink and said, "Fucking girl."

"About the girl, Richard…"

"Like to kill her."

"Do you know who she is?"

"A Yank tart, that's who she is."

"Not exactly, Richard." Black sighed.

"Something wrong?"

"Not exactly, Richard. But I have some serious news."

Richard waited expectantly. Black let him wait, let him get a bit nervous.

"I've just been told," Black said, "that the girl is traveling incognito."

"Oh?"

"Yes. She is sole heir to the Mitchell Mining fortune. She's a millionaire."

Pierce laughed. "Impossible."

"Quite true, I'm afraid."

"Why are you afraid?"

"Because she is here to sell some stock in Copper and Brass, Limited."

"Say," Pierce said, "we own that, don't we?"

"Until now."

"What do you mean?"

"I'd better explain," Black said.

And he did, quickly and tersely. He explained about the Dutch, and about the decision of the board. He put it with the proper degree of subtlety, and the proper degree of bluntness.

Finally, Richard said, "What you're saying is that Shore Industries, Limited, will be sold off."

Black looked down at his hands. "Yes."

"That decision is final?"

"I'm afraid it is."

"And they can't be…uh, persuaded to change their minds?"

Black shook his head. "Impossible."

"Shit," Richard said.

"There's no way out," Black said.

"There must be a way out."

"There isn't," Black said.

"There *must* be. Because I must retain control of Shore Industries. There is too much at stake."

Black shrugged.

"What you're saying," Pierce said, "is that the girl will ruin me."

"Well, perhaps not—"

"Yes. Ruin me."

"Richard, there are other avenues, other ways to explore—"

"Don't say it," Richard said. "Don't bother."

"I'm not trying to kid you. I'm trying to make you understand."

"That everyone is screwing me."

"No, indeed, Richard. It is a simple matter of business…"

"The hell." He frowned, lit a cigarette, and sipped his drink. "Tell me," he said. "If the girl is not around, what happens to the deal?"

"I am not certain. She may or may not have signed power of attorney."

"And if she hasn't?"

"Naturally, any sale would be delayed in her absence."

"That's interesting," Richard said.

"But I would strongly advise you, Richard, to avoid any contact—"

"Don't worry," Richard said, standing up. "Don't worry about a thing. I'll figure this out for myself, and I'll take care of it."

"You mustn't be rash."

"I won't be rash," he said, with a slight grin. "I'll be effective."

"Richard, please—"

"Don't worry," Richard said. "Just don't worry about a thing."

He stalked out, leaving Black alone in the room. Black reached into his pocket and removed the small vial of white powder. Dezisen: the perfect treatment, for the perfect condition.

He would use it tomorrow.

14. KIDNAP

She came down the street in front of the hotel shortly before noon, and Raynaud was astonished. She was wearing a vinyl dress of bright red and black checks, cut low in a V between her breasts, and high over her hips. She was wearing bright red velvet boots, knee length, and her long legs straddled a shiny chrome Triumph Bonneville.

She roared down the street and pulled up in front of where he was parked. He leaned out the window of his car and said, "Hey, lady."

He was wearing sunglasses, with a fat cigar between his teeth.

She brushed back her hair with her hand. "Yes?"

He opened the door and growled, "Get in."

She laughed.

"I'm kidnapping you, sweetheart," Raynaud said. "Now move it."

"But I have things to do."

"Too bad. When you're kidnapped, you have to do as you're told."

She laughed again and got in beside him. "Where are you; taking me?"

"To the country."

"Why?"

"To make a pass at you."

"That," she said, "you could do in London."

"But the country is more romantic."

She smiled wryly. "Are you a romantic?"

"That's for me to know, sweetheart, and you to find out."

He drove north and east, up the Kingsway to Southampton Row and right on Euston Road, past King's Cross and St. Pancras. A dingy, depressing part of town, but he regarded it benignly.

"Where in the country?" she said.

"Cambridge. I'm told it's pretty."

"Who told you that?"

"Richard." He laughed.

They picked up the A10 on the northern outskirts of the city and passed through a succession of small towns: Cheshunt, Ware, Buntingford. The land was farming country, perfectly flat.

"Nice day," she said.

"Very nice for a kidnapping."

Overhead the clouds were soft, like pulled cotton, and the sky was light blue.

"I thought as long as you had a gun, you might as well see what a real kidnapping was like."

"It's exciting."

"It will get more exciting."

"Will it?"

"Yes," he said. "By the way, where'd you get your machine?"

"The Bonneville?"

"Yes."

"Bought it a few days ago. You like?"

"I like. You know how to drive?"

"More or less," she said, stretching her legs and pulling her red boots up.

"You make a good impression," he said.

"That's the idea," she said. "I only bought it to impress future kidnappers."

They were caught in a traffic jam in Royston, and stopped for a sandwich and a pint in a roadside pub. It was filled with local laborers and rock 'n' roll from a jukebox.

"Good sandwiches," Jane said. She munched and smiled.

"What's funny?"

"You. You look very earnest today."

"All kidnappers are earnest."

"But your cigar has gone out."

"You can't have everything."

"When are you going to make your pass?" she said.

"When I work up the nerve."

"Oh?"

"Yes. You see, my governess used to beat me with a metal-studded whip. She turned me off women for years."

"When was this?"

"When I was a little boy."

"So now you kidnap girls?"

"Yes."

She smiled and drank the beer from the heavy mug, licking away the foam from her upper lip.

"Could we stop this?" she asked.

"What?"

"This kind of talk. Let's stop it."

"All right."

"Let's say that we've known each other for two weeks, that you've taken me out every night to all the best restaurants, and called me every day, and sent me flowers and passionate, cryptic notes."

"Why would I do a thing like that?"

"Let's just say you did."

"All right. I did. Now what?"

"Now you're taking me into the country for a day. I'm sitting here expecting you to say something important to me."

"Oh."

"Well?"

"I'm trying to think of something important," he said.

"Is it so hard?"

"Yes," he said. "As a matter of fact, it is."

Back in the car she said, "I'm sorry about last night."

"Why?"

"I didn't mean to get so stinking."

"We both were."

"And I didn't mean to say all those things."

"You were very amusing."

"That's good," she said. "I think." She took the cigar out of his mouth and threw it out the window. Then she lit a cigarette, and placed it between his lips.

"Thanks."

"Any time."

"You have nice hands."

"Don't be corny."

"You do. Scout's honor."

"Cornier and cornier."

"Passionate hands. Lusty hands."

"Listen," she said. "The last useful thing these hands did was chop up a horse."

"What kind of a horse?"

"A nice one. But old."

"Where was this?"

"On the ranch. We—"

"You have a ranch?"

"Yes, I was raised on one. And we had this horse—"

"Montana?"

"No, Wyoming. And we had an old horse that broke his leg."

"So you chopped it up."

"No, I killed it first."

"You shot it?"

"No, gave it an injection of Demerol."

"You're a very good shot."

"Thank you."

"Go on."

"Well, the horse died, and we had to get rid of it. *I* had to get rid of it. I was the only one on the ranch at the time. But it was heavy as hell. Have you ever tried to lift a dead horse?"

"No. Never tried to beat one, either."

"There you go again. Corny."

"Sorry."

"Anyway, the pickup was high off the ground, about four feet—"

"You have a pickup?"

"Yes."

"At the ranch?"

"Listen," she said, "are you going to let me tell the story, or what?"

He smoked the cigarette. She said, "Anyway, the pickup was high, so I had to cut the horse into small chunks in order to lift it into the truck, and even then it was heavy. The head, for instance, weighed—"

"Please. I just finished lunch."

"—about fifty pounds. It was really a struggle for a young girl."

"How young were you?"

"Fifteen, at the time."

"You're joking," he said.

She shook her head.

"That's a terrible story," he said.

"I suppose it is," she said. "I had nightmares for months later, but I got over it eventually."

"Like numbers one through five."

"Yes," she said. "Exactly." She smiled: "Some day," she said, "I'll tell you about my ocelots."

Raynaud parked the car and they walked through the Backs, the fields behind the colleges, along the River Cam. Horses and cows grazed in dappled sunlight that filtered through the trees.

As they walked, she said, "You're the quietest kidnapper I ever met."

"We kidnappers are a thoughtful bunch."

"What are you thinking about?"

"The ransom note," he said.

"What will it say?"

"I'm not sure. How much are you worth?"

"Oh," she said. "Not much."

"Then I'll ask for something reasonable. Twenty thousand dollars."

With mock outrage: "I'm worth more than that."

"Okay. Fifty thousand."

"And will the note have a threat?"

"Oh, yes. An awful threat."

She smiled. They walked on. A cow behind St. John's College looked up at them, mouth full of grass. It watched impassively for a moment, then turned away. Birds chirped in the trees overhead. They walked through the formal gardens behind St. John's and sat on the grassy banks of the river, in the shade of a willow. Students punted on the Cam, the girls reclining in the square-ended boats while the boys poled behind.

"It's peaceful here," she said.

He nodded.

"Seriously," she said. "Why did you bring me here?"

He looked at his hands. "I'm not sure."

"You must have had a reason."

"Yes," he said, "I suppose I did."

He put his arm around her and drew her close, feeling the bones of her shoulder. She rested her head on his chest and they looked out at the river. Her body was relaxed against him, and he sensed that she was trusting him in a very deep way, and it gave him a strange, powerful feeling that was almost sad.

"I don't understand any of this," he said.

"Any of what?"

He stroked her hair. "You."

"There's nothing to understand," she said. She put her hand on his chest. "Your heart is beating fast. I can feel it."

"Don't pay any attention. It just likes pretty girls."

"Does it?"

"Yes," he said, and he kissed her.

Whistles and catcalls from the punters interrupted them. They lit cigarettes and stared out at the river, both suddenly uneasy.

"You scare me," she said. "I hope you know what you're doing."

"I don't."

"Then do it again," she said, "and find out."

He lay down on the grass and she bent over him, her short blond curls glowing in the sunlight. He kissed her again, longer. When she broke, she kept her eyes on him.

"Did you mean that?"

"Yes."

"This is serious business."

"Yes," he said, and pulled her down again. There were more shrieks and whistles from the river, but they paid no attention.

Finally, she said, "You're a good kisser, for a kidnapper."

"Takes two."

He smiled. "I think you're sexy."

"I don't mind."

"Neither do I."

Another kiss. He ran his hand down her back, feeling the ridge of her spine, her shoulder blades, the soft hairs of her neck, trying to get used to everything.

"Say," he said, when they broke again. "I think you're habit forming."

"What does that mean?"

"What do you think?"

She brushed her hair back from her face and said, "Say something important to me."

"I love you," he said, and kissed her again.

"Jolly good show!" shouted a voice from the river.

Room 14 of the King's Arms Hotel looked out onto the street, and it was noisy. The furniture was nothing much; her vinyl dress was thrown over the back of a chair, adding a touch of color to the room.

"What are you doing?" she said.

He was touching her lips, and the small indentations left from her teeth, when she had bit down. Then he touched her cheek, the angle of her jaw.

"Casing the joint," he said.

"Sometimes you make me afraid."

"Don't." He placed a finger over her lips, then brought it down, tracing over her chin, down her neck, to her breasts. Her skin was light gold, and there was a faint paleness from a bikini.

"Do you like me?" she asked, in a hesitant voice.

"I love you."

"I mean…"

"Yes," he said. "I like you."

"I worry," she said. "Why should I worry?"

"Because you are a silly girl," he said, touching her knee, feeling the bones, her thigh, the muscles of her hip. Skin. Beautiful, smooth, soft.

"Nice hands," she said.

He smiled. "Corny."

"Nice hands." She sighed. "Touch me again. You have a nice touch."

"So do you."

"I'm glad."

She had mysteriously changed, becoming almost a child, hesitant and offering, waiting for approval. He wanted to reassure her.

"Don't worry," he said.

"I won't," she said. "If you won't."

And then later, in a surprised voice, but a pleased voice, she said, "Again?" and he said, yes, again, if she didn't mind too much, and she said that she didn't mind at all, that it would be a great pleasure, and he said he hoped it would be a great pleasure, and later on she said in a very loud voice that it was a great, oh, yes, a great, yes, a pleasure, great, yes, great.

"I'm sorry," she said.

"About what?"

"Being so loud. And all."

Curled up on her side, legs drawn up into a tawny bundle, she watched him.

"Who's listening?"

"The neighbors," she said, and giggled.

"What neighbors."

"I don't know. Do you love me?"

"Yes," he said.

She let her body stretch out, slowly, luxuriantly, and pressed up against him, fitting herself to him, smoothly and gracefully.

"Christ, you scare me."

"Why?"

"Because I love you."

"That scares you?" He kissed her breast below the pink nipple.

"Hell, yes, it scares me."

"What can I do to reassure you?"

She was quiet a moment, then said, "Well, it will sound funny, but…"

"At your service," he said.

*

She walked to the mirror, her eyes smoldering with a dark, sexy look, walking in a certain way because she knew he was watching and wanted him to watch.

"You were showing off," she said.

He grinned. "I suppose I was."

"But I don't mind," she said. She looked at herself in the mirror. "Do I look different? I feel different."

Raynaud laughed.

"That amuses you?"

"It pleases me."

"It should." She stepped close to the mirror and checked her eyes. "I'm a mess. Did I get mascara all over the pillow?"

"Yes. That's what you get for crying."

"I couldn't help it. I always cry when I'm happy."

"I'll remember that."

She said, "I'm going to take a shower now."

"I'll help you."

"It's not necessary. Aren't you tired?"

Raynaud smiled. "I'm exhausted."

"You ought to be. I can hardly walk."

"Crude girl."

"Oversexed bastard."

She went back to him and kissed him on the cheek. "You're going to think I'm terrible…"

"I do, I do."

"…but I'm starved."

"That's easily taken care of."

"Is it?"

"Yes. There's a restaurant downstairs."

"I didn't notice," she said, and giggled.

They had a corner table and sat grinning at each other, wrapped in their private secret. They rubbed knees under the table. The food, when it came, was ordinary, but it seemed excellent; their conversation seemed fascinating and witty.

After an hour, a tall, strikingly beautiful girl came over to their table.

"Hello, Charles."

Raynaud looked up. "Hello, Sandra." He stood, feeling suddenly awkward, aware that Jane was watching him closely "Join us? Jane Mitchell, Sandra Callarini."

The girls exchanged slight nods and cold, appraising glances.

"No, I can't, thanks. I'm here with friends."

"Ah."

"I just came by to say hello."

"How have you been, Sandra?"

"All right. It's off, you know."

Raynaud shook his head. "I hadn't heard."

"Yes. I called it off yesterday."

"I'm sorry."

"Don't be." She extended her hand. "Let's have lunch some time."

As he shook her hand, feeling the slight squeeze, he said, "I'd like that very much."

"Goodbye."

"Goodbye, Sandra."

"Miss Mitchell."

"Miss Callarini."

Sandra went back to her table; as Raynaud sat down, Jane said, "Very pretty. Was she number four hundred seventy-four?"

"No."

"A friend?"

"She was Richard's fiancée."

"Ah. He has good taste."

"He has money."

After dinner, they went back to the lobby. Raynaud glanced toward the stairs, and back at Jane. She shook her head; he paid the bill, and they headed back in the car toward London. Jane looked out the window at the spires of Cambridge as they left.

She lit a cigarette and said, "Do you know Reggie Stone?"

"No."

"He's a photographer. Fashion. With a very large ear for gossip. He told me all about Lucienne Pierce. Richard's stepmother."

"What about her?"

"Do you know who her latest lover is?"

"No," he said.

"Somebody named Charles Raynaud," she said.

"Incredible," he said.

She shook her head and smoked the cigarette. "I know quite a bit about Charles Raynaud," she said. "In college, I knew a girl from Texas. Her father was an oil millionaire. Her name was Lisa Barrett. Father named J. D. Barrett. An art collector."

"Oh," Raynaud said.

"So you see, I knew about you, from the start. Last week, when you were in Mexico. I knew all about you."

"Terrible."

"And now I want to know," she said, "what's going on with you and Richard Pierce."

He was silent a long time, driving the car, thinking about the hotel room, about London, and Paris, everything.

"You really want to know?"

"I really do."

He sighed. "I was brought here as a dupe," he said. "By Lucienne Pierce. She arranged for me to spend time with her stepson Richard, whom I had known years before. She gave me a song and dance about protecting Richard; she offered me a lot of money. Obviously she doesn't intend to ever pay off. She is carefully arranging a huge scandal involving Richard, me, you, and probably several other people. She is setting it up, and then arranging for it to explode. The idea is to get Richard jailed for twenty years or so."

"That means murder."

"Yes. And meantime, Richard knew all along what was happening. He hired me in order to arrange a kind of reverse play —set up a murder attempt by me, using fake bullets. He also arranged several other murders, very inept. Hired a man to do it."

"Sounds complicated."

"It is. But you forget the stakes: half a billion dollars."

"And you?" Jane said. "What is your plan?"

"I have no plan."

"Why did you take me to Cambridge today?"

"For the same reason I beat up Richard yesterday."

"To force the issue?"

"Yes," he said. "To force the issue."

"When will it happen?"

"Probably," Raynaud said, "tonight."

"How?"

"I haven't the faintest idea," he said.

15. STIMULUS

Jonathan Black sat in his flat and glanced at his watch. It would not be long now. Within an hour, the trigger, the mental firing mechanism, would be activated. And the emotional charge would be discharged.

The Scotch would taste sweet, nothing more. Richard would never know what had hit him. He would react unreasonably, in a furious, uncontrollable rage.

Quite satisfying.

There only remained to provide the direction for that rage, and he was certain that his plans would be adequate. The fury would be channeled, directed, concentrated.

And Richard would never know what had hit him.

16. RESPONSE

Richard Pierce sat naked in the living room, beneath the painting of the enormous hamburger, and tickled Dominique. He was very drunk, drunker than he could remember, so drunk he could hardly talk, but he didn't give a damn. Dominique was laughing, pleading for mercy, trying to roll away from him. Finally she did, and fell on the floor.

He laughed and patted the sofa alongside him. "Come on back."

She rubbed her bottom where she had fallen, and pouted. "No."

"Come on."

"No."

"Coward."

Still rubbing: "Look who's talking."

He stared at her in stony silence. "What," he said slowly, working to form the words, "what, pray tell, do you mean by that remark?"

"Nothing."

"Bloody hell. Tell me."

"I mean nothing."

"Listen, you little bitch—"

"Don't call me a bitch."

He reached out and grabbed her arm.

"You're hurting," she said.

"Tell me."

"I was in the beauty parlor today," she said, standing up and pulling her arm free. She rubbed it. "Everybody was talking."

"Oh?"

"About you and Charles."

"I want to forget that. It was all her fault."

"They talked about you," Dominique said.

"Me?"

"They said things that were not nice. I want another drink."

"You can't have one."

"I want one, Richard."

"Listen, Snapper, you don't get a drink unless I say so. That's the way it is. Now come over here."

"And do what?"

"Earn it. Play the flute."

"Ugh."

She hated to play the flute; he knew that.

"Earn it."

She shook her head and walked across the room, sitting down in a leather chair. "No."

"What did you say?"

"I said no, you drunken fool."

He could hardly believe his ears. "Do you know who you're talking to?"

"A drunken fool," Dominique said.

"Listen, Snapper, if I become tired of you, I won't pay—"

"Oh? You are so generous?" She laughed. "You have no money. You spent it all on the Italian."

"I have plenty of money."

"Whenever you want money, you must run to the skirts of your mother."

"Stepmother." He said it slowly.

"Mother," Dominique said.

"Be careful, little girl."

"Such a big man," Dominique said, "around women. You're very brave and tough around women, aren't you? But what about men? What about Charles? How tough were you then?"

He got up, unsteadily, and walked toward her. He bent over and drew his hand back to slap her.

She kicked out her bare foot, catching him in the stomach, and he toppled backward to the floor, feeling ludicrous.

"Drunken fool."

"Why did you do that?"

"Because you are a fool."

He got to his feet. "I'll beat you for this."

"You will beat no one."

She stood and walked toward him. He swung at her, but she ducked away easily: he was too drunk. He almost lost his balance. She slapped him twice, hard, stinging across his face.

"In the beauty parlor," she said, "I listened to them and I thought they were wrong. Now, I know they were right."

She swung again. A sharp, burning slap.

"They were completely right. You are a fool."

Slap.

"And a drunkard."

Slap. He was moving backward, holding his hands up, protecting his face.

"And a coward."

Slap.

"And it is good that Charles slept with Sandra, and it is good that he is sleeping with Jane—"

"They know that?"

Slap.

"Everyone knows that. And it is good, too, that she will ruin you."

Dimly, through his intoxication, he understood what she was saying.

"You mean…"

She pushed him disdainfully down on the couch, and stood over him, hands on her hips. "It is all over the city. Mitchell is selling stocks, and your fortune will be destroyed. Everyone is laughing at you, calling you a coward and a fool."

Abruptly, she leaned over and spat in his face.

"And I call you a coward and a fool."

He wiped the spittle off his cheek. The little bitch, the stupid, ignorant, ungrateful little cheap cunt. Before he was through with her, she'd be nothing, just nothing, a body in the gutter. She would pay for her arrogance, her stupid, childish…

"Where are you going?"

"I am sleeping in the guest room tonight. And tomorrow I return to Paris. Good night."

She stomped into the guest room. He heard the lock turning in the door.

Fix her, the little bitch. Show her who had the last word.

His first thought was the gas. He could turn it on and leave the apartment, going to Yvonne's—going anywhere, anywhere at all—and coming back in the morning to find her dead. But no: a moment later, he heard her opening the window in the bedroom.

He got up and poured himself another Scotch.

His umpteenth. It tasted sweet. Jesus, Jesus, sweet Scotch, what were things coming to? When Scotch tasted sweet, the end was near. That was what they all said. Perhaps an ice cube.

He went into the kitchen, wincing in the harsh light, and got a cube. He sipped the drink: didn't mean a damn.

He shook his head. Damn them all. Damn Dominique, and Charles, and the cause of it all, Jane. Damn the beauty parlors of this world, with the catty women and their damned dryers telling tales out of school.

Two days! That was all it had been since the fight. Two days, and it was all over London. They were laughing at him, snickering behind their hands.

They hadn't used to do that. Once he was a leader, an admired playboy, he had his pick of the women—hell, he still did…

"Everyone is laughing at you…"

Let them. Hollow laughs. Soon he would be rich, and they could all go to hell. He would live in Morocco or Beirut and forget London, forget everyone who lived here.

"Everyone is calling you a coward and a fool…"

Talk was cheap. Only money counted. Certainly they were pleased to see him fall, they were waiting for it, hoping for it. They thrived on misfortune.

"And she will ruin you…"

Jane. The cause of it all. Before Jane, everything was good. He had good times with Raynaud in Paris, and with Dominique, and with the others, and everything was happy. He was respected, even admired, by Raynaud. And the others. And he was going to be rich.

Until Jane.

Stupid, sly, stinking bitch of a girl.

Jane.

Jesus Christ, the Scotch was like molasses, it was so sweet.

And it had a funny color. He gulped it down, shuddering, and poured vodka. He wanted to forget it all, but he was unpleasantly awake. Feeling less drunk by the second. He swallowed two shots of vodka neat.

Still awake.

Grass: a stick in the bedroom. He smoked it quickly. But it did not help, his mind kept coming back in slow circles to Jane. Jane. Jane. Jane. He hated her, he loathed her, she was even blond, like Lucienne. He hated her, wished he had never met her, never set eyes on her.

If only Jane wasn't there. How pleasant it would be. Raynaud would be his friend again. Dominique would be his friend again. Beauty parlors would stop talking. The world would be a happy place again, without Jane.

On the counter in the kitchen was a long knife, a butcher's knife with a heavy wooden handle and a finely honed, short blade. It glinted in the light. He picked up the knife, closing his fingers around the handle, staring closely at the blade. And thinking. And thinking.

He was suddenly so furious he could hardly speak.

17. THE NEEDLE

Jonathan Black sat in his car with his hand placed over his heart. The pains worried him; they were getting worse, and more frequent. It was all a very bad thing.

As he sat there, brooding, Richard came hurrying out of the apartment, swaying drunkenly. He bent over his car and put the key in the lock but apparently did not get it to open immediately, because he stopped to kick the car in blind fury. A moment later he had opened the door, started the engine, and roared off. Black had not been able to see if he had a gun with him, but he was certain he did. A gun, or a knife, or something.

Ten minutes later, wearing a raincoat and probably nothing else, Dominique came out and walked directly to his car. He opened the door for her and she got in. "How did it go?"

She shivered. "All right."

"Was he mad?"

"He was furious. Insane."

"You put the powder in a drink?"

"Yes. Scotch. He drank a lot."

"And you talked about the girl?"

"I did just what you said. Now, please." She pulled up the sleeve to her raincoat, holding out her bare arm.

"Yes," Black said. He withdrew the bottle and syringe from the glove compartment, filled it, and squeezed out a few drops.

"Not too much," Dominique said.

"Never fear." He tied the rubber loop around her forearm until the veins stood out. Then he slipped the needle into the crook of her elbow, and squeezed in the morphine.

"There you go." He withdrew the needle, put a cotton pad over the puncture, and pushed her wrist up to her shoulder. "That should do it."

She sat in the car. "Wait a minute. We agreed—"

"On ten doses, yes. But I don't have it now. I'll bring it tomorrow."

"Oh, no—"

"Dominique," Black said patiently. "Trust me. Trust me."

He looked at her eyes. Already the pupils were constricting, and her stare was turning glassy. In a few moments, she would not care. She would trust him.

"Promise?" she said.

"I promise."

"And a needle, too. I don't have a needle."

"Yes. A needle, too. Now go back into the apartment."

She returned. He waited until she had gone up the steps and closed the door behind her. Then he started his car and drove straight home.

It was finished.

Everything, every small detail, even Dominique, was finished.

18. SHOTS IN THE DARK

Fortunately, Jane Mitchell was a light sleeper, awaking instantly with no trace of grogginess or fatigue. When she heard the pounding at her door, the hurried urgency in the knock, she assumed that it was Charles, and that something had happened. She got out of bed, wearing a pale yellow Dior nightgown, and went to the door after pausing long enough to see by her watch that it was 12:35.

She threw the latch on the door and opened it. She could not see the person standing before her; his face was in shadow from the hall light behind, and her eyes were not used to the light. She stood for a moment, slightly confused, blinking.

"Yes? What is it?"

Then she saw the arm come up, and the sharp, straight blade of the knife. She stepped quickly backward as the knife swung down; it missed her but caught the nightgown, tearing it.

She backed off quickly and the man came in, panting, obviously excited. She moved to the right of the bed and he followed her. She climbed quickly over the bed, and he swung again, burying the blade deep into the mattress, ripping the sheets with a jagged sound as he pulled it free.

At no time did she scream; she was not given to screams, but made for her purse as the man clambered over the bed toward her. He was unsteady, breathing heavily, his breath rasping in his throat.

Just as he came off the bed and prepared to slash again, she opened the purse, gripped the gun purposefully, and fired four times in rapid succession. The first shot snapped the man's head back. The second doubled him over with a sound like a cough. The third sent him stumbling and sagging toward the floor. The fourth hit him moments before he collapsed like a sack of grain.

Suddenly, there were shouts all around her. Another man

appeared silhouetted in the doorway. She fired and missed, the bullet splintering the wood of the door. The man ducked back and shouted, "Madam! Madam! It's the manager!"

Jane said, evenly, "Come in with your hands up."

A moment later, he came in, slowly, trembling.

"Turn on the light," she said.

He did, flicking the wall switch. The room filled with light and she saw a pale man in a tuxedo, his eyes wide and staring. She put the gun down.

"Who let in this creep with the knife?" she said, and then looked at the body near the bed.

Richard.

"My God," she said.

The manager approached her like a man cornered by a tiger. "If you'll put away your pistol, madam…"

She handed it to him silently.

"I…I'll just call the police."

She sat on the bed, not looking at the body or the blood and brains on the floor, and waited while he dialed. People were pouring into the room—maids, room-service men, guests from nearby suites, drawn by the gunshots. They all stood in awed silence until someone with a brisk manner, who seemed to be the house detective, pushed them all out.

After the manager had dialed the police, she said, "I'd like to make a call."

"You'd best wait," the manager said, "for the police."

The first to arrive was a bobby who burst into the room, had one look, and became deathly sick. While he was retching in the bathroom, with Jane looking tired and the manager looking embarrassed, another man in a raincoat arrived and began to ask clipped, precisely obnoxious questions while he took notes on a small pad. He was asking her things like whether she had ever shot anybody before, and whether she had ever used a gun before. Foolish questions. She stood it for fifteen minutes, then began to get hold of herself, to think straight.

"I want to make two calls," she said.

"You have the right to legal advice," the detective said. "Whom are you calling?"

"My fiancée, Charles Raynaud," she said smoothly, "and Lord Overton."

The name of Lord Overton caused a visible reaction in the detective. Lord Overton had been head of the committee of the House of Lords which had written the scathing report on Special Branch and MI6 the year before.

"Lord Overton is an acquaintance?"

"Lord Overton is a close friend of the family."

"Yes," said the detective, closing his pad. "Well, then."

She made her calls.

As it turned out, neither Charles nor Lord Overton was much needed. At the station, there was ample testimony from the hotel staff to indicate the following points: 1. That Miss Mitchell had retired to bed at 11:10 that evening, alone. 2. That the deceased, Mr. Pierce, had entered the hotel obviously intoxicated and nervously excited at 12:34. 3. That the night manager had been in his office necking with a certain Miss Conover, from the kitchen staff, and so had seen nothing. 4. That the bell captain, in charge of the desk, had left his post momentarily to relieve himself, and so had not seen Pierce enter the lobby and go up the stairs. 5. That a Mrs. Lewiston, from Ely, had been sitting in the lobby nursing a brandy and soda and had observed the deceased, Mr. Pierce, who walked as if concealing something in one hand, and that Mrs. Lewiston had been alarmed by his manner and appearance, and went to the desk only to discover that the bell captain was not there. 6. That the night maid, Mrs. O'Herlihy, a sixty-year-old woman of good character and, surprising in an Irishwoman, a teetotaler, had observed Mr. Pierce banging on the door to Miss Mitchell's suite with the wooden handle of the knife. 7. That Mrs. O'Herlihy had telephoned the police at 12:35 to report the incident, but that the call was still being acted upon at the time the manager called, at 12:39, to report the death of Mr. Pierce.

By 1:40, the police reluctantly agreed to release Miss Mitchell

without bail into the custody of Lord Overton, with the under-
standing that she would not attempt to leave London without
permission, and that she would not, under any circumstances,
attempt to leave the country.

Outside the police station, Raynaud said to her, "What do you
want to do?"

She said, "I want to walk."

They walked aimlessly, down dark, damp streets in a fine
drizzle. She paused once to light a cigarette, and her face in
the matchlight was drawn and tired. Raynaud remembered his
brief conversation with one of the detectives who had examined
the body. Four shots: one through the abdomen, just below the
diaphragm; one in the head; one in the neck below the jaw;
and one in the left temple. The detective stated that, from the
position of the body, the last three shots had struck Richard while
he was already falling from the impact of the first.

"I feel queer," Jane said at last. "I wish I knew why he did it."

"Was he drunk?"

"Yes. You could smell it, very strong. But still…"

"What?"

"He didn't act drunk. He acted crazy. Insane."

Raynaud frowned. He had been bothered by a persistent
thought for nearly an hour now.

"Do you think he could have been drugged?"

"How? On what?"

"Dezisen," Raynaud said. "A new drug, extracted from snake
venom. It's being marketed as an experimental compound for
research purposes."

"But who…"

She stopped. Raynaud nodded. "Yes," he said. "Richard's uncle,
sweet old Jonathan Black."

"But why would he want Richard dead? You told me before—"

"The point," Raynaud said, "is that Richard wasn't going to
die. You were. He was going to kill you. And that would get
him thrown into prison after a long, messy scandal involving you,
him, and me."

"That was why you beat him up, and took me to Cambridge?"

"Yes. I set up the scandal."

"But it backfired," Jane said. "I killed Richard."

"Yes, and that changes everything."

A cab cruised by; Raynaud stuck out his hand and hailed it.

"Where are we going?"

"To find the next body," Raynaud said.

As the cab moved through dark streets, Raynaud said, "You see, it's all a set-up. Planned months in advance. Very carefully engineered, with all the little checks and balances neatly arranged. Now they're fouled up, and we've got to move quickly."

"And do what?"

"Find the body of Dominique."

"How do you know she's dead?"

"I would be very surprised," Raynaud said, "if she isn't."

The door was locked; he leaned heavily against it and broke it open. The wood was old and it splintered easily. They walked into the apartment.

"You never met Dominique," Raynaud said, "but she was Richard's girl. A tart from Paris..."

They searched through the rooms, moving quickly. Nothing in the living room, the kitchen, the master bedroom.

"Richard couldn't figure out how she got a visa into England. Or how she got her fixes—she was an addict, you see. But I think I know—"

He stopped. They had come to the guest room. Dominique lay there on the bed, in her underwear, not moving. Her lips were purple; otherwise she seemed asleep.

Jane stepped forward. "Is she all right?"

"Don't touch," Raynaud said. "Don't touch anything."

He moved closer, and looked at the face. There was no movement, no breathing. He carefully felt for a pulse at the neck. Nothing. The skin was cold.

"Dead," he said, stepping back.

"How?"

"Overdose."

He hurried back to the kitchen. If Dominique had given the poison to Richard, how would she do it? Food? Not likely.

He looked around the kitchen. A bottle of Scotch and a bottle of vodka stood open on a counter. He bent over them, not touching, and sniffed. The vodka seemed to be all right. But the Scotch had a sweetish odor and looked cloudy.

"I think that's our answer," he said.

"Don't you think you'd better call the police?"

"No," he said. "Not yet"

He went into the bedroom and found the tape recorder, then took the tape out from its hiding place over the refrigerator. He slipped the cartridge into place, picked up the phone, and dialed.

"What are you doing?" she said.

"Saving our skins."

19. SKIN SAVING

Jonathan Black was at home, in his bedroom, lying quietly in bed. He was not asleep, but he was careful not to move. When the call came, he wanted to be sure his cheek had the pink creases of sleep. Small touches, but important touches. Detectives noticed so many things.

And sleep, he thought, was the best kind of alibi. A guilty man did not sleep well on the night of the murder. A guilty man did not have wrinkles from the pillow on his face.

After driving home from his meeting with Dominique, Black had wiped down the car carefully, removing any fingerprints from the girl. Then he had had a glass of milk to settle his stomach, and gone to bed. He had been waiting in bed ever since.

The call came at five. That, no doubt, would be Richard. Calling from the police station to announce that he was being arrested for the murder of the Mitchell girl.

He let it ring five times, then answered it with sleepy irritability. "Hello? Doctor Black speaking."

"Doctor Black. Charles Raynaud."

The voice sent a small shiver, a slight premonition, down his back. "Charles, it's rather late—"

"This is rather important," Raynaud said. "Richard is dead."

For a moment, he could not believe what he had heard. It was impossible, incredible, unthinkable.

"Richard? Dead? Oh, my God."

"I'm sure it must be a shock," Raynaud said. "It will be less of a shock to hear that Dominique is dead."

"Dominique?" His mind was churning; he would have to be careful of what he said. "Who is Dominique?"

"The little girl you gave an overdose to. Tonight."

He's guessing, Black thought. He sat up in bed and reached

for a cigarette on his night table. Guessing. Very astutely, but still guessing.

"I'm afraid I don't understand you."

He chose his words carefully, making certain there would be no slips.

"I'm not through," Raynaud said. "There's also the bottle."

"Bottle?"

"It's cloudy. Did you know it turned liquor cloudy?"

Black frowned. Impossible that he should know...

"Charles, whatever are you talking about?"

"Dezisen," Raynaud said.

The bastard. It was inconceivable that he should know about that, without being told. Someone must have told him, and nobody knew.

Except Lucienne.

The sneaking bitch.

"Charles, this is all very confusing, and I really—"

"It's all blown up," Raynaud said. "Everything has gone wrong. Richard is dead, the estate goes to charity, and you go to jail. As soon as the police find the Dezisen in the bottle. And in Richard. The police will be fascinated."

"My dear Raynaud, you must be under some terrible delusion. Police? Dezisen? I don't have the faintest idea what you're talking about."

"I just want you to know," Raynaud said, "that Jane and I are going to keep out of it. If we can. And only you can determine that."

"I?"

"Listen," Raynaud said.

There was a moment of silence, and then a mechanical scratching sound. Black poured himself a brandy, stubbed out his cigarette, and was lighting another when he heard Lucienne's voice. On a tape recording. Lucienne was talking about the will, about hiring Charles, about the death of her husband and Black...

Good Christ.

"I just wanted you to hear that," Raynaud said, clicking off the tape. "There are, by the way, two copies of the tape. They have been left with friends outside London. There is also a tape of my explanation of this affair, which has been left with another friend. All three tapes will be handed over to the police should anything happen to me, or to Miss Mitchell."

"Charles, how absurd—"

But the phone was dead in his hand.

20. A QUIET DRINK

"Damned unfair," Peter Dickerson said, rubbing his eyes. "The whole thing."

"Shut up and drink," Raynaud said, "and call the manager."

The three of them were sitting in Dickerson's hotel room. Dickerson wore a bathrobe, a wrinkled face, and an unhappy expression. They had just woken him up.

"Call the manager?"

"Yes."

"But it's five in the morning."

"Call him," Raynaud said, "and have him up for a drink."

"In God's name why?"

"We need an alibi."

"Now? At five in the morning?"

"Yes," Raynaud said. "Now."

Jane said nothing. She sat in a corner and stared at her glass.

"Jane, what the hell is happening? Who is this person?"

"She killed somebody," Raynaud said.

"Who?"

"Your client. Miss Mitchell."

"Killed somebody? How ridiculous."

"Four shots. One through the heart," Raynaud said.

Dickerson stared at him. He turned to Jane. "Is this true?"

She nodded.

"Who did you shoot?"

"Whom," Raynaud said. "Richard Pierce."

"Richard Pierce? *The* Richard Pierce?" Dickerson said, his voice rising.

"None other."

"My God, but the stock we are selling is—"

"Precisely," Raynaud said.

Dickerson dived for the phone. "I have to call New York,"

he said, picking up the receiver. "I have to get through right away."

"Call the manager," Raynaud said.

His voice was flat and tired. Dickerson stopped, hesitant.

"Do as he says, Peter," Jane said.

There was a moment of silence. Then they heard Dickerson say in a calm voice, "I'd like to speak to the manager, please."

21. TRAP

At five-thirty in the morning Black had finished half a pack of cigarettes and most of a bottle of Armagnac brandy. He was pacing up and down his study, thinking furiously, his mind darting from Raynaud to Lucienne to Jane, and around to Raynaud again. He was searching for a weakness, an escape, a way out. There had to be one; there *had* to be. He could not accept the possibility that so simple a fool as Raynaud had trapped him. Had figured it all out.

But Richard was dead. That was the kicker: that shot everything. The whole plan, his hopes, his expectations. With Richard dead, the estate went to the Chelsea Home for Consumptive Children, and the Westfield Old Soldiers' Hospital for Chronic Illness, and other equally worthy causes.

He shook his head. Insane, all of it. That tragic list of tragic charities, with old Herbert signing it all away…

He was lighting another cigarette, raising the match to the butt, when the pain struck him. He was unprepared for it, a sharp, excruciating, squeezing vise that wrapped around his chest, doubling him over.

He dropped the match on the carpet, where it started a small fire. His eyes were filled with tears of pain, but he managed to stamp the fire out. The cigarette fell from his grimacing lips, and he collapsed into a chair.

His immediate thought was the nitrogylcerine pills, though already he felt the pain shooting in long, agonizing streaks down his left arm to the elbow, and he knew the pills would do no good. Still, he took one pill, and a second, washing it down with brandy.

He sat in the chair, hoping the pain would leave. It did not. It was steady, sharp, like needles plunged into his chest, tensing his muscles, forcing him to breathe in small stabbing gasps.

For a time, he thought he would die, or lose consciousness. His mind became fixed on one thing: morphine. He had it downstairs, in his dispensary, but that meant walking one flight down. He was not certain he could do it. He sat in the chair, fighting the pain, and finally decided he must try. He went to the stairs, leaning heavily on the bannister, and made his way down slowly. Near the bottom he tripped, dizzy, sweating, and fell the rest of the way. He had a sudden attack of nausea, but struggled to control it.

Leaning against the wall, wiping the chilly sweat from his face, he made his way to the dispensary. He clicked on the light, and saw the room, green, spinning. He tumbled to the floor.

He did not know how long he was unconscious. When he came to, he was lying in a puddle of vomit. He pulled himself up, the pain still there, and crawled toward the cabinet of medicines. Morphine, he kept thinking, morphine. He found the colorless ampoule, filled the syringe, and injected it into his arm. The pain continued, squeezing tight around his lungs, and he was still lightheaded, but he began to feel a little better. He sat down and waited several minutes, and the pain began to ease. The shooting pains down his left arm stopped, and he began to breathe more regularly.

With his stethoscope, he listened to his heart, though there was no doubt in his mind as to what had happened: massive coronary. His heart was already weak, and the tension, the drinking, and the smoking hadn't helped. Through the stethoscope he heard a gallop rhythm and a bad murmur.

Some cold, logical corner of his mind told him that he was already a dead man. Perhaps not immediately. Perhaps he would live a day, or a week, or a year. But his hours were numbered.

He could think of only one thing, and the bitterness of it, the horrible twisting agony of it, distorted his mind: Lucienne, though she would not inherit the estate, at least would live. She would survive, and that, in a sense, was success.

He could not permit this to happen. Through his mind flashed a series of images of Lucienne, on the bed, on her stomach, raising her buttocks obscenely, Lucienne with her mouth open, her tongue flashing out, curving, slurping, Lucienne with him, Lucienne with a hundred others, always the same...

He could not permit it. Not after his work, after his efforts and his planning. If Black died, she might fix all the blame on him. And then she might attempt to break the will. The lawyers had said that the will could be broken. Not for certain, but there was the possibility.

So Lucienne might inherit the estate after all.

And Black would die.

No, he could not permit it.

He felt another gasping pain, and another. Despite the morphine, he did not have long. Desperately, his mind cast about for an answer. And desperately, he fixed on his final chance.

It took him two minutes to climb the stairs back to his study. There, he rang for Burgess, the butler. Undoubtedly, Burgess would be asleep; Black had never rung for him before at this hour.

Ten minutes passed. When he heard Burgess' steps in the hall outside, he picked up the phone and began talking to the dial tone.

"Yes...yes...quite dead...yes, well, we have to implicate her ...there's no other way...Lucienne must be fixed..."

Burgess waited politely in the doorway. Black looked up, pretending to notice him for the first time. He said, "Well, I'll call you back shortly," and hung up.

"Burgess, bring me water, would you?"

"Of course, sir."

"Thanks. I'm afraid we've got something of a crisis."

"Yes, sir," Burgess said neutrally. He walked away, down the hall, and Black wiped the sweat from his brow. He had no doubt that Lucienne would be called immediately.

Black timed him: six minutes to bring a glass of water. So he had called Lucienne—perfect. He took the glass, and Burgess said, "Will that be all, sir?"

"Yes, thank you."

"Very good, sir."

When he was alone, Black got up, leaning on the desk, still

dizzy, still in pain. He looked down the hall, making sure Burgess was gone, then he went down to Belinda's room.

Belinda had been his maid for four years. She was a simple-minded, somewhat avaricious girl with no modesty at all, which was why he had originally hired her. She was sleeping; he shook her awake.

"Belinda."

"Wha—"

"Belinda."

She roused slowly. The effort of waking her nearly made him faint, but he kept his control. He shook her until she sat up.

"Belinda," he whispered, "I am afraid something terrible is about to happen."

"What?"

She was instantly awake, sensing his mood.

"Come with me."

He led her to his bedroom—she had been there before—and went directly to the wall safe, which he opened. He removed two packets of fresh bills.

"Here is a thousand pounds," he said, giving it to her. "I want you to hide it carefully. I am afraid, Belinda, that something will happen to me very soon. You have been good and faithful, and I wish you to be rewarded."

Her mouth hung open in astonishment. She took the money numbly.

"Get dressed," Black said, hoping she would not notice that he was in pain, or that the sweat was pouring off his face, drenching his collar. "Wait in your room. If you hear any disturbance, run for the police. Do you understand?"

"Yes…yes, sir."

"Good girl."

She started to leave.

"Oh, Belinda. One other thing."

"Yes, sir?"

"Burgess is not to be trusted. Will you remember that?"

She was obviously confused, but she nodded vigorously.

"Good girl," he said again, and returned to the study.

❀

He sat at his desk, staring at the telephone, trying to focus his eyes on the dial. His head was pounding, his chest was on fire, his arm was virtually paralyzed by pain. The morphine was no longer helpful. He had a terrible desire to pass out, to slip into oblivion. He found himself digging his fingers into his palms to keep awake, to fight off the gray drowsiness that threatened to creep over him.

Fifteen minutes passed, then twenty. He took more pills, and an amphetamine. They did not seem to help. He wondered if he could hold on, or if Lucienne would arrive to find him dead…

The sound of a car in the drive.

The sound of a door opening.

Black picked up the phone and dialed WEA-2211, the automatic recorded service which reported the weather. A pleasant female voice began, "Good morning. Here is today's weather forecast. In London, the four A.M. temperature is fifty-one, the relative humidity is sixty-seven, and the barometric pressure is twenty-nine-point-five, and falling. Wind from the west—"

Black began talking. "Yes, we can arrange it. Lucienne is a fool, that's why. Richard's death will be easy. Everyone knows that she hated him. We will have no difficulty leaving a small clue, a hint…Besides, old Farnsworth at the Yard is one of her rejects. Only too happy to put on the screws."

From the doorway, Lucienne said, "Good morning, Jonathan."

Black looked up in astonishment, quickly cupping his hand over the phone. "Lucienne!"

"I just thought I'd stop by."

"This is certainly a surprise." He smiled, trying to ignore the pain in his chest, the dizziness in his head. He could not really see her, and wished he could. He wanted to gauge her expression, her mood…

"Won't you sit down?"

"No," she said. "I won't."

He returned to his phone call. The voice said, "Tomorrow, scattered showers in East Anglia and Devonshire, clearing by midday—"

"Well," he said into the phone, "I've got to ring off now. Good-bye. Yes. Goodbye."

He hung up and looked at her, folding his hands across his stomach and trying to control his features.

"Well now, Lucienne. What brings you here at"—he glanced at his watch—"six in the morning?"

"What do you think, John-love?"

"I haven't the slightest."

"So Richard is dead, is he?"

He appeared surprised, though it was an effort. "You know that?"

"I know everything," she said.

He smiled at her. "Oh?"

"I know about you, too."

"Oh?"

She shook her head. "Innocence doesn't suit you, John. Really it doesn't. An old murderer like you."

"Me? A murderer? Preposterous. Lucienne, you need sleep, you're overtired. You're imagining things."

"Am I?"

Her voice was sardonic, cold, tense.

"Yes, indeed you are. Bursting in here, distraught…"

"And what were you doing?"

"Just a call," he shrugged.

"To whom?"

"A colleague. Actually, I was arranging a new series of experiments."

"A new series of experiments." She laughed. "John, do you think I am so foolish?"

"Foolish? Heavens no. We're old friends, Lucienne."

He had a particularly sharp, stabbing pain in his chest. It was all he could do to keep from doubling over. As it was, the sweat poured off; he wiped it with a handkerchief.

"You're sweating, John."

"Yes. A small cold."

"Oh?"

"Yes."

"It couldn't be that you're afraid?"

"Afraid? Why should I be afraid?"

"You tell me."

Lucienne stood in the doorway, holding her purse in her hands. She tried to hold it casually, but could not; it was heavy. Good.

"I don't follow you, Lucienne."

"Richard is dead," Lucienne said, her face taut, "and something must be done to explain it. To explain *your* bungling. But you have a plan, don't you?"

"A plan? No."

"You have a scapegoat."

"I wish I did." He laughed, easily.

"And the scapegoat is me. You've been waiting for the chance, the chance to take over the fortune yourself. This is the perfect opportunity. Isn't it, John?"

"Lucienne, really—"

He stopped. She had opened her purse, and produced a gun.

"What are you doing, Lucienne?"

Quavering fright in his voice. Rather good, actually. Though the pain helped.

"I want the truth, John."

"What truth? You're making all this up."

"Are you framing me? Are you planning—"

"Lucienne," he said soothingly, getting up from behind his desk, and walking toward her. "Lucienne, my dear, don't be silly…"

"Stay away from me."

She backed off, holding the gun.

"Lucienne, darling, don't be so suspicious, so absurd…"

"I'm warning you!"

"Lucienne, Lucienne, Lucienne—"

The first shot from the little .22 derringer hit him in the shoulder, spinning him around to the floor, toppling him, and he thought, Oh, Christ, you missed, you stupid bitch, you missed, can't you do anything right, you stupid bitch, can't you even do this?

The next shot penetrated his brain, killing him instantly.

Lucienne stared in horror at the crumpled body and the smoking hot gun in her hand. It had happened so quickly she had not had time to think.

Burgess burst into the room, took it all in, in a glance. "Madam, are you all right?"

"Yes, I'm all right."

She felt weak, dizzy. She sat in a chair as Burgess bent over Jonathan.

"Is he…"

"Dead," Burgess said, straightening. He looked at Lucienne.

"Burgess," she said, "you have worked for me for some time…"

"Yes, madam."

"I think we can arrange further, very comfortable employment."

"Madam, I—"

"At a handsome salary, Burgess."

"Really, I think that—"

"Burgess, name your price." Her voice was sharp and cold. It stopped him. He hesitated, then smiled. "Shall we say a hundred thousand pounds?"

"Let's say two hundred."

"Indeed, madam, that would be most agreeable."

"Then call the police. Only remember. You never saw me here tonight, you saw a burglar, an unknown man, who was rifling the flat. Understand?"

"You can count on me, madam."

"I'm sure I can, Burgess."

She stood to go, and looked toward the doorway.

The maid was standing there, watching them, and looking at the body of Jonathan. Her fist was pressed to her mouth.

She let out one high-pitched scream and ran.

"Burgess. Get her!"

Burgess was too stunned to move.

Lucienne fired at the fleeing girl, but the gun had no accuracy at that range. The maid scampered down the stairs. She flung open the door and ran out into the street, shrieking, "Help! Murder! Police! Help!"

Lucienne ran to follow her, and saw her reach the end of the block, where the frightened girl collided with a bobby.

A moment later, police whistles began to blow.

22. THE VENOM BUSINESS

Jane sat with him in the open-air café on High Street, reading the newspaper. It was a bright, cheerful day; the girls were out in their short skirts, walking, talking, being chatted up by the boys.

"Stop staring," Jane said, without looking up from her newspaper.

"Wasn't."

"You were."

"Wasn't."

She turned the page of the paper. "It's all here," she said, "all the grisly details."

"The English love a good murder," Raynaud said.

"Or two," she said, "Or three."

She set the paper aside and looked at him. "Charles," she said, "were you telling me the truth about all this?"

"Yes."

"You're quite sure?"

"Quite sure."

"Why were you here, at all? Why did you come in the first place?"

"Money," he said.

"But that doesn't make sense."

"It does to me."

In a quiet voice she said, "I have plenty of money."

"Yes, but it's yours. Not mine."

"It's legal."

"So what?" he said, watching a girl with long legs and a Marimekko.

"You mean you really don't care?"

"Not particularly."

"Well," she said, "did you make a lot of money this time?"

"A reasonable amount."

He hadn't totaled all the checks yet. But it would probably come to about fifty thousand dollars. Not what it might have been, but still…

"You could be in jail now," she said, "or dead."

"But for the grace of God."

"Charles." She touched his hand and looked at him seriously. "I wish you wouldn't be like this."

"It's the only way I can be," he said. He leaned over and kissed her on the cheek.

She accepted it coolly. "I was going to reform you," she said.

"And I was going to enjoy your attempt."

"But it won't work, will it?"

"No," he said, lighting a cigarette. "It won't."

"You'll never change?"

"Oh, probably I will. When I'm older, and tired."

"I don't believe you," she said.

A few minutes later, when she got up to leave, she folded her newspaper very carefully and set it down on the table.

"If you ever want to try your hand at catching snakes…" he said.

"Maybe I will," she said. "Some day."

"Okay," he said, nodding.

"Okay," she said, and walked away, down the street. After a moment she was lost in the crowd of bright young girls in bright cotton dresses. There seemed to be hundreds of girls out that day, all over London. Hundreds of girls.

He felt sad for a moment, and then amused.

And then he laughed.

Monday: Principauté de Monaco

Victor Jenning, tanned and very fit, walked down the steps of the Casino into the cool night air. They were already bringing his blood-red Lamborghini around from the lot. It was a new car, and Jenning was pleased with it—Carrozzeria Touring body mounted over a 3.5 liter V-12 engine that ran smoothly at 240 kilometers an hour. It was a hardtop, of course. Jenning loathed driving fast in an open car—unless he was racing—and he had rolled enough cars to have a healthy respect for solid protection overhead.

People were gathering to admire the car as he came to the bottom of the steps. It was only natural; the car had never been produced prior to 1965, when old Ferrucio Lamborghini, the tractor and oil burner tycoon, had established a limited production shop in Cento, just a few miles from Ferrari's plant at Maranello. Three hundred Lamborghinis were made a year, so it was still quite a rarity. It had cost him $14,000.

As he made his way around the crowd, he answered their questions with smiles and a slightly bored voice, then got in behind the wheel. He was a jaded man, and so felt only mild pride, but it was sufficient to make him forget—momentarily at least—the ten thousand dollars he had just dropped that night at baccarat, in a particularly poor run of luck.

He started the engine, listening with satisfaction to the bass growl from the twin exhausts. The crowd parted, and he reached down for the lights. His hand flicked on the windshield wipers, and he had a twinge of embarrassment. Damn! It was painfully obvious that he'd owned the car just a week. He bent over to peer at the switches.

At that moment his windshield shattered in front of him.

The crowd gasped; somebody screamed. Another shot, and Jenning, who had immediately dropped as low as he could, felt pain in his right shoulder. He turned on the lights, released the brake, and put the car quickly into reverse. Still hunched over, he roared backward, sat up, spun the wheel around, and tore off into the night. Air blew through the gaping hole in his windshield, and he swore to himself.

Victor Jenning was a man accustomed to attempts on his life. There had been four in the last two years. None had come close to succeeding, though he had a slight limp as a result of the second. In a strange way, he did not mind the assassination attempts—they were part of the game, one of the risks in his line of work. But he hated to see his new car damaged. It would take weeks, now, to get a new windshield fitted properly.

As he drove through the dark streets of Monaco toward the doctor, he was so furious that he did not bother to reflect that, had he known how to work his lights, he would probably be dead.

Tuesday: Cairo, Egypt

One of the Arabs held a gun. "It will not be long now," he said pleasantly.

In the back seat of the taxi, the European stared at the gun, at the Egyptian holding it, and at the back of the neck of the driver. They sped through the dark streets of the city.

"Where are you taking me?" he said. He was French, and spoke Arabic with a slurred accent.

"To a meeting. Your presence is desired."

"Then why the gun?"

"To assure…punctuality."

The Frenchman sat back and lit a cigarette. He remained cool; it was part of his training. He had been in tight situations before, and he had always managed to escape safely.

The car left the city and headed south, into the desert. It was a moonless May night, black and cool. The French man could see the outlines of the palm trees that lined the road.

"Who is this person I am meeting?"

The Arab laughed softly: "You know him."

They drove for ten minutes, and then the Arab with the gun said, "Here."

The driver pulled off the road, onto the sand. The Nile was a few hundred yards away.

The car stopped. "Out," the Arab said, motioning with the gun.

The Frenchman got out and looked around. "I don't see anybody."

"Have patience. He will be here soon." The Arab drew a pair of handcuffs from his pocket and handed them to the driver. To the Frenchman, he said, "If you please. Our man is rather nervous. This will reassure him."

"I don't think—"

The Arab shook his head. "No arguments, please."

The Frenchman hesitated, then turned and held his hands behind his back. The driver clicked the handcuffs shut.

"Good," said the Arab with the gun. "Now we will go to the river, and wait."

They walked silently across the sand. No one spoke. The Frenchman was worried, now. He had made a mistake, he was sure of it.

It happened with lightning swiftness.

One of the Arabs tripped him, and he pitched forward on his face into the sand. Strong hands gripped his neck, forced his head down. He felt the grainy sand on his lips, in his eyes and nose. He struggled and kicked, but the Arabs held him firmly. His mind began to reel, and then blackness seeped over him.

The Arabs stepped back.

"Stupid fool," one said.

The driver removed the handcuffs. Each man took one leg,

and they dragged the body to the river. The Arab put his gun away and held the body underwater with his foot until it sank. It would rise to the surface later, when it was bloated and decomposing. But that would not be for several days.

The body sank. A few final bubbles broke the calm water, and then, nothing.

Friday: Estoril, Portugal

The man walked across the rocks in his bare feet, looking into the setting sun. The waves of the Atlantic crashed into the rock. He was an American, a minor consular official attached to the office in Barcelona. He had received news of his transfer to Nice just three days before, and had decided to relax for a few days before moving. He was accustomed to traveling, and did it easily, so there were no major preparations to look after. Lisbon had been the perfect choice for a short break. He had been here during the war, and loved it deeply. Particularly this stretch of coast, west of the city, past the point where the Tagus River emptied into the ocean.

He smiled, breathed deeply, and reached in his pocket for cigarettes. To his right, the rocky shelf leading up from the sea ended in a sloping pine grove; to the left, the water rushed up against sharp, eroded stone. He was alone—few people came here at evening, this early in the season. He felt relaxed and cleansed after the bustle of Barcelona. The match flared in his hand, and he touched it to the cigarette. What the hell was he going to do in France, where cigarettes were so expensive?

Offshore, a fishing boat started its motor, and he listened to its faint puttering as it pulled away. He would have lobster tonight, he decided, in a little place in Cascais. Then he would return to his hotel and compose a letter to his girl in Barcelona, explaining that he had been sent away, suddenly, and was returning to the United States. The Spaniards were accustomed to hush-hush, sudden maneuverings among any kind of government officials; Maria would take it well. And although he would miss her, he was confident he could find a suitable replacement on the Riveria. Hell, if you couldn't find a girl there, you couldn't find one anywhere.

Behind him, there was a sharp *crack!* It was a sound he did not hear, for by that time, the bullet had entered the back of his head, smashing the occipital bone and burying itself deep in his cerebellum. He felt a momentary twinge of pain, and was pitched forward onto the rocks. His face smashed down hard, breaking the bones of his nose and jaw. Blood flowed out.

Two other men, neatly dressed in sport clothes, viewed the fallen body with satisfaction. The tide was coming in; within an hour, these rocks would be submerged, and the body carried out to sea. It was a good, clean, neat job. They were pleased.